THE
DARK QUEEN

To Johnny,
Enjoy!

Joseph

THE
DARK QUEEN

JOSEPHINE BOYCE

First published in 2018 by Josephine Boyce
All rights reserved
© Josephine Boyce, 2018

Josephine Boyce asserts the moral right to be identified as the author of this work.

This novel is entirely a work of fiction.
The names, characters and incidents portrayed in it are the work of the author's imagination. Any resemblance to actual persons, living or dead, events or localities is entirely coincidental.

All rights reserved. No part of this publication may be reproduced, stored in a retrieval system, or transmitted, in any form or by any means, electronic, mechanical, photocopying, recording or otherwise, without the prior permission of the publisher.

Formatted by Eight Little Pages.

Printed and bound in Great Britain by Clays Ltd, Elcograf S.p.A

To the darkness that allowed me to write a queen like Amarea.
Please go back now: I'm scared.

Character List

Aiden – Queen's illegitimate half-brother
Amarea Saffiere – The Dark Queen
Bassiri – member of inner circle
Captain Fletcher – Captain of the Port Guard
Commander Denmer – Head of palace barracks
Degat Kureen – Hyrathean lord
Degat Soligan – Hyrathean lord
Dideum – Young mage
Dolsan – Hyrathean King
Gallia – Niseem's wife
Ithrael Ethea – Captain of the Queen's Guard
Koharu – Yuto's cousin and second-in-command
Lisette and Leonius – twins, members of inner circle
Lord Tiemenin – Primlect
Niseem Hassan – leader of inner circle
Saia – strategist for inner circle
Terro – Hyrathean guard
Tristam Condessa – Queen's cousin
Vulma Supreme Leader – Ruler of Vulma
Yeela Hassan – Niseem's sister
Yuto – Jaien captive of Hyratheans

Daeneah Realms

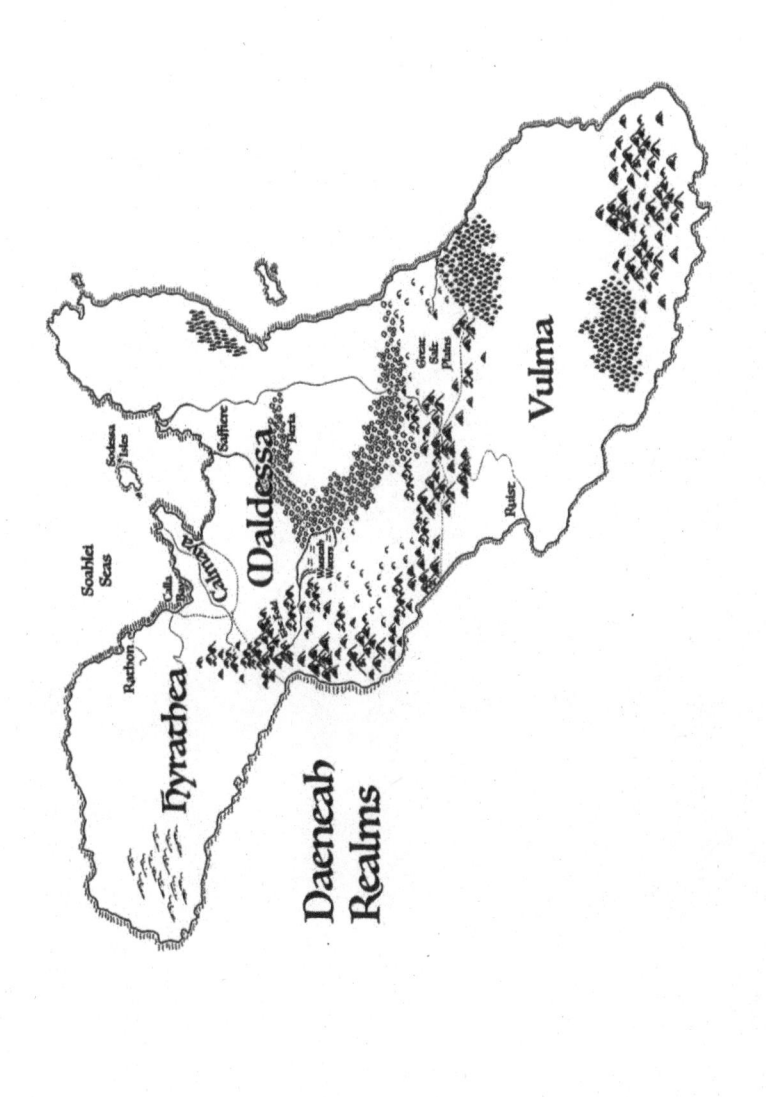

Hyrachea

Maldessa

Vulma

Soahlei Seas
Sodesa Isles
Cairuru River
Suffiarre
Ruchyn
Great Salt Plains
Ruise

PART ONE

Prologue

They told her that she had the face of a goddess and that it made her the most dangerous person in the entire kingdom. It was the second part that had always interested Amarea Saffiere, future Queen of Maldessa. She would much prefer to be considered dangerous than beautiful.

Amarea was sent to the convent for her own protection aged fourteen; she hadn't even been given the chance to grieve the deaths of her parents and sister. They told her it was the plague that had killed her family, but few within the palace were affected and she understood why she'd been spared. She reasoned that she only survived the assassination of the royal family because they wouldn't want to murder a child who had the face of a goddess, even if it wasn't the face of the deity they worshipped. They, as far as she was concerned, were the Church.

From the moment she stepped inside the Daylarian abbey, she knew to be on her guard. Zanzee, her country's regent and leader of the Atarix Brotherhood, highest order of the Church, held her small hand in his as he walked her through the cold stone hall towards her new room.

"Being in the hand of Daylar, the house of our true god, will heal your broken soul."

But Amarea knew that only her goddess, Neesoh, could save her.

On her first night at the abbey, she stood before the High Priest.

"It is a call from Daylar himself, this face of perfection before me. We shall protect her within these walls. Our future Queen. Our salvation."

She kept her eyes on him and ignored the rows of priests behind her in the hall, all of them leaning forward with eagerness to see the face the High Priest spoke of with fervour.

"We must teach her to be humble, to be righteous, because her beauty is too great a gift to bear without being tested." He looked down at her, drinking in her youthful features. "Kneel, child."

Amarea knelt and was made to stay there through the rest of the day to reflect on the burden of her beauty and how she must avoid all vanity.

Things didn't improve for Amarea. She was made to kneel before the statue of Daylar from sun up to sun down, wearing only a white robe, even in the freezing months, to make penance for her sin of vanity each time she caught sight of her own reflection.

As she began to blossom into womanhood, she noticed that the priests found it harder and harder to be near her. Her face became too bewitching, the magic in her veins too powerful. As penance for their own lustful thoughts, they forced her to strip naked and made her stand nightly before the brothers of the Church as they exalted heaven over her child body, her cursed flawlessness. She kept her eyes raised to heaven, praying to Neesoh as she heard the slapping of their flesh.

Sometimes she vomited. Sometimes she couldn't stop the tears. She hated these weaknesses in herself but she felt horribly trapped and alone. She was grateful that at least they didn't touch her. They didn't dare: her mother had taught her, before anyone could take advantage of her, how to fight against the men of this world, weak to their urges, and so she always kept her nails long and filed into claws.

Late one night as Amarea was kneeling alone in front of the statue of Daylar and wondering whether she could smash in his smug face, one of the brothers entered the room. He was panting and sweating as he approached her; she knew now what this meant. She rose to her feet and turned to face him. He reached forward for her breast and she slapped his hand away. Despite the rules, despite the claws she flashed at him, the lust in his eyes didn't fade.

"No," she commanded. Her voice was firm, deep.

"I must have you."

Amarea's eyes narrowed. No one would have her against her will. She slashed her nails across his face, drawing blood. "No," she repeated. A long burning fierceness began to rise up within her. Why had she endured their ill treatment for so long? She was to be Queen. No more.

He lunged again, anger now mingling with his lust. She kneed him in the groin. He bent double, gasping. She held his head in her hands and smashed her knee up into his face, breaking his nose with a satisfying crunch. Blood sprayed across her white shift dress. A smile tugged at her lips. She pulled him to his feet and took out her rage at her imprisonment, pounding her fists into his weak body. Her knuckles split and so she let him fall to the floor.

He splayed his palms on the flagstones to push himself up but she grabbed him by his right shoulder and dug her nails in until they broke his skin. She felt them sink in and she knew they would scar. The thought pleased her.

Amarea whispered into his ear. "Let these be a reminder to you that you are to touch no woman without her permission."

After she'd nearly killed Brother Tobias, they didn't punish her as much for the beauty she didn't ask for, but she did not stop hating the priesthood.

A few weeks later, from across the dining hall she saw in the eyes of one of the priests the same burning lust that Brother Tobias had exhibited. She would endure the Church no more. Alone in the main hall that night, when she knew all within the abbey were asleep, she made her way to the kitchens. She took flints and kindling and she started small fires, beginning outside the rooms of the brothers of the Church. She wanted to burn the abbey to the ground, hoping she would die alongside all the men who had been her jailers, her persecutors. But alas, her will was too strong. As the heavy wooden beams collapsed around her and the smoke found its way into her lungs — the heat singeing her eyebrows, cracking her lips — she was still able to cling to life. In the heat and fog of the smoke, she crawled her way out of the wreckage, listening as the cursed men screamed to their puny god. She hoped Daylar heard because she was sending him a message. She was coming for him.

Chapter One

AMAREA

Amarea was to be Queen only in name, a fact she understood all too well as she prepared for her coronation. Her ladies of Astree dressed her in an outfit of white and gold and brushed gold dust across her palms to signify that the touch of their soon-to-be Queen was a blessing, a privilege. A mask of gold covered her face, a face that was too beautiful to behold, a face that bewitched anyone who looked upon it. The Daylarian Church had continued to insist that to expose her face was a sin. She had no right to control others with the magic in her blood, and on this she agreed with them, sometimes. After all, what was the point of having such power if she never used it?

One of Amarea's ladies secured a jewel-encrusted headband over the top of a white shani veil that was added as extra protection for those around her. The circlet was made up of a design in gold of thorns that strangled blooming roses. Amarea brought her hands up and under her veil to adjust the mask, the weight of it uncomfortable and hot against her skin. Her ladies fetched her shoes and placed them upon her feet.

She was pampered here in her palace, the cold floors of the Daylarian abbey a nightmare that didn't visit her as often any more.

Two ladies held out the dress Amarea had chosen, and she stepped forward for them to start tying her in. The bodice was cut low with intricate beading, gold leaves and roses arrayed the fabric, and a tangle of golden thorns snaked around Amarea's waist. It fitted her tightly until just past her hips, from where the beading faded and fell into the frailest white shani fabric — delicately soft, and even though it was whisper thin, light could not shine through it. Despite the jewels and precious metals she was bathed in, the shani fabric was the most expensive thing Amarea wore.

One of her ladies stepped forward and secured a cape around her neck; the collar was high and decorated in the same pattern as her bodice. The sleeves of the shani cloak rested over Amarea's upper arms, and the train fell below the hem of her dress. Amarea checked her reflection in the polished glass in front of her: she would almost be the image of the young Queen the Church wanted her to be if it weren't for the revealing nature of her gown. With a small satisfied smile, Amarea approached the door to her chamber, which opened before her. On the other side stood Zanzee, the regent.

"Beautiful," he said in appreciation.

Amarea tapped one of her sharpened gold nail attachments against her thigh. Zanzee knew not to comment on her beauty, and she was sure he did it to challenge her, to remind her who really held the power. He stood before her in his blue and white robes of the Atarix Brotherhood. It still revolted Amarea to see any symbol of the Daylarian Church, and not for the first time she was grateful she didn't have to school her expression of distaste. Amarea ignored his comment and swept past him down the hall and made her way to the grand central staircase of her palace. Her elaborate costume clung to her body and she felt the cape flowing behind her in rippling, offensive luxury. She knew the outfit affronted Zanzee and those of the Church: they wanted her to appear as their young virginal Queen, an illusion they were desperate to weave for the people, for their foreign neighbours. She never saw the need, and it gave her satisfaction to be able to defy them in some way. *Besides*, she thought. *This is one of my demurer choices for today*.

Her personal bodyguard, Ithrael, fell into step by her side, and she allowed him to be close as she walked down the stairs; he was the only male permitted to be in such close proximity to her, and she craved the nearness more than she'd care to admit even to herself.

Amarea entered the council chamber where the High Sancees, the senior members of her council and the men who helped rule her queendom, waited for her. They stood and bowed, a mere formality; she was no leader to them. The Sancees, the government of her limping, suffocating queendom, sat, their eyes following her lithe, perfect body as she lowered it into her elaborately carved, high-backed chair. Every one of these *men* wanted to know what rare beauty lay behind the veil and whether it really was beauty or whether Amarea hid her face from vanity because of a disfigurement. They need only to have asked her ladies, who could not look at her for long, whose eyes remained lowered when they served her. To never be seen was her curse.

"My Queen." The Primlect stood and bowed briefly to Amarea, his grey hair tied low and his white official's robe clipped in place with the deep-blue crystal emblem of the queendom. "You called us here today as you wish to make an announcement, is that correct?"

In her own country, inside her own palace, at her own table, she was not allowed to speak first. She inclined her head and the Primlect sat back down. Amarea ran her talons along the armrests of her chair and spoke slowly.

"I will not grant the Daylarian Church any more land. The balance between the Daylar and Neesohan Churches is shifting far too much in favour of Daylar, and if we allow that to happen, we risk instability. We do not want an unhappy population."

Ruling wasn't the bloodthirsty vengeance she'd dreamed of. Sadly, to make her queendom heal she needed to be a politician first and an avenging demon second. She looked forward to the second part.

The Primlect, head of the council, started to speak but Amarea held up her hand and glared at him hard enough to know he felt it through the veil.

"I may have had most of my political power taken from me when I was a child, but tonight I become Queen in my own right. But even then, the land that this country is built upon is the Crown's, and *I* say how it is to be used. There will be no more churches, no more abbeys. The Daylarian Church will just have to make do." She rose to her feet. "Now, *gentlemen*, if you'll excuse me, I have a ceremony to attend."

That small act, that one defiance, was the start of her true reign, for she would *reign* and she would bring damnation to all those who called themselves men of god and preyed upon the innocent. She would burn every single symbol of their house to the ground.

Chapter Two

AMAREA

Amarea stood by the balcony doors, the Primlect behind her, his heavy breathing irritating every one of her nerves. She rolled back her shoulders and walked forward as the doors opened before her. The crowd below cheered for their soon-to-be-crowned Queen — for her. The joy didn't reach Amarea and she could hear, even under the cacophony, the rumble of discontent. Amarea waved and smiled despite knowing they couldn't see the false joy pasted across her face. She wanted to run through the palace halls, tear off her ridiculous outfit, put on some simple clothes and stand before them as their true Queen — the Queen who wouldn't bow to the tyranny of a religion, who wasn't clinging on to her rule because the High Sancees on her council were taking more and more control of the queendom under the watchful eye of the Daylarian Church.

But she didn't run. Amarea stayed on the balcony, waving to her people, and vowed to every single one of those before her that she would be the Queen they needed, not the Queen they wanted to love.

In the throne room Amarea sat, bored and uncomfortable, holding onto her sceptre whilst waiting for Zanzee to finish his pontificating.

She was to be the first ruling Queen the kingdom had known, and so she had ordered that they melt down and refashion the old crown for her. The Church had of course refused, but they did agree to her using some of her own jewellery to create the crown she desired. She'd inherited a lot of pieces from her mother: rubies as large as plums, diamonds as clear as mountain water, emeralds as vibrant as the lushest day in spring, and gold, chests full of it. Zanzee turned to her with the crown set safely on a blue velvet cushion. It was glorious.

In the centre of the crown, made up of gold raven feathers, thorns and roses nestled amidst a tangle of nature, sat the largest diamond ever seen — the Siren, one of the crown jewels that had been placed in a glass case, never used. It was being used now, in her crown.

Despite the best efforts of the jewellers who had crafted the masterpiece, it sat heavy upon her head, but she didn't mind. The weight reminded her of what she bore, of who she was. The first Queen of Maldessa.

She held her head high as the room bowed to her, their Queen, and she watched as Zanzee took a beat longer than everyone else to submit. Finally, she could begin her true reign without her regent deciding everything.

The banquet was large, the small ballroom filled with tables of dignitaries from each of the Daeneah realms; even a representative from Vulma was there, and some from across the Jaidic seas. The food was rich and plentiful. Glazed suckling pigs sat atop the centre of each table, surrounded by steaming meats and fishes of every variety — no expense had been spared, and the alcohol was even more abundant. The Primlect sat to her left, Zanzee on her right, and Ithrael stood behind her.

The Primlect leaned towards her and muttered in that loathsome way of his, white spit in each corner of his mouth. "It has been decreed that the Calmayan people shall not be granted refuge in our land. It doesn't make sense to bring their plight to our shores." He licked one of his greasy fingers. "We do not want to welcome the wrath of the Hyrathean nation — we will protect our people first and foremost."

Amarea lifted her chin slowly. The Calmayans had always been peaceful neighbours; the Hyrathean attacks were unwarranted.

"And when, pray, was this decided?"

"Whilst you were preparing for the ceremony, your Majesty." He left a slobbery mark on his glass as he took a large gulp then placed it back in front of himself.

"I see." Amarea speared a piece of meat with her nail, lifted her veil, and chewed the roasted boar carefully. "I also see that you invited the Hyratheans here tonight, despite that decision being a politically dangerous one."

"We felt it best, for the sake of peace."

"And for access to their indispensable luxury goods trade?" The Primlect wisely stayed silent, knowing that the Hyratheans had no real trade; they merely sold on what they plundered.

Zanzee, however, had never been one to observe such prudence. "And the Hyrathean prince is here and has requested the first dance."

"Has he now?" She sounded bored even though she knew an opportunity when it presented itself.

When the meal was finished, they all moved to the large ballroom. The ostentatious crystal chandeliers gave the room a soft glow and made the light refract off the thousands of opulent pieces that adorned women's necks, so that the room sparkled. Amarea made her way to her throne, nodding and smiling at the greetings. Her crown no longer sat upon her head; she would only use it ceremoniously from now on. There was no way she could get anything done with that weight on her head.

One of the guards escorted the Hyrathean prince to her. He was handsome, strong and barbaric looking, which Amarea didn't mind in the slightest.

"Your Highness." Amarea inclined her head.

"Your Majesty." He gave her the bow of a soldier.

He led Amarea to the dance floor and they took their places in the centre of the dignitaries.

"You look exquisite tonight, your Majesty," he drawled as he placed his hand lower than was necessary for the dance they were engaging in.

"Why thank you, my lord, how kind of you to say."

"I was considering leaving tomorrow but now I think I might stay a while."

She brushed her body against his as though by accident but enticing him all the same. "You are quite the flatterer."

"And you are quite the beauty, I hear. But I wondered, how are we to know if that is indeed true if we are to never see your face?"

"Some may, with my permission, but I cannot risk it if anyone else is around." She tried to sound innocent and unaware of the allure of her words. He pulled her against him and she could feel his thrill at the prospect of getting her alone. "And how goes your war, my lord?"

His expression darkened. "It goes well."

"Ah, good, I'm so glad to hear it. Wars can really be such a drain on your treasury." His expression darkened further. Yes, she may be a Queen with no real power, but she read the reports; the Hyratheans were haemorrhaging money. She pulled him closer. "I don't like war." His expression changed instantly, clearly enjoying the press of her hips against him.

"Not many women do."

"All those people killed or hurt. It saddens me." She leaned towards his ear. "My lord, I would *hate* for you to come to harm." He had expertly led them towards an alcove as they danced, away from too many prying eyes. Amarea ran her hand up the back of his neck and let her breath brush his ear ever so slightly, sending a shiver through him. "End this war, make peace. I can't bear the thought of ..." She let her voice catch and pulled away. His breathing was ragged and his reaction evident. Men were hopelessly weak. The music had stopped and Amarea found herself blessedly free. She had always hated this kind of politics, although unfortunately, it seemed to be the only way she had ever been able to make any impact.

Not long after, Amarea managed to escape to her room. She had no time to change before there was a knock on her door. Amarea opened it to find Ithrael standing behind the prince. She indicated for Ithrael to go, and the look he gave her was murderous. She ignored the twinge she felt from the judgement; he was just a guard, after all. Instead, she walked towards the prince and gently laid a hand on his chest.

"My lord, I've never allowed a man such as yourself to see my face."

"Only the Brothers?"

"Yes," she whispered, shyly.

He cupped her cheek over the veil, then bent forward and kissed her through it. She had to admit it was an elegant move, even for a murderous barbarian like him. He pulled away and gently gripped the veil, then slowly lifted it away from her face. Amarea tipped her face forward and removed the mask, and finally looked directly at him. He stopped breathing as he took her in.

"My Prince?" Amarea asked, deeply concerned. She truly hoped she hadn't given him a heart attack. That really wouldn't help her plan, and it had, annoyingly, happened once before. He sucked in some air and then his hands were cupping both her cheeks as he drank her in. Amarea was surprised he wasn't aggressive with her; some were when they saw her because the want was so severe. He began to breathe more rapidly and so she leaned forward and kissed him. He moaned in pure ecstasy and she pulled back, afraid to end things too soon without achieving her goal.

"Let me worship you, my Queen."

My Queen. Oh yes, things were working out well. She stepped backwards and allowed him to take in all of her. She could see how overwhelmed he was and so she turned away and took off her veil, unclasped her cape, and peeled herself out of her impossibly tight dress. When she turned, naked save for her jewels and gold paint, he was kneeling before her.

"My Queen," he whispered, trembling.

"Will you do anything for me?" she asked, her voice now firm, her own, and not the simpering weak thing she used in public.

"Yes, my Queen."

"What would you wish your reward to be?"

"To pleasure you, my Queen." Which was what they always wished and what she took, if she desired. She looked at him in his trance, gripping his knees with white-knuckled fists, holding himself back despite his raging desire, and she supposed she should feel guilt for her bewitchment of him but she didn't; she never manipulated someone who didn't deserve it and in truth, they always seemed happy about it. She lay back on the bed and opened her legs, and he knelt before her on the floor.

"You will end your war with Calmaya and you will enact a peace treaty. You will pay them reparations and you will not invade another country."

"Yes, my Queen."

Amarea could hear the tremble in his voice now, his craving for her so strong. She placed her feet on his shoulders, a signal that he may touch her. She lay back and enjoyed the pleasure that he gave, her eyes shut, imagining another man between her legs, and as she found her release, so did he. Amarea sat up as her body shuddered, dropping her legs to the floor. She gripped his right shoulder, digging her nails in, breaking skin and spilling blood — marking him as she had marked others, the sign of a contract with the Queen of Maldessa.

She sat up fully, pulling her robe off the bed and wrapping herself in it. She stood and handed him a goblet of wine and watched him drink. Some of the glassiness faded from his eyes, but when she stepped forward and he took her in again, he was lost once more.

"We have a contract."

"Yes, my Queen."

"If you break it you will never get to experience me again, do you understand?"

"Yes, my Queen."

"And you might want to go back to your room and change your trousers before you let your party know of your decision." He looked down, some clarity coming back. She pulled the hood of her robe up and over her face so that only her lips were visible. She could hear his breathing begin to even out.

"What did you do to me? Was it some kind of a drug?"

"Oh Prince, do you really think I hide my face to be mysterious? A beauty such as mine is a weapon. I use it when I must."

"I need to have more of you." He stepped forward and his hand went to her waist, and she couldn't deny that she was tempted to try something different this time, maybe something more. But no, she knew how to play this; she would not be reckless with the Calmayans' lives.

"Honour our agreement and you may, but until then you must leave."

The door opened as she pulled her dark hood fully over her face, allowing her to still see through the specially woven fabric, and Ithrael threw her a look that was distaste mixed with anger — he had heard everything. No wonder he was put out by her invitation to the prince.

Amarea shut the door on them and walked to her bathing chamber where her ladies had filled the small pool with steaming, scented water. She dropped her robe to the floor and stepped down into the soothing warmth to cleanse away her remaining distaste she felt for taking pleasure in the way that she must to get the results she needed. She loathed that it was the sole weapon at her disposal, at least for the time being.

The look Ithrael had given her was stuck in her mind. She knew why he looked at her that way, knew what he saw, but she wouldn't apologise. She wouldn't forgo the power she had over people just so she could act in a more appropriate manner. The Calmayans could heal — so what if she sliced off pieces of herself to achieve that? She was all too aware that what she was doing removed consent and made her actions distasteful, and there was no real justification, but she would squander her morals and subvert what was right to protect her people and those of a vulnerable nation.

Amarea sank down under the water, and despite how much she tried to justify it, she couldn't help but feel revulsion at her actions, the actions of someone who had fought so hard not to be treated thus. She dug her nails into her thigh and breached the water. She would find a better way now that she was truly in power. She would no longer have to whore herself, and others, to make change.

Chapter Three

ITHRAEL

Ithrael finished his shift guarding the Queen early, making some excuse that he needed to check over the palace security. In truth, he needed to be as far away from her as possible and to walk off his anger and distaste. He understood that she was trying to save the Calmayans, but her methods ... Anger rose up inside him and so he headed to the barrack's training grounds. He needed to beat this feeling out of himself because her moans, her cries of pleasure, they taunted him.

Despite deciding to alleviate his frustration with an aggressive training session the previous evening, Ithrael's mood hadn't improved by morning. He was aware he was particularly brutal when he trained Amarea in combat, but he was unable to control all of his rage. He was, as always, blindfolded, worried that when they fought her bindings might come loose and he would gaze upon her face and lose the thing he treasured most: his self-control.

Amarea seemed to feed from his anger, even managing to land a few blows. He was all too aware that nothing gave her greater satisfaction than hearing the sudden exhale of air and held-back grunt from him when she took him by surprise.

He defeated her and she lay beneath him. "Do you yield?" His voice was deep, coarse.

"Never."

He smiled at her roguishly. She lifted her body up against his in response and put her mouth to his, only a whisper of fabric separating their lips. Ithrael didn't allow himself time to think; instead he pulled back violently and marched to the other side of the room. This was the cruel game she played, always taunting and teasing him and him always, always resisting. He hated her for it. He knew she did it partly for that reason, but there was something else there, something he had to constantly fight.

Ithrael joined Amarea later as she rode to the Neesohan Church, her church. He was struggling more each day to suppress his desires and he sat stiffly on his horse, making it pull at the bit. He had to conquer these feelings; they would do him no good.

He focused on their destination, trying to distract his mind. Instead of not thinking about Amarea, however, he remembered when he had first begun to work for her — he hadn't been able to understand why she was so loyal to the Goddess of Night, of darkness, and so she had explained it to him. "Because Neesoh, Goddess of the Night, is my goddess and my ancestor, the woman whose face it is said I wear, whose power runs in my veins and allows me to heal faster than any ordinary being."

She'd come across as haughty as she spoke and he hadn't particularly liked her at that point. She had continued to try to explain, registering his expression of disbelief. "She is denounced by the Daylarian Church because she fought for her people and condemned her lover, although the reason for this has never been unearthed. Neesoh was the wife of Daylar, God of the Light, said to be more powerful and deemed the greater deity — for daylight surely must mean goodness." She shook her head at that, as if she couldn't believe such ridiculousness. "By walking away from daylight, Neesoh is seen by the Daylarian Church as evil and those who follow the God of the Light as walking the path of righteousness. I prefer to walk in the darkness with my goddess at my side."

"But how can you be sure you follow the right church?"

Her body tensed and her shoulders rose a fraction; he'd started to read her moods through her body language. "Because I *feel* her. She is not who the Daylarians claim her to be. And neither am I." Over the years, he had often thought of those words and how true they had proven to be.

Amarea rode wearing a hooded cape to hide the fact she was hiding her face, but it wasn't hard for people to notice their Queen was passing; maybe he should have advised her to stop adorning her clothes with spikes and jewels. They rode fast, having learned early on that any other speed meant attacks from the locals.

At the Neesohan church, the High Priestess of Neesoh greeted them at the door and the Priestess and Queen bowed to one another — Amarea bowed to no one but the High Priest and Priestess. The High Priestess touched the top of Amarea's head and they then followed her inside to where the High Priest was waiting; he was old and could not get up to greet them at the door. Amarea knelt before him and kissed the ring on his hand, and he gave her a fatherly smile. This man cared for her and had tried to save her from the Daylarian Church many times, but Ithrael didn't fault him for his failure. The Neesohan Church was small and didn't have the power it should, and the High Priest had tried when no one else had.

"We will call them in now," the High Priest said to Amarea.

Ithrael stood near the door, keeping watch as five people entered: two men and three women, all dressed as priests and priestesses of the Church, all her spies.

"What have you learned?" Amarea enquired, looking at each in turn. Ithrael knew they were her most treasured advisers, each of whom she had spent many an hour with, going over plans for their once-great nation.

The leader of their group, Niseem, stepped forward. "My Queen." She bobbed her head in the way of all Maldessan soldiers, a brief, efficient sign of respect. "The distribution of aid to the Calmayans has been successful. Rumours state that the Hyratheans are pulling out." Amarea nodded and Ithrael was grudgingly impressed. The prince had moved quickly; her plan had worked.

Bassiri then stepped forward and nodded quickly. He was the largest of the group, black, and despite being muscular, he was not a warrior — he was a political manipulator who charmed men and women out of their secrets. He could do what Amarea could do only when her face was unveiled. "The high circles are uncertain what your reign will bring. They fear retribution for their lifestyle. They have been seeking the Daylarian Church's guidance and the Atarix Brotherhood is assuring them their positions won't be affected."

Ithrael looked to Amarea and she seemed to sense his need to speak, nodding her head to give him permission. "My Queen, if this is the case, you need to prepare for opposition."

"What kind?"

"Every kind."

She sighed. It wasn't the first time she'd had to plan for physical and political threats. The rest of the news told them what they already knew, that the poor were getting hungrier, the taxes too much a burden, children were no longer attending schools as parents needed them to work or help out at home. Living conditions had worsened; there were fewer merchants and middle class, and the gap between the rich and the poor had widened dramatically in recent years, all because of the greed of a too-powerful Church. Ithrael knew that this all weighed greatly on Amarea, and because of the Daylarian Church she was powerless to do anything about it.

"What policies would be best to address first?" Amarea asked the room, but Ithrael noticed she directed her question mainly at Saia, whose keen intellect saw ways through complex policy that not many could find.

"You're not in a position to alienate the Sancees and those in the high circles — it's too great a risk so early in your reign, but with the poor as they are, a revolt is imminent. The uprising may only have held off to see what you would do."

"A personal fund, then?"

"Yes, I believe so, my Queen."

"Saia." Amarea removed a velvet pouch from her pocket. "I'd like you set up a charity for the poor but keep my name from it, find people to distribute funds and aid." She handed Saia the pouch and Saia slipped the contents into her hand. Ithrael couldn't help involuntary raising his eyebrows — apparently, Amarea was able to keep things from even him, even though he was always at her side.

"But ..." Saia couldn't form words as she looked at what was in her hand — the Siren diamond.

"The other is just glass, no one will notice. It's only a temporary fix, though."

"You'll need to levy the high circles at a higher rate."

"I look forward to it. Can we implement some kind of pay-off if they donate to a charity?" Amarea posed the question to Saia, but it was clear she would have been happy for input from anyone in the room. It was one of the things Ithrael respected most about her: her willingness to listen to others' opinions, even though she was the most powerful person in the country.

"They'll just put it back into the Daylarian Church." Saia was right; the high circles would.

"You'll just have to use the taxes to improve schooling and to alleviate the strain on the lower classes," Niseem consoled.

"Put it in motion," Amarea told the room.

Lisette and her twin brother Leonius had remained silent throughout the briefing, but that was part of their charm. They still knew what part they played, what they would have to do. They bobbed their heads along with the others, and they all exited the room.

For the first year of his employment as Amarea's personal guard, Ithrael would stand by the window, but he now stood behind her chair so that he could read every report, something she allowed, encouraged even. Ithrael let out a small huff of disbelief as he saw what Amarea was writing.

"What, Ithrael? Out with it," she snapped. She hated paperwork, and even though she had sought his counsel, she hated interruptions.

"You should be integrating your sick houses with the care houses," he pointed out, slightly pleased by how easy it was to rattle her when she was doing paperwork.

"Why?"

"If you keep them separate you'll have them competing, passing the sick off onto each other. If you make them one entity under the charter then it will work better. There will be a better level of care all round."

Amarea didn't say anything, not being one to admit outright when someone else had a better idea than she did.

Instead, she began to redraft her work. Ithrael didn't allow himself to feel smug; he knew she'd sense it and find a way to punish him over it.

Amarea signed her last letter and sighed. "If only it was as easy as just killing Zanzee." Ithrael's hands instinctively went to his daggers; he would love to kill Zanzee — all she had to do was order it.

"You could always burn all their abbeys to the ground. You're quite adept at it, if I remember correctly," he offered helpfully.

"I would, but I have a feeling the people would object."

Ithrael started to pace the room. He hated to feel impotent over a problem.

"Aren't you supposed to be *standing* guard?" He could hear the smirk in her voice so he ignored her comment. He would always protect her and he didn't have to be standing right behind her to do that.

"I know we must tread cautiously, but my Queen—"

She coughed as a reminder.

"*Amarea.*" He spoke her name reluctantly, not liking the informality as it blurred the line that he was trying to keep very firmly drawn. "I fear that caution won't serve us."

She tilted her head slightly, which meant she was contemplating his words seriously. "What about creating councils in each of the cities, with lead representatives from all manner of backgrounds?"

"In principle it will help, but ... *Amarea* ... the fact remains that the Church and the high circles are too powerful." She sat back in her chair and tapped her nails on her desk, considering Ithrael's words. "Besides, do you really think you will get any of these bills passed through your council?" She stopped moving her fingers at that.

"I have to try, for the sake of the people."

"I don't disagree, but we need to take greater action."

Amarea stood and joined Ithrael in his pacing. They crossed paths in the middle of the room and continued their ponderous walking.

"The Fold?" she asked.

"Bring the outlaws in?" Ithrael frowned at that.

"We need more men."

"To do what exactly, Amay?" He didn't notice that the nickname from her childhood, the one he'd heard her cousin use often, had slipped out; he was too preoccupied with his thoughts of the queendom. "Marshall rule?" He continued past her, their backs now to each other.

"To remove the high circle."

Ithrael stopped and turned to face Amarea. "Slaughter them instead of going after the Church?" He was intrigued.

"The Church has influence because of the control it has over the high circles. If we harm the Church, we upset the people who worship its god and we risk retribution from anyone else who might hold claim to this throne. If we strike the houses, we strengthen my position here so that I may begin to do good."

"It could start a war."

"My people are starving, what would you have me do? You are the one who suggested action." Amarea flung up her hands in frustration.

"This feels wrong, even for us."

Amarea hesitated, but only for a moment. "Have Niseem make contact but let's not move forward yet. We need to be ready for any eventuality," she commanded, reminding him that she was Queen, something he told himself he must never, ever forget. He could not risk seeing her as a woman, ever.

"And if we cannot find another solution?"

"Let's hope their god is merciful in their afterlife."

Amarea was standing close to him and asked, "Rael, if I fail, who will be there to defend my people?"

"They will fight for themselves."

"And would you lead them?"

Ithrael was standing close to her. Despite what she was asking, he didn't hesitate with his response. "Yes, my Queen."

She stepped closer to him. "Really, if you think about it, you wouldn't be fit to lead them, seeing as you weren't able to keep their Queen alive."

His lips twitched, holding back a smile. "It's likely she made a reckless decision and took action when the cover guard was on duty."

Amarea placed her hand on his chest, over his heart. "You know, if you would just sleep in my room then I wouldn't be able to wander off at night, or have a reason to."

He didn't smile, just raised one eyebrow and leaned forward until their faces were so close he could sense her pulse quicken. "But if I were in your bed, you wouldn't be able to run this country."

"How so?" she asked, distracted.

"Soldiers of the Maldessan army are known for their stamina."

She laughed softly. "Prove it."

"Duty first." He moved forward, responding as though he was going to kiss her, but instead he put his lips to her ear. "You have a meeting with the Primlect." He smiled as he felt the slight shudder run through her body. He had to stop playing these games of hers. He had to remember she was his Queen and nothing more.

Amarea reacted by standing on her tiptoes and touching her cheek to his, letting the soft fabric of her veil brush his skin as she put her lips to the side of his ear. He couldn't help the tremble when she whispered into his ear all the things she would do to him, and all the things she would let him do to her, before pulling away and exiting the room. For the first time ever, he wasn't instantly by her side.

Chapter Four

BASSIRI

The dining table was long and the food plentiful — flavoured rice dishes with large slow-cooked farm birds. Bassiri was carefully cutting up his roasted slice of pheasant as he listened to Lady Gallistry brag about her new diamonds. He knew, just by paying attention at these types of gatherings, that the Gallistrys were struggling financially, thanks to Lord Gallistry's penchant for the gambling houses and the women and men they supplied. It peaked Bassiri's interest that she had new diamonds; some of the other women around the table commented on them, but their interest in the jewels wasn't for the same reason. He didn't have a way in with the Gallistrys — not yet, anyway.

Conversation turned to the Hyratheans and how they were a barbaric race. Bassiri had always hated how the Maldessans could speak of a people in such a way; he didn't like the superiority of it. Even so, he was relieved that the Calmayans would no longer have to suffer the pillaging from their neighbours, whose greed had far exceeded their own borders. As he ate, he dipped in and out of conversations. He was able to do that, be aware of so many things at once — it was what made him so valuable to his Queen. As he looked around, he noticed new clothing and jewellery on some of the other men and women of the party. This was odd, as they were the ones he knew also had financial difficulties. Being a member of the high circles was a birthright, one that didn't always come with the appropriate amount of coin. They were also too stupid to hide their newfound wealth within the high circles — they'd rather preen than be prudent.

After dinner Bassiri approached one of the newly adorned women, one he knew was infatuated with him.

"Gisella, how fine you look this evening. The emerald of your gown really does set off the colour of your eyes."

Gisella blushed at the compliment. "My husband bought it for me."

"He is a generous man."

She was a little drunk, her eyes slightly glassy, which was why Bassiri had chosen to speak with her. "Hardly — it's only because he's now become religious he's being generous."

"Religious? What do you mean?" Bassiri asked, steadying her by gently placing his hand under her elbow. Her blush deepened at his touch.

"You know, Ricard, he wouldn't spend so much as a penny on me, but he's been having meetings with some of the Atarix Brotherhood recently and suddenly he's buying me clothes, redecorating the old house — he's even planning on throwing a ball." She beamed at Bassiri. "You'll come, won't you?"

"It would be an honour. I'm so pleased that your husband has also found his way to our god."

"Who would have thought religion could change a man so?"

"Who indeed."

Bassiri made his way through the party, hearing similar accounts of newfound wealth and religion. It wasn't hard to piece the information together. The Daylarian Church was buying the loyalty of those in the high circles who could be bought. He had to tell the Queen.

Bassiri left the party, slipping out unnoticed, and made his way to the palace through the wide, open paved streets of Saffiere. He loved his city with its pale stone buildings, grey slated roofs. There was something bright and welcoming about the streets, even when you were further away from the palace where the roads became narrower.

It was late but he knew the Queen would be up or would not mind the disturbance. Even at night, the white building shone like a beacon, the gleaming towers reaching towards the stars, a symbol of the power of the crown or at least who owned the crown. Apparently, it was the Church.

The Queen was awake and in counsel with Niseem, and Ithrael was in the room on duty when he reached her study. Bassiri nodded his head in abrupt greeting, having long since been told not to bow before her as others had to.

"I have news."

"Would you mind waiting a moment?" Amarea asked. "Saia is on her way."

Bassiri sat in one of the armchairs positioned near the fireplace. The entire room was a library, each wall covered with books. He'd always liked the Queen's choice of office. They talked of other matters until Saia arrived and he could inform them of the Church's manoeuvre.

"It doesn't surprise me," Niseem remarked as she sipped her wine.

"I don't think any of us are much surprised, but it does mean they're making their move, whatever that move might be," Amarea said, tucking her feet underneath her, a relaxed gesture and something she would never do in anyone else's company. Ithrael watched the Queen as she made herself comfortable and Bassiri could see the struggle on the man's face. He felt sorry for him. It would do him no good to love a queen. There was only heartache in it.

"They plan on blocking any edicts you try to pass to do with education and health," Ithrael said, speaking what they were all thinking.

"Is this to be my life as Queen, to be constantly held back by paperwork?" Amarea rubbed her face under her veil. She was exhausted. Bassiri didn't envy her duty, which was why he worked so hard for her. He knew that she wanted the same things as him, to see the people treated better, to have the education they deserved, to be able to get medicine when they were sick and to have meals on the table. She didn't want to control them as the Church did, to only repay them for their loyalty. She wanted them to have their freedom to live, and that was why he loved his Queen, because he knew that despite appearances, her intentions were good. However, he didn't always approve of her actions.

"We will find a way to move against the Church — just give us time," Saia said soothingly, her eyes bright and alert.

"I fear time is what I don't have." Amarea was looking into the fire as she spoke, her shoulders dropped slightly in defeat.

It was the same fear they all shared. The Church was planning something and Bassiri just hoped they could discover what it was before it was too late. They would have to put a plan in motion to make sure they were ready for whatever was coming.

Chapter Five

DALIA

There was a rapid knock on Dalia's front door. She opened it to find Sofia standing there, barefooted and out of breath. She must have run from her small apartment all alone through the cobbled streets of Fieria.

"It's Mama," Sofia said, barely able to catch her breath.

Dalia grabbed her bag and cloak and followed Sofia straightaway, holding the child's hand as they ran through the streets together. Dalia could still smell the same strange sweetness in the air that had settled over their town a few days ago. It clawed at her, made her nauseated, but she didn't have time to worry about what was happening. Sofia's mother was dying.

In the cramped room Sofia shared with her mother and baby brother lay Missinda, feverish and moaning.

Dalia knelt beside Missinda and touched her sweat-soaked brow. She was muttering to herself.

"The smoke will kill us all. The smoke will kill us all."

"Hush now, you have the fever. I have something for you." Dalia opened her bag and removed a small vial with a dark-green liquid inside.

"Sofia, boil some water for me, will you?"

The small girl went to the hearth and placed the heavy cooking pot onto the grate. When the water had boiled, Dalia poured some into a cup, added three drops of her tincture and carefully fed Missinda the mixture. The same sickly smell that had been lingering in the air was more present in this part of town and seemed to sit heavily in the small, stifling room. Dalia opened the one window to air it. The moonlight fell upon a tapestry Missinda had been working on. She'd always been a gifted seamstress but had struggled with work since her husband's passing in a farming accident. The tapestry showed Fieria aflame. A chill ran through Dalia.

Dalia made sure to feed the children and took her time tidying and making the small apartment cleaner. People had so much less these days, and Dalia was lucky to have her hut and garden. Many couldn't pay but there was always food given to her, and logs chopped and left at her doorstep. These were her payments and it was all she needed. But others weren't so lucky; they didn't have skills that were so desperately in need.

Before Dalia left, she bathed the baby and made sure Sofia washed as well. When they were both pink and clean smelling she kissed them each goodbye and promised to be back later to check on them all. Missinda was breathing easier, the sweat on her brow less now that her fever dream appeared to have eased, and so Dalia went out onto the streets of Fieria. The sickly scent wasn't as strong: whatever had fallen over the town was lifting. She smiled to herself. Maybe the bad omen she had sensed was gone.

As she walked home, Dalia allowed her mind to wander to more pleasant things, like Tomas, the man who left logs by her front door. He had strong farmer hands and kind eyes. *He would make a good husband,* she thought to herself, and had to stop herself from laughing at her foolishness. If her sister could hear her, she would tease her mercilessly.

When she reached her cottage, dawn was approaching. The blue light settled over everything, and the smell of fresh dew made her smile. Dalia stopped at her front door and turned, wanting to take in the morning, enjoy the contentment she got from the peace of the early hours. That was when she saw the first flames. The same flames that had been stitched into the stretched cloth at Missinda's.

Dalia dropped her bag and ran towards the flames, towards the small apartment where two children slept with a mother too sick to get them out. By the time she reached the apartment, the air was thick with smoke.

"Sofia! Sofia!" Dalia yelled from outside. The small pale face of the child came to the window, terror in her eyes. "Open the door." Sofia nodded, and not long after the door opened. Dalia ran across the room, which was beginning to fill with smoke from outside, and gathered the sleeping baby into her arms, making him squawk and wriggle.

"Missinda, wake up." Dalia shook the woman until she awoke, the drug she'd given to calm her fever still making her drowsy. "The city is aflame. We must go."

Missinda sat up and threw her shawl around her shoulders, the fog of fever and sleep leaving her instantly. Missinda took Sofia by the hand and they ran down the stairs together.

"Cover Sofia's face from the smoke," Dalia managed to choke out as she placed the baby's muslin over his nose and mouth. She pulled her own cloak up to cover her own — the smoke so thick now she could barely see. And the heat: stifling.

Everyone in the city was asleep and would die in their beds, the smoke silently killing them before they were even aware of the flames that climbed the buildings around them. The bell. She had to get to the bell.

She handed the baby to Missinda. "Get to my cottage, and then keep going until you're at the trees. The fields in between will stop the flames. Wait for me there."

"Where are you going?"

"I have to warn everyone."

Missinda was looking panicked but she took her baby in her arms and began to run. She had her children to think of and both of them understood that in that moment, saving them mattered most.

Dalia knew the bell wasn't far, but she could barely see now. She stumbled her way towards the central town square, the smoke in the air making it more and more difficult for her to breathe.

As she made it to the square, the bell was still visible in the centre, its iron dome reflecting the light of the flames that were now all around her — every single building that surrounded the square was alight. She reached the bell and with two hands pulled down until the first clang rang out. She continued to pull on the rope, the sound ringing out across the burning town. She began to hear shouts and wails, people waking; some would be able to save themselves.

The smoke was getting too much and so Dalia stopped pulling on the rope and turned to make her way back to her cottage. Her head swam and she knew why. She'd inhaled too much smoke. It was too late for her but she wished, she hoped that others were able to escape.

She stumbled forward as far as she could before she collapsed, and then she crawled, not ready to give up on herself. She'd never given up on a patient and she knew there would be many who would need tending to.

Dalia managed to make it out of the square, and on the other side, she couldn't believe what she saw. People running from their homes only for robed men, *priests,* faces covered, to cut them down. They were being murdered, every one of the people who were trying to escape the flames. Across the street, she made out a large man with strong hands and kind eyes, running towards the chaos. Dalia managed to stand, the smoke thick all around her, and she caught his eye and she knew he was coming to save her, even though he would have been safer on his farm. She shook her head. He had to go; they would kill him. There was pain in his eyes, true pain. But she shook her head again. There was nothing he could do. She gave in then, for his benefit so he knew it was no use, and collapsed to the ground. She hoped he'd turn back; it was all she could hope for now.

Dalia wasn't sad to be leaving such a world behind, only the man with the pair of kind eyes who had come to rescue her. She prayed to her goddess then to protect him. As she slipped into unconsciousness, the world around her burned and blades cut down innocent lives, the sound of their screams the last thing she would ever hear.

Chapter Six

AMAREA

Early in the morning Ithrael entered her chambers when she was barely dressed; that's how she knew something awful had happened.

"What?" she asked, not angry but afraid.

"The fever."

There had been an outbreak in a small town not even a day's ride from the capital. Although her healers didn't think it to be a plague, they had taken precautions nonetheless.

"Has it spread?" Amarea asked. They'd quarantined the area and sent as many healers as the capital could spare.

"My Queen, Fieria has been razed."

"Razed?" Amarea didn't understand; she pushed her flapping ladies away.

"The people were hemmed in and butchered, the whole place torched. There were no survivors."

She grasped hold of her bedpost for support.

"My Queen, they're saying you did it." His expression was pained.

"What?"

"They're blaming you."

"Oh, Gods." She sat down on her bed and ordered her ladies to leave. "How many died?"

"Nine hundred and sixty-eight."

Amarea's hand went to her mouth. "So many." She paused. Her mind emptied, and she felt as though her heart had stopped and she was locked in the horror. And then a breath, and another. "Who is to blame? The Church?"

"I have people investigating but that's my guess. But Amarea." He knelt before her and took hold of her hands; the gesture was so unlike him that she stiffened. "The people are already taking to the streets. They already believe it to be your doing, and even if we can prove it's the Church …"

"We won't be able to alter their opinion of me. It'll be too late." He nodded and she hated the apology in it. She didn't want him to feel sorry for her. She wanted him to fight alongside her. She stood up and began to pace.

"Going out to them won't do anything, and neither will remaining here. I want to visit the site of the massacre to see what has been done to my people. Will going there make things worse?" Amarea clenched her fists; fortunately she wasn't yet wearing her nail spikes.

"There is no way to dispel this now and I feel you must do what you wish. I will take you there, but you'll need to be disguised."

"Give the order that no guards are to raise arms against my people unless they breach the gates. Let them be angry. They should be."

Amarea opened the concealed door in her bathing room and made her way down the short passageway to Mierdas' chambers. He was the highest-ranking mage in the land and kept residence at the palace instead of at the House of Mages. Amarea often felt that he was more important than she, because he kept the elements balanced. This balance was essential for their crops to thrive, so that her people would not starve. In her land, magic untamed and often unchecked could create an imbalance. In the past the sky had burned with fire, the earth had opened up beneath their ancestors' feet and the water had risen so high that it had taken entire cities, pulling them back into its depths. That's why his role was crucial, and that of all the other mages who assisted him in this precise elemental magic, but Mierdas was the one who ensured the stability in this land. Moreover, he had a few other interesting tricks up his sleeve.

Amarea greeted him and kissed his cheek, and his wizened face crinkled in appreciation.

"What can I do for you, my Queen?"

"Have you heard?"

"I have. Such tragedy." He shook his head sadly and shut his already unseeing eyes — his eyelids looked like they'd been folded over, two peaks pointing to one another.

"I need to go to the site, to see for myself what has been done to my people, but I won't be able to get through the streets right now. Might it be possible for you to alter my appearance so that I can see this devastation for myself?"

Mierdas smiled. "It would, your Majesty. Give me an hour."

"Not too hideous, though," she said, unable to help herself.

"Of course not." He chuckled, and she left him as he ran his fingers along his carefully organised shelves, occasionally opening a bottle and sniffing to double-check its contents.

Back in her room, she opened the trunk that sat at the end of her bed, storing blankets for the winter months. Beneath them were her 'sneaking around' clothes for when she needed to escape the palace. But she couldn't risk having a face covering; today she needed to blend in. She put on the loose riding tunic and tight trousers, and pulled on her riding boots. They were expensive leather but she didn't need to pass for a peasant, just a normal person.

She became restless waiting for Mierdas and almost stormed down to hurry him up, but she soon heard his shuffling footsteps along the hidden corridor. She went to the door and opened it, and helped the old man through.

"One drop on your tongue should last you four hours." He held up a vial of deep-purple liquid. "It will transform your face and mask the magic in it."

"There's magic in my face? Is that what it is?" she asked, wanting, as always, to understand all she could about what flowed through her veins.

"What else?" He reached forward to find her hand and patted it.

"Thank you," she said to his parting form, and he held up his hand as if to say, "It was nothing." The idea that her face had magic in it had her thinking but she didn't have time to pursue what it might mean for her. She used the pointed glass stopper to drop a single bead of liquid onto her tongue and placed the bottle securely into a lined pouch, which she then tucked into her cleavage.

She removed her veil and watched as her face transformed. It was a strange sensation but not a painful one, as her features still seemed the same but the luminescence disappeared: her skin became dull, her eyes seemed a little smaller as did her lips, her nose a little bigger, her face a little rounder. She was by no means ugly now, but she'd become pretty, she was normal, and she felt oddly relieved. Amarea opened the door to her room to where Ithrael was standing alone in the hall outside.

"Time to go." He looked up and into her face for the first time and froze momentarily before recovering his composure.

"How much of it is you?"

"It's pretty close."

Then he did smile. "It's good to finally meet you."

He opened the door opposite to hers, the one that led to his chambers, and she stepped inside. Amarea had never been in his room before. It was smaller than hers and far less luxuriously decorated. The bed had a dark wooden headboard, and a dark-blue blanket covered it. There was a desk in the window, polished knives on a dresser, and a door she could see led to a bathing room. He led her to the corner where a dresser stood and pushed on the wall. Behind the hidden door was a passage that led downward and eventually outside. So that was how he was always sneaking around. Amarea was jealous. She was Queen and she didn't have her own private escape, but it was no doubt intentional for her to have chambers that she couldn't sneak out from easily.

They stepped out into the gardens and made their way to the stables. Ithrael disappeared for a moment and came back in normal clothes, having changed out of his uniform. They mounted their horses and headed out. No one seemed to have noticed a thing.

Their ride was long and so it was mid-afternoon when they arrived. They dismounted and tethered their horses in the woods on the outskirts of Fieria. As they walked, the first signs of devastation presented themselves with the smell of smoke and flecks of ash dancing in the breeze. The closer they got the more cinders circled their feet, until they broke free of the trees and before them lay a barren landscape. A landscape that was once so rich with life was now desolate. The bones of houses jutted from the scorched earth like the jagged tines of a pitchfork. They stood on the edge of the town, the woods at their backs, and let the silence settle into their bones. She knew who did this; there was only one group who would do such a thing. She knew she'd never be able to prove it, or even if she could, she would never be able to convince the people that their Church, people of faith, could do something so barbarous.

Amarea knelt in the ash and dirt and pushed her fingers down, whispering a prayer to Neesoh. Her blood felt hot in her veins as she prayed for the innocents. Their screams began to echo in her ears, making her eardrums throb. Neesoh was with her, fuelling her hatred. The Daylarian Church must be stopped.

"I need to see Niseem." Ithrael didn't protest, even though he understood what this meant. She was ready to fight back.

Niseem met them in the woods away from the city. She already knew what had happened.

"Find who did this," Amarea ordered.

"Yes, my Queen." Niseem bowed lower than usual, her eyes burning. There would be bloody retribution that night.

When they returned to the city, there was chaos. People hadn't tired of their protests against the Crown, against Amarea, despite the late hour. It would appear that alcohol had helped to continue fuelling the mood, and in that moment, Amarea had half a mind to join them. She quickly dropped another dose of potion onto her tongue, fearful she'd be trapped within the city mid-change and then there really would be a frenzy. It was almost impossible to anticipate exactly how someone would react when they saw the real Amarea, but it definitely wouldn't be anything good, that was for sure.

Worried for the horses, Ithrael and Amarea dismounted and began to lead them through the city. The animals were restless and she could tell Ithrael was too, despite him hiding it well. She knew that for him, this was far from ideal; he took his role as her protector a little too seriously. A group of drunken men jostled past Amarea and knocked her, nearly tripping her up. Ithrael threw expletives at them and checked Amarea for damage — as if she could even be damaged.

"If you carry on like this, people will get suspicious."

"Just pick up the pace, okay?"

As they neared the city's main square, the noise level rose steadily until they could see the centre of the gathering — at least they weren't outside the palace. Standing on the back of a stone panther that guarded the central fountain was a man whose face she couldn't see. He was speaking to the crowd, and as they neared, she could hear what he was saying.

"We cannot allow this to continue! She takes our money in taxes and spends it on jewels and shani dresses that barely cover her body, flaunting her wares for all to see. Has she no shame? She takes from us to live in luxury, sleeping with any man who will pay her attention whilst her people starve! And then when sickness comes to her country she *burns* it out, pretending to send healers to help when in fact they are too afraid to even enter the sick houses!" That was news to Amarea; she was going to have to have words with a few people.

"It's time to take back what's ours. It's time to overthrow the high circles and make this a place where everyone can prosper!" There were enthusiastic cheers from all around.

"You know," she said to Ithrael as they passed the square by, "If I bring down the high circle, the Church will attack me. If I bring down the Church, the high circle and the people will attack me. If I supress the people's revolt, as is expected, the people will attack me even more."

"Then you shouldn't attack anyone."

"That's not my point. My point is, yes, I can manoeuvre to try and improve my situation but I won't be able to stab Zanzee through the hands next time he places them on the table and uses them to push himself up into that slow rise before he starts to condescend me."

"So you're mainly upset that you can't inflict pain yourself?"

"Precisely."

"It's an unfair and cruel world."

She looked around at the thinning crowds. "Will this pass?"

"For now." They walked back to the palace gates in silence and without further incident.

The reports of the treasurer's death reached Amarea by first light. A heart attack in the dead of night. No one was surprised; the man had been grossly overweight and had the propensity to suck the fat from a suckling pig. Disgusting. And by some strange coincidence, one of the other High Sancees was attacked on the same night as he left a gambling house: he was currently lying in his bed in a life-threatening condition; apparently, he owed a large amount of money to quite a few of the city's lenders.

When she was alone she allowed herself to smile at the news. Did they really think she would retaliate in a way that they could trace back to her? She was strangely grateful for the timing of her people's riot. They would not be able to prove a thing. Just because she was a woman did not mean she was not intelligent enough to manipulate the board. Those two initial moves were the most important: the treasurer because, well, he controlled the government's money, and Lord Eamos because he was the one High Sancee who seemed the most adept at bribing everyone on the Church's behalf. Two main players were out of the game; it was time for her to move her pieces into place.

She walked into the council chamber covered head-to-toe in a veil secured in place by a simple, twisted-gold crown of rose thorns. She liked the idea of being a haunting figure on the day after the death of two High Sancees. The council stood as she entered and she could feel their unease at her attire. The greatest benefit of being a woman, one so beautiful she had to hide her face, was that they never quite knew what to make of her, and that gave her power.

"Gentlemen," she said, before the Primlect decided to continue with the tradition of speaking first. The council sat and she remained standing at the head of the table. "The news today has indeed been shocking. And even more sadly, I don't believe in coincidences." Amarea turned her head so that they knew she was looking around at each of them. "Someone in here has made a deadly mistake. I will discover who sought to gain power and in doing so manipulated my council, the highest order in the queendom." She noticed some of them cringe at the mention of their kingdom now being a queendom. "This also leaves two seats that need filling — I suggest this is done by the end of the week to prevent any ... instability."

Every man in the room wanted the treasurer's job so that he could skim money and increase his already expansive wealth. The time had come to put forward names. Amarea didn't suggest anyone; she kept silent. If she were seen to prefer any one person, they would never be elected. The names were drawn and she already knew whom her pick would be, but they were not on the list. She allowed the rest of the meeting to continue without any intervention from her. Behind her veil, she began to plot and plan. How foolish of these men to underestimate a woman.

Niseem came to Amarea's study later that day.

"We've discovered who attacked the village. We found a few eye witnesses but they've been too afraid to come forward." Niseem hesitated. "Too confused by what they saw, that they believed the perpetrators had dressed up as Daylarian priests, until one man was spared by his own brother who is a priest in the Church."

"He admitted he saw his own brother?"

"He told his wife. She didn't feel the same loyalty as him — her sister was in Fieria when it burned." Niseem swallowed hard, fighting the emotion they were all feeling.

"Oh, Gods."

"It's the proof you wanted, though — it was orchestrated by the Church," Ithrael responded.

"And probably the order came from that snake, Zanzee." Amarea dug her nails into her desk in anger.

At nightfall, Amarea rode hard with Ithrael at her side. When they arrived at their destination, she slipped from her mount, a flask of oil in one hand and a tinderbox in the other. Ithrael helped Amarea pour a trail in oil but stood back to allow her the privilege of striking the first flint. Amarea watched as it fell from her hand, falling end over end until it landed in the saturated ground. It caught the oil instantly, and she stood back to admire the path of destruction as the flames raced along the course they'd drawn, trapping the brothers inside. The first scream brought a smile to her face.

They waited until the last cry had died down and then checked to make sure none of the priests from the burning abbey had escaped. It didn't right the wrong the Church had committed, but it was a start.

Amarea was working at her desk, the late winter sun warming her back, when the duty guard opened the door and her cousin Tristam sauntered through. He bowed deeply as was expected, but when the door closed behind him, he pulled Amarea into a hug.

"Did you not eat at sea?" she asked him, relieved to see his sharp features after two long years but surprised how rail thin he'd become.

"Unfortunately the sea didn't always agree with me." His hands went to his stomach and the corners of his mouth turned down.

"Goodness, I would never have sent you away as my envoy if I had known you'd suffer so." He sprawled himself across her settee and his mouth sliced into his naturally sharp smile, a smile that meant mischief and secrets.

"Suffer? My Queen, I positively thrived." There was a daring twinkle in his eyes. "But I am sorry I missed your coronation. We had a little trouble in Tangua."

"What in Neesoh's name were you doing there?" Amarea was excited by the distraction Tristam brought.

"I thought it might be fun."

"Tris, only you would think a pirate port would be fun ... *Was it?*" she asked, desperate to hear of his escapades.

"Immensely." He began to regale her with his misdeeds, most of them so outrageous even she almost blushed. Almost.

Amarea had been told her cousin was a terrible choice for an emissary of the Crown — he was too fickle, too reckless, too flirtatious. But what she saw was his guile and his ability to put anyone he met at ease with his seemingly harmless charm, beneath which he could be as ruthless as she was, and he had a far keener mind. But it was his ruthlessness that she understood and valued best.

"How's ruling treating you, Amay?" His tone was light but she could hear the interest beneath it.

"Oh, you know, Church and State getting along as well as can be expected. In fact, today we have been putting forward names for the new treasurer. Unfortunately, poor Sebastian had a fatal heart attack last night."

"Did he indeed? How unfortunate. I wonder — did news of my intended arrival reach you in time?"

"It did, late the night before last."

"Well, that was lucky." He tapped his chin thoughtfully. "Dear cousin, I was thinking, now that I've returned and I am next in line to the throne … would a High Sancee position be available to me? Although I have adored my travels, I do miss home." He pouted theatrically.

"But of course. You are from the greatest house in the land. You must have a position on the council. In fact, dear cousin, how are your numeracy skills?"

"Now you ask, my Queen, they are very proficient."

"Excellent. I suggest you go and speak with the Primlect immediately because no other house should be considered for the position now that you've returned."

"I'm glad we see it the same way." He kissed Amarea on her veiled mouth and left, but not before eyeing up her current guard with obvious appreciation. Amarea wished she could see the Primlect's face when Tristam walked in and laid claim to the new title. Council meetings were about to get far more enjoyable. But for now, there wasn't much she could do. Politics moved slowly and so must her scheming; otherwise, she was at risk of being caught and would lose whatever power she'd managed to grasp in her few short weeks as ruler. Her country was in turmoil and the Church was trying to destroy any support she might have. She paced around her room, her veil stifling her; she didn't know if she needed to fight someone or fuck them.

Chapter Seven

AMAREA

The following night Amarea was in her room with nothing to occupy her time and anxious about everything that was happening in her queendom. She needed to let off some steam and Ithrael was off duty so she had no one to torment. Without thinking it over too much, she uncorked the potion Mierdas had given her and put one drop onto her tongue, then changed into her 'ordinary' clothes. Amarea checked her hands for remnants of gold dust and then turned to look in the mirror. Her face was even plainer this time; she must have accidentally taken a larger dose. She was still pretty but definitely plain, and Amarea felt relief to be less than she was. She would never renounce her title, her obligation, but she would renounce her beauty in a breath.

Amarea opened one of the many arched windows in the curved wall where the tower connected to her room, which gave one part of her bedchamber a half moon of glittering glass. She leaned out and looked down to the balcony below; the drop wasn't too great. She climbed out onto the window ledge, crouched down, grasped the sill with her gloved hands and then let herself drop. She was wearing supple riding boots, so when she landed her feet didn't make too much of a sound. Across from the balcony was a tree, just about in reach. She took a deep breath as she teetered on the stone railings, then launched herself forward — leaves tore off the branches as she slid and fell until she had a firm grasp. Her heart pounded with adrenaline but she had a huge smile. She'd missed doing stupid and rebellious things — it had been far too long since she'd been out alone. She swung and dropped to the ground and made her way through the arches that led to the main hall. No one recognised her; in fact, their gazes slid over her as if she was nothing. She made her way out of the palace and into the city. Into her city.

Amarea knew of the drinking establishment that Ithrael preferred — it was the one all the soldiers preferred, the one where the whores were 'clean'. She removed her gloves and tucked them into the belt tied around her tunic and pushed her thin dark trousers into her boots. Her hair was loose, so she quickly plaited it as she walked and tied it with a thin strip of leather from her pocket. The fashion for women wasn't often trousers — most preferred a more feminine dress — but Amarea had always chosen the clothes of a traveller, finding more comfort in them, and she was better able to move if she encountered trouble.

The roof of the drinking house was low; in fact, the entire building appeared as though it had sunken into the ground, making it seem seedier than it might otherwise have appeared. Amarea opened the door to a room that felt humid and reeked of stale alcohol and flatulence. She marched straight to the bartender, confident that she had another four hours before her glamour wore off. She ordered a beer and it came slightly chilled from the barrel, which was pleasing. Only after her first taste did she turn to take in the room. There were men, whores, women, even a child in the small room with sawdust-covered floor. And there, in one corner, was Ithrael.

He looked up, sensing Amarea's presence, and their eyes locked for a moment before she looked away disinterested, even though he would have recognised her disguise from the other day. Those piercing gold eyes didn't miss a thing.

A conversation with a group of three men, one of them handsome, drew her attention, and she toyed with the idea of having some fun even if Ithrael noticed. Amarea laughed at the handsome man's joke and from the corner of her eye, she saw Ithrael stiffen. She assumed he didn't like the attention she was drawing. She could feel his glare, then, but she ignored it and continued her conversation. The handsome one invited Amarea to sit at a table with him that had just become free, and she didn't decline.

Ithrael wasn't in her line of sight and so she propped herself forward on her elbows to talk to the man she was with to keep an eye on Ithrael's movements. The man's eyes dropped to Amarea's cleavage; she didn't pull away. In fact, she found it thrilling to be appreciated as another person, the other version of herself, instead of being revered. As the man talked about himself, something about the conversation on the table next to Amarea's snagged her attention. Two young men, maybe even boys, and a girl, not quite a woman, were talking and something they'd said had caught her consideration. Their clothes were travel-worn and they looked as though they'd barely slept in days. They'd been talking about the Queen, about Amarea.

"She's bewitched the kingdom, you know she has. That's why there's so much poverty. If we can just counter the magic she wields, then we can rebuild this nation." The only way they could possibly do that would be to chop off her head, *silly children*. Amarea noticed the way both boys looked at the girl, both clearly in love with her, both going to suffer heartbreak until she had chosen. *Such foolishness, such naivety.* Amarea hadn't poisoned the queendom — the Church had. If only Amarea had the power they spoke of. But she would. She would.

The handsome man hadn't even noticed that Amarea hadn't been listening to him. He reached forward and playfully tugged on her braid. Amarea smiled at him in a way that said he could tug harder if he liked, and that's when she felt the presence behind her, the one so familiar, so comforting.

"It's time to go." Amarea looked up at him and scowled.

"Who are you to tell me what to do?"

"Amay." His voice was stern, as if he were talking to a child.

Amarea crossed her arms and sat back. "Come, have a drink with us Rael, it would do you good to relax." She enjoyed using his nickname; she liked the way it sounded.

"I was supposed to be having the night off."

"Do you two know each other?" the handsome man asked.

"We're old friends. He can be a little protective." Amarea smiled seductively at the man as she rested a hand on his arm, and rolled her eyes for good measure.

"*Amay.*" Ithrael was getting really pissed off and Amarea couldn't help but be thrilled by the exchange, by being able to look Ithrael in the face without the blur of her veil.

She stood and rested her hand on his face. "It's good to see you." He sucked in a breath, part anger, part surprise, and she began to weave her way through the revellers, the handsome man calling out protests as she went, until she was out in the cool night air. Ithrael wasn't far behind. Amarea turned to face him. "It's okay, I'll go back now."

"What were you thinking?" He gripped her arm in frustration, the only person who would dare to do such a thing.

"You didn't object before."

"Because I was with you. You cannot leave unguarded, not at a time like this." He took her in. "Mierdas has a lot of explaining to do. He shouldn't let you have control of such magic."

"It was just a bit of fun. I got bored. You need to lighten up, Rael."

"You got *bored?* You have a country to run — try filling your time with that." His grip on her arm tightened and his face was so close to hers that she could smell the alcohol on his breath. He was a little drunk, and the thought of him being even slightly out of control excited her.

"Can't we just go back inside? Have some drinks, talk about everyday things? Do things other people do?" Amarea leaned towards him, her lips nearly touching his. He pushed her back against the wall.

"Gods, Amay! You have to stop this."

"Why? What harm will it do?"

"I'm supposed to protect you. I can't protect you if I'm fucking you."

"Actually, I think that would be a wonderful way of protecting me." She smiled teasingly at him. "And with this face you won't be in any danger. It'll be like screwing one of your whores."

"I don't screw the whores," he said, offended.

"Maybe not, but that's how you see me, isn't it? The woman who whores herself for her country." He slapped his palm against the stone wall behind her and leaned in.

"You are not a whore, but dammit Amay, if I have to listen to you, you—"

"What?" she asked, breathing the word out slowly, arching her back towards him. His teeth were clenched so tight the muscle in his jaw began to spasm. She brushed her lips against his ear and felt him shudder. "What are you so afraid of?"

"I can't." He was barely able to speak the words as he looked into her eyes.

"It isn't a crime. We both want this." She managed to slip her hand under his top and rested it on his hard stomach.

"I have a duty."

"Yes, but I still don't see the problem." Her fingers pulled at the waistband of his trousers and she brushed them against his bare skin. He loosed an agonised breath and so she whispered into his ear, "I always think of you when I come." And that did it, finally, after months of taunting his self-control cracked, and oh, Gods was she glad for it. His lips smashed against hers, his anger still hot and evident in his kisses — they were fiery and desperate and exactly what she'd always wanted from him. He pressed his whole body onto hers and she was fumbling at his belt when she heard a girl and a boy laughing because they'd caught them. Ithrael pulled back and watched them leave.

"They were the ones talking about me." And the moment was broken; she'd inadvertently brought the soldier back.

"What were they saying?"

Amarea rested her head back against the wall, trying to catch her breath, clear her thoughts. "I'm poison to this kingdom."

"Fools." He looked at her then, really looked at her, cupped her face in his hand and ran his thumb along her cheek. "I like this face." His smile was small, shy even.

"So do I." Because she knew her beauty frightened him. He kissed her, gently this time, and the tenderness annoyed her. She wanted him to want her, not to love her — what good was that? She fumbled for his belt again, but he pinned her arm above her head and when she tried to use the other, he pinned that one too. She was angry but she knew from far too many sparring sessions that she wouldn't be able to fight him off if he didn't want her to. She hooked her foot around his leg to bring him closer but he pulled back and chuckled.

"What's the rush?"

"I only have three hours left."

"Plenty of time." He kissed her neck with soft caresses and she snarled at him. "Always so impatient." She could feel his smile in his next kiss so she bit him. He pulled back in shock and then glared at her. "I think it's time you went home."

"Don't talk to me like I'm a child." All thoughts of getting him into bed vanished, replaced by her irritation.

He picked her up before she had the chance to defend herself, slinging her over his shoulder, and began to carry her like a sack of potatoes. Her, the Queen, being carried like potatoes — it was unheard of.

"Put me down this instant!" she hissed.

"You're not my Queen. You can't order me to do anything."

"Ithrael …" Her voice was threatening.

"You've clearly had too much to drink and need to be taken safely home."

"I've only had one beer! Besides, your training isn't doing me any good."

"What do you mean?"

"You kidnapped me far too easily."

"Hmm, good point. I'll increase your training. Better see me in the training room at 5 a.m." She groaned childishly. "You're the one who wanted to be trained."

"Yes, but I'm also the one who has to read through countless documents and talk to countless men about countless policies. 5 a.m. is too early."

"Only time I can do I'm afraid — I'm too busy escorting the Queen around to meetings the rest of the time."

When they reached the palace, Amarea still thrown over his shoulder and beginning to feel like she might actually be a sack of potatoes, he stopped, plonking her at the base of the tree she'd climbed down.

"I'm assuming this was your route?" Ithrael raised an eyebrow at her.

Amarea crossed her arms. "I'll see you in the morning." She didn't look back as she turned and began to climb, but she knew he was watching her, unable to leave, forced to be there to save her in case she fell. The boundaries of their relationship angered her, but she couldn't help a swoop of triumph as she leapt from the tree to the balcony without a misstep and then, pulling a short dagger from each of her boots, slammed one into the mortar between bricks, and then the other. Using her feet, she expertly scaled the tower, using her momentum to prevent her from slipping. She reached her window, hauled herself through and looked down from the window, triumphant, but Ithrael had gone. Amarea paced her room for a while, emotions swirling inside her, and then she heard the door across the hall click shut — Ithrael's door. She peeked through the keyhole and saw the guard on duty, and let out an aggravated sigh.

Amarea didn't sleep well, so when she was standing in the training room at 5 a.m. her mood was foul. Ithrael was unusually chipper and she missed his sombre seriousness. She hated this new, teasing side to him.

They were allowed exclusive use of the room without an additional guard when they trained because of the risk of Amarea's face becoming exposed. She'd removed the tunic she usually wore as training gear, and underneath she was wearing a top that had been cut short and sewn tight to hold her breasts in when she exercised. Her stomach was bare, she was wearing loose trousers cuffed at the ankle, and she wasn't wearing any shoes. Her scowl was thunderous but her aim was true. Amarea's state of undress threw Ithrael momentarily so that she had the opportunity to strike him when his guard was down. She kicked out his leg, and for the first time she was able to knock him onto his back. Fortunately for him, the floor had special matting so that he didn't end up injured; this time it saved him some bruises.

"Not so clever now, are you?" Amarea said through her veil — it was hot and uncomfortable. Ithrael hadn't had time to blindfold himself yet, so she could see his eyes glitter as she held him pinned to the floor. Amarea mistook the meaning because the next thing she knew, she was on her back and he was kneeling down, looming over her, his legs straddling her.

"I'm always clever."

Amarea was breathing heavily and she could see his eyes catch on her cleavage; she took advantage of the moment once again and swiped out one of his arms so he was off-balance, and forced her body weight up. Her hips slammed into his and she could feel his arousal; surprise halted her momentum so that he landed back on top of her. They were frozen in the unexpected moment of intimacy. There was only a wisp of fabric between them and Ithrael's undoing.

"We can't. We shouldn't."

"I don't care about what I should be doing. I only care about what I want."

Amarea lifted her veil so that only her lips were uncovered and she kissed him, the sensation different this time, as though before the potion had numbed her lips.

"Amay... the Church would forbid it." He sounded pained as he spoke.

Her hackles rose. "Why does the Church scorn such a thing as pleasure?" She leaned back so she could take in his face. "What's so wrong with it? It's an act of worship, of showing the other person your devotion to their body. It's an act of exploration of each other's desires, of knowing someone as others could not. It's an act of release and completeness. Is that not religion of a kind?"

"Yes." He pulled her veil back down. "And I would worship you fully but it's my duty to protect you. My duty comes first." With that he stood and walked away. The rejection burned Amarea. She felt humiliated and angry.

She straightened her veil and clothes and stormed out of the room. Ithrael was waiting on the other side of the door and he followed her, as he always did. His proximity made her want to scream.

Amarea had to endure the rest of the day with him constantly nearby. By the time she went to bed, she was exhausted — she'd spent the entire day resisting scraping her claws down his arm in retaliation to his rejection. Him and his cursed *duty* and *honour*. She went to sleep with the bitter taste of his dismissal coating her tongue.

Chapter Eight

ITHRAEL

The smell of smoke woke Ithrael. Moments later he burst into Amarea's room to make sure she was safe. She sat up in shock, and fortunately for him the darkness hid her face but she still covered it quickly.

"The people are rioting." He threw her clothes from her chest and turned his back to her as she dressed. He watched as the crowds gathered around the outer gates of the palace. Huge pyres burned. They were trying to breach the wall. Amarea dressed and allowed Ithrael to lead her through her bedroom and bathing room and into Mierdas' chamber.

"Where will we go?" Amarea asked him as they burst into the magician's laboratory.

"The sea."

Amarea yanked her hand from his. "I will not leave my people."

He tempered his anger. It was his instinct to protect her and it was hers to protect her people. "Your people want you dead."

"As does everybody — that doesn't mean I'm leaving."

Ithrael stared at her but relented, knowing he couldn't win an argument when it came to her queendom. "The mountains, then." She didn't answer but he'd persuade her. The mountains would do for now; at least there he could find a way to better protect her. Mierdas emerged from his adjoining chamber wearing a robe.

"You're coming with us," Ithrael told him after quickly explaining the situation, but the old man shook his head.

"I will only slow you down. Before you go, my Queen, I must have a word." Mierdas took Amarea aside and spoke quietly and quickly, so quietly even Ithrael couldn't hear. Ithrael began to get agitated; whatever Mierdas was telling Amarea it was taking an age. He needed to get her out of the palace, to safety. Rebels could burst through the doors at any moment. Finally Mierdas pressed a small, ancient, leather-bound book into Amarea's palms and kissed the back of each of her hands. "A lot depends on you." Ithrael didn't want to hurry their parting but he was conscious that the main doors would be breached by now. He had to get Amarea to safety.

"If I flee, then the High Sancees will take over again and Zanzee will resume control. I cannot give them even the smallest advantage."

"If you die then they take more than an advantage."

"I won't go to the mountains." Her tone was enough for him to know she wouldn't budge on the matter. She turned over in her hands the leather book Mierdas had given her.

"Summon the others." She swept past him and back to her chambers.

Ithrael swore under his breath. "We need to chain the door."

"You'll find some in one of the trunks in the corner," Mierdas said.

"Why do you have chains?"

"For securing my goods when I travel."

"Right, of course." Ithrael began to open Mierdas' trunks in search of the chains.

Ithrael refused to speak to Amarea as he secured her door and stood guard.

"They're here." It wasn't so much a sound but a feeling — he could sense their approach. Amarea straightened her clothes as Ithrael unbolted the door he'd just locked.

Niseem and Saia nodded their respect. Everyone in the room waited for Amarea to speak first.

"It's time to enact the rest of the original plan — all of it, tonight." She turned to Ithrael. "Maybe I should be grateful to the people for the uprising — after all, it is the perfect cover for our scheme." There was a smile in her voice. Niseem accepted the instruction instantly, but Ithrael could see Saia considering, as she always did when anything was presented to her.

"To have it seem like the people took out key members of the high circles is dangerous. What repercussions will they have to endure?" said Saia.

"Zanzee won't decree anything that will harm the people. He'll leave that to me and I have no intention of them taking responsibility for my actions."

"It's a risk." She pursed her lips in thought, not in disagreement. "Have you another way out of this situation?" When Saia thought, it was as though you could see her brain working.

"Not one that holds a better outcome. At least this way we eliminate part of the problem," Amarea said. "However, Lord Tiemenin and his family are to remain unharmed."

Ithrael bit his tongue — sparing Lord Tiemenin created a risk to Amarea and what she was trying to do. Ithrael knew she did it for Estelle, her ex-lover, and so he kept quiet, despite his misgivings.

Amarea turned to Niseem. "Make sure the kills don't seem professional. I want them to look hurried, desperate, and if I hear that anyone other than our targets has been harmed, please let our contractors know I will happily send my entire army to help me take back The Fold. It is mine, after all."

"Yes, my Queen." They turned to leave and waited for Ithrael to undo the chains.

"And be careful." It wasn't like Amarea to offer sentiment, but Ithrael knew that she treasured these two women, and she would need them more than ever in the coming days. "Stay close by in case I need to get a message out." They left without another word. Ithrael would know where to find them if needed.

Chapter Nine

AMAREA

Amarea joined Ithrael at the window and considered him as he looked out over the riot outside. The gates wouldn't hold for much longer. They were running out of time. He was blessed with eyes that saw better in the dark than any other soldier she knew, and it was this gift that allowed him to keep track of events unfolding out in the darkness. It was clear there was something different about his eyes — they had a ring of fiery gold around the pupils, eyes that seemed strange in one with white hair. They said he was born with hair as black as night, but that when he was sent to his trials his father had wanted to test him to prove his family was the strongest, and so when he was only thirteen years of age, he made him fight three snow lions. He came back from the fight covered in scars and hair as white as freshly fallen snow. Some said the fear did it, others a sign that the spirits of the snow lions were in him. Amarea just believed he was born with unusual white hair. Either way it didn't matter; it made him distinct, made him seem all the more fierce.

"There's something I need to tell you." She hated the tension that had fallen between them but she knew she was about to make it worse. It didn't matter; suppressing the Church was all that mattered.

"What is it?" Ithrael asked, and Amarea could see he was hoping she'd changed her mind about escaping the palace.

"There's something you need to know." She fetched the small book from her dresser.

"The book Mierdas gave you?"

"It's a diary, actually."

"You've read it?"

"Mierdas told me what was in it." She tugged on her veil, feeling uncomfortable. "It's Neesoh's."

"The Goddess — she had a diary?" Ithrael appeared unconvinced.

"Protected by magic so it wouldn't deteriorate, apparently." She was sure her tone conveyed her own scepticism.

To his credit, Ithrael didn't show his own cynicism, even though she knew he'd feel the same as her. Instead, he touched the ancient journal carefully. "Why is this of importance?"

"Because of what Mierdas learned from it, long ago. As have all the royal mages. It's about her magic, my magic." She'd found it all a little hard to accept when Mierdas had whispered it to her. But having glanced through the book, she had to admit it was possible it had belonged to her ancestor.

"The one that heals you?"

"And bewitches those who see my face." He looked at her expectantly, waiting for her explanation, waiting for the revelation Amarea needed him to hear. "There's a way for you to be immune and for you to share in the magic that heals me." Despite her hope that it was true, she still struggled to keep some of her pessimism from showing.

He didn't respond instantly; instead, he considered her words. He replied tentatively, "I don't need healing, but I would like to be done with the veil. What do I have to do?" He took her hand in his but Amarea pulled it away.

Amarea felt uncharacteristically nervous. She cleared her throat and tried to add more conviction to her tone because whatever they believed, she needed to try. "We must be linked."

"Linked? Linked how?" She could hear his hesitation.

"Linked by Neesoh, and if one of us dies, so does the other."

Ithrael huffed a laugh. "Even if it was true, I wouldn't put you at risk like that. How would I defend you if I was worried my own injuries might become yours?"

Amarea continued reluctantly, finally revealing her true desire. "Because your magic will become mine."

"My magic?"

"When you killed the snow lions you drew out Daylar's dormant magic — you became the first vessel for his power since he left this world."

"You're saying I am the embodiment of Daylar and you are the embodiment of Neesoh? We are the ... what ... second coming of our gods?"

"Something like that."

She could tell he was struggling with her revelation. He breathed out with an expression of incredulity.

"I want to give you my healing power, Ithrael, and I want your strength to help defeat the Church." Amarea smiled, but she knew she was asking to take something that he may not be willing to give, that she'd weaken him by linking them, because her life was perpetually in danger. This was not an ideal arrangement for him. It was a selfish want of her own, but Gods, she did want his strength and to be rid of her gods-damned veil when they were alone. She wanted him to see her. Maybe then he wouldn't be so reluctant to be with her.

"You want me, the man holding Daylar's power, to give you what you need to destroy his Church?" His eyebrows were raised, his lips quirked in a rueful smile. Oh yes, she saw the irony too. "If I did this, what would it entail?"

And so she told him of the ritual, of how their blood had to mingle to bind them, how their bodies must be joined. To his credit, he didn't react when she mentioned the final, sexual element.

"What is it?" she asked, irritated, thinking he wasn't paying attention.

"If you are Neesoh reborn and I'm the reincarnation of Daylar, then surely I heal as you do? I haven't scarred from injury since that day, and you have the same strength. Maybe you can't beat me in training because I'm just physically bigger than you? Maybe if you fought a mortal man …" He said 'mortal man' with a self-satisfied smirk. "… you would beat him."

"I hadn't thought of that … Maybe, but my face. What of that?"

"You know… there is another solution." She hated the hope she saw in his eyes. She hated that she would have to crush it.

"That's just an old tale." An old tale of Neesoh and Daylar, of when he was first able to behold her face without falling under a spell. Her beauty was so pure even a god couldn't look upon her face without falling under her enchantment.

"But for you to be born with the face of a goddess and the tale to pass through countless generations before coming to fruition, surely it's a history lesson."

"It's a story of a god and a goddess, not a history lesson."

He held up the book. "This diary might prove otherwise." They stood there facing each other in silence. Amarea was reluctant to deliver his wish.

"It's still a binding."

"Amay …" He wasn't scolding her; he appeared upset she would think that of him.

"It's a lot to ask."

"And linking our lives together isn't?" He threw up his hands in exasperation. "If you don't want this to go any further, I understand. I know that—"

"What? I have a propensity to take whomever I want to my bed?"

"Yes." He glared back.

"Fuck you, Rael."

"What are you so afraid of?"

"Men! Of the control they have had over me my entire life," she yelled.

"I have never controlled you. I'm asking you to be with me."

"And I want to be with you but not like that. You don't know what that power would do to you."

"Then we don't do it!"

"There has to be another way, without the linking or me having to marry you." Ithrael looked like Amarea had slapped him. He looked as though she'd rejected him entirely.

"I thought I was the one person you trusted, the one person you were your true self with. My mistake." He turned away from her and she wanted to throw something at him, to scream, maybe even to beg for him to see reason, but that was something she would never do.

"I will not hide out any longer. I'm going to prepare myself. Summon the twins." Amarea went to her bathing chamber and seethed. Neesoh had left Daylar because he'd controlled her, abused his power. He couldn't accept that she was as powerful as he was, maybe even more so. Amarea would not have a man undermine her reign.

Amarea stripped off and using a basin of water, not having time to fill her bathing pool, she washed quickly. Using her thin blade with a mother-of-pearl handle, she shaved most of her body hair away. It was the new fashion and she rather liked the feel of her silken skin. Amarea dried herself, then oiled her now-smooth skin with the oil of jojoba.

Whilst her skin was still slick with oil, Amarea pulled on her tight-fitting outfit. She wore leggings adorned with small black plates of metal that looked like scales. The bodice was more like armour, plated in smaller pieces around her hips and waist, but over her breasts were gold raven feathers, razor sharp. The sleeves were separate from the bodice and were in the same design as her leggings, but they finished at the wrists with cuffs of small, gold raven feathers. Instead of her usual nail extensions, she wore gold filigree gloves with talons. Amarea sat down at her vanity and began to apply make-up.

Amarea finished making up her face and stared at herself in the mirror, at a face that could stop a heart from beating, that could kill, excite, torment. Her curse, her blessing. Amarea placed the black veil over her head and tied it at the base of her neck to hold her veil in place. Next, she clasped her cape on, the black shani fabric falling around her in ripples of blackness so absolute it was as though night-time's shadows had been woven into each thread.

Then Amarea placed her crown upon her head — there must be no mistaking who she was to the queendom on that day.

"It's time to go." Despite his reservations earlier, Ithrael fell into step behind his Queen, the twins behind him. It was time for Amarea to make her entrance.

Chapter Ten

AMAREA

The hallways were empty as they walked towards the throne room. Adrenaline sang through Amarea's veins; she had been waiting for this moment since the day she'd stepped inside the abbey, since the church of her people took control of her land. Amarea walked down the hall, the shattered glass of the large mirrors that had adorned the walls covering the floor. There were two Maldessans at the door to the throne room. They weren't soldiers but they were holding the swords of her personal guards. They didn't bar their path as they reached the throne room; instead, they opened the doors and stepped aside.

Amarea walked into the room at a leisurely pace, a nightmare in black and gold. The room fell silent as they all turned to her, and froze. This was the power she had; she could stop a room just by entering. Amarea walked through the crowded room and stood before her throne, then slowly sat, Ithrael at her side, the twins nowhere to be seen.

Amarea took in the scene before her. It was filled with an angry mass of her people. She saw the fever in their eyes. They were out for blood. Amongst them, she even noticed some of the elite. *Smart.* They wanted to be there if she was overthrown so they could muscle their way into a strong position. Instead of addressing the room immediately, she waited. There was power in silence — something you only learn when you can wield it. A boy close to manhood stepped forward when the silence had been stretched so long it was uncomfortable. He was one of the trio Amarea had seen at the inn.

"I'm here to claim what is rightfully mine."

"And you are?" She didn't hide the derision from her voice.

"My name is Aiden and we have the same father."

Amarea laughed long and hard. "You're an *illegitimate* son. You have no claim to this crown, child."

"I do. I have the backing of the people and the blood of the king in my veins."

Aiden couldn't see her smile but it was a cruel one as she said, "Ithrael, if you wouldn't mind testing his claim?" Ithrael stepped forward and the boy proffered his arm. Amarea was reluctantly impressed to see he didn't shake when the warrior with eyes that burned as molten gold sliced his hand. She watched as he bled ... and started to heal. It wasn't irrefutable proof, but it did mean something.

"So, *brother*, how will you rule?" She made sure to sound amused.

"Fairly. I will help the people, the poor." Aiden tilted his head back and raised his chin defiantly.

"A noble gesture. And how do you intend to do that?"

"By only taxing the rich and giving that money to the poor houses."

"Oh, the ones run by the Church? Interesting." She sighed and sat back in her throne. "Dear *brother*, if you don't tax the people, how are you going to pay for infrastructure that helps the people? If you only tax the rich, don't you think they'll ask for more of everything because of their contribution? The rich are also powerful — you risk alienating potentially powerful allies. If you give money to the Church, how can you be sure it's not going to go to the high circles and bolster their position in government? Do you think ruling is just giving things away?" Amarea bent forward. "Politics is dull, child. It's paperwork and slow, painful negotiations. You live in a fantasy, boy. You will ruin this queendom."

"You murder your people! You have watched as they suffer and starve. You even burned down another abbey, filled with holy men who helped my friends and me. And you've just killed off most of the High Sancees." His eyes were scorched with righteousness. Such fire — what a shame she would have to snuff it out.

"*Brother*, you mustn't listen to everything you hear — did no one ever teach you that?" She relaxed back on her throne. "Oh yes, father wasn't around for you, was he? I suppose he wasn't much around for me either, what with him being dead. Neither could he have been around for my mother for that matter, what with him bedding your mother."

Aiden seethed. He had a pretty face; maybe he was her brother after all.

"You see, what I've learned, here in this palace, surrounded by men, is how to rule." Amarea slowly rose to her feet. "What I have learned is that the Church has this country in its grip and is suffocating it." She could see where Zanzee stood, then. His face didn't hide his fury at her slight. "What I have learned is that there is no way to stop the men who stand in my way unless I silence them, permanently, myself." She was on Aiden in a second, her hand at his throat, her nails sinking into his skin.

"No!" screamed the pretty girl from the inn. She ran forward, the other boy at her heels.

"Is this who you choose, girl? A boy with big ideas but no inkling how to rule, who would destroy this country? Not the stoic friend who is always there for you? Who, I imagine, treats you far better." The girl's eyes went wide, clearly surprised that Amarea could see so much of their relationship, not knowing that she'd seen far more from their behaviour at the inn than they would have liked. "This boy knows *nothing* of what it is to rule, the sacrifices you have to make." Amarea dug her nails in deeper. "*Kneel.*" Her voice fell into a quiet, resonating command.

Amarea could see he wanted to resist her but she forced him down to his knees. Maybe Ithrael was right; maybe she did have the strength of her goddess in her. "You are right about one thing. Sometimes politics just won't suffice." She pulled her nails free and watched as the blood dripped from his neck and then quickly halted. He'd paled slightly, but she'd hardly weakened him.

Amarea straightened and looked at the room. "Do you follow this *boy*?" His blood slowly dripped from her nails.

"Do you follow this idealist?" She placed the pointed heel of her shoe in his shoulder and pushed him back. Her strength was too much for him and he toppled pathetically.

The twins stepped forward, cloaked in black shani capes Amarea had gifted them. Between them, they held the Primlect. "You want your country back?" The faces in the room were confused, but in an instant, Amarea was before the Primlect and she ripped out his throat in one swift movement. His eyes bulged as blood gushed from his neck. She dropped his flesh to the floor and then held her hands out wide. "This is what I do for you, my people. The council is gone. Only the corruption of the Church remains. Together we can rebuild, remove the hold they have over us."

"Stop this madness at once!" Zanzee couldn't hide the almost scream from his voice. He stormed towards her.

"Will I have to kill you too, priest? It won't be the first time I've had to kill one of the Brotherhood."

"We all know what you've done to my brothers. We all know you slaughtered an entire abbey full of peaceful, religious men. Not once, but *twice*. You are an abomination! You are not fit to rule."

"And how do you intend to stop me, Zanzee?" The Primlect's blood had soaked into the hem of Zanzee's white robe and was starting to spread further up the material. Amarea found it oddly satisfying to see.

"If a ruler is seen to be unfit, the Church can stand in until such time as a replacement is found." He rested a hand on Aiden's shoulder. "The legitimacy of this boy will be granted and he will be properly educated until such time as he's ready to take the throne." Amarea began to laugh; she couldn't help it. It was all too ridiculous, too perfect. This was his plan all along — to discredit her, to show her as bloodthirsty to her people. Oh, how gloriously she'd underestimated him.

"Zanzee, you clever man." There was a moment of silence, a calm before the chaos that she knew was about to erupt. She could hear the warm blood dripping from her fingertips, hear Zanzee's ragged, excited breath, feel Ithrael just a step behind her. Amarea nodded once, signalling him. She slashed her nails across Zanzee's throat. The wound was superficial — she knew it would be — but she needed to get herself in a better position if she was to survive this fight, and although she relished the thought of ending Zanzee for good, she didn't have time to kill him. She stepped back so that she was beside Ithrael.

"I presume this is what you were training me for?" The crowd was surging towards them. Amarea removed her crown and placed it carefully on her throne.

"Well, I hadn't thought you'd do this, exactly, but yes." Amarea could hear the smile in his voice. He didn't judge her for the blood she'd spilled, not him. She knew the monster that lurked within, the one that he held back, his wild and untapped violence, the ferocity she couldn't wait to see unleashed. She could feel the power in her blood now, Neesoh's blood, and it was calling to her.

"Try not to kill all my subjects. I would like to have some people left to rule over."

"Yes, my Queen."

The moment came; the first strike. It was from a wild-haired man, his clothes ragged and old. This man had suffered under her reign, but no more. She would end his suffering on that day so that she could rebuild. She blocked his sword with her arm, then ripped it from his grasp and ran him through with his own blade. "Neesoh take you," she uttered as she turned and sliced across the belly of her next attacker, a woman, broad-shouldered and fierce. She was sorry for her death, and she once again spoke a quick prayer to her goddess, the Goddess of Darkness.

At her periphery, she could see Ithrael fighting with all the wildness of his savage heart and all the control of his soldier training. Amarea wanted to be able to stop and watch him in that moment as he took on the hoard, her king, her god. She spun and sliced off an arm. She ducked and severed a heel tendon. She rolled and hammered the hilt of her sword into a kneecap, shattering it. Ithrael and Amarea were fury itself, fighting against a storm, and by the gods, they were winning.

But then, something went wrong and Amarea was on her knees, and she didn't know how it had happened. She'd trained for this, though; she was about to jump back up when something held her in place. She could not move. Aiden, her supposed brother, stepped around to face her holding a sceptre in his hands: Amarea's sceptre.

"Crafted by Daylar himself, I'm told." He smirked at her with all his youthful arrogance. "Zanzee showed me a little trick the other day." Amarea noticed then that the blue stone that sat encased at the top of the staff was glowing. Her strength was no match for the magic within the stone, but she continued to push against it.

"You are not fit to be Queen any more." He had raised the sceptre as if to strike her when a dagger whipped through the air and sank into Aiden's wrist. Amarea managed to catch a glimpse of the attacker from the corner of her eye and saw that it wasn't Ithrael who had thrown it; it was Tristam.

"I think I might have just as much a claim to the throne as you." The look in Tristam's eyes told her all she needed to know; he was buying her time. She kept trying to move, an arm, a hand, even a finger, but nothing. Amarea felt as though she'd been turned to stone. She couldn't even blink. As always, she felt Ithrael's presence before she saw him. And she knew then that all was forgiven, that they were one. His bloody hand slipped into her own.

"I am yours," he whispered.

As I am yours, she wanted to say. All her anger was gone, and she knew that despite their argument they were going to be okay. They were one, with or without a binding. She realised what he had planned but she could not be afraid for him, not now. He sliced through the back of her veil and it fell from her face. Amarea looked upon the blue stone with eyes unguarded and she blinked once, twice. She was free. Amarea stood, Ithrael's hand in hers, and the boy turned to her having sensed her movement. Tristam turned away, his jaw clenched, but Aiden could not turn back once he saw Amarea's true face.

"What's the matter, brother? See something you like?"

Her face, exposed in that room, was an act more violent than her slaying each one of them because she was taking away everything they stood for by forcing them to be beholden to her, their true Queen.

"This ends now," Amarea commanded, and the room was filled with the sound of metal clattering to the floor — every weapon relinquished except for Ithrael's whose eyes were closed. Amarea's hand slipped from Ithrael's as she approached Zanzee and watched him fight against her power. "How does it feel to know my true power? Do you feel as your brothers did? Do you need to exalt your god, on your knees, spilling your seed onto the floor as they did? Do you feel the need to punish me for the sin of my face, for what it does to people? For what it does to you?" She had to give Zanzee credit; he continued to stand his ground. Amarea walked back to her throne, stepping over bodies and severed limbs as she went, Ithrael following her, stepping exactly where she had trodden. His blindfolded training sessions had prepared him for this very moment.

Amarea stood before her throne and looked over the carnage and the faces of her people as they struggled with the vision before them, dressed in black and gold with a face of death and beauty. Some had fallen to their knees in worship; others were clawing at their own skin. Some looked ill, from either injury or the effect of her. Most were lusting for her, their Queen.

Before them, they saw their own vision of their goddess, of Neesoh. Her face. Amarea's face. Looking upon her was not something a human was supposed to be able to do. The divine were never supposed to be seen by mortal eyes. And so to look upon their Queen was to be bewitched by the magic that ran through her veins from her ancestor, the magic that was stronger in Amarea than in any descendant before her, the magic that had made her face that of the divine, which made even the strongest fall before her.

"Be still. Be calm." The room settled a little. "I am your Queen. I will remain your Queen." She paused and took in a breath, feeling distaste at what she was doing. She would rather kill a subject than bewitch them. At least when they fought, they did so for their own purpose. This victory felt hollow.

"The boy, Aiden, will join Tristam on my council as a High Sancee. Tristam will arrange for each town to put forward a representative who will also have a place on the council." Amarea turned to the boy, blood stains smeared across his neck. "But if you fuck with me again I will have your head." He looked suitably frightened.

"Zanzee, the Church no longer has a place in my council or in this palace unless invited. Your funding will be significantly reduced and you will go back to simply worshipping your god." His face was filled with beautiful damnation for her soul. "I was really looking forward to killing you and replacing you, but better to have an Atarix I know and distrust than any other. Be warned. If you disobey me I will visit you, my face unveiled, and make you wish you were dead. The things I will make you do to punish you for your disobedience would make even Neesoh renounce me. But I would do it, for my people."

"You won't get away with this, Amarea."

"Careful, Zanzee." Amarea smoothed her hands over her hips and let out a seductive sigh. "You have no idea what I'm capable of." He broke out into a sweat and Amarea felt satisfied. She really did think she was rather good at her job.

Amarea left the room, her face still exposed, and Ithrael followed her out into the hallway.

"One more thing, my Queen," Zanzee said from the doorway. His hands were behind his back, and Ithrael, who was standing in front of Amarea, drew his sword and stepped forward. Ever her guard, despite her own strength.

"You cannot have it all," Zanzee said. She didn't understand what such a frail-looking man could do to either of them until she saw what was in his hands. Zanzee held up a large shard of mirrored glass, a piece that he must have retrieved from the floor, which was still covered in shattered pieces of the mirrors that had once hung intact upon the wall. Amarea's reflection was revealed to Ithrael in the splintered piece of mirror in Zanzee's liver-spotted hands. Ithrael's eyes went wide.

"No!" she said, her voice merely a gasp, and covered her face. "Rael ..." She heard him turn quickly and he pulled her hands away and stared into her eyes.

"Beautiful."

"No, Rael, no." Amarea found herself sobbing. She hadn't cried since she was a child and had found herself unharmed by the destruction of the abbey. This couldn't be happening, not to Ithrael.

"Amay, it's me." He kissed her tenderly, not wildly or passionately. There was no madness in his burning eyes. He then turned of his own free will, stepped forward of his own free will, and drove his blade through Zanzee's heart of his own free will.

"But how?" wheezed Zanzee.

"I've relinquished myself to him in body and soul," Amarea said as she stepped forward to stand beside Ithrael.

"No magic, no ritual," Ithrael said as Zanzee slipped through the blade onto the floor. "But you tried to break her heart and for that you must die."

Amarea knelt before Zanzee's dying form. "Look into the eyes of your god, Zanzee. He has slain you. There will be no afterlife for you." He was horror-stricken as he gulped his final breaths, gazing up at Ithrael as realisation dawned: that Daylar lived on. Amarea stepped away from him, letting his life drain away across the marble floor of her palace.

Ithrael and Amarea stepped into her room alone. He closed and locked the door before pulling her to him and kissing her with the desire of a thousand nights spent apart in longing. She knew that his duty no longer mattered. All that mattered was that they belonged together. He could see her when no one else could. They tore at each other's clothes until they stood naked, truly naked, before one another.

"Let's do things that'll make even our gods blush." His smile was wicked and feral as he lifted her up and she wrapped her legs around his waist and felt him push inside her. Amarea let out a cry of pleasure, not even a little bit sorry for the blood of those they had slain still covering their naked, intertwined bodies.

PART TWO

Chapter One

BASSIRI

Bassiri lay with his head resting against his arm, watching as Lord and Lady Gallistry left his room. To them he would have appeared a man contented, sated from their night of revelry. But with Bassiri, looks were often deceiving.

Bassiri's presence was hard to miss and yet he could slip through a room as though a whisper in a rowdy crowd. His cheekbones were high, his lips full and his skin tone marked him as a man from the prosperous nation of Assisa. There was no doubt that Bassiri, the son of a wealthy merchant, was beautiful. Lady Gallistry looked back once at his recumbent figure, his dark-purple sheets barely reaching his torso, and he knew that she wished she could go back and leave her husband on the other side of the door.

Such was Bassiri's effect, and it was a weapon he chose to use most. The parties he attended were one thing, but between the sheets was where he extracted the most secrets. His Queen had never asked him to use such methods for his spying, and she would never expect it of him. The way Bassiri saw it was that if he was going to obtain information from the rich and powerful, he may as well enjoy himself whilst doing it.

Once the door clicked shut, he headed straight to his bathing chamber. He kept no servants; the secrets he acquired were too precious to be overheard and so he washed and dressed himself. He wore a tunic of midnight blue over matching trousers, and a dagger at his waist. In the queendom of Maldessa, it was foolish to think you didn't need to be armed at all times.

He strode through the opulent halls of the palace's western wing, the wing reserved for the Queen and a few of her inner circle. His soft-soled shoes barely made a sound on the high-polished, grey-veined white marble floor, shoes he always chose to wear for their discretion. Outside the entrance to the throne room, two guards opened the heavy doors and let Bassiri pass without question. There were few granted such privilege.

The Queen was sitting on her throne, and although Bassiri couldn't see her expression behind the black veil that hid her bewitching beauty, he could tell she was annoyed: her posture straight, hands clenched around the ends of her armrests, the gold tips of her nail extensions digging into the wood.

"... and if your Majesty would grant us the right of way then we would much better serve the queendom," the man in front of her protested. Bassiri managed to hold back his smile, even when he caught the eye of Ithrael. She hated small pettiness being brought to her but she had agreed, once she had rid herself of opposition, she would hear her people out, once a week, to show them that she cared. The trouble was, she just didn't care for the trivial.

Bassiri stepped forward. "Excuse the interruption, my Queen. I'm afraid I have some urgent business to discuss with you." Amarea turned her head slowly; her shoulders sank just a little, which told him she was relieved for his interruption.

She stayed facing him as she spoke. "Tristam, would you be so good as to take over?" There was a saccharine sweetness in her tone, one he knew she put on to irritate her cousin, now officially their country's treasurer.

"Of course, my Queen." Tristam bowed from the other end of the hall and managed to keep his expression neutral, even though Bassiri knew he hated these sessions as much as Amarea did.

Bassiri would like to pretend that he hadn't seen Tristam there from the moment he'd stepped into the room, but somehow, whenever Tristam Condessa was in the same room as Bassiri, he always knew where he was.

Amarea rose from her throne, a fluid and powerful movement, and walked towards the eastern door that led to the council chamber. Ithrael fell into step behind her, and Bassiri followed. The meeting room was plain by palace standards. It was a place of business, not for show. Bassiri waited for the Queen to sit before he pulled out a leather chair and sat at the large wooden table.

"I do hope you have something to tell me, but if you don't I'm still grateful for the escape." She removed her jewelled circlet and stretched out her neck.

"Our suspicions were correct." Her body stilled as he spoke; he had her full attention. "The Gallistrys were approached a few weeks ago to relay a message from one of the brothers of the Daylarian Church to the city of Ruist. The Church has been funding them to be go-betweens for months."

"*Ruist.*" Her words were almost a snarl.

"It appears the Daylarians have found a formidable ally."

"And the message?"

"They will support any action the Vulma Supreme Leader may take, so long as the Church's status within Maldessa is restored." Bassiri crossed his hands and waited. Ithrael sat down next to the Queen and let out a breath.

"Do you think they plan to invade?" Ithrael asked Bassiri.

"Possibly, but the Vulch don't like to be seen invading nations — they're more likely to find another way." Despite the threat, Bassiri didn't feel concerned, not when he was in a room with the two most powerful people he knew.

"We're barely on our feet after everything the Daylarian Church and high circles did to this country. They may choose to invade … We'd be an easy target, too." The Queen rested back in her chair and turned her head towards Ithrael. "How large is their army?"

"Last report from the High General, one hundred thousand men. Well-trained, well-armed."

"Neesoh help us," Amarea said with a hiss.

"I think we should include the others in this discussion, my Queen. Niseem and Saia might have some more insight, but I do not feel the Vulch strive for all-out war. The Vulch don't like to be seen as the aggressor they are. We should be more concerned with how else they might try to take your throne." The Queen listened as Bassiri spoke, and agreed. That was why he had been amongst her advisers for so long; she listened to him, although she didn't always heed his advice.

Chapter Two

AMAREA

Amarea made her way down the hall to her private study. Ithrael, as always, was close behind. Once the door had clicked shut, she removed her stifling veil and shook out her dark-brown hair. She rested her hands on her desk, the one her father had ruled his kingdom from, the one she now sat behind and tried to make things right from. Ithrael placed a hand upon her back.

"We'll find out their plans before they attempt anything."

She let out a sigh and turned to face him. She loved his face, the silver scars that ran across his skin like the lines of a river on a map, his golden eyes that spoke more to her than words ever could. She rested her head against his broad chest. "Will we ever get a moment's peace?"

"No." She leaned back against the desk and scowled at him. Laughing, he pulled her towards him. "You're a Queen. Queens don't have the luxury of a quiet life."

"Is there anyone I can kill to make this problem go away? I have enough to deal with here without having to worry about foreign invasions and your church resurrecting itself."

He let go of her, his expression changing in an instant.

"It's not my church."

"You have the spirit of Daylar within you. Of course it's your church," she countered, spoiling for a fight.

He crossed his arms and gave her a levelling look. "I may be the ..." He waved his hand around, trying to think of the correct terminology, "... *personification* of Daylar, but they're not my church. They're a corrupt organisation that uses religion as a weapon."

"Fine." She threw up a hand, not sure what she was angry with him for.

"I'm sorry there isn't anyone you can kill." He pressed a kiss onto the top of her head. "But I'd be happy to spar with you. I'll even let you draw some blood."

She looked up at him, relieved by his distraction. "Such sacrifice. Must be that godly essence." She looked towards his crotch with a cocked eyebrow.

"If only you had more of Neesoh in your essence, maybe then you wouldn't have such a filthy mind." He pulled her towards him and she smiled into the kiss he gave her. Gentle, tender, maddening. She would have had him then and there but footsteps were approaching; she could tell he heard them too, by the slight clench in his jaw.

"What did I tell you? No peace." She kissed his cheek and picked up her veil and placed it over her head as she went to sit behind her desk. Ithrael took his place behind her as a knock sounded on the door.

They had only heard one set of footsteps approach, but as the door opened Saia stepped forward, with the twins Lisette and Leonius waiting behind her.

"My Queen." Saia curtsied. She was the only one of her inner circle who did; having been brought up in the palace as a serving girl, she couldn't get out of the habit. But long ago, Amarea had discovered the woman's intellect and recruited her. She was skinny, and Amarea often wondered if she was too distracted with work to remember to eat. Her chest was almost flat, her hair a dark blonde and her features plain. Amarea had always thought of Saia as pretty, and she liked that she didn't conform to society's demands of being preened constantly. Saia was wearing a plain, charcoal grey, loose-fitting tunic and trousers. Ever since Amarea had removed Saia from cleaning duties, she'd worked with Amarea and the Neesohan Church.

"Bassiri informed you of the situation?"

"Yes, my Queen. Niseem is still in Fieria overseeing the rebuilding of the town." Despite the deference Saia showed her Queen, she spoke with confidence. Amarea had always admired her for her sharp mind but she respected her more for her ability to speak it without fear.

"I'll have a message sent to her to let her know what's happening." Amarea would never leave Niseem out of anything. Since the events that took place eleven moons ago, she planned everything with her inner circle. "Lisette, Leonius — I need you to go to Ruist and see what they're planning with the Daylarian Church." They acknowledged the order with a nod of their heads. "And be careful. I want you both home, and soon." They bowed their heads to her and left the room. She always found their silence, their stillness, strangely comforting.

"My Queen, I believe Bassiri to be correct. The Vulch won't attack outright — it's not their style. They prefer to use methods that are more subtle. They seem to worry about the way they are perceived by the other Daeneah realms."

"But not ours, it would seem." Amarea tapped her taloned nails against her desk. "Can you look into methods they've used in the past? It might shed some light on how they will come at us."

"I've already begun looking. I should have something to you by morning." She curtsied, readying to leave.

"I'll have a plate sent to you in the library." Saia smiled, a blush on her cheeks, and left.

"You embarrassed her," Ithrael reprimanded.

"She doesn't eat enough. It concerns me."

Ithrael began to massage her shoulders. "Another worry you've decided to take on."

"Tell her to take better care of herself, then! I can cross it off my never-ending list of things to worry about. Are all my people eating well enough, including Saia? No, not really, must do better! Do all the children have access to schooling? No, not yet, must do better! Do I have an army big enough and strong enough to defend this realm? No, not yet, must do better! How are people feeling now I've started to implement taxes? Terrible! They hate me! Must do better!" She threw up her hands, her voice almost raised to a shout.

"Want to postpone your meeting with Aiden? We could spar, or spar naked?" Ithrael's smile was wicked.

Amarea groaned. "I'd forgotten I had to meet my worm of a half-brother."

"He's not that bad."

"He's so whiny."

"He's young and learning."

Amarea pulled off her veil once more. "Let's spar in here, on my desk. Aiden will just have to wait." Her smile was wild, and so was his.

Chapter Three

ITHRAEL

Ithrael made his way through the palace following his Queen's every move. Before she'd claimed back her queendom, being her shadow had never bothered him, but lately — lately, he felt differently. He continued to follow her to her chambers and then waited outside as the ladies of Astree, those whose husbands Amarea hadn't slaughtered when establishing her reign, removed her formal attire behind the closed door. When they'd gone, he stepped inside the Queen's personal chambers. She was sitting by her window, looking out over her city. Her hair was down, no make-up upon her face. As the nights were getting colder, she was wearing a loose-fitting yellow tunic with loose, matching trousers. She was breathtaking. Sometimes he wondered if he was, in fact, bewitched by her beauty as others were, but then he remembered Mierdas' words: "When she relinquished herself to you fully, the power in her magic no longer touched you." And she had relinquished herself to him, in body and mind, as he had with her. So why wasn't it enough?

He knelt before her and took the cup of warm spiced milk from her hands. "Amay."

She smiled down at him. "Everything alright?" Her voice was soft, tender. He was the only person she spoke to in this way.

"Marry me." Her body stiffened, her chin lifted slightly. His heart clenched.

"No, Rael. You know I won't." She loosed a breath and cupped her hand to his cheek. "Please stop asking me." There was pain in her eyes. He knew she didn't like hurting him but even so, every rejection stung more than the last.

"I want to be at your side."

"You are at my side."

"No, I'm at your back." He stood but kept his eyes on her.

"I'm not having this conversation again." Her tone was dismissive, the one she used as Queen.

He clenched his fists and his response came out harsher than he intended. "Of course you're not, because everything has to be on your terms."

Her eyes turned cold. "I have given myself to you. Is that not enough?"

"No." He forced himself not to feel the ache that was building. How could she not see what this was doing to him?

"I will not have a man undermine my reign." The softness was gone from her voice.

"I've never asked to be king, merely your consort so that I can stand *beside* you when your enemies are near, not behind you."

Her eyes threatened tears but Amarea didn't cry. "Have I not given you enough? Do I not make you feel my equal?"

He turned to look out of the window at the soft glow of lights in the windows of Saffiere. A city of her people. He knew they would always come first, as his duty as her protector would always come first for him. But he deserved to be treated as her equal, and not only that, he wanted her to be his wife — a normal symbol of their union where nothing else about them was normal. He wanted to celebrate their love with their friends. He wanted for them to be their own family, when she had none. He wanted to give her that, at least. There wasn't much that he could give his Queen.

He turned back to face her. "I can't do this any more. I want more than you can give."

She stood up and clasped his face in her hands, tears spilling down her beautiful face. "Rael, what are you saying?"

"I'll be your personal guard — I will always protect you — but I can't be with you in this way."

She brushed her tears away with the backs of her hands. Gold dust that had been painted onto them and not properly removed transferred to her cheeks, making them shimmer. "Is your pride so wounded?"

"Not my pride. My heart." She stepped back as if he'd inflicted a physical blow.

"I don't understand, Rael." She shook her head. "I really don't understand. You know I can't give you what you want, and you know why."

"Because of all the men who have harmed you. Yes, I know, Amay." He stepped forward and brushed away another tear that had escaped. "But I am not those men and I can't spend my life as anything but your equal."

"You are my equal! Why else can you look at me when no one else can?"

"I don't doubt your love for me, but your fear of men will drive us apart and I can't bear for us to break on bad terms."

Her body went completely still; she was a deadly snake about to strike. Her voice came out low and cold. "You are no longer my personal guard. I no longer want to see your face inside *my* palace. You shall return to the barracks and return to your rank of captain, the rank you held before becoming my personal guard."

"Amay!" He let out an exasperated huff. "Don't be unreasonable. No one can protect you as I can."

"Unreasonable? *Unreasonable?*" She glared at him for a brief moment before yelling, "Get out!"

He stood his ground for a moment, ready to argue, but the fight quickly left him. Amarea was stubborn; he wouldn't win this argument. He turned around and left, closing the door behind him.

He made his way down to the barracks and as he walked, he made sure there were enough guards on duty in his absence. He stepped into the eating hall filled with off-duty soldiers sitting around laughing and drinking together — the barracks often became a makeshift drinking house in the evenings. He spotted Niseem sitting talking to her wife, Gallia, and headed over to them.

"You're back."

Niseem looked up at him, her dark eyes alight. "Just back. It's good to see you."

"How are things in Fieria?" He sat down next to Gallia and poured himself a mug of ale from the jug on the table.

"Progressing much better now." She gave him a wry smile and Gallia snorted a laugh.

"So modest my love."

"Modesty?" Niseem raised an eyebrow. "Didn't you claim the other day you could beat Ithrael in a dagger-throwing contest?"

Gallia shrugged. "He may be gods-blessed but I have better aim." She drank from her cup and looked up at Ithrael, a smile in her eyes.

"A challenge, Gallia? Really? I trained you to be a soldier." His tone was dry but he felt relief to be distracted.

"And it still stings that a man five years my junior taught me to fight."

"Well, I am ... what did you call it? Gods-blessed." He finished his ale and poured himself another glass. Niseem studied him.

"You're supposed to be on duty tonight ... *What happened?*" Ithrael shrugged and decided to avoid Niseem's gaze by looking into his drink. "Oh, you didn't ask again did you?"

"Can you blame me?"

He didn't miss the look that passed between Niseem and Gallia. "I don't blame you but you know she won't change her mind."

"Oh, I know. She's demoted me." He swirled his ale before he took another long drink.

"I was going to report on Fieria and find out more about this Vulch threat, but now ... I think now I'll leave it until morning." Niseem shifted in her seat. Ithrael didn't blame her for being wary of Amarea when she was in a mood.

"Did she throw anything at you this time?" Gallia asked, her lips quirked in a barely suppressed smile.

"Just words."

"She's good at throwing them, too." Gallia remarked, having spent many hours working in the palace as a guard.

Ithrael let out a sigh. "Can we talk about something else?"

"But I heard the Queen kicked you out!" Ithrael turned to see Tristam standing behind him.

"Oh good, the news is spreading already." He went back to his drink, threw it back in one and poured himself another.

Tristam slapped him on the shoulder before sitting down next to him. Wine appeared in front of him with a crystal goblet. Ithrael looked over at the retreating servant. "Our ale not to your taste, Prince?"

"That warm horse's piss? I prefer my grapes to my grains." Tristam took a sip of his wine and straightened his deep-red tunic that had elaborate gold embroidery along the cuffs and neckline. Although he was the Queen's cousin, Tristam didn't look much like her; his skin was lighter, his hair a softer brown, and his nose was on the larger side. "So, what did you do this time?"

"How was your trip to Calmaya?"

"I know you're trying to change the topic of conversation but I'll bite because I do so love talking about me." Tristam regaled them with his usual over-exaggerated tales — drunken bar fights, being chased down the street by an angry lover, lavish parties.

"Tristam, we all know there weren't any lavish parties — the Calmayans are barely functioning after the Hyratheans nearly destroyed their entire kingdom." Niseem levelled him with a look that was akin to that of a schoolteacher. They had grown up together — her father was friends with his parents, and Niseem never let Tristam get away with tall tales.

Tristam let out an exaggerated sigh. "Do you want some wine, Nissy? It might relax you." Gallia pouted at her wife.

Niseem threw up her hands. "Why does everyone think I need to relax?"

"Because you do," they all said in unison, which made even Niseem laugh.

"I'll relax when we don't have threats on every border and down every street."

"My love, you'll never relax if those are your parameters." Gallia stretched over the table and gave Niseem an affectionate kiss. Ithrael looked on wistfully.

"Don't sulk, mountain goat, she'll come around eventually." Tristam poured him some more ale. "Let's get you drunk. Have you ever been drunk?" Tristam ignored the large soldier's glower. "No, I don't suppose you have. I think it would do you good. Stop you being so brooding all the time. Makes people sad seeing you loping around after the Queen, giant sword in hand."

Ithrael looked at Tristam in a way that he was sure conveyed how many ways he was planning to hurt the prince. Tristam cleared his throat. "Maybe you need to relax as much as Niseem needs to."

"I don't need to relax!" Niseem protested.

"Really, then why have you started shuffling in your seat? You're desperate to go home and read all the reports that came in whilst you were gone." Gallia waited, eyes bright, for her wife's response.

"There's a lot going on at the moment," Niseem said in a quiet voice.

"That's it!" Tristam slammed his palms down on the table. "Gallia, we're going to teach these two how to have real fun." Ithrael didn't have the energy to protest any more and so he allowed Tristam to lead them to his favourite tavern where he drank and drank, but no amount of alcohol dulled the pain in his heart. He had lost his Queen, and this time, it was for good.

The following morning, with a pounding head Ithrael made his way to report to the commander of the palace guards. As he walked through the tunnel that led to the senior military compound, he found that he was at least grateful Amarea hadn't banished him from the palace. She could have gone so far as to send him away from Saffiere entirely.

Commander Denmer was sitting behind a large oak desk that wore the years of its service to many a commander by no longer holding any varnish; the wood had split in places, and in front of where the commander sat there was a groove in the surface, as though every order signed had slowly worn away the surface.

"I cannot say I'm surprised to see you but still, you are the last person I'd ever have expected to be demoted within my ranks." Denmer looked up at him, his pale grey eyes of those from the mountains bore into him. Denmer's face was lined with age, his nose red and slightly bulbous, his teeth small and yellowed. In his youth, he would have been a formidable figure — age had shrunk him somewhat, but he could still command a room filled with soldiers and have them do his every bidding.

"Where will you send me?"

Denmer's face didn't betray much, but even so, Ithrael could tell he wouldn't like what he was about to hear. "You're to be on duty at the port."

So she did want him out of the palace, after all. At least she hadn't sent him to a barracks on the outskirts of Maldessa.

"Very good, sir."

"Gallia is to take your place as Captain of the Guard." Commander Denmer's tone was reassuring; it was what Ithrael needed to hear. There was no one more dedicated than Gallia.

"Thank you for that."

"Well, she's one of our best, and as deference to you …" There was the unspoken "and your father" hanging in Denmer's pause. "… I thought it best not to promote Kasabian." Kasabian was a handsome, typically rakish guard who no doubt would have enjoyed serving the beautiful Queen.

"Gallia is a strong choice. She will do her duty well." And she would, but he knew no one could protect his

Queen as well as he could. Ithrael took his leave and went to collect his possessions to take down to the small quarters that sat by the docks. It was going to be a long winter.

Chapter Four

AMAREA

Amarea couldn't sleep. She was too angry to even shut her eyes. Instead, she stared up at the thin gossamer canopy that draped over her bedframe. *If only her magic would allow her to vaporise people with a single look.* She would have enjoyed watching Ithrael vanish into a puff of ash. How dare he want to force her to marry him? How dare he believe he wasn't her equal! She'd never seen him as ambitious with regard to the throne, but now she wondered what his true motive was. That's all men wanted, to take, take, take. Well, she wasn't going to give up her throne for anyone, or anything. Even with this vow to herself, she still couldn't sleep.

She was in a foul mood by the time morning came. She batted her ladies away as they tried to dress her in a gown that was in her usual revealing, overly tight style. She couldn't bear the idea of being in anything constricting. She insisted, instead, on a simple gown of midnight blue with an attached train that hung from her shoulders. She made them clasp on her most vicious gold talons — filigree gloves of gold that ended in sharp points. She'd often considered dipping them in poison, and today she was very taken with the idea.

"The delegation from Hyrathea arrives soon. Would you wear your crown?" one of her ladies of Astree asked.

"Yes, have it brought to the throne room, but I can't abide wearing it for long, particularly today." Amarea rolled her shoulders. It was going to be a long day.

"I have arranged for there to be a formal introduction and for you to then carry out your discussions with the Primlect and select members of your council in the state room. Your crown need only stay on for the introduction." Her lady gave her a small smile and didn't even hesitate when she noticed Gallia change places with the guard on duty and then follow closely behind as they made their way through the palace.

Amarea's chin was high and her crown steady when the Hyratheans arrived. They stood before her, their light-brown, muscled bodies on display despite the cold weather. They wore animal pelts thrown back over their shoulders and secured in place with leather straps. She did like the barbarians' style, even if they could be … difficult.

"Gentlemen, how good of you to visit. Your absence from this court has long been missed."

One man stepped forward and thumped his fist to his chest, over his heart. "Your Majesty, it is an honour to be granted an audience."

"It has been such a long time, Degat Soligan." Amarea's voice was soft and placating.

"Not since the terrible incident between our princes. I am sorry that their dispute was brought to your doorstep." It was fortunate she wore a veil as her face may have given her away; her scheme to have them kill each other still made her smile, which she was doing in that moment.

"Let us not speak of the past. Let us speak of the future." She stood. "Come — let us discuss matters somewhere more comfortable." She held out her hand to indicate the door they were to take and watched as they were led through. A lady of Astree approached with Amarea's replacement crown, a piece in solid gold, simple compared to her usual choices, with spiked peaks rising up from the circlet. Despite choosing blue over black, despite toning down her outfit, there would be no doubt that she was the powerful Queen that people knew her to be.

The room fell silent when she entered. She had waited to make sure they would all be seated once she walked in and have to rise upon her entrance — she loved small power games. There was no high table between them; instead, there was a lower one, piled high with a variety of drinks, savoury and sweet treats, all of which Amarea couldn't consume until after the meeting as she couldn't risk anyone catching a glimpse of her face in a diplomatic discussion — it would be seen as coercion. To save herself the pain of having to stare at the delicacies, she sat in the armchair furthest away. Each chair was high-backed and upholstered in different colours of velvet fabric. Amarea had found that making people comfortable when discussing uncomfortable topics made for a more agreeable resolution.

After enduring the usual dull discussions of economics, Degat Soligan spoke. "We've heard rumour the Vulch have designs on your queendom, your Majesty." She was impressed he managed to keep his obvious smugness out of his tone.

"Don't they have designs on us all?" There were polite huffs of laughter from the room full of men.

"The Vulch have always been friends of ours," Degat Kureen said, his tone cocky. Not surprising, Amarea thought, from such a young lord.

Amarea sat back, giving off an air of ease and comfort. "Is that so, Degat Kureen?"

Tristam was trying not to smile into his sparkling wine, whilst Aiden looked bored and Primlect Tiemenin glowered at the Hyrathean lord. Tiemenin had been the first elected Primlect in her country's history, and even though he was still relatively new to the position, she was rather pleased with the choice. He was, after all, Estelle's father.

"It's unseasonably cold for this region, don't you think Primlect Tiemenin?" Degat Soligan remarked. Amarea stilled. Her neighbours weren't ones for pleasantries and talk of the weather. They were barbarians, fighters. She wondered what his meaning was.

"If you say so, Degat Soligan. I wouldn't be one to contradict you," Tiemenin countered.

"We stopped off in Calmaya on our way here. Your neighbour's climes are far better than yours."

Before anyone could respond, Amarea spoke. "And how do you find our neighbours? Recovered from their recent ordeals?" Amarea stroked her hand along the soft velvet arm of her chair.

"We have offered aid to them, your Majesty," Degat Soligan replied with an edge in his voice.

"Aid? Indeed, Degat Soligan, you impress me."

His smile was all teeth but no emotion. "A peace offering, for past wrongs."

"How noble of you. And pray, what do you hope this will gain with us? For us to open trade with you once more? For us to look past your slaughtering of a people?" Her voice was cool and calm.

Degat Kureen sat forward, his expression furious. Soligan held up his hand to him. "Have we not paid for our transgressions by being blocked from trade with all nations of the Daeneah Realms?"

"My lord," Amarea said through gritted teeth but managing to keep her tone even, almost civil, "a few sanctions will never be enough to compensate for the loss of so many lives."

"And yet there are no sanctions on you, your Majesty. I hear you had quite a *hand* in the events of the night of the Blood Moon." Niseem had been correct; the people were calling the night she'd killed the last primlect the night of the Blood Moon. Supposedly, the moon had turned red that same night. She liked the idea that she'd made the moon bleed.

"And what sanctions would you have my country endure, when the events of that evening were domestic and didn't infringe upon any other kingdom?" She hoped he heard the vicious smile she now wore.

"I would disagree. You removed key figures who were essential to trade and diplomatic relations within Daeneah. The impact was felt across all the realms." He interlaced his fingers as if he were observing a manoeuvre in a game.

"Soligan, we're here to discuss your position, not ours. As far as the other realms are concerned, they have no issue with our Queen or her past actions." The Hyrathean lords were wearing down the Primlect's patience.

"Is that so? But don't your people now refer to you as the *Dark* Queen because of that night?"

"Enough," commanded Tiemenin. "You do not come here and insult our Queen. The sanctions will not be lifted, as I'm sure the other nations will tell you, until we are confident you will stay within your borders." The Primlect's directness was one of the things Amarea appreciated about the man helping to run her council.

The Hyratheans left soon after, and she couldn't imagine they would stay past the state dinner they had planned for that evening. They would try their luck elsewhere, no doubt. Maybe even manage to broker a small trade agreement somewhere. Probably with the Vulch.

"Do we need to be worried?" Amarea asked Tiemenin, Tristam and unfortunately Aiden, but only because he was in the room.

"They'll try and win favour with the Vulch, there's no doubt about that, and the Vulch, if they are indeed looking to take your queendom from you, will use them to do it," Tiemenin said.

"Should we be more lenient on them in that case?" she asked.

"I don't think it will make a difference," Tristam said. "The Hyratheans are a proud people. They know you were the one who brought the case of sanctions against them to the court of the Daeneah Realms. They won't forgive, or forget."

"And so I now have two enemies who plan on attacking my weakened queendom. Wonderful." She wanted to take off her veil, wanted to breathe properly. She was so tired she couldn't think straight.

"We'll know soon enough what they plan," Tristam said.

Amarea removed her heavy crown and placed it on the floor next to her feet.

"Why are they so desperate for this nation, anyway? It's not the largest, doesn't have the best agriculture or mining, or anything." Aiden looked around for an answer. Amarea was tempted to throw something at the idiot boy but she didn't have the energy to do even that. Fortunately for Aiden, Tiemenin responded, "The magic."

"The Queen's and the Guard's magic? That's just those two, though." Aiden looked confused.

"The land beneath our feet was the land where the god Daylar and the goddess Neesoh first fell from the sky. Daylar fell during the day, a spark of the sun, and Neesoh at night, an evening star."

"I know all this."

Amarea was amazed by Tiemenin's patience with the boy. Tristam was already distracting himself with eating the food laid out in front of them. "Of course, it's a well-known story. But it is said that when they landed they jolted the land beneath their feet awake and some of their magic seeped into it. It is why we have the strongest mages, a Queen descended from the Goddess herself and the spirit of Daylar within one of our greatest soldiers. They see that as power, and power is what the Vulch will always want more of," he said.

"Yes, but it's only a few people who have some of that magic," he said, and to Amarea it sounded a lot like whining.

"Boy, you say we have poor agriculture ..." Tristam shook his head at him, tutting. "But that is purely because our people were exploited by our greedy high circles. The crops we produced during those years matched that of other nations in quality and quantity. As you're young, you won't know what our land can truly do. Our soil is the richest around. The fruits, vegetables and grains we can grow are the greatest in the known world. Just you wait, when we're back on our feet you'll see why this land is so desirable, what we can produce. Have you tried vintage Maldessan wine?" Tristam tipped his head back and groaned in ecstasy. "Now that is what I call gods-blessed."

"And where do you think your Queen gets all her gems from?" Tiemenin asked, as though he were the boy's schoolmaster.

"Inheritance?"

"Mines that are now inaccessible thanks to the mercenaries living in The Fold. They laid claim to the richest seam of mountain ranges in protest against the elite, the same mountains where Ithrael Ethea fought and killed three snow lions at thirteen years of age, unleashing the spirit of Daylar and absorbing it. That's how it happened — isn't that correct, your Majesty?" Tiemenin looked to Amarea.

"So Mierdas believes." Amarea didn't like that the conversation had turned to her ex-lover.

"Do you see now, Aiden, why this land is desired? When working properly, it is the richest around. So, not only does magic hold physical power but wealth, too."

"I see now," Aiden said, his eyes slightly wider. *Wide with greed*, Amarea thought. Fortunately, she'd already taught him that he could not defeat her. At least that was one threat she had managed to take care of.

Tiemenin and Aiden left to attend further meetings. She was glad the Primlect had taken it upon himself to educate Aiden; she wasn't sure anyone else would have had the patience for it. Tristam stayed behind and Amarea insisted Gallia sit and help herself to the food and drink. "I hate to see any of it wasted."

"I'll make sure the cooks know it can be taken home by the staff," Tristam suggested. Amarea slumped down in her chair as there was a knock on the door. Saia stepped inside, looking like she'd barely slept, with Niseem and Bassiri. Amarea didn't miss Tristam react slightly at the sight of Bassiri, but he recovered so quickly she doubted anyone else noticed.

Saia looked as wrung out as Amarea felt and so she thought it best to hear what she had to say first. "What did you discover about the Vulch?"

"Their methods are clever, there's no doubt about that. In fact, it's hard to prove that they were behind the sacking of Ruist when it was once Bayoan, the removal of King Tesud from Calmaya, the destruction of Hyrathean ports after a heated trade dispute or many other events." Saia rubbed her face. "But, they make sure that people understand to fear them, that they are likely the force behind these events, to keep the fear alive. To keep their dominance."

"And so if you were planning how to go about attacking Maldessa, as a Vulch, what would you do?" Amarea asked her.

"Rile the Hyratheans, have them do something stupid and aggressive as a diversion tactic. Then, enact my true plan, to remove the Queen who has the power of a goddess ..." Saia paled.

"It's okay, Saia. I know that they could only do that by killing me. Don't be concerned about saying it out loud. I just need to know how they intend to do that."

"The only way they could would be to capture you or find a way to neutralise your magic so they could kill you. And even you don't know enough about your power to know how to stop it." She was right. Amarea barely knew anything about the magic in her veins. She had read Neesoh's diary hundreds of times but it didn't make anything clearer.

"There is a third play," Niseem said. "They could use what you love against you."

Amarea's head snapped up. Saia looked guilty, as if she'd been thinking it too but couldn't face saying it. Ithrael.

"They wouldn't dare."

Niseem's expression was soft as she spoke. "If you don't attack a queen but someone she loves then you aren't instigating war — you're making it personal. People make mistakes when it's personal."

"And what if the person our Queen cares most about is the embodiment of a god himself?" Tristam asked as he inspected the bubbles in his wine.

"They would have to find a way to overwhelm him. But with him in the palace, they will struggle to reach him," Bassiri noted.

Amarea went cold. "I … I sent him to the barracks at the docks …" She looked at her room full of friends, hoping they weren't thinking what she was thinking. The atmosphere had changed; it was dread that laced the air. "Gallia, send a guard to bring Captain Ethea to the palace immediately." Amarea's voice wavered. Had it started? Had she been too focused on looking in at her own land to see the enemies circling outside her borders? If it were she who was circling, she would have snatched the opportunity. She hoped that she wasn't too late.

Chapter Five

ITHRAEL

Ithrael pulled his jacket tighter around himself as he made his way to the docks. The cold had seeped into his bones. It must be a side effect of his hangover as he didn't usually feel the cold so badly. He hefted the strap of his pack more securely onto his shoulder and pulled on the heavy wooden door of the barracks.

It was nearly as cold inside as it was out. He made his way through the small dining room and found the captain's quarters. He'd be working alongside three other captains so that two were always on duty. Unfortunately, because of the size of the docks' barracks, it meant sharing a room. He was already missing the palace. He sighed and left his pack on the end of the vacant bed and went to find Captain Fletcher whom he'd be on duty with.

Outside the wind had picked up, the icy blasts lashing against his cheeks. Amarea was really getting her own back, he realised. She was far too calculating, but then again, that was what he loved about her. He spotted Fletcher further along the docks talking to someone who appeared to be a merchant. Ithrael made his way over to him, his head bent against the wind.

"Like I said, you can't dock here any more unless you pay us for today." Fletcher sounded fed up.

"And like I said, I already paid for the week." The merchant's voice was beginning to rise.

"There is no proof of your payment in the ledger and I've spoken to everyone on duty this morning and none of them took your money." Fletcher spotted Ithrael and acknowledged him with raised eyebrows.

"May I ask what the person who took your money looked like and what they were wearing?" Ithrael interjected.

"Dark-blue overcoat with red piping. He was tall with red hair, freckles." Fletcher's eyes narrowed.

"Not one of ours?" Ithrael asked.

"No, this has been happening more and more. Okay sir, we'll track down the culprit. In the meantime you can stay docked until we sort this out." Fletcher made a note in the ledger and called over one of the dock guards and explained the situation.

Ithrael followed Fletcher to the guard's house, a small shed-like structure with windows on all sides, which sat in the middle of the stretch of land in front of the port. Inside it wasn't much warmer, but being out of the wind was a relief.

"Been having issues with our people not being as alert because of this weather. It's allowing grafters to get a little bolder," Fletcher said whilst blowing into his hands. "At least when it's like this you can't smell the fish — just wait until summer." Fletcher smiled to reveal he was missing a lateral incisor that somehow made him seem endearing, although Ithrael knew from training that Fletcher was a ruthless, competitive fighter.

"Well, that's something for me to look forward to then." Ithrael looked out over the ships and the water. On the far right were the fishing boats, but in front of him and to the left were the merchant ships. Further to the left sat some of the Queen's fleet, large vessels ready to defend at any moment. "So, want me to track down your thief?"

"If you want to go back out there be my guest. I'll write down a few of their known hideouts, and take one of the duty guards with you."

Ithrael approached the first guard he saw, who introduced herself as Yeela.

"You've worked with my sister," she remarked after he'd asked her to join him.

Ithrael examined her features. "Niseem?" She had the same brown skin, dark eyes and aquiline nose.

"Yes!" She tipped her head back and smiled up at him. She was shorter than her sister. "I don't think our father planned for his daughters to grow up to be an adviser to the Queen and a soldier when he moved here. He probably wanted us to be seamstresses instead."

"Have you been to where he's from, to Issabad?" he asked as they bent their heads against the freezing wind.

She shook her head. "No, not since I was a baby and so I don't remember a thing about it. Maldessa is my home. Niseem remembers some things, but not many. She says she misses the warmth." Yeela laughed and pulled her jacket tighter. "Is it possible to miss something you don't remember? Because I think I miss that, too."

Ithrael smiled. "I think so." He started to relax. Yeela was easy to be around and she enjoyed talking, unlike most of the soldiers he spent time with when he was on duty.

"Turn right here — this is their usual hangout." Yeela pointed to a rundown tavern with no sign hanging from a frame, just two chains swinging in the wind.

Ithrael went in first, pushing on the stiff wooden door. There were around twenty people in the small, dark tavern. The smell of salt, sweat and stale ale hit him the moment he entered. The room fell silent as soon as they took in his and Yeela's uniform. Ithrael approached the barman, stopped and then examined the room, his gold eyes fierce. He couldn't see anyone with red hair.

"We're looking for someone — tall, red hair, freckles. Took a docking fee this morning." Ithrael's voice was deep and commanding.

"Don't know anyone of that description," the barman said, not even flinching at the sight of the renowned warrior.

Ithrael had found in his time working in the Queen's Guard that certain people needed to be treated with gentleness, whereas others only responded to aggression. He wasn't in a particularly gentle mood, and these people were the latter of the two. Ithrael reached forward and grabbed the barman by his collar, dragging him over the counter, dropping him at his feet. "Are you sure about that?"

One of the larger men in the room stood up. "Hey, what do you think you're doing?"

"Trying to find a tall man, red hair, freckles who took dock fees. Did you not hear? Want me to speak louder?"

Ithrael was spoiling for a fight and he would have been happy to take on each and every one of these men.

"Uh, Captain?" Yeela whispered.

"Not now."

"But Captain ..." Yeela's tone made him look to her. She lifted her chin in the direction of the fire where a gentleman was sitting. His hair was a muddy brown, greasy looking, but the fire kept catching it, revealing a reddish hue.

Ithrael face slashed into a smile. "I owe you a drink, Yeela." He strode forward and hoisted the young man up from his chair, held him up in the air and shook him up and down. His pockets jingled. There was a snigger from some of the men in the room. "That sounds to me like enough coin for a week's docking fee, don't you think, Yeela?"

"Exactly like that." She had her hands on her hips and wore a satisfied expression.

Ithrael put the young man down and held out his hand, and eyes that spoke of a power beyond any mortal man's bore into the now nervous-looking thief. "Hand it over."

The thief looked around for support but he'd clearly lost the backup he was hoping for and emptied his pockets for Ithrael.

"And the rest." The thief pulled off his boot and dropped two more coins into Ithrael's open hand. Ithrael put the coins into the leather pouch attached to his belt. "This time I'll let you off, but if I catch you ripping people off anywhere near the port again I'll enjoy taking you to the prison myself."

The thief rubbed the back of his head, and looking down mumbled, "Yes, sir."

The room was still silent when they left and stepped out into the biting wind. "You made quite an impression. They may actually think twice about grafting on the docks."

"I doubt it." Ithrael pulled up the collar of his coat to stop the cold air slipping down his back.

"What's with this weather?"

"If I were still at the palace I'd have a word with Mierdas — bet it's another one of his training weeks for a mage and he's letting them control the balance."

"I hate training weeks." Yeela shivered and blew into her hands.

"Don't you have any gloves?"

"Nope." Ithrael pulled his off and handed them to her.

"I couldn't, Captain."

"You're the one who has to stay on duty outside. Keep hold of them until you get your own."

Her lips quirked into a half smile. "Thanks. Niseem was right about you. Beneath the terrifying exterior, you're a good guy."

"Terrifying exterior?"

"Yeah — all the scowling, the scars, the weird yellow eyes and white hair."

"Weird eyes?" Ithrael raised an eyebrow.

"No one has white hair and yellow eyes. No one. You kind of stick out a bit." She spoke with sympathy, as if sticking out were a bad thing. He supposed that maybe it was; he'd never bothered to consider it before.

"Oh, well thanks for making me feel welcome in my new position."

"No problem, sir, I'm here to do as you command." She bowed as he laughed, feeling an unusual sense of lightness. He hadn't felt relaxed in a long time. He'd been spending all his energy worrying about Amarea and the queendom — being at the docks, he didn't feel it so keenly. He had been right when he said he couldn't stay in her shadow; it really was turning him into a brooding, ill-humoured man.

They rounded the corner into a dark alley, which Yeela assured him was a short cut. Maybe if she hadn't been talking so much he'd have heard the approaching footsteps. Maybe if he hadn't been so determined not to think about Amarea that he'd been listening intently to Yeela's chatter, he'd have been more aware of the change in his surroundings. He went through a lot of maybes in the ensuing minutes.

He was alerted too late, and it was only because of their pursuers' mistake — a piece of shingle from the roof one of the assailants was climbing across fell at Ithrael's feet. He looked up as the first man dropped to the ground and at the same time, a thick grey smoke began to fill the air around him and Yeela. The smog clawed in his throat making him choke out a cough. He felt pressure in his lungs such as he had never experienced before.

He reacted on an instinct borne of years of training and threw his dagger before drawing his sword and awaited the next attack. The first man was down and Yeela had her own sword drawn. The next attacker went for her and Ithrael was pleased to see she could hold her own as three more fell upon him. He slashed and parried, never letting up, but the smoke grew thicker, his lungs felt heavier and a fog seemed to seep into his brain. His arms began to feel weak as it became harder for him to catch his breath. He kicked off a new attacker and glanced to the side to see Yeela continue to hold her own despite beginning to cough badly. Her last attacker was down and she was hammering blows onto a new one. The smoke didn't seem to be bothering the attackers much, although they did have cloths tied over their noses and mouths.

"Yeela, try not to breathe in the smoke," he yelled, and sliced his sword across the throat of the man to his right. Behind him he spotted a lantern that appeared to be the source of the noxious smoke. Ithrael batted off two more men as he went for it, knowing that if he could just breathe properly he could dispatch each and every one of the mercenaries. He now knew that's what they were; he could recognise their kind, especially after having hired their services not too long ago. But the closer he got to the source of the smoke, the more his head swam and his legs no longer felt like they could hold up his weight. He could barely breathe. He reached out with his sword, hoping to knock over the lantern and in doing so extinguish the flame, but as he reached forward, something large and heavy was smashed across his head and Ithrael Ethea, a near god in a world of men, fell to the ground unconscious.

Chapter Six

AMAREA

Niseem wiped Yeela's eyes with a wet cloth as she coughed to clear her lungs of the foul smoke that still lingered. Amarea could smell it; there was a cloying sweetness to it that made her feel nauseated. She really needed to get more sleep.

Niseem put the cloth down and looked at her sister with concern. "Say that again, Yeela."

"Captain Ethea was taken."

"How?" Amarea commanded, making the young guard flinch. She hadn't meant to frighten her but her emotions were coursing through her body and she wasn't able to control herself.

"They took us by surprise, overwhelmed us. The smoke made it hard to see and breathe, but for Captain Ethea, I don't know, it affected him more. There was nothing I could do, but I could see him getting weaker and weaker. I saw him go for the lantern that was making the smoke and I tried to intervene, to warn him even, but I wasn't fast enough. They hit him over the head with a metal bar and he went down. He stopped moving." Her voice caught but she carried on. "I went to try and help him but then they overwhelmed me and tied me up. I was helpless and watched as they carried Captain Ethea away." She looked down at her hands, which held Ithrael's gloves — Amarea recognised them. The girl clutched them so tightly her knuckles turned white. "I'm sorry I failed you, my Queen."

"You didn't fail me." Her response was automatic. She didn't blame the young guard; she blamed herself. Amarea took a breath, trying to focus her mind. "If they were able to overpower the captain they were well prepared — there was nothing you could have done. I'm grateful you tried to intervene." Amarea rested her hand on the young woman's shoulder and noticed that Niseem looked far more shaken than Yeela. "Niseem, take your sister home. She's to have a week's rest to recover from this ordeal."

"My apologies but no, my Queen. I want to start looking for the captain. The sooner we begin, the sooner we will find him."

"I have people looking already and there is nothing you can do without rest. If you wish to be involved in the search, I will recommend you to Denmer. You might be able to give him some clues as to who the kidnappers are." The soldier's face brightened.

"Thank you, my Queen."

Niseem led her out and Amarea collapsed into her chair.

"Can I get you something, your Majesty?" Gallia asked, her voice gentle.

Amarea shook her head. "I should never have sent him away when I knew there was a serious threat."

"You couldn't have known that they would take him, or even that anyone would be able to take him."

"But we did know, just too late."

Saia was sitting quietly in the corner of the room. Amarea had almost forgotten she was there. "How did they know they could take him? What was the smoke?"

"I don't know but even the smell of it made me nauseous," Amarea noted.

"I found it nauseating, as well. Gallia, how about you?" Gallia shook her head. "And Yeela found it bothersome, too … but it *incapacitated* Ithrael." Saia sat quietly for a moment, thinking. "I need to see Mierdas and catch up with Yeela, get her clothes and see if any of the smoke still clings to the fabric. Mierdas might be able to ascertain what was used." Saia was almost talking to herself.

"Take them to the House of Mages, Saia. Mierdas is brilliant but there are others in the House who may be of help." Saia stood and left the room without so much as a goodbye.

"Do you know what the hardest part of this is, Gallia?"

"No, my Queen."

"That because of my position I cannot go and find him myself. Instead I must stay here and do *nothing*." Amarea clenched her fist so tightly that she pierced the skin of her palm with her metal claws. Blood pooled but she barely registered the wetness in her palm. The Vulch had taken Ithrael to get to her. They must not have been paying attention to the events that unfolded on the night of the Blood Moon.

Chapter Seven

YEELA

Niseem was fussing over Yeela, and even though Yeela knew she was doing it out of love and concern, it was really starting to irritate her. Her sister had taken her back to their father's house. That was the first black mark against her. The second was not intervening when their father started fussing and complaining about how he knew she shouldn't have joined the Guard. The third was when she wouldn't leave the room as Yeela changed out of her smoke-laced clothes, which she placed into a satchel to take to the House of Mages.

Yeela only had the patience for three such incidents, and besides, she had a job to do. She dressed in her spare uniform, which made Niseem protest, and then marched out of the house, back to the barracks. Yeela could hear her father yelling at Niseem for getting her little sister into dangerous situations. She couldn't help the smile that tugged at her lips.

She stopped off at the House on the way to the barracks and handed over her clothes. Once at the barracks she went straight to the commander's quarters. She'd never had a one-to-one with him before.

"Yeela Hassan," the commander stated, much to her surprise as she had no idea he knew who she was. He stood up from his desk and strode around it to shake her hand.

"Commander." She shook his hand with a firm grip and made sure to keep eye contact.

"A few months on the job and you're unlucky enough to be caught up in this." Commander Denmer shook his head. "So, what can you tell me about the assailants?"

"They were mercenaries for sure. Once they tied me up and began speaking I could tell all their accents were different, but the leader, he had that guttural accent of a Vulch and the colouring too — blonde hair, pale skin, blue eyes."

"So it's as we suspected. Did you see where they took him?"

"Just towards the port. I'm afraid I can't say more than that. At least, that was the direction they took." She wished she could say more. She'd been careful to pay attention to as many details as possible but none of them were any use now. She felt useless. "Sir, might I request to be part of the team tasked with finding the captain?"

"You've already been assigned." Yeela realised that a smile wouldn't be appropriate but she did allow herself to feel a little pride. "Report to the palace. The Queen's Guard will be instructing the team that is to search outside of Maldessa."

"Thank you, sir."

Yeela left, pride swelling. She was to leave Maldessa. She hadn't been past the borders of Maldessa since her father had first brought her and Niseem to the queendom. She'd always wanted to travel but it was hard enough to get her father to accept her being a soldier; she didn't think he'd have been too happy if she'd been a sailor.

She made good time getting to the palace and waited with a group of five guards for Gallia to arrive. She'd always looked up to Niseem's wife — it was part of the reason she'd joined the Guard — but now she felt a swell of honour when Gallia entered in her Captain of the Palace Guard uniform. That was her sister-in-law, the woman who was currently commanding the respect of the selected soldiers tasked with retrieving one of Maldessa's most renowned men. She looked around at the four men and one woman with whom she would travel. They were all older than her. She recognised the woman and one of the men; they were definitely some of the better fighters within the Guard.

"You've all been selected for your skill as soldiers and your language skills. Between you, you can speak enough languages to blend in, and we need you to blend in. This is a mission of the utmost secrecy; the captors cannot see you coming." Gallia looked at each of them with an even gaze. "We have a team staying in Maldessa to make sure they haven't attempted to hide him here, but reports seem to indicate he was taken on a merchant ship heading to Assisa."

The island of Assisa was much further away than Yeela had expected to travel. Niseem had made it clear that it was a possibility the Vulch had taken the captain, and it was strange they would head to Assisa as they weren't an ally.

"I know you're all thinking that he's probably been taken to Ruist, but we cannot make that assumption. The Vulch will almost certainly hide him somewhere other than their land, somewhere where they have strong allies."

Yeela frowned. "Captain, when did the Hyrathean delegation leave?"

"They have yet to leave."

Yeela curled her hands and clutched at the sleeves of her uniform to steady her nerves at speaking out. "Aren't they a close ally of the Vulch?" She didn't say what she was thinking; it was better if someone more senior made the assumptions.

Gallia cursed. "Errol, you speak Hyrathean?"

The youngest of the five cleared his throat and confirmed he did. He had skin a lighter shade of brown to Yeela's, and now that she considered him, he looked Hyrathean. Well, that was handy.

"Yeela, Errol, you go to Hyrathea. We'll establish your cover in a moment. The rest of you follow the other lead — you best leave now to catch up. Yeela, Errol, wait here. I need to speak with the Queen."

Yeela watched as everyone left and her stomach fluttered with anticipation. She was going to go on her first mission and as a spy, no less. She was a little disappointed that she wasn't going to travel all the way to Assisa, but Hyrathea would do. She'd heard that the wild lands were beautiful, untamed horses galloping through the plains. It sounded wonderful.

"How long have you been in the Queen's Guard?" she asked her new travelling companion.

"Two years." His voice was deeper than she'd expected. He held himself almost to attention. He seemed the serious type.

"And you're Hyrathean?"

He looked offended. "Maldessan. I was born and raised here. My father was a Hyrathean trader."

She noted the "was" but didn't comment on it. "Lucky that there's someone who's a good fighter and can speak Hyrathean. I'm sure the Queen will be very grateful."

"If we find him."

"Oh, we will. I have a feeling." And she did, right in the bottom of her stomach, the same feeling she'd had the night of the attack, that something was off. She'd only ignored it because she'd been with the land's greatest fighter. But that feeling had never let her down. She *knew* that they were on the right track. The Hyratheans had Ithrael and she was going to help get him back.

The Queen entered covered head-to-toe in midnight-blue silk, no crown or circlet on her head. Although her sister had worked closely with the Queen for a long time, Yeela had never been in the same room as her. She was instantly awed; she had even more of a presence than Ithrael. There was something almost approachable about him, but the Queen — she was most definitely a queen. The room felt like it was humming with her power, or maybe it was anger that emanated from her. Yeela knew that the Queen's magic was in her face, but Yeela was sure it was more than beauty that made the woman before her powerful.

The Queen approached Yeela and reached out a hand. Her skin was as dark as Yeela's but the tone was slightly different. She felt a sense of pride that she almost had the same colouring as her Queen, who Niseem had told her wasn't as evil as people would have her believe, that she loved her people and did what needed to be done to protect them. She touched her hand to Yeela's cheek and Yeela looked directly at the veiled face.

"You are brave and wise, Yeela. Niseem has always spoken of you with great pride. Listen to your instinct when you journey. It will save your life." She leaned forward and whispered into her ear, so low Yeela only just heard her. "Bring my love home."

Yeela's heart thundered. It was true that the Queen and her guard were lovers. There had been months of rumours but Niseem would never confirm them. Yeela simply nodded once. "I will, my Queen."

The Queen turned to Errol and placed her hand on his shoulder. "Listen to Yeela — she has good instincts." The Queen stepped back and nodded to Gallia to brief them.

"You're to travel as newlyweds to Hyrathea. The story is, Errol is a trader and you want to bring your new bride home. We have a horse and cart for you, including some wares that are currently being collected. You will have coin but feel free to trade anything within the cart if needed." Gallia looked at each of them intently. "And I need not tell you the importance of this mission. If you are captured, no one can know that you were sent by the Queen." She paused to let her meaning settle — no matter the torture, they were not to speak of their Queen. They would have to be willing to die for the mission. "As it happens, the Hyrathean delegation is leaving at first light but we have no idea where they are keeping Captain Ethea. It is possible they are hiding him nearby and they will collect him on their way home.

"We want you to go ahead of them. They came by land and so will leave by land, and the only way across is the Northern Pass. But we don't believe they'll go back through Calmaya. You're to travel to the North Post Inn and stay the night, rise early and wait further up the road. We want you to feign wagon trouble, and we hope either you'll be invited to join their party or you can at the very least establish whether they have possession of Captain Ethea. Is all of that clear?"

"Yes, Captain," they said in unison. It no longer felt to Yeela like she was going on an adventure; the weight of what she was about to undertake settled on her. She could feel herself becoming overwhelmed. All this time she'd wanted danger and adventure and now that it was right in front of her, she was scared. Then she caught Errol's eye and the strength of purpose and the unspoken assurance in the man's eyes calmed her enough that she was able to leave her Queen and Gallia without her entire body trembling.

Yeela followed Errol down to the stables where their cart was waiting.

"This rickety thing is supposed to take us all the way to Rathon?"

"If we're even going to their capital, if they even have him. Who knows where they'll keep him," Errol replied, his expression serious.

"Let's hope our horse, is in better condition." Yeela looked around for the horse, and a stable hand led a mare towards them. She was old, no doubt about that. They were going to a land of wild, beautiful horses and Yeela was concerned about how their poor mare would look in comparison.

"Will she make the journey?" she asked the stable hand as she fed the horse an apple. She'd always had a soft spot for animals.

"How far you plan on going?"

"It's a three-day journey to my husband's parents." Yeela figured she may as well start the pretence now, best to smooth out any shaky parts of the lie early on.

"Oh, there's no doubt Apple will manage that, so long as you don't push her too hard and she's only pulling the cart."

"Apple?" Errol asked.

"She was the Queen's first horse, bit old for her style of riding. She named her when she was a child on account of her liking apples."

Yeela's face lit up. "She was the Queen's?"

"Aye, and a fine Hyrathean breed. Won't get a more reliable horse. You must have pleased the Queen for her to lend you one of her favourites." Yeela turned to Errol with a bright smile but he didn't seem in the least bit impressed. He still appeared put out by the horse's name. Yeela let Apple smell her palm and then rubbed the horse's nose.

They helped load up the cart and changed into the clothes they'd been given. Yeela folded away her uniform carefully, almost reverently. She paused as they were about to leave, looking around, hoping to see her sister before she left, but they were alone in a barn by the side of the stables. It was past dusk and they needed to start their journey, and so she climbed up next to Errol and placed a blanket over both their legs and let him snap the reigns.

Just past the palace gates, she saw someone running towards them, her long brown hair loose and streaming behind her. Niseem. Yeela told Errol to stop and she jumped down and into Niseem's arms. Niseem's face was blotchy and tear-streaked.

"I won't stop you from going but I want you to know that if you get yourself killed for that idiot Ithrael, I'll never forgive you."

Yeela laughed through her tears into Niseem's neck. "I'll keep that in mind."

"I love you La-La." Yeela's heart squeezed — Niseem hadn't called her that since she was a child.

"I love you too, Nissy." They held each other tightly, and then Yeela let go and climbed back onto the cart. She didn't try to hold back her tears as they began to move again, keeping her head turned, watching as Niseem's figure got slowly smaller. Only when she was completely out of sight did Yeela turn. Her tears dried and her determination to succeed doubled.

Chapter Eight

AMAREA

As soon as she was inside her chambers, Amarea tore off her veil and made her way through her bathing room and entered the hidden tunnel that connected her rooms to Mierdas'.

"My Queen," the old man greeted her. Even though her tread was light and he was blind, Mierdas always knew when it was she who entered. That, or he called everyone who walked into his chambers "my Queen".

"Have you a way to track him?" she asked, trying to keep herself from demanding anything of one of the most respected men in the queendom.

"I've tried to track his magic but …" He turned his head towards her, his blind eyes not meeting hers, the milky pupils barely revealing the blue that was once there. "I'm afraid, your Majesty, I can't."

She sat down heavily on one of the wooden benches. Mierdas' main chamber was more of a laboratory, filled with books he'd memorised as his sight began to vanish. Bottles of potions, vials of experiments, covered most surfaces. Something noxious was always bubbling away.

Amarea often had to come and open the windows to stop him from poisoning himself. On a pedestal was the Book of Balance. It was the oldest book in the land and was preserved through magic, like Neesoh's diary.

"The smoke?"

"I believe so." He patted the clothing in front of him. "Fortunately I've got some of the young guard's clothing here. I have some of my more talented mages working to find out what it might be, as well. But, it will be hard. There is very little left on the clothing. We're having to extract what we can but—"

"It might not be enough. Can you speculate at all?" She knew he disliked speculating but she had to ask.

"What do we know about magic?"

Amarea almost groaned — he always insisted on making everything a lesson, even when Ithrael's life was in danger, apparently.

"That it's contained within all the elements." He raised an eyebrow expecting more, and she pinched the bridge of her nose between her fingers. "And those of us that have magic also have it contained within our very being. No one knows how to control or release the magic — the knowledge was lost with the gods." She waved her hand dramatically even though he couldn't see her do it — there was no doubt he could hear her sarcastic tone, though.

"Very true, which is why we don't know how your magic works, or that of Captain Ethea. What concerns me is that someone has found a way to interfere with magic, and if they know how to interfere with it …"

"Then they might know how to wield it."

"Precisely so." He nodded, his face falling into a frown.

"Is that what they want? To control our magic, to take it?"

Mierdas rubbed his hand along the bald top of his head; a half halo of white, fluffy hair covered the rest of his head. Amarea always had the urge to touch it but had never dared. This was not a man to be petted. "To control it, definitely. But to what end? Hard to say. They are indeed controlling it by cutting it off so that Captain Ethea was incapacitated. Whether they want to snuff magic out altogether, well, that remains to be seen."

"But if magic is in everything, in our ... our ... *essence*, then how does this smoke work?"

"I don't precisely know, yet. When inhaled it must bind to the magic, rendering it useless. I'd go so far as to say it may even be poisonous, for one Captain Ethea without his magic is still a match for five men."

Mierdas complimenting Ithrael's ability didn't make her feel better about the fact he'd just revealed Ithrael had been poisoned. "Could it kill him then? This smoke?"

Mierdas opened his mouth to respond and quickly closed it again, his face falling into an expression of deep thought. He raised his frosted eyes to her. "I'm sorry, my child, but that's a strong possibility." Amarea thought she might vomit; bile rose up into her throat but she swallowed it down. "The more urgent matter is what they plan to do with this smoke with regard to you, your Majesty."

"I hadn't even—"

"I know, but I must. You are the leader of this nation. We cannot risk this smoke poisoning you."

Amarea's head swam. "The Vulch ... Saia said they'd find a way of getting what they wanted without being noticed. Is this the way?"

"If that was the case they would have used it on you first." She wasn't sure if he was trying to be reassuring. It didn't feel like he was. It was unlikely; Mierdas wasn't one for being gentle about an issue.

"But I'm well protected. What better way to test whether their concoction works on the Goddess Queen than by testing it out on the godly guard?" She stood up and began to pace. "No one else is the embodiment of the gods as we are. Certainly, people have some magic but not in the way we do. This is how they will take my throne." She paused, considering, and then reluctantly continued. "Is there a way to protect me from the poison?" And although her heart clenched to be so selfish, Amarea knew that for her queendom to survive, she had to survive, and that made her life a priority.

"The more I know of the substance, the more able I'll be to find a cure."

"And when we find Ithrael, you'll be able to help him to recover?" He reached for her hand, and when she offered it to him, he gave it a squeeze.

"He is the strongest of men. I will do what I can but I believe that he will survive on his own." She allowed herself a small smile at the words. They were the truth. If anyone were to survive such a poison, it was Ithrael.

Chapter Nine

YEELA

The inn was a lot more comfortable than Yeela had imagined it would be. The two fires in the main room were lit when they entered and the room they were shown to was comfortable, if a little cold, and only contained the one bed. Yeela decided to worry about that problem later; first, there was food to eat. The innkeeper provided them with hard bread and stew at a reasonable price. There wasn't much meat in it but at least the meat that was in there tasted familiar and not gristly. It really wasn't as bad as she had expected. The only thing to dampen her mood was Errol. He didn't seem pleased by their horse, the inn, their room or the stew.

"Do you always scowl?" she asked after she'd mopped her bowl with her bread, sitting back in satisfaction.

"I'm not scowling," he said with a scowl.

"Yes you are." She considered him a moment. He was handsome but not conventionally so. His nose was large, not unlike hers but wider around the nostrils. His eyes were more of a dung brown than the rich brown of her own. She decided she'd tell him that one day, that his eyes reminded her of dung; she was sure it would rile him. His ears stuck out just a little, making his face seem gentle, which may be why he adopted a scowl to look more fearsome. His hair was long and braided in the style of the Hyratheans and how Captain Ethea wore his. She had always assumed the captain wore his hair long as a badge of honour, to not shy away from the fact that it was ghostly white. She assumed Errol wore his long because of his heritage. Most men in Maldessa wore their hair to their shoulders and tied it back, but Errol's went to the base of his shoulder blades. He wasn't tall, though, only a couple of hands taller than her, and she was relatively short herself.

"Are you ready to turn in?"

"Not just yet. I'm not tired. Why don't you stay down here with me and hear what stories people have to tell?" She couldn't hide the excitement from her voice. She'd always loved listening to stories in taverns. She'd sneak into them as a child until her father had caught onto where she was going and had started to keep a closer eye on her.

"You stay here, then. I'm going up to bed."

Yeela frowned at him. "You'll leave your wife here alone?"

Errol gave her an incredulous look. "I think you'll survive." He stood up and made his way towards the stairs. She watched him go and couldn't help but feel flattered that he thought she could take care of herself. Of course she actually could; she was a trained soldier, after all. But it was nice when people treated her like a member of the Guard and not Niseem's shorter, "adorable" little sister.

Far too many people felt the need to rub her on the head, as if she were a puppy.

Yeela looked around the tavern, which was relatively quiet. Not many travellers had stopped in overnight and there weren't many locals. In the far corner, two young men were laughing together — they seemed like the sort who would have good stories. She made her way over to their table. "Good evening, gentlemen, would you mind if I joined you? My husband's weary from the journey and I'm not ready to retire just yet."

Both of them looked like they were from Calmaya, their skin lighter than hers, hair a lighter shade of brown and noses smaller. Not that she minded the size of her nose.

"How could your husband abandon you so!" one of them cried in mock alarm. He was slim with dancing eyes and a broad smile. Yeela decided she liked him. "I'm Rikko and this is Bel."

Yeela shook both their hands. Bel's was a little on the clammy side but he blushed when she touched him and so she forgave him. "Where are you both headed?"

"Just dropping off some supplies at the inn here and a few along the way," Rikko replied.

"Farmers?"

"Brewers!" Rikko cheered as he held up his drink.

Yeela laughed and then gasped dramatically. "And I haven't even tried it yet!" They insisted on her having some from their jug and she took a sip. "I bet they drink the same ale in the palace."

"They do! We supply the barracks there." Rikko couldn't hide his pride.

Even though she already knew this as she recognised the taste, she made a good show of being surprised and impressed. "So not only are you brewers, but you're master brewers." Bel blushed into his drink whilst Rikko guffawed with glee.

"So where are you headed …?"

"Yeela," she offered.

"So where are you headed, Yeela?" Rikko repeated.

"To meet my husband's family."

"Are you newly wed?" Bel appeared to be overcoming some of his shyness as he was finally able to speak.

"Very newly, and I have no idea if they'll like me." Yeela shrugged as if she was pretending she didn't care but cared very much. It was a skill to produce such a layered performance.

"How could they not like you, mistress?" Bel asked, looking very earnest.

"You're too sweet." Yeela rested her hand on Bel's arm, which brought back his blush.

Rikko was looking pensive. "Newly wed? And you're not up there with him?" He pointed a thumb towards the ceiling. "And he's not down here having fun with you?" Rikko shook his head. "I'm sorry to hear that Yeela, I truly am. A woman as lovely as yourself deserves a doting husband."

"You don't need to concern yourself — he's just tired. Besides, have you seen a Hyrathean without his shirt on?" Yeela fanned herself with her hand. "Oof! I do love a barbarian."

Rikko slapped his hands on the table top and howled with laughter. "And here I am trying to watch what I say."

Bel began laughing, too. Soon they were sharing stories that would definitely have had Bel blushing had he not already turned completely red thanks to his ale consumption.

They were in the middle of a particularly loud fit of laughter when Errol appeared at the bottom of the stairs. The scowl he usually wore was extra severe. Yeela choked on her laugh. "Oh dear, looks like I'd better go to bed."

"Sure you can find a way to cheer him up, Yeela."

She smacked Rikko over the head. "Watch your mouth." But she smiled at him and waved them both goodnight as she made her way to the stairs. Errol stood aside to let her pass and gave a meaningful look to the two brewers. Yeela rested a hand on his arm and into his ear whispered, "Excellent way to get into character."

He turned to look at her, their faces close. "Character?"

"Of the jealous husband." Errol looked like his head might explode; she sucked in her lips to keep from laughing and then ran up the stairs.

In their small room, she could see Errol had made up a bed on the floor. She put her hand to the boards and they were terribly cold. They must be over a room without fires. She picked up his blanket and wool-stuffed pillow and placed them on the bed.

"What are you doing?"

"It's cold and uncomfortable. Don't get fussy about propriety now, we're soldiers, we can share a bunk. Besides, we're married." She winked at him and then went behind a screen to change into her underclothes and then dashed across the cold room and into the bed. All the while Errol just stood there. "Don't be a prude."

He went back to his signature scowl and then climbed into bed next to her. She instantly felt warmer and let out a contented sigh.

"How much did you drink?" he asked whilst facing away from her.

"Only one cup. On a mission, remember? Gotta keep a clear head." She turned around so they were back-to-back and quickly fell asleep.

The next morning Yeela was woken by the sound of the innkeeper throwing pots around in the kitchen downstairs. Or at least, that's what it sounded like. She was annoyed with herself for not realising the moment she was roused from sleep that Errol was snuggled up against her and he was, well, *happy* to be awake. She scooted away from him quickly and bashed her head on a strut.

Errol's eyes flew open as Yeela grabbed her head and winced.

"What are you doing?"

"What am *I* doing? What are *you* doing?" She looked pointedly at his crotch. Errol looked down and then pulled the blankets over himself.

"It's ah ..." He cleared his throat. "Something that just happens, in the mornings. It can't be helped."

Yeela's eyes widened. "It does that? Every morning?" Her friend at school, Jasmine, had educated Yeela on all things men and sex because her father would never have spoken to her about such things, and Niseem was always too busy to realise there were things Yeela needed to know. But Jasmine only knew so much and generally, it was acquired knowledge. This was obviously something she hadn't learned yet.

"Yes, for every man."

"Oh …" She wasn't quite sure what to do and he clearly wasn't ready to go anywhere, so she crawled inelegantly to the end of the bed, grabbed her clothes and made her way to the bathing chamber at the end of the hall. She couldn't help the giggle that escaped when she shut the door. Men were such strange creatures.

Breakfast was a plain omelette, no shredded pork or cheese that Yeela was given in the barracks, but it was still good food. They ate in silence, the awkwardness not having quite vanished. As Errol paid the innkeeper, Yeela went to bring Apple and the wagon around and to make sure she was well fed and watered before they went on their way. She was pleased to find all their wares still inside the cart. They were mainly fabrics but there were also a few other items that might have attracted a thief. Errol joined her out front just as Rikko and Bel emerged from the inn. They gave Yeela a cheery greeting, which she returned. Errol didn't even bother to acknowledge them.

"How are we supposed to convince the delegation to allow us to join them if you can't even be civil to two brewers?" she asked as Errol climbed up onto the cart and snapped the reigns.

"Brewers?" He frowned and looked behind at the retreating men. "They aren't brewers. They're simply delivery men from the brewery."

Yeela opened her mouth to protest and then considered ... They were quite young, about her age, and to be supplying so many ... She decided not to let Errol know that he was right and she'd not been as observant as she thought she'd been. Feeling put out, she remained quiet whilst they made their way towards the Northern Pass. She watched the road, looking for areas where it might be good for them to stop. They rounded a corner blind, and in front of them was a small clearing. It was impossible to miss and if they positioned the wagon in the right place, the party would be forced to stop or they'd crash right into them.

"Here."

Errol nodded, and she felt a little bit of pleasure because he'd listened to her. The ground was fairly rocky as it was at the base of the start of a mountain range. They climbed down from the cart and together carried a large boulder to just past the corner. Fortunately, Hyrathean men tended to forget that women could be strong, and they would know Errol couldn't have moved a boulder that size, but they would never think a woman would have been able to help him. It was a good plan. They tested the visibility a few times to make sure it was in the right place, then led Apple past the boulder but made sure the cart wheels ran into the giant rock.

"Nothing happened," Yeela said as she examined the wheel.

"See there?" Errol pointed at the axle. "See how it's bent slightly and the wheel has warped a little?"

Yeela looked a little closer. "Yeah?" It was hardly noticeable and she wasn't sure what good it would do.

Errol took out a hammer from the small bag of tools on their cart and began hitting the wheel and axle. The spokes splintered when the wheel bent enough and the axle looked like it may not ever be mended. They then dragged the cart along further to create tracks in the ground.

Yeela examined the scene. "Something's missing." She looked around and began gathering up loose bits of scree from the side of the slope and scattered it around the boulder and made a faint track in the rubble to make it seem like the boulder had rolled down. "Better."

Errol took a moment to take everything in and then nodded. Yeela dusted herself off and then sat on the cart to wait.

It was late morning before they heard the sound of horses approaching. Yeela's heart thundered — what if it wasn't the delegation? Anyone could be using the path. What if it was them and they didn't have Ithrael? Surprisingly, her thought wasn't *What if they realise we're spies and kill us?*

When the sound of hooves got closer, she ran out to the side of the road and waved them down.

Their horses slowed. "What is the meaning of this?" asked the man leading the group. He wore usual Hyrathean attire but for once, his fur was wrapped around his body. Yeela assumed he was the soldier in charge of guarding the party.

"There's a boulder. We couldn't move it and we didn't want anyone to get hurt." He dismounted from his horse and went to investigate. When they went around the corner together, Errol was on his knees in front of the half-collapsed wagon trying to straighten the axle.

"Our horses should be able to get around this." Yeela's heart began to pound. They were just going to pass them by. "But our wagon might end up like yours."

He shouted over to Errol. "You. Give us a hand with this boulder."

The two men together moved the boulder with relative ease and set it far enough away from the road so that no one else might accidentally crash into it. The soldier looked at their cart and sighed. "You're not going to have any luck fixing that out here. You'd better abandon it."

"But all our goods — we can't leave them!" Yeela protested.

"I can fix it," Errol objected to Yeela, not the soldier.

"I told you you wouldn't be able to. You've been trying all morning!"

"Well, if you actually helped instead of complaining, maybe it would be fixed by now." He was pointing a finger at her and his expression was so serious that she wanted to laugh, and so she did.

"Look at us, newlyweds and already bickering like my parents." Errol's face broke into a smile, the first one Yeela had seen. It made him look younger and his ears stuck out a little more in a way that was disarmingly charming. She flushed a little; she couldn't help it.

The soldier looked between them and then muttered something under his breath. "You Hyrathean?" he asked Errol.

"Ka," which Yeela knew meant yes in Hyrathean. The only other word she knew was no — *knon*.

The soldier went back around the corner and Yeela shrugged. She wasn't sure if that was a good thing or a bad thing that Errol was a countryman. Two different soldiers appeared, and they, too, had covered their chests. Yeela was a little disappointed.

"Been told to take your things onto our wagon, give you a lift to Rathon if that suits?"

"Thank you!" Yeela gushed and began passing the men bundles from their cart.

"Tes rous sor?" Errol asked in Hyrathean. Yeela assumed Errol was checking it was okay for them to get a lift. Hyrathean was surprisingly similar to Maldessan if she listened carefully.

"If your wife doesn't mind riding behind me." One of them smiled lasciviously at her.

"She can ride with me, on our horse." Errol smiled back but there was a warning there.

"Let's hope your mare can hold you both." Yeela looked over at Apple. She was sure the old girl could handle it, so long as the pace was slow. But then a thought occurred to her. She'd once again have to be close to Errol. Last night she hadn't minded it but now, well, she felt strange about it for some reason. Yeela carried a bundle of textiles down the row of men, waiting for them to load up their things. The wagon was canopied but she wasn't allowed to see inside. Instead, her items were taken from her but she could smell something horribly sweet coming from inside, like a cloying incense. She knew that smell.

As she passed all the men, she took in their features to see whether any of them had been there the night they'd taken Ithrael. None of them were familiar. She relaxed a little. No one would know she was a guard.

Errol helped her up onto Apple and she was annoyed, not for the first time, that she was in a dress. She had to bunch it up and her exposed ankles became cold very quickly. By the time they had made it through the pass and into Hyrathea, her legs were completely frozen. It was going to be an uncomfortable journey to Rathon.

Chapter Ten

AMAREA

Ithrael had been gone for an entire day. Once again Amarea had barely slept, and when she had, feverish dreams of a sickly and dying Ithrael had hunted her. In her dream he was so diminished by the poison she barely recognised him. At sunrise she rose from her bed and changed into her training clothes: tight bandage top to secure her breasts, loose-fitting trousers and top, and a veil she could tie around her face. If she couldn't fight the men who were targeting her and those she loved, well then, she'd have to pretend to fight them.

She was surprised how unenthusiastic the soldiers looked to have her join their session. In fact, they suggested the recruits spar with her first. Either they didn't want to harm their Queen or they knew how strong she was. Either way they were all cowards.

She fought off the trainees easily and even encouraged them to attack all at once, but it was like flicking away ants. She wasn't even out of breath. It made her miss Ithrael even more.

Gallia joined her. "I heard you were out here destroying morale."

"Maybe I should have requested a guard who shows more reverence," Amarea countered.

"Maybe, but you'd have thrown them off a balcony within a day." Amarea smiled behind her veil. Yes, she probably would have.

"So, do you want to fight?" Amarea hoped Gallia did; she was a strong fighter and might actually prove somewhat of a challenge.

"I didn't think it would overstretch you, and so I've arranged for some visitors." The quad where the soldiers were training cleared and they began making their way up to the surrounding viewing balcony.

"Gallia, what did you do?" Gallia would hear the vicious smile she now wore in her voice.

"Remember that horrible pack of wolves that tore through an entire family?"

"Yes ..."

"Well, they were captured as they were terrorising villages. Thought you might want to play with them." Gallia walked away and Amarea's blood began to pump. A whole pack of wolves, and wolves that deserved to die, too. She was going to enjoy this.

When Gallia was safely on the balcony, the wolves were released from a cage. From across the clay courtyard she could see the madness in the eyes of the predators. They were not ordinary wolves, these wolves; they were out for blood, not food. They were her kindred spirits. It would be a shame to kill them — they were beautiful beasts, after all. But she remembered the reports. There was a baby and a young child amongst those killed. As Queen, she deserved to enact an appropriate punishment. Was it so wrong that she was going to enjoy it?

The wolves circled, seven in total. Each wolf bared its teeth at her, its intension clear. She stood still and waited.

They attacked as one; some charged, some leapt, some stayed low. A full body assault.

Gallia had kindly given her two daggers before she departed. Amarea spun, the blades sharp enough to slice through the fur and skin, her movement fast and sure enough to be a killing blow. The first wolf was down on the ground in an instant. Her other dagger ripped through the belly of a second that was lunging at her. Only five to go. It was too easy. She hadn't even spun a full circle yet; time had slowed for her as she slammed her dagger down and through the skull of a wolf about to go for her calf. She continued turning as an open maw went for her middle. She twisted the daggers in her grip so that they were lodged into the tight sleeves of her top, and using her now free hands she tore the wolf's jaw apart, dropping its limp body to the ground. The blades came back out as she kicked another in the head; it fell back, stunned, but quickly regained its composure. Another went for her arm but she pierced a dagger through its eye.

The remaining two attacked together. They wanted to topple her, to get her on the ground. She wouldn't have her soldiers see her rolling around on the floor. Queens didn't fall. She adjusted her stance and ducked, allowing their jaws to miss her. She reached out and grabbed one by the back of its neck, and using her other hand to gain a better grip, she threw the animal against the opposite wall. The resounding crack was assurance enough it wasn't getting back up again. The final wolf's hackles were raised, its yellow teeth bared, and it let out a low growl. Amarea watched the animal and felt a sadness for the lovely creatures she'd destroyed. So instead of fighting it she crouched, holding out her palm flat in a stop motion. The wolf continued to snarl but Amarea didn't move, the blood of its brothers and sisters already cooling and drying on her out-held hand.

"Sit," Amarea commanded.

The wild wolf, leader of its pack, sat. Amarea stepped forward and ran her fingers through the soft pelt on top of its head. She was the alpha now.

There was silence in the arena. Amarea didn't look up; she simply turned towards the exit and walked. She heard the soft pad of the wolf as it followed her. She didn't need their applause, only their understanding that as their Queen, she was in complete control.

Gallia met her just outside the training grounds, and the wolf at her heel snarled. Amarea held up her hand and it ceased.

Gallia raised an eyebrow. "Will your companion now be joining us everywhere you go?"

Amarea looked down at the wolf. "I don't think he'll appreciate being a pet." She thought for a moment. Releasing him wasn't possible, not when he had shown interest in human flesh. "He can stay in the barracks, join the Guard dogs."

"Is that a good idea? Won't he attack the soldiers ... and the dogs?"

"Not if I introduce them." Amarea made her way to the kennels and enjoyed the sound of the paws trotting behind her. Ithrael would have laughed at her new companion, and the thought made her heart ache.

Chapter Eleven

ITHRAEL

Ithrael came to with a heavy sack over his head, secured around his neck. His head hurt and he had a sour taste in his mouth. The cloth smelt of wood smoke and horses, but underneath that smell there was a cloying, sweet odour. He swallowed hard; he knew why he tasted vomit. The smoke from the alley, it had done something to him. He felt weak and his entire body ached. He was lying on his side but he had no idea where. He felt around with his hands, which were tied uncomfortably behind his back, and felt the grains of wooden planks beneath his fingers. He wasn't on a ship as there wasn't any rolling motion, which he was very glad of in that moment. The area was small, as when he managed to stretch out his legs his head and toes reached either end. He had to rest for a moment after that, which worried him. He'd never been this weak; even as a child he'd been strong. He lay still and listened. There were voices, deep ones, but he couldn't make out the words. If he had to guess he'd say they were Hyrathean, which made sense. The Vulch were bound to have the Hyratheans do their dirty work. The fact that he was still alive was a positive; it meant he might just be able to escape. However, it also meant there was a strong possibility of torture. In his weakened state that didn't sound particularly appealing, and so he gathered his strength and began to test his bindings.

Chapter Twelve

AMAREA

Amarea was soaking in her bathing pool when a knock sounded on the tunnel door. She'd barely slept again and it was beginning to take its toll on her mood and body. Her head ached as she tipped it back and let her hair fan out around her like seaweed.

"I'm in the water — you can come in if you want." The door opened and Mierdas entered. Even though she knew he couldn't see, it felt odd being naked in front of the old man, and so by the time he'd entered she'd wrapped herself in a drying robe.

She walked over to him, her wet feet slapping slightly against the black marble floor. "Have you found him?"

"No, but there's been a development." Mierdas' face was crinkled with ... was that worry? Mierdas never worried. "For a time, the House and I have noticed something a little ... awry with the weather patterns. Nothing alarming, but last night a heavy frost fell."

"Frost? We don't get frost past the mountains at this time of year."

Mierdas nodded. "A frost so heavy I fear many crops have suffered."

"We have stores, though, we always prepare for the winter." But she knew that the stores were lower than usual after the treatment of her people under the Daylarian Church.

"The balance is off."

"How off?"

"I can feel the scales tipping. I can taste a sweetness in the air." Amarea's eyes widened. She had been aware of a strange sweetness that morning. "The smoke."

Mierdas ran his hand along his bald patch. "It is as I feared. They have found a way to poison our land."

Amarea began to pace. "But how? Surely such smoke would poison their own lands? They can't control the direction the wind blows."

"I don't know how, yet, but whatever it is, it has started."

Amarea felt a wave of dizziness, a sensation that was foreign to her. "Mierdas, I want you to go to Calmaya. If this smoke only affects us here, then go to where the air is clear. Take everyone from the House with you."

"My Queen, that's hardly necessary."

"And how are we to redress the balance with our mages sick from the air in this land? And if Calmaya is no better, get on a ship to Assisa — they are our friends. Get as far away as you can and once there, find a way to fix this."

Mierdas was troubled; she could see that. But he couldn't argue with her logic. It was the only way they would be able to reverse the blight.

"And what of you, my Queen?" His voice was soft, sympathetic.

"I will not leave my people when there is an attack on their home." Mierdas let out a sad sigh but seemed to know that's what she would say. "As you wish. I will begin preparations for us to leave immediately."

Amarea stood alone in her bathing chamber. The skin on her arms rose up with the chill in the air. She felt powerless. She *hated* to feel powerless. How could she fight an invisible force? Why was there no one she could kill to make herself feel better? She clenched her fists. There was always an enemy to fight; she just had to find them.

Amarea swept into the throne room. Her dress was black and backless which hugged her figure then fanned out into a short train at the back. Her shoulders were covered with gold studs, her forearms encased in gold armbands, her fingers adorned with gold talons. Her veil was black, the circlet her usual one of golden roses, leaves and thorns. She was the vision that her people had come to recognise as their Queen — an uncompromising force.

Gathered in the hall was every member of the council, every senior member of her army who was within half a day's ride, every person of note that her inner circle could think of. She stood before her throne and looked out at the crowd, questions in their eyes.

"I don't want to alarm you all but an attack has begun upon our home." There were shocked whispers and mutterings, and she held up her hand for silence. "A poisonous smoke has been released and is causing disruption to our weather." The room stilled with surprise. It was unheard of for the weather to be disrupted; everyone had so much faith in the House of Mages. "If anyone has begun to experience nausea, weakness and headaches, they are to report to a guard station that is to be set up. Those who are affected we will try to move outside of the radius of the smoke."

"Will not everyone be affected?" one of the representatives of a town asked.

She hadn't been sure how much to tell them but disliked the idea of keeping this a secret. "Those who have any kind of magic will be affected. The House of Mages is being relocated so they may work to resolve the balance without being affected. The more magic someone possesses, the worse the symptoms will be."

The head of education stepped forward. "But my Queen—" Amarea liked her; she'd always been pragmatic and kind. Amarea shook her head. She knew what she'd say, that Amarea had more magic than any. Now wasn't the time.

She watched as the room began to empty and waited until only the council and army commanders were left in the room.

"The source of the smoke must be found. They have to be near our borders. I need scouting parties to go to the outskirts of our land — to the mountains, to the sea — and find it, or them. But only send those who seem completely unaffected — as soon as they get closer it will only get worse." The commanders took their leave to begin organising the searches.

"And what of the destroyed crops?" Aiden asked.

"We begin rationing food now. We cannot say how long this will last and we need to prepare."

"I'll draw up an announcement to be given to each town and village," Niseem offered.

Commander Denmer had stayed behind at Amarea's request and spoke. "You will need soldiers to help facilitate the distribution of rations. The people won't like it, even if it is for their own good." Amarea agreed.

"And how are you feeling, my Queen?" the Primlect asked.

"Like I have an enemy to fight. I expect all of you to do your utmost to help me find them." It hadn't been what he meant but she wouldn't let them see weakness in her. "We knew that the Vulch would find a way to target us that would make it difficult to prove it was them. In the past they've been fiercely opposed to magic — they've gone from refusing, to acknowledging its existence, to actively preventing any form or sign of magic within their nation." She was beginning to feel light-headed but she wouldn't let it show, so she continued, her voice never giving an indication that she wasn't herself. "This attack is an attack on our people, on those who are unable to defend themselves. We will stop it. We will protect our people from those that wish them harm."

She swept from the room, not, for once, for a dramatic exit, but because she needed to lie down. Her head had begun to spin. Wherever the smoke was coming from, it was spreading. She could taste it in the air.

She slept for longer than she'd intended. *At least*, she thought, *she'd finally managed some sleep, even if it was in the middle of a busy afternoon.* With aching limbs and a sickly-sweet taste in her mouth, Amarea dressed in her riding clothes and made her way to the stables. Gallia joined her as she rode to the House of Mages.

Once inside, Amarea could see on the faces of those inside that they were suffering as she was. They walked with a shuffling pace, sweat shining on their brows. She found Mierdas at the bottom of the stairs, directing everyone. He looked frail and was leaning against the bannister.

"You need to leave, it's getting worse."

"I know, I know. We're nearly ready." He reached for her arm and patted her hand.

"Let's get you in a carriage, they know what to do." Amarea, weak herself, led the old man outside and helped him into his seat.

Mierdas feebly grumbled protests about being the last to leave. "Mierdas, without you we cannot hope to defeat this threat. You're to go ahead of the rest of the party. Every moment counts." She gave instructions to the driver and ignored the mage's protestations. She was Queen, she outranked him; and so the carriage, with its guards, set off at speed towards Calmaya. They would have to travel through the night but she hoped that the further Mierdas was from Saffiere, the better he would feel. He was too frail to endure much more of the poisonous air. She looked up at the sky, dusk far enough away for her to know that the darkening above them was unnatural. Her thoughts turned to Ithrael. She had ordered for him to be brought home, but now she wasn't sure it was such a good idea.

Chapter Thirteen

YEELA

Yeela was pleased to discover that once they were past the mountain range the air became milder, which meant her ankles were starting to thaw. They stopped for a night in a clearing just off the main road, hidden from view of passing travellers by a wood of evergreen trees.

She was the only woman in their party, something she was comfortable with as she was often placed in teams with only men for guard duty or training. However, amongst this party she felt less at ease, especially around one of the degats — Kureen, she believed his name was. He seemed to watch her every move with eager interest. She did her best to ignore it, and as she was supposed to act how Hyrathean men saw women, she got to work preparing the fire and the men handed her food parcels to make a stew.

"Can you cook?" Errol whispered to her as he handed her a large pot and a large skin of water.

"No ... I mean, all you have to do is throw it in, right?"

Errol's scowl was slightly different to his usual scowl, more surprise than annoyance. "I'll help."

"You know how to cook?"

"My mother taught me. Besides, I'll make it with the spices they're used to, they'll appreciate that." He began unwrapping the cured meat.

"You'll have to make it seem like you're the one helping me because, you know, it's how the barbarians see women."

Errol flinched. "Don't use that word."

"Why?" she asked. She hung the pot over the fire.

"It's offensive." He uncorked a glass bottle of oil and passed it to her.

"Niseem always said the Queen described your people as barbarians with a kind of affection." She poured the oil into the pot and Errol tapped her arm to tell her to stop. She recorked it and passed it back to him.

"It makes it sound as though we're savages." He passed her a small pouch of mixed spices and indicated five pinches.

"No it doesn't, it's saying you're fighters who are a little wild." He passed her some onions, cloves of garlic and carrots to chop. The Hyratheans came prepared for the trip, but she supposed they were a delegation and were used to finer meals, even when travelling, because in the Maldessan army she'd always been given dried pork, stale bread and maybe, if she was lucky, some cheese.

"It makes it seem as if my people are uncivilised." The spices had started to smell and Errol nodded to her to add the onions and garlic.

She stirred the pot. "I'm sorry, I never thought of it that way. I've always thought barbarians were kind of attractive."

She flashed him a smile but it didn't remove his scowl. "I won't use the term any more. I'm sorry I offended you." And she really was sorry. She knew the hurt words could cause, and it wasn't for her to say if they were offensive to him or not. She'd used the term because Niseem had told her the Queen had, but that didn't make it right.

He passed her the meat without another word and she added it to the pot. The food already smelt amazing. She stirred whilst he poured in a skin of wine. It began to bubble and he indicated she was to add the water. She did so until he nodded that she'd poured in enough. They tidied everything away and then joined the others who had finished with the horses and were now sitting around the fire.

"You help your women to cook?" one of the men asked Errol.

"She's learning to make real food," Errol replied, an arrogant look on his face that Yeela hadn't seen before. She wondered if this was a side to him she didn't know or an act. It was hard to say. She couldn't separate the Maldessan soldier from the Hyrathean man, despite her previous apology. The man laughed and slapped Errol on the back. Yeela scowled at him, giving him a taste of his own medicine.

"And what's wrong with Maldessan food?"

"Not enough spices," the man replied.

"What's your name, friend?" Errol asked.

"Terro."

"How is it you speak Maldessan so well?" Yeela asked whilst trying to find the rock that was digging into her.

He shrugged. "Because I'm a guard to the delegation."
She felt bad; she'd made an assumption again about the Hyratheans, that they weren't educated. Of course they would be educated. She was ashamed of herself. She would have to do better, have more of an open mind. The Hyratheans had been an enemy for so long she'd become prejudiced without even realising it. She stayed quiet after that, listening as Errol and Terro spoke in both Hyrathean and Maldessan. Listening to the Hyrathean language around her, it sounded similar to Issish. A few words she could discern as she started to hear the patterns that were similar to Issish and Maldessan.

When the stew was ready Yeela served it to the men with a slice of their hard, dark bread that had a slightly sour quality but tasted just fine when dipped in the stew. She had to admit, Errol knew what he was doing; the stew was good. She received approving nods from the others.

When it was time to turn in, even the lords, or degats as they were called, laid out their sleeping mats in the open. No tents or shelter for anyone. It would make it difficult for her to investigate the wagon if everyone was out in the open nearby. Errol placed their sleeping mats side by side, slightly further out than the others.

"Won't we be cold?" she asked.

"We'll have each other for warmth." She heard a chuckle from nearby and turned to see Terro listening in.

"I've married a scoundrel." She playfully slapped Errol on the arm and was given a smile in return. She couldn't quite comprehend how much his face transformed when he smiled. She found herself watching him a little longer than was appropriate then quickly turned to ready her bed. Yeela couldn't sleep. They were too far from the fire and the temperature had dropped dramatically. Errol noticed her shivering and moved closer, pulling her into his arms.

"What are you doing?" she whispered harshly, uncomfortable with the intimacy.

"Trying to prevent you from getting ill." His breath was hot in her ear and tickled.

"If I wake up with you sticking into my back again I won't be happy." He was silent; she could imagine the blush on his cheeks and smiled to herself. "Do you think they're asleep?"

"Not yet and they have a guard outside the wagon."

"How are we to find and free him?"

Her body shuddered violently from the cold, and so he pulled her closer, curving his body around hers. She began to enjoy the feeling of him holding her and before she knew it, she was in a deep sleep.

She woke up with a stiff neck and coldness against her back. Errol was already up and so was the rest of the camp. She rose and packed her things away and went to relieve herself before the journey, wishing it was still dark so she didn't have to worry about any of the men seeing, although she did now see the benefits of a skirt.

Errol helped her onto the horse, something that was necessary with her full dress, and she felt conscious that she hadn't washed. The Maldessan army was very strict about cleanliness and she was used to her routine. *They should prepare their soldiers for warfare when such routines aren't possible*, she thought. Her skin felt greasy and she had the horrible taste of salt pork lingering in her mouth from their rushed breakfast. The Hyratheans set a faster pace and she was worried for Apple having to carry them both, but the horse seemed content to have riders instead of a cart. The wagon was behind them but she heard nothing from inside. Whenever she'd managed to get near, she'd smelt the sickly smell of the smoke. Just the scent of it made her feel nauseated but nowhere near as badly as when she'd been in a cloud of it in the alley and it had felt like she was being choked. She began to despair. They wouldn't have an opportunity to free him with so many men around, and once they were in the city, the chance would be lost. They had to get Ithrael out, and soon. If only she could get him away from the smoke.

Chapter Fourteen

AMAREA

By the next morning, Amarea's body ached as though she had trained for two days solidly. She couldn't eat and she could barely stomach fluids. She looked out of her windows across the city to a sky filled with heavy clouds of smoke that were so thick she couldn't see a scrap of blue anywhere. The sun was a white ball against the poisonous fog. Amarea rested her head against the cool window. She felt weak and helpless. There had to be something she could do; she couldn't just wait for her soldiers to find the source. She hated an enemy she could not see or fight.

Niseem joined her in her chamber. She looked well, which was a relief.

"Where's Saia?" She hadn't seen her in a while.

"In the library. She was up all night researching ..." Niseem hesitated. "She doesn't seem well. More than just tiredness." It was as she feared; Amarea had always sensed some magic in Saia.

Amarea sat down and put her veiled face in her hands. "I need all my strength to fight this, and I need all of my top people at their best." Reluctantly she said, "Have her and any of my inner circle or council who are suffering sent to join the mages."

Niseem shook her head. "You know she won't go, but I do have something slightly positive to tell you."

"Oh?" Amarea lifted her head up so she could see Niseem, and the action was more physical effort than she'd have liked.

"Reports have come in that the air in the mountains is clearer. You could go to the winter palace, keep your strength up." There was hope in Niseem's voice.

"I won't leave the city." Even Amarea could hear how weak her protest was. She hated herself a little for it.

"My Queen, with respect, you are no good to your people in a weakened state, and it will only get worse," said Niseem.

"And what of those left behind to suffer whilst their Queen runs away?"

"It's not running away. Think of it as a tactical relocation." Amarea wished Niseem could see the expression on her face, but somehow she felt that Niseem didn't need to see her expression to understand Amarea's mood.

Amarea would usually pace in this situation but the thought of moving made her want to weep. Niseem was right; in this state, she was no good to her people.

"Have the worst affected brought to the winter palace. There should be room enough for everyone if we only take limited staff." She stood up slowly. "Have my ladies pack my things. I want Bassiri and Tristam with us. Obviously you'll come with Gallia." She paused and reluctantly added, "And I suppose my brother will be affected too, so he'll have to come." She made it as far as the bed before having to sit down, her breathing ragged.

"We need you out of here as soon as possible." Niseem went to the guard stationed outside her door and ordered him to get a carriage ready and to send the ladies up.

"A carriage? I've never travelled by carriage," Amarea protested in a voice she found revoltingly pathetic. She really needed to get away from the smoke so that she could, at the very least, speak with some authority. Niseem turned around, a hand on her hip and an eyebrow raised. Niseem could say a lot with her body.

"Fine. But if anyone *helps* me there or *into* it I will have them executed."

Amarea was ashamed with how long it took her to make it out of the palace. Unfortunately, the carriage had been brought around to the front entrance and she cursed the sweeping staircase that led down from the main doors. Every step was a jolt of agony in her bones, and by then the day had darkened dramatically. At one point she'd had to pause, fearing she'd faint. Gallia's hand had begun to reach for her but the hiss that had emanated from Amarea had made her pull back instantly.

Amarea nearly wept with relief when she was finally in the carriage and seated. Niseem and Gallia joined her, the others to follow later with their belongings. The priority was to get out of the city.

"Where's Saia?" she whispered, her throat hoarse.

The carriage door opened and a grey, sweating Saia started to climb in, and Gallia helped her through the door.

"I'm glad you can't all see how I look," Amarea remarked. Saia replied with a weak smile and then tipped her head back and shut her eyes, panting. Gallia instructed the coachman to go.

"What's in the bag?" Niseem picked up the satchel and baulked. "You carried this when you're so unwell? She opened it to reveal thick, heavy books.

"I need them for research." She wiped her face with her hand. "I feel like I have the worst fever in history. I can't imagine how you're feeling, my Queen." Amarea simply grunted back in response. "Oof, that bad."

"So this is going to be a fun journey. So glad this trip is going to take the whole day," Gallia quipped.

"Hopefully the closer we get the better they'll feel." Niseem patted Saia's hand in sympathy as she groaned with the rocking of the carriage. Gallia handed her a special lozenge for the nausea. Amarea had already eaten two. They weren't helping much.

"Distract us," Amarea requested, hoping that their inane chatter might divert her from the feeling of her body being on fire; her veil was suffocating and all she wanted to do was rip it off. But even now, she wouldn't do that to those she cared about. "And if any of you see me vomit you're never to speak of it. Queens don't vomit."

"I really hope you don't vomit. Firstly, it'll set me off, and secondly, this is a small carriage," Saia protested.

"How about the story of how I met Gallia?" Niseem offered.

"We all know the story. She was new to the Guard and thought you were a thief and tackled you to the ground trying to arrest you. It happened in front of me." Amarea rolled up her sleeves; she felt like she was suffocating from her own body heat. Niseem handed her a soft cloth to wipe herself with.

"I know, I just wanted to remind you of my wife's shame." Niseem laughed at Gallia's outraged expression. Amarea smiled behind her veil. She always felt at home when she was with them.

"Just think, Aiden is suffering as much as us," Saia said with a slight smile.

"It's all that's keeping me going," Amarea replied.

"Tristam was upset he's not unwell. He complained with great vehemence. He's *really* not unwell," Gallia said.

"Poor Tristam, he'll be devastated to have it proven he has no magic." Niseem sighed, but there was a twinkle in her eyes.

"How was Bassiri?" Saia asked. Niseem and Gallia shared a knowing look.

"He had a slight headache," Gallia replied. With her eyes still closed, Saia nodded as if confirming something she suspected.

"Are either of you upset you aren't affected?" Saia asked.

Niseem and Gallia looked at each other. "No," they said in unison and then laughed.

"Why not?"

"Ummm." Niseem smoothed back her hair. "It doesn't change who we are because we don't have it. I mean to say, we are who we are. Magic wouldn't make us any better. Besides, look at what it's doing to you two poor women." Saia was shivering, and even though Amarea was in black it was evident her clothes were drenched in sweat.

"Good point," Saia said.

"I've never been more relieved to be 'not special'," Gallia said as she started tucking into some of the food she'd brought, which granted her a foul look from Saia.

The first half of the journey was torturous for Amarea. No position was comfortable, every part of her body felt bruised and painful. Niseem and Gallia kept insisting she drink water, but every time she swallowed she gagged, which made the others protest. She managed to keep it down each time; she didn't want to think about what would happen if she vomited into her veil.

Niseem had been right, though. After a few hours she just felt terrible, not like she was near death, and the sky had lightened slightly. From that moment onwards, the journey became more bearable. Eventually she heard Saia sigh as she relaxed into sleep. Her skin no longer looked pallid, and the sheen of sweat was gone from her brow, although her hair had frizzed terribly because of it. Amarea rolled her shoulders and neck and took a deep breath. She didn't feel well, but she felt better and as though she could face the challenge ahead of her. She didn't expect a miraculous recovery, or to even recover whilst the smoke still hung in the air, but she could cope; she could think. That was good enough for now. Niseem had been right. Leaving the city was the best thing to do — now she'd be able to take on their enemy.

Chapter Fifteen

ITHRAEL

Ithrael awoke to realise they must have burned more of whatever it was that was affecting him. He'd passed out again and he was feeling worse than before. He couldn't tell how long he had been unconscious, but the air felt warmer — that or he was running a fever. He'd made little progress on his bindings, so despite how weak he felt he began to work on them again. Sweat slipped down between his shoulder blades, his breath ragged. He paused what he was doing; he had heard a voice he recognised. Or was he delirious? There it was again, a voice, rich and full, and she was speaking Maldessan. Yeela? Had they captured Yeela, too?

His heart pounded. He had to help her. But then he heard her laugh. Had she betrayed him? He focused his fever-fogged mind. No. She'd fought with determination in the alley. What on earth was she doing there? It didn't matter; he had to concentrate on getting free of his bindings so that when they next brought in the smoke he could smother it. He couldn't fight off his captors in such a weakened state.

Using all his strength, he focused on working at the bindings around his wrists, but it was no use. There was only one option available to him; he was going to have to dislocate his thumb, which wouldn't be too much of a problem but he suspected he wasn't going to heal like he usually did. It was just a dislocation ... he could deal with it. Or so he thought. His magic must have been a barrier to pain because as soon as he managed to dislocate his thumb, he passed out again.

When he awoke he was ashamed of himself, but he didn't let that stop him from slipping his hand from his binding and clicking his thumb back into place. The ache and throb was not as severe as it had been, which he hoped meant some of his strength was returning. He made quick work of the other fastening and then removed his hood and leg ties. He felt like he could breathe for the first time in days. He sucked in large gulps of air and wondered how Amarea was able to suffer wearing a veil every single day.

He took in his surroundings and established that he was in a covered wagon. He peeked through a slit in the canopy towards where he'd heard Yeela and saw a group of Hyratheans, Yeela amongst them wearing a dress. He didn't take her for a dress wearer. He observed their interactions; she appeared demure, which from the short time he'd known her seemed to be completely out of character. So, she was there to break him out. A small smile of affection on his lips.

The sun was past its zenith; he would have to wait for nightfall. He prepared his bindings so that he could slip them back on if anyone came to check on him, then carefully widened all the gaps between the canopy covers so that the sickly-sweet smoke that clung to the air inside the wagon began to lessen. He wanted to stick his head outside and drink in the clean air but he managed to resist the urge.

He took his time, slowly stretching his muscles to ease the tension of having been tied up. His bones still ached but it felt good to be doing something. It felt good to be preparing himself; it's what he'd always done. He'd trained to be the perfect fighter, which in itself takes time and dedication. He knew that to enter into any battle you had to strategise, and that took its own kind of groundwork. And so readying his body made him feel good, made him feel like he had purpose again instead of being trussed up and useless.

His father had always taught him that half a battle was won in the mind: if you felt defeated then you would be beaten. Ithrael wouldn't allow himself to feel defeated. But the sense of hopelessness was there — never had he been this weak and he didn't enjoy the sensation. He continued to stretch and went through how many men were in the camp and how he might fight his way out with Yeela's help. Surprise was always a great advantage, and usually he was also an advantage in himself; however, as another wave of dizziness washed over him he realised that for the first time in his life he'd be more of a liability. He didn't like the idea.

The camp began to move, a welcome relief as it brought more air into the wagon and the throbbing in his head began to subside. Unfortunately there was nothing inside the cart that he could use as a weapon aside from his bindings: they would be useful enough, though. He soon discovered that one of the boards was loose so he pried it upwards until the nails gave and he was able to pull it free. Not only could the board be used as a weapon, he was able to put his face to the gap and breathe more clearly, even if he did inhale dust from the road. Feeling a little better, he also realised that he'd unearthed an escape option. He managed to pull up enough boards to allow him to slip out, and with the rattling of the wheels against the uneven road no one would hear his escape in action.

He stopped. He couldn't escape whilst Yeela was in their camp. He swore under his breath; he couldn't leave and have her stuck with a group of Hyratheans. He replaced the boards, loosely. Feeling much more like himself, he decided the best course of action was to sleep and restore his strength so that he could get Yeela out under the cover of night. The only issue facing him now was his white uniform and hair, glowing like a beacon in the night.

Ithrael awoke when the wagon stopped. He slipped into his bindings and waited. It wasn't long before a guard entered with the foul-smelling incense. Ithrael held his breath and waited for the guard to leave. He crawled over to the lantern, his lungs burning from holding his breath. Ithrael opened the small metal door which squeaked slightly but he didn't have time to worry about it as he was running out of air. Spitting on his fingers he tried to smother the smouldering block inside. It continued to smoke until he squeezed it desperately between his palms, feeling the heat sear his skin. He gritted his teeth against the pain and continued to hold it, sure his hands were blistering and bleeding.

Just when he thought he couldn't endure any more, the smoke halted. He lifted one of the boards and sucked in the air from beneath the wagon. He opened his palm and examined the small black cube that lay in his bloody and blistered palm. He didn't recognise the now grey block in his hand, and so he pocketed it. The Queen would need to know about it. He closed the door to the lantern. It was made of brass and would do considerable damage to a Hyrathean guard if swung with enough force.

He listened intently to the sounds of the camp and the smell of food cooking. His appetite was definitely back, which was a good sign but it meant his strength was low. Soon he could tell they were turning in for the night. He'd need a horse for Yeela and himself. That would be his first task.

Ithrael dropped through the gap he'd made in the floor of the wagon and watched as the feet of the guard on duty passed by and went to the camp perimeter. On trained silent feet, Ithrael made his way around to the back of the cart. The soldiers' horses were tied to trees nearby. He watched whilst the guard went into the trees to take a piss then slipped through the night like a ghost glowing against the black sky. He untethered two horses and led them away. Passing back towards the camp, he noticed one of the horses was Apple, Amarea's horse from childhood. He knew he shouldn't deviate from the plan but he couldn't leave her favourite horse behind. He went back and untethered her and hoped that she would follow them out.

The guard was returning to his duties and so Ithrael hid near the nickering horses and waited. The Hyrathean went back to the wagon and stood outside. Ithrael took in the area. Yeela was sleeping further out from the camp, an Hyrathean at her side. The sight made him freeze — *had* she been a spy? Betrayed him, his Queen? It didn't matter if she had; he needed to find out what she knew. Spy or not, Yeela was coming with him. He might just have to use a little more force than originally intended.

He timed his movements to the bored guard's pacing. Every time his back was turned, Ithrael would move. He reached the tree closest to where Yeela was sleeping. The guard had tipped his head back and was humming to himself. Ithrael made his way forward and slipped the knife from the belt of Yeela's companion. He didn't stir. Ithrael placed his large hand over Yeela's mouth; it was the same size as her face. Her eyes flew open, a dagger held to his side in an instant. Her eyes widened in shock and then in them he was sure he could see a smile. He relaxed his grip as Yeela gently woke her companion. Ithrael's expression was stern; Yeela simply rolled her eyes.

The man awoke and took Ithrael in with surprise, and then what seemed like relief. They stayed low as they watched the guard. When they felt he was distracted enough by examining what was in his trousers, they moved as one further into the trees, taking a slightly circuitous route but a safer one, to where Ithrael had left the saddled horses. The

Hyrathean held up his fingers indicating two with an incredulous look. Ithrael merely scowled at him, which made Yeela smile far more than he deemed appropriate. He mounted one horse and held out his hand to Yeela. She climbed up behind him and the other man climbed easily onto his waiting horse. They walked the horses through the trees alongside the road until they were well beyond the view of the camp. Only then did they pick up speed. It wasn't until Ithrael deemed the distance great enough that he spoke.

"Who's the man?"

"Captain, this is Errol. He was sent here with me to retrieve you." Ithrael nodded in Errol's direction. He didn't feel the need to point out that he hadn't needed retrieving.

"We heard something this evening, in the camp," Yeela began to explain. "The House of Mages has been evacuated from Maldessa and moved to Calmaya. The air in Maldessa, they were saying, has become poisonous."

"The smoke?" Ithrael asked, and Yeela confirmed his realisation. "The Queen, she cannot stay there."

"They laughed about it, as if they knew more." Ithrael glanced behind and saw Yeela looking over to Errol. "They joked about how all it took to defeat the Dark Queen was blowing smoke up her arse." Yeela didn't sound amused.

"Did they say anything else about the smoke?"

"No," Errol said, "but I got the sense they knew a lot more."

Ithrael reigned in his horse until he was at a standstill. "I have to go back."

"Back?" He didn't need to see Yeela's face to know she wasn't excited by the idea.

"If they've found a way to poison the air in Maldessa we have to find out all we can."

"So you'll go back, into imprisonment?"

He climbed down from the horse and passed the small grey cube to Yeela. "Give this to the Queen — she must learn all she can from it."

"No."

"No? It's an order."

Yeela lifted her chin. "And I have direct orders from the Queen to bring you home."

Ithrael looked over to Errol, who simply shrugged. "She's right. We have orders from the Queen, and if you're not leaving, neither are we."

"Can I just get this clear in my head, though? We're to re-join the kidnapping party?" Yeela looked concerned.

"If we don't, we'll be hunted, and I'm hardly one who can blend in to spy in Hyrathea," Ithrael pointed out.

"We could put horse dung in your hair," Yeela offered, somewhat helpfully. Ithrael gave her his most unimpressed look. "Honestly, I think Errol's been taking inspiration from you on giving dark looks."

Errol responded perfectly by scowling. Yeela held out the grey cube to him. "Keep it, I might get searched."

"So, what, we're to let them take you to Rathon and imprison you? Maybe even torture you. Then they'd execute you. We're just going to let them do that?" Yeela asked, her expression filled with concern.

"Yes, but I'd like you to help me get out before the torture and execution, if possible. Unless you learn anything valuable before we get to Rathon."

"The Queen is going to kill me."

"Your sister is going to kill me for not offering for you to leave right now."

"I wouldn't."

"I know, that's why I didn't ask."

Errol was watching their exchange with a bemused expression. "How will we free you from a Rathon prison? They're known to be particularly ... violent places."

"So long as I'm not near any of the smoke, I'll do most of the work for you." Ithrael displayed no arrogance, just fact. He was the best after all. "And if we need to get out sooner, I've loosened a large section of floorboards in the wagon." Without further discussion, Ithrael turned his horse around and started to gallop back to the camp. He just hoped they'd arrive there before anyone had noticed their absence.

Chapter Sixteen

YEELA

As they'd planned on their way back, Yeela emerged from the woods with Errol's arm draped around her, and she was giggling softly. The guard looked up from his perch against the wagon, frowning.

"Where've you two been?"

"None of your business," Yeela replied hotly. She looked at Errol who had plastered a very satisfied smile on his face. The guard scoffed and then scolded them for running off. During their exchange, Ithrael slipped back into the wagon. It was a miracle no one had noticed their absence.

The following morning when Terro was teasing them about wandering off into the woods, Degat Soligan had given one of the guards a loaded look and he'd headed towards the wagon. Yeela knew that they would find Ithrael bound and asleep. Even so, her heart raced as she pretended to be affronted by Terro and Errol's lewd jokes.

They would make it to Rathon that evening and there were two options before them: delay, or try to get one of the degats to reveal something. Soligan didn't seem like the best target to Yeela but she'd noticed Kureen paying close attention to her over the last two evenings. He was younger than Soligan and seemed hot-headed, often disagreeing openly with the other lord.

Yeela made sure to accidentally brush up against him when she was helping to pack up the camp. She rested her hand on his chest. "My apologies, Degat." She lowered her eyes and went back to clearing away the cooking implements. She headed over to Errol who was readying Apple, who had fortunately decided not to run off in the night. Foolish horse.

"What are you doing?" Errol snapped under his breath.

She ran her hand up the base of his neck, her hand tangled in his hair, and leaned forward as if to whisper a secret between husband and wife. "He's our best source of information. I need to find a way to get closer to him."

Errol's lips went to her ear and she put the tingling sensation she felt down to his breath tickling her ear. "I'll think up a way to slow us down."

She backed away laughing and finished packing. She could feel Kureen's eyes on her and so she allowed the occasional furtive glance back. She knew the game she was playing was dangerous to herself; leading on a man like Kureen was not a risk she'd usually take. But there was more at stake than her personal safety. Her Queen needed her; her country needed her. She wouldn't let her fear get in the way.

Sharing a horse with Errol made it difficult for her to work on Kureen but they rode with the guards, whose mood was now higher as they were nearing home. The weather had improved and Yeela couldn't help but prefer the temperature in Hyrathea. She even enjoyed the changing landscape from woodland to drier scrubland with the distant mountains as a backdrop. There was something untamed about the land and she found her soul recognising the wildness as a kindred spirit.

They stopped for lunch and ate the last of the salted pork, hard, dark bread and dried fruits. Yeela left the men and headed towards a boulder to relieve herself, and when she emerged Kureen was waiting for her, as she had anticipated. She smiled at him.

"Where will you stay in Rathon?" he asked, not looking directly at her.

"With my husband's family." She was surprised to find him struggling for conversation; he'd always seemed so brash and confident. "And you, my lord, will you return to family?"

"I return to the palace to work with the Dolsan, our king."

Of course she knew their king was known as the Dolsan, it was common knowledge, but that didn't stop him from explaining simple things to her — it clearly made him feel important. "That is a very privileged position indeed. You must be privy to many things."

He smirked. "More than you could believe."

"And do you make important decisions, too?" She made her eyes wide and wondering. How Niseem would have laughed to see her sister this way. She was always the soldier, not the flirt. Even as a child she'd preferred to play with a wooden sword than with anything considered appropriate for little girls.

"Of course." He flicked his fur back over his shoulder as it had slipped to cover part of his torso. He wasn't as broad and strong as the other Hyratheans but he was still an impressive figure. A little slighter but that was likely because he spent his time being a politician.

"What sort of things? Anything I might have heard of?" She rested a hand on his arm encouragingly but he began to tell her something incredibly boring to do with his court. She only half paid attention; he was going to be of no use to them. Maybe she wasn't the best person to approach the Hyratheans — she was a Maldessan after all. But that gave her an idea. They began to walk towards the camp.

"My husband despairs of my heritage. He hates our Queen. He calls her a whore, a witch and a murderer." Yeela hated to speak of the Crown she served in such a way, but it was necessary. "You've met her. Do ... do you think she's that bad? Is my Queen who they say?" She hoped she gave the impression of a woman wrestling with her conscience.

"We respect the strength of your Queen, but she has made powerful enemies."

"The Church?"

He nodded. "Yes, and some outside of your land. They will want retribution."

She halted and turned to him, eyes filled with worry. "Retribution? Will there be a war?"

He stroked his hand down her arm. "Don't fear, you're in Hyrathea now — the smoke won't touch us here."

"Smoke?" She looked confused.

He stuttered over his words. "I ... I mean war."

She tilted her head to one side. "Is that the smoke they were talking about the other day, the one that made the mages leave?" The order had been called for everyone to get ready to leave. Yeela clutched his arm. "My mother is still in Maldessa! Will harm come to her?"

His face filled with concern for her. "It's magic-suppressing smoke. If she has no magic she will be okay."

Yeela relaxed and let go of his arm. "She has no magic, only a sharp tongue." He laughed, delighted by her. She frowned. "How can smoke stop magic?"

He shrugged. "Something the Vulch invented. They're always finding new ways to do things, and they found a way to suppress magic."

"But how? Surely the smoke will go everywhere?" She waved her hands in the air towards the sky, amazed by the complexity.

"I have no idea. It's something to do with the position of the five towers — they somehow link and nothing outside of them is affected, only everything inside of them."

"Oh, well that sounds simple enough. Now tell me, Degat Kureen, do you have a wife to keep you company? It must be weary work that you do." The quick subject change had the lord preening under the attention of a young woman, and she hoped he wouldn't realise his blunder.

"No wife." He reddened slightly. "I've no charm for women."

"No charm! My lord, I've never heard such nonsense." She smiled prettily at him.

"I talk too much about political matters. It bores most women."

She gave him a shy smile. "Well, I find it fascinating."

She left him looking pleased with himself and made her way to Errol. He helped her mount and then climbed up in front of her.

"I wish I could ride in front for once," she said.

"Keeping up appearances." He snapped the reigns and Apple began to walk, and she wondered whether Errol actually liked being in charge as the other Hyrathean men did. "Any luck?" he said at barely a whisper.

He kept their horse apart from the others. She leaned into him, linking her hands around his waist. "Five smoke towers."

He huffed out a breath. "I don't think it's enough — we need to know how to counter it. I heard the others saying that the smoke has altered the weather balance in Maldessa and a heavy frost is killing the crops."

Yeela swore under her breath. "The captain was right — we can't go back. We have to find out what we can, how to stop the smoke from poisoning our people and our land."

"Can't we just snuff it out?"

"I think if it were as simple as that they would have tried a different way of claiming our kingdom." Yeela began to worry; what if the smoke, once inhaled, left permanent damage. What could it have done to Ithrael, her Queen, her home? She looked over at the Hyrathean warriors and her familiar hatred bloomed. Being with them in a friendly capacity had made her forget that they were the enemy. They would always be the enemy, and Yeela didn't let the enemy win.

Chapter Seventeen

AMAREA

Stepping out into the cold evening, Amarea felt relief at being able to breathe without her chest feeling like there were thousands of tiny blades inside of it. She didn't feel completely recovered: there was still the slight throb of a headache, a dull ache in her bones, and she felt weak, but her head was clear and she could think. That was all she needed to take down her enemy. Even weakened she was better than the best of them. They should never have underestimated her.

The winter palace had a view of the Waeseah Waters, a lake said to have healing properties. Neesoh and Daylar were supposed to have swum in its waters naked and made love there for the first time, blessing the water. The palace itself was backed by mountains, and you had to approach it from a steep path. The stone was white, making it gleam like a snowcap. The turrets weren't as high as her palace in Saffiere and she almost preferred the winter palace for it. It managed to both belong to its surroundings and stand out.

She kept a small guard and staff at each of her palaces and so by the time she arrived everything was ready for her. A fire had been lit in her rooms and she'd requested her travelling companions join her for a meal in the adjoining chamber, which usually had a sofa and armchairs but a table had been brought in and was laden with hot food.

Saia sat down and started to pile her plate with steaming meat, potatoes and vegetables. "I don't think I've ever been so hungry." The others followed suit. Amarea had requested long ago that her friends shouldn't stand on ceremony around her, particularly where hot food was concerned. She piled her own plate high and ate by holding her veil out with one hand. It wasn't elegant, it wasn't convenient, but it protected those she cared about. Being able to eat again restored more of her strength and soon she was able to slow her eating to ask the questions that had begun to plague her.

"We need to open up faster communications between us and the House of Mages. Any ideas?" She sipped at her wine and waited. They all fell quiet as they considered the question. Sending out riders was slow, as were pigeons, and they were invariably intercepted. And although her hawks were more reliable, she wanted a new way to communicate that the enemy couldn't intercept. Signal fires were useful for alerting an attack but they needed another method.

Saia furrowed her brow in thought. "I read once about a magical receiver they used in Assisa which worked on vibrating magical frequencies between the two posts. It linked blue stones to create a connection and then different parts of the machine moved a certain amount of times to indicate a letter of the alphabet." She went over to Amarea's writing desk and retrieved some paper and an ink pen. She began to draw a contraption. "For instance, all vowels are different amounts of rotations of this wheel." She began to explain the ins and outs as the others looked on.

"It seems a little over-complicated," Amarea said. "If we're sending a signal, you say it mimics the movement at the other end, correct?"

"Correct, like pulling on a piece of string that's attached to both machines but the string is actually a magical frequency."

"So, why can't the machine be designed with the full alphabet — won't that be quicker?"

"In other words, you pull the 'h, e, l, l, o' strings and the corresponding ones are pulled the other end?" Niseem asked whilst examining Saia's drawing.

"Yes, exactly."

They all looked to Saia. "It's possible. I'd have to get to work. It's a shame there aren't any mages here to help."

"I'll do what I can to assist you," Niseem said, and Saia gave her a grateful smile.

When they'd all left, Amarea made her way to her bedroom and was finally able to remove her veil. She examined her reflection and pondered whether the smoke meant she could reveal her face without entrancing those around her. Her skin was a rich brown and fairer than Neesoh's, whose skin was the same black as those of Assisa. But over the generations, through marriage, the beautiful colour of her origins had been lost. Secretly she envied those who wore the skin of her goddess, even if she did wear her face. Her eyelashes were naturally curled and thick. Her nose straight, perfect. Her lips were full, her chin small, her cheekbones high, her jaw not too wide, or too round, or too slim. Just right. She examined her features in the mirror, finding nothing remarkable about them. She understood her own beauty: she saw the symmetry there, and she knew there was nothing she wanted to change, but she couldn't see the magic. To her it was her face, nothing mystical about it. Ithrael had once told her it wasn't her features so much as the power that they emitted combined. The sheer perfection in one place was too much for the human mind to comprehend.

"So if I break my nose my magic will vanish?"

He'd laughed and kissed her nose. "Maybe if it stayed broken."

She turned away from the mirror, revolted by her face, the one that brought men and women to their knees. The face that ruled a queendom and had led her lover to his capture. Tristam had told her time and time again that she was being unreasonable refusing Ithrael, but she'd been so stubborn; she wouldn't listen to reason. But now, with him gone she understood what it must have felt like to be anything but her equal. She was ashamed of herself.

Amarea removed her clothing and walked naked to her bathing chamber where a steaming bath was waiting for her — the water was milky with oils. She stepped down into the hot water and sank her body below the surface. The heat soothed her tired and sore body. When Ithrael returned she'd apologise. She'd do whatever he wanted; she needed him back. She came up for air and a sob escaped her lips, and then another. Her body bent in on itself, wracked with grief for the loss of her love, her pain so deep and raw that sound no longer escaped her lips until she gasped for air. She had never known pain like it. She'd kept going and going because she'd had to. But in the dark of the night, surrounded by water, her fear and loss overtook her.

Somehow she managed to climb out of the pool, dry and dress herself. She curled up in her bed and rode wave after wave of her misery. She wanted him back. She wanted him home.

Finally she slept and awoke in the morning with gritty eyes and a tiredness that had nothing to do with the smoke — it was exhaustion of her bruised soul. She felt as though she was tied together with strands of silk and could easily collapse at any moment. She didn't know how she was going to face the day, how she was going to plan for an attack against their enemy, how she was going to do any of it. All she knew was that she had to, that she had no choice. She dressed in a gown of black velvet that was high-necked, the sleeves long, as was the skirt. She tied her black shani veil around her face, a black circlet atop her brow and secured black talons on her nails. If they thought the black smoke was dangerous, they were in for a surprise.

The grand hall had been made into a war room overnight at her request. She was pleased to see Bassiri and Tristam had arrived, less thrilled to see Aiden. By Aiden sat a young man she didn't recognise, so Gallia whispered an explanation. "He's a mage in training — his name is Dideum, who insisted on staying behind in case he was needed." She must have seen him at the House before.

"Does Saia know?" Amarea looked around and saw the young woman enter. She looked like she hadn't slept much, again. Amarea muttered a curse. Saia needed her to take care of herself; she was one of her most valuable assets.

"Can someone please get her to take a sleeping draft tonight?"

Gallia gave Amarea a wry smile. "I'll try my best."

Saia approached them. "My Queen, I've drawn up some plans that I'm confident will work."

Amarea didn't doubt her; Saia was touched by magic. "We're lucky enough to have a mage here. Speak with him and see if he can assist."

Saia looked over at the group already sitting at the table and her eyes fell on the mage, obvious by his clothing that marked him as someone from the House. Without hesitation she approached him and Amarea watched as his face lit up at the sight of her. Saia didn't notice in the slightest, and for some reason this softened Amarea's heart. She continued to watch as the mage's expression turned from interest in Saia to interest in her project. He began talking animatedly with her and they both left the room, still talking. Amarea smiled to herself despite everything; she was glad Saia had someone to keep her company and to share some of the burden of her work.

Amarea greeted her cousin. "When did you arrive?"

"Not long after you — we rode up with the remaining guard." She didn't think too much about how the journey between Bassiri and Tristam had gone. Neither spoke of what had happened between them that had caused such tension, and if Tristam wanted to speak of it he would tell her.

"Have any of my people needed to be evacuated?" she asked them both.

"Only five needed to come with us immediately. They've been housed with their families," Bassiri said, his voice deep and rich but soft at the same time.

She took her place at the table next to Tristam and the Primlect joined her. More people began to file in until everyone she needed was in the room, save for Ithrael.

"Does anyone have anything new to report?" She placed her hands on the table and clasped them together.

Three of her generals were in the room and her breath caught when a fourth walked in: High General Ethea, Ithrael's father. He was tall and broad-shouldered with dark, prominent features and a nose that had probably once been broken and not set properly so it had a curve to it. His hair was now grey but she knew it had once been black; she remembered him from her youth when he used to meet with her father. He was the leader of her combined army and navy and had been away for months. She felt both relief at his return and worry. Did he know about his son?

He stood opposite her and bowed, deep and quick. She inclined her head. "High General, thank you for journeying back so quickly. What news?"

"I managed to hear word on my way through the port from a party sent to find the source of the smoke. One has been located upon the Sodessa Isles."

There was a collective intake of breath from around the table. The Sodessa Isles were hallowed, said to be the final resting place of Neesoh. Only those of the Church of Neesoh ever stepped foot on its sacred shores.

Amarea had to ask the question but fear gripped her. "The priests and priestesses?"

The High General couldn't look at her. "Slaughtered, your Majesty." There was pain in his voice, something she never expected from a man of his reputation.

A gasp of horror escaped her lips and she clenched her hands together tighter and bowed her head. The priests and priestesses of the Neesohan Church were all that were good and pure in her country, and her enemy had killed them. "Neesoh carry them home," she whispered and then raised her head. "And what was the cause?"

"A tower. They tried to extinguish the source of the smoke but neither water nor sand would stop it. They couldn't get close enough to investigate further as the smoke was so thick they began to choke."

"Was there flame?" Niseem asked.

"None that they could see."

"Like the amber incense used in the churches." Niseem lifted her eyes to Amarea.

She was right; it appeared to be some form of resin. "Have someone contact the House, see if they have any ideas. Don't let the soldiers stay too long or too close to it, but I want them stationed on the island if they can bear being so near to the source. Anyone suffering should be replaced."

"Yes, my Queen."

"I take it no word from the House?" She looked around the table and no one seemed to have any news from the mages. No news didn't worry her as she knew they were safe, but it did irritate her. They were probably all running numerous experiments and forgetting to send reports on their progress. "We need a liaison, someone who will actually let us know what is happening there, but …" She held up her hand before anyone was recommended. "They will need to wait until Saia has come up with a communications device. They may as well take it with them and know how to use it."

"And Dideum should be the one to deliver it to the mages as he will know how to use it," Tristam said.

"Agreed," Amarea replied, noticing that Dideum had paled slightly. But she didn't have time to worry about the young mage's relationship with the House; there was too much to do.

The Primlect moved the meeting along but Amarea couldn't concentrate. She loathed sitting and discussing plans when her people were being targeted.

"… and we had the mages take samples of the soil before they left," one of the counsellors for agriculture was saying. "The rations have been badly received but are being well managed."

"Any word from the Vulch?" Amarea asked the room.

"They've offered aid," the Primlect said with disdain.

"Oh, I bet they have. I'm sure they'd love to send in a contingent of soldiers under the guise of aid." She loosened the bow on her veil slightly. "I want to make sure we're rationed here as well — any excess is to be distributed. If the people are hungry, so are their leaders. We will be unable to understand their plight unless we feel it for ourselves."

"We'll hardly starve — the rations are fair and plenty," assured a counsellor with a smile.

"I'm sure they are." She ensured her voice was gentle. When people can't see your face it's easy to have your meaning misinterpreted. "High General, how is the mobilisation of our soldiers looking?"

"There are ten thousand men on route to the winter palace as we speak. Ten thousand more are headed to the Northern Pass. Smaller numbers have been sent to be stationed at outposts to warrant we have all areas covered." Anticipating her next remark, he continued, "Yes, we are spread thin but at this stage it's all we can do to prepare. When we have a better indication of the threat, we can work quickly. At least this way we have every station covered and you will have an army at your direct command, your Majesty."

It would have to do, she supposed. "And I imagine you will all council me against marching our entire army into Vula?" There were awkward coughs and shuffles in response. "Pity."

She stood alone in her private study, looking out across the water and to the tainted sky that seemed to cease midway over the lake. She stepped closer to the window and looked at the skyline; it was almost as though there was a clear boundary where the smoke stopped. She looked out towards the mountains to where The Fold was, and froze. It was darker there, definitely darker. She stripped off her dress and donned her black trousers from the night of the Blood Moon, the fabric like the scales of a snake. It was both armour and a uniform. She was the Dark Queen and she would make her enemies tremble before her.

Chapter Eighteen

AMAREA

Amarea swung her leg over her black mare, a small guard accompanying her as she rode out. The High General had attempted to protest against her actions but she wouldn't be detained. She'd seen something in the sky and she was going to find answers. She didn't care that she was Queen and she was supposed to stay inside her ivory castle. She had to *do* something, and this was what she was going to do.

Their horses were steaming in the cold late afternoon air by the time they arrived at The Fold. Amarea slowed her horse but didn't stop, even though she was aware she was being watched and that no one could pass into The Fold uninvited, not even the Queen. She kept going, her guards at her back, Gallia to her right.

"Sometimes I wish you would think things through, your Majesty," Gallia remarked in a low voice.

"Then you'd just get bored, dear Captain."

An arrow flew and Amarea kept her horse moving forward, unflinching as it landed inches before her. Her horse didn't flinch either, having been battle trained. They were far enough past the entrance that they were now within The Fold; mountains towered either side of them as they made their way along the valley that led to the outlaw encampment.

"Your men will have to do better than that, Boothrod," she called. A second arrow landed even closer but she didn't stop. A third flew directly at her heart and so she snatched it out of the air and dropped it at her horse's hooves.

A laugh echoed off the mountain walls. "What is it you want, *Queen*?"

She halted her horse and rested her hands on the pommel, calling out her response. "I thought you hated the Vulch more than me, Boothrod?"

A man stepped out from hiding. He wasn't particularly tall but he was broad with a bald head and a beard of red and brown. The top of his head was tattooed in blue with markings that bore no meaning to anyone but those of The Fold. "Those pale assholes? What's to like?"

"So why have you let them build a tower on that mountain?" She pointed to the west to where she had seen what she could only describe as the corner of where the lines of smoke joined. It was clearly the location of a tower.

He crossed his arms, his large biceps bulging, and smiled, but there was no humour there. "What of it?"

"You have dealings with them now?"

"When the coin is right. I believe I'll even work for our loathsome Crown under the same conditions." He licked his lips in satisfaction.

"It's still my mountain. What made you think you could give them permission to build a toxic tower on top of it?" Her voice was cold and there was no mistaking the threat.

"I've always considered myself the landlord to these mountains, seems that I can rent them out to whomever I please." He matched her tone, his stance wide, unmoving.

Amarea slid down from her horse faster than humanly possible and strode towards him, her black outfit gleaming in the golden light of the late afternoon. He stood his ground but she saw a subtle flinch. She did enjoy being feared.

"Do you realise what you have done?" Her voice boomed through the valley as she approached him.

"Apparently it was to weaken the Queen. I didn't see any harm in that." The *nerve* of this man infuriated her.

She slapped him across his cheek, the force of it strong enough to cause him to step to the side, the insult clear. You don't slap a Maldessan man; it's demeaning to them.

"You fool. That tower has poisoned the *entire* land. Any family you have beyond that smoke may starve, or worse if there is any magic in their veins."

"Elo." The name came out as a breath, a prayer. He swore.

"You're to help my men try to bring it down but if anyone feels unwell close to it they're to return to the valley. You're to report your progress to the winter palace, daily." She turned towards her soldiers.

"I don't answer to you or take orders from you, Amarea."

She spun on him, her fury coming off in waves of unchecked power that vibrated through the air. "I can force you to my will, Boothrod, but I have respected your choices until now. I allow The Fold to exist, for you to rule these people." She indicated those who were surrounding them but remained hidden.

He snorted at her.

"Do you wish to kneel before me? To grovel at my feet and become less than you are? To worship me as a goddess and lose all control?" She began to untie her veil. "Do you know why I hide my face? Because this is the only cruelty I will not commit unless absolutely necessary, because your freedom lives in your choices. I *will* take that from you."

His face didn't leave hers, his jaw set. The fool believed he could resist. "Have you always wondered at my beauty, is that it Boothrod? Have you always wanted to see what others have spoken of? Will you allow your curiosity to damn you?" Her rage was so great she was going to do it, reveal her face and have the leader of The Fold fall under her spell.

"Stop!" The call came from her right. Amarea stilled her hands and turned. The woman was old but there was still strength there in her broad shoulders, in her purposeful walk. She was tall with grey hair in a long plait down her back, and there was fierceness in her eyes. "Fool man to allow your pride to do such a thing."

Amarea took her in; there was something familiar about her. "Yes, you know me. I was in the king's guard when you were a child. I saw your face when you were young. It was enough to make you weep, even then, before the magic had fully taken hold." Amarea remembered her now; she'd had red hair and worked inside the palace.

"Catarina, I remember you." But she didn't know why she had chosen to leave the palace for The Fold.

The woman nodded as if it was right for her to remember. "The smoke, it's poisoning the land?"

"It's caused a frost that's killed all the crops and makes anyone who has magic sick."

Catarina turned her piercing gaze on Boothrod. "You'd allow that smoke to poison my grandchild just for your foolish pride? Take it down, Booth."

"Ma ..." Boothrod looked embarrassed.

"Want me to slap you too, you silly idiot? I told you no good would come from deals with the Vulch." She spat on the floor at the name of their enemy. She glared at him a moment more, and seeming satisfied said to Amarea, "We will destroy the tower."

"If you can. The other we've found seems to be resistant to all methods of extinguishing smoke and the tower is unbreakable. We must try everything to bring it down. And have your granddaughter brought to the winter palace — she will be away from harm there."

"I thank you, your Majesty, but if it's all the same we will have her brought here."

Amarea re-tied her veil. "I'll meet you at the tower at first light, Boothrod. I hope you'll bring some ideas on how to destroy it."

She returned to her horse and mounted it in one fluid movement, turned her around and walked her slowly out of the valley. Amarea could feel the eyes of the outlaws on her back. She was almost relieved to have a tower so close by; it meant that she could oversee its destruction. Catarina was right. Her son was a fool to trust the Vulch.

CHAPTER NINETEEN

YEELA

Yeela was concerned. She could see Rathon in the distance and Errol hadn't come up with a plan to slow them down, as far as she was aware. It seemed foolish to keep Ithrael locked up. They should let him escape back to Maldessa whilst she and Errol stayed on and tried to discover more. She wanted to go and tell him to run but there was no way to do it. She felt helpless and useless, a feeling she hadn't felt since she'd joined the Guard.

She shouldn't have doubted Errol because moments later there was a groan from one of the soldiers, Dekkon. She wasn't particularly fond of him. He made remarks about her gender often, something she hadn't ever encountered with men from Maldessa, where they saw her as an equal. He halted his horse and ran off into the brush as far as he could and squatted behind a scrubby bush. Yeela turned away, revolted.

"What's wrong with him?" she said as she put her hands over her ears, not wanting to be witness to the man's bowel movements.

"We spotted some cip berries earlier, and Errol was saying how he'd eaten them by accident as a child and was violently ill for days. Dekkon bet us he could eat them without getting sick because he has the stomach of a true Hyrathean," Terro said with a laugh and then grimaced as he heard Dekkon retch.

"My love, can we move further away please, I can't quite bear it."

Errol moved them further up the path and past where the wagon had stopped. From there they couldn't hear or smell anything, which was a blessing and it got them closer to Ithrael. They both dismounted, as others had done.

"That was your plan?" She stifled a laugh by sucking in her lips. She hated to admit it but despite its childishness, it was effective.

Even Errol struggled not to smile. "Worked didn't it?"

"I thought it was going to be some great strategic move, not a schoolboy trick."

"Technically I didn't trick him. I told him exactly what would happen. I just know his type."

Yeela looked over at the Hyratheans; the degats were looking seriously displeased.

"How long will this buy us?" she asked.

"Not long. They'll likely leave him here and have him follow us slowly."

The Hyratheans were talking amongst themselves, so Errol and Yeela approached the wagon slowly. When they were close enough, in a whisper Yeela relayed the message of the five towers and that she felt Ithrael should leave with them straight away. She wasn't sure exactly how, but she knew if he didn't, things were going to go badly. Errol all the while pretended that she was telling him something. It was strange talking to him, but not.

"We need more information. Don't worry about me," he said quietly.

They stepped back and Yeela stroked Apple's nose.

"He's our captain — we have to listen to his orders."

"I know, but I have a bad feeling."

Errol frowned. "The Queen said to listen to your feelings on things. Have you magic?"

"I don't know. The smoke makes me feel a little unwell." She'd never considered such a thing before. She'd always had good instincts, it was true, but she had never considered that to be anything to do with magic.

"It must be some kind of magic." Her heart hammered at the thought. She never saw herself as different to any of the other soldiers. "The Queen must have sensed it."

"So what do we do?" She was getting worried now.

"We stay the course. We prepare as best we can and we be as careful as we can. It's a dangerous mission — I never expected it to go smoothly." He squeezed her arm gently and she felt better for having him there with her. Despite his scowls, Errol was a Maldessan soldier too, and she felt safer with him by her side. Not that she'd ever admit that to him.

As Errol had suspected they were told to move on and Dekkon was left behind to fend for himself. The other soldiers threw insults and jeers at him as they left, a lot of them about him being bitten on the arse by a snake. There was no response from behind the bush, only a pathetic whimper. Despite the short interlude, it had allowed them to pass their message on to Ithrael and Yeela felt better about proceeding knowing that it was what her captain had ordered. She always felt better when she was following an order; there was something easy in letting other people make decisions for you.

Night began to fall and the lights of Rathon guided their way in the increasing darkness. There was something beautifully magical about a city glittering against a night sky, and despite the circumstances Yeela was excited to be visiting a foreign capital. They'd only passed small villages and homes on their way to Rathon and hadn't stopped in any of them. She wondered what new things the Hyrathean capital would hold. Even though she'd always wanted to explore, she'd joined the palace guard because part of her could never quite leave her family. Now, though, she was finally experiencing true adventure and her heart sang for it.

"Have you ever been?" she whispered close to Errol's ear. She felt him shiver slightly at the tickle of her breath.

"No, never, but I do have an uncle we can stay with. I'd been planning on visiting at some point so I know where to find his home."

She sat back in the saddle and took in the city as they passed through. It was different to Maldessa: the buildings were sand coloured and tightly packed together, with flat roofs. The roads weren't cobbled but flat and dusty so that the horses kicked up small clouds of dirt. The side alleys were tight and small but the main streets were wide enough for a wagon and cart to pass one another. She wished she were passing through in the daytime as there were carvings above doorways and windows that she couldn't make out by the soft light emanating from windows.

The roads led down towards the sea, but their caravan took a left turn up an incline where the thoroughfare stayed wide and the houses grew larger and were better maintained. It wasn't long before she had her first glimpse of the palace. Against the night sky she couldn't make out much except for the shape. It was a large building and wasn't as tall as the Maldessan palace but it covered more ground. Instead of turrets, it had wide, square towers with crenulated top.

There were numerous guards outside the palace walls, far more than they had in Maldessa. Yeela took in the exterior layout, and what she could see of it informed her it was going to be hard to spring Ithrael from the palace prison — but nothing was impossible. Well, nothing had been impossible *yet*. Errol dismounted and helped her down from Apple. She couldn't wait to be back in Maldessa where she was able to do things for herself; the Hyrathean idea that women were fragile was incredibly irritating.

"We'll get a cart for you — just be sure to bring it back tomorrow," Terro said as he rode through the gates. They waited for him to return and Yeela's unease grew. She felt watched, assessed. Terro had been the one who'd befriended them, but there was something about the atmosphere that made her think they were finally beginning to realise it was strange to have a Maldessan woman amongst them when they had a Maldessan prisoner.

The cart soon arrived and the soldiers unloaded their things into it. They said their goodbyes and harnessed Apple. As they rode away, Yeela whispered her fears to Errol, leaning against his shoulder to give the impression of an affectionate wife.

"They'll have us followed."

"Even I felt it that time. They'll watch our every move from now on." Errol's grip tightened on the reigns, and Apple nickered.

Errol's uncle's house was on the far side of the city, near the outskirts. He had a small tavern with a stable for horses, which was incredibly fortunate for them. They settled Apple in the stables and went to the kitchen door. Errol knocked loudly and a man pulled it open, looking irritated. She saw the family resemblance immediately. The man squinted and then beamed broadly. "Errol?"

Errol smiled and gave his uncle a hug. "This is my wife, Yeela."

Yeela stepped forward into the light and Errol's uncle slapped him on the back. "Come in, come in." They shut the door behind them and Yeela hoped that the greeting had seemed to those watching as a father welcoming his son home.

"Yeela, this is my Uncle Tret."

Tret pulled her into a hug. "Welcome to the family." He turned and called, "Kalla! Kalla!"

A woman appeared. "There's no need to yell like that!" She stopped in the doorway and a hand went to her mouth.

"Errol?" His name came out in a gasp and tears sprang from her eyes. She rushed to him and hugged him against her substantial bosom. "You look just like your father." She sobbed loudly and Errol looked a little uncomfortable from receiving so much affection from someone he'd never met.

"I can't get over it. I thought it was Jerr standing outside my door." Tret shook his head in disbelief. "What brings you here, boy?"

"I've always wanted to come here and I thought, since I got married, now was the perfect time." Tret nodded as though he was doing exactly what he was supposed to do.

"I'll make up a room for you. Our best is taken but we have a lovely one that will suit you well." Kalla patted him on the cheek and rushed off to prepare their lodgings.

"How long will you stay?" Tret said as he went over to take a pot off the stove that was close to boiling over. He began serving up bowls laid out on the counter.

"A few weeks, and we'll pay, of course."

"Don't offend family with such words." Tret frowned at him and went back to spilling stew over the counter. Yeela's stomach growled: it smelt amazing, of meat and spices and something sweet, too.

Tret placed two bowls on the small kitchen table covered in onionskins, carrot peelings and a dusting of different spices.

"Eat. We'll talk more when my customers have left." He carried out four bowls and a young girl came in soon after and took the remaining four out.

The stew was richly spiced lamb with chickpeas and apricots. Yeela felt warmed to her core by the food and it helped to ease her worry. When they were finished, not knowing what else to do they began to clear up the kitchen in companionable silence; it was the least they could do for the free room.

"Where do we go from here?" Yeela asked Errol when she knew they were completely alone, not enjoying how pathetic the question made her sound.

"Tomorrow we visit the markets, we go to the coffee houses, we listen to what people are saying. We make a decision from there."

It didn't feel like a plan but it was something. It was a step forward at least.

Chapter Twenty

AMAREA

Amarea was awake before dawn and rode out with five guards towards the tower. Gallia had insisted on joining her even though she deserved the rest. Amarea hadn't protested; she wanted someone she trusted completely to be there.

She was surprised to find Tristam galloping to catch up when they were near the mountain pass. She slowed so his horse could reach her.

"What brings you here?"

"I wanted to come and see for myself. I just didn't realise you would leave at *such* an ungodly hour." He did look a little rumpled, as if he'd rolled out of bed and onto his horse.

They reached the summit just as dawn was breaking, and Amarea was relieved to discover that she only felt ill towards the final ascent. Whatever they had done to ensure the smoke didn't spread had also made it possible for her to get close to the tower. It helped that she knew the way she was feeling would vanish once she was halfway down the mountain — she could endure the pain temporarily.

The tower was large and would have taken some time to construct. It concerned Amarea that wherever the other towers were, whoever built them had been given access for an extended period of time, meaning there was a loyalty issue still within her realm.

The tower was made from a blackened wood, not the stone they used for their own signal towers. It was wide at the bottom and narrowed near the top, only to widen out again. The smoke billowed out upwards and then spread towards the centre of Maldessa, despite the wind blowing in the opposite direction. Amarea couldn't fathom how such a thing could be possible.

Amarea approached the tower, and with each step her body felt as though a weight was pressing in. Despite the smoke being carried up and out, a small amount still seeped from between the cracks in the wood, weakening Amarea.

A searing pain sliced through her temples as she reached the door but she pulled it open nonetheless. Agony slammed into her as a cloud of noxious fumes enveloped her entire body. She didn't scream; she wouldn't let herself. She had control over that at least. Her body wanted to crumple to the ground, the pain immeasurable, but she was a Queen and she didn't bow down to any threat. And so with her body in torment she took a step forward, the initial haze of smog clearing enough for her to see.

Before her was a large, glossy black block that smouldered and puffed out the thick smoke, which appeared almost oily close up. Her body convulsed as if to vomit but she managed to hold it back. Appearance was everything and there were outlaws watching; she couldn't let them see her so indisposed. She took a moment to take in what was before her and the strange carvings in the chamber, and then walked back out, her pace slow, purposeful. To anyone watching she was completely in control, every step measured, but all she wanted to do was collapse and weep from the agony.

She took steady breaths of the clearer air before she spoke to those gathered, pleased to see Catarina amongst them. "Before any attempt to destroy the tower is made I'd like all the markings inside to be written down to be studied. Those of you least affected should start on that now."

Gallia sent in two men and the outlaws sent in two of their own, clearly not wanting to be outdone. Gallia approached Amarea with a skin of water. "How did you stand it?" she said so only Amarea could hear. "Even I felt sick being so close by."

"One thing I've learned as Queen is that to be a ruler you have to be more determined than anything that stands in your way."

Gallia let out an unprofessional snort. "Niseem said you were stubborn."

Amarea couldn't help but smile. "You have no idea how stubborn I can be."

One of the outlaws came out of the tower coughing and gagging and Boothrod ordered him back to the valley. A woman was sent in his place.

"What ideas for extinguishing the smoke do you have?" Amarea asked Catarina instead of Boothrod. She saw him tense when she approached his mother and couldn't help but smile. Men were too easy to toy with.

"We assume you tried water and sand," Catarina said. "We also brought tightly woven blankets to try."

"Salt."

Amarea turned her attention to the sulking Boothrod. "Salt?"

"Salt puts out an oil fire but we don't have enough for something so large." He crossed his arms, making his observation into a challenge.

"We'll have salt brought from the Great Plains." Gallia nodded at one of the soldiers who'd come with them to deliver the message to the winter palace.

The scribes exited the tower, coughing from the smoke but seeming well otherwise. The outlaws kept their copies of the writing, and Amarea was handed the copy made by her guards. She frowned; she hadn't recognised the lettering inside and she was none the wiser with it all down on paper. She handed it over to Gallia who also looked perplexed.

"I'll give this to Saia and Dideum. Hopefully their work will be done soon." Gallia slipped the notes into the inside pocket of her winter coat.

They stayed a while and watched as the soldiers tried smothering the smoke with blankets, but they caught fire as soon as they touched the black rock-like substance.

They all leapt back. "The blankets shouldn't have caught so quickly," Gallia said, stepping back from the temporary furnace.

"Try the snow. Water may not work but maybe frozen water will," Catarina said. It took the soldiers some time to gather enough: despite being high up during early winter, there hadn't been much snowfall. With their piles of snow ready they began to quickly shovel them onto the source, but it merely sizzled and spat and created a steam that caused everyone to cough and wheeze.

Catarina crossed her arms, her lips turned down. "'Tis a dark magic indeed that turns water into gas that harms."

"You think it's magic? They used magic to suppress magic?" Amarea was surprised; it was completely illogical. She'd assumed they'd found a natural substance that was poisonous to those who had magic in their blood.

"How else could such a cursed thing still burn?" Catarina tutted.

"But the Vulch have no magic — their land is barren of it."

"Aye, but magic can be made through other means. Unnatural means."

"Blood magic doesn't exist, Catarina." Amarea dismissed the woman's fears. It was superstition, that was all.

Catarina gripped her arm and stared at her as though she could see past the veil and into her eyes. "And did you not feel the power that flowed into you the night you burned those men alive?"

Amarea pulled her arm free but didn't reprimand her for touching the Queen without permission. "Be wary of the words you speak to me."

"I left the Guard when you were sent away as they wouldn't allow me with you. I knew those priests. I heard the stories. I thought I had failed the family when I couldn't keep you from those monsters. When I heard you'd killed every last one of them, I laughed with glee. But lives taken in such a way creates an energy that needs somewhere to go, so I ask you, did you not feel the power that night?"

Amarea took a moment to think back to that night. She'd been covered in ash, the men screaming from within the burning abbey. Had she felt power? Yes, she had as she had knelt before the pyre, the last breath finally extinguished. She'd felt it but she'd been on her hands and knees and she'd prayed to her goddess, to Neesoh, to protect her. The surge of whatever it was had left her. Had she poured it back into the ground? Had she poisoned the earth?

In answer to her unspoken question, Catarina spoke. "They say nothing grows on that site, that the earth remains blackened."

Amarea was lost in thought when Gallia asked her, quietly, "What of the abbey near Fieria?"

She'd prayed to Neesoh then, too, felt the fiery hatred leave her as she'd muttered the words, Ithrael's hands in hers. Had Neesoh cleansed her of the dark magic that rose up from those deaths? And what of the other lives she'd taken? Had her magic been tainted by them? Had Ithrael's? She reflected back on the night of the Blood Moon. No, she hadn't felt any strange power rise within her; somehow, there was a difference in the kills. Maybe she should refrain from mass slaughter in the future.

Chapter Twenty-One

ITHRAEL

Ithrael had the hang of the smoke and had managed to avoid its full effects since returning to the captivity of the wagon. He could tell when they finally reached the city by the sounds from the streets and knew that he would have to mentally prepare for whatever the Hyratheans had in store for him. He tried not to think about it but he couldn't help feeling a little anxious about not being able to escape the smoke. He feared it more than any torture — it diminished who he was, who he'd always been.

The wagon stopped for a while and he heard Yeela and Errol leave. He replaced his hood and bound his hands as the wagon moved again. It soon stopped, and two men removed him and took off his hood. Ithrael kept his body limp so as to appear unconscious. They struggled to carry his large frame and they quickly dropped him in the dirt. He let out a whoosh of air and stirred, taking the opportunity to look around and examine the palace's set-up.

He pretended to attempt to stand and then collapsed. They each lifted one of his arms over their shoulders and began to drag him towards the large metal doors in front of him. He let out a groan for effect, doing his best not to overdo it. Two guards opened the door and Ithrael was dragged down the stairs that were just inside the entrance, his feet bouncing painfully against each step. At a short landing the guards needed a rest and so they propped him against the wall. The walls were a dark-reddish brown with iron sconces that held flaming torches. Fire was always useful to have around; he appreciated the lack of orob lamps which they used in Maldessa.

The guards, having recovered, dragged him down a spiral stone staircase that led to a dungeon with rows of iron-barred cells. He counted at least ten before he was dropped inside one, the door slammed and locked with a key that was placed on the guard's belt.

Ithrael waited for the guards to leave before he stood. There was one man on duty but his back was to him; his feet were up on a small table and he was looking out into the distance. Ithrael took his time to inspect every inch of his cell. There was no window, the walls were thick, the hole in the corner for waste was too small to make his way down and out. It would have to be the door; he could pick the lock easily if he had something to pick it with. He sat with his back against the far wall, watching the guard and conserving his energy. He didn't plan on leaving yet anyway; there were things he needed to find out. For his Queen. For his love.

They brought the smoking lamp soon after, just as Ithrael was drifting off to sleep, still sitting up against the hard wall. A bed of any sort would have been nice but he could endure. The lamp was hung from a hook in the ceiling outside his cell. He couldn't reach it but at least there was some distance between him and it.

"Er, what is that stuff?" The guard dragged his feet off the table and turned in his chair, looking up at the smoking lantern.

"Keeps this one weak so he doesn't cause trouble." The guard pointed his thumb at Ithrael.

"Stinks though. I gotta put up with that shit as well?" he said.

The guard shrugged. "Degat's orders." He walked off, leaving the other guard grumbling about being stuck on the shittiest duty just because of one small incident.

"What did you do?" Ithrael asked, more out of boredom than curiosity.

"Shut your mouth — you don't talk in here."

There was a cackle from a cell opposite Ithrael's. "He got so drunk he shat in his superior officer's bed."

Ithrael and the other prisoner began to laugh. "I'll have you beaten! The both of you!" The guard was going purple.

"And they knew it was him because there was still shit on his trousers the next day. Literally walked around with the evidence on him!" The other prisoner howled. Even though Ithrael's head was beginning to throb from the smoke, he laughed harder. The guard was clearly incompetent and stupid, which worked in his favour. The guard unhooked the lamp and dangled it closer to Ithrael; Ithrael recoiled and pretended to be affected instantly by retching and clutching his stomach. A sick grin spread across the guard's face.

He pulled the lamp back and re-hung it. "Not so smart now, are you?" He laughed to himself, taking pleasure in his power over Ithrael. Ithrael relaxed back against the wall and waited for the guard to fall asleep. He watched as the guard drank from a small flask he kept inside his jacket. It wasn't long before he'd nodded off.

Ithrael stood and went over to the bars, holding his shirt over his mouth and nose in the hope it would reduce his inhalation of smoke. Although the room was dark and there was a haze in the air from the substance burning in the lantern, he saw someone rise in the opposite cell and approach the bars. He was older than Ithrael but still young, his black hair matted, his beard long and unkempt, his clothes filthy. He must have been in the prison for some time.

"What's your name?" Ithrael asked.

"Yuto. Yours?"

"Ithrael."

Yuto snorted softy. "Fancy name for a man who can't handle a bit of smoke."

Ithrael kept his voice level. "It's a targeted poison for people like me." He glanced over to the still-sleeping guard. "How long have you been in?"

"Let's see ... I was taken in for piracy about ..." He looked up, thinking. "Nine moons ago, maybe more."

Ithrael squinted at him. "Where are you from? Your accent, I can't place it."

"Jaien."

"You're a Jair? Long way from your island." Despite Maldessa having people from many lands living there, few were from Jaien. Not only was it the farthest island, its people didn't like those from the Daeneah Realms because they had their own god and they saw the worship of any other gods as blasphemy.

"An opportunity arose. Unfortunately I was apprehended before my job was complete. Pity, really — it was going to help me get me more riches than I could ever dream." He had a dreamy look on his face. He was tall for a Jair and it was possible he was fit before his imprisonment, but months in captivity had begun to make him waste away.

"So you're a thief?"

Yuto smiled with his top and bottom teeth on show — they were white and straight and caught the light, a sign of wealth. "Need something stolen, *Ithrael*?" His fingers twitched in the air as if in anticipation of the deed.

"Possibly."

"Unfortunately they are too aware of my ability to lift anything within my grasp and tend to keep a good distance. I haven't had so much as a chicken bone to pick the lock." He examined his finger. "I considered breaking one of my own off and stripping it of the meat to use as a pick, but I thought that might be just the madness setting in."

"Very likely. It's a good thing you waited. We won't be needing your finger."

"I should warn you, the last man to try and escape was cooked alive on a spit in the grand hall in front of the king's guests," Yuto said sadly. "I doubt poor Herron tasted that good. There was hardly any meat left on him."

It was beginning to concern Ithrael that Yuto really was insane. "No need to worry about that. I can get us out of here but I need information. How much do you know about the palace?"

Yuto explained in impressive detail the layout of the palace from what he'd discovered before he'd been caught.

"So you can get me to the Dolsan's private study?"

"Only if you can get me out of here."

Ithrael looked around. "I can, but I'll need your help."

Ithrael had just finished explaining his plan when they heard footsteps approaching. Ithrael went to the back of his cell and sat down, waiting. Five men walked into the dungeons and three of the men approached the bars to his prison: one was dressed as a degat, the other was a guard and the third was wearing a crown and so it was easy to surmise he was the Dolsan.

"So you're the Dark Queen's play thing," he said. "The white hair is ... interesting."

Ithrael remained seated, an insult he could see the Dolsan had noticed.

"Drug him further, he looks too lucid to me. Afterwards bring him to the chamber. Let's see how the slayer of panthers feels about being skinned himself."

Yuto was watching through the bars and sucked in a breath through his clenched teeth. "Sorry mate, that's a bad way to start your time here. *Really* stings."

The Dolsan whirled around and bit out, "One more word and you'll be joining him, rat."

Yuto held his tongue but Ithrael could see he was struggling to keep quiet. The Dolsan left, not before telling the degat who was with him to have the prison guard reprimanded for sleeping on the job. He was probably heading to his chamber to prepare himself for an evening of torturing Ithrael.

The guard entered the cell with the lantern, opened it and threw a fine dust over the smouldering resin. The effect on Ithrael was instantaneous. The dust turned into thick smoke that made him choke and gag until he was too weak to even stand. His vision swam and he heard the degat order the soldiers to remove him. He was dragged once again but this time his knees knocked against the stairs as they took him up towards where he was to be skinned. He didn't like the sound of that but his body was limp and wouldn't co-operate. If he was honest with himself, he was fucked.

Chapter Twenty-Two

BASSIRI

Bassiri found it most infuriating when the Queen didn't behave like a queen and ran off into danger. She didn't hold enough value to her existence and it was a problem, one he'd often argued with her over. When he saw her return from the mountain with a weary-looking Tristam in tow, he wasn't impressed and he didn't hide his feelings.

The Queen held up her hand to him. "I don't want to hear it. I need you to do something for me … but you're not going to like it."

"Anything for you, my Queen." He bowed his head in respect.

"I need you to go to the site of where the Daylarian abbey burned down, which means going through the fog. I wouldn't ask, considering the effect it has on you, but that's exactly the reason I need you to go."

He didn't like the idea of having to venture back into the smog but he was intrigued. "Oh? Why's that?"

"I need you to look around, see if you feel worse when you're there, see if any of the remains or the soil looks like a type of black resin." She was clenching her hands together, not a good sign. She was worried. "I have an idea and I need to see if it's correct. Anything you find that you think is odd, bring it back. Just, wear gloves when you pick anything up." She approached him and gave him a hug, something she hadn't done since they were young. "I hate to ask, my friend, but I trust you to have the right judgement on this matter." She kissed his cheek and stepped away.

"Of course, my Queen."

Tristam stepped forward. "And I'll go with him. I saw the black resin. I'll be able to help identify it if I see it."

Amarea was the only one in their small party whose shock was not evident. Tristam had been avoiding Bassiri ever since he'd returned and now he was volunteering to be alone with him? Bassiri didn't know how to feel but politely accepted the offer; there was nothing else he could do.

They saddled and packed their horses with supplies in case they had to stay overnight. The ride would only take a couple of hours but they weren't sure what they would find within the forest. They mounted their horses and set off in silence. It wasn't like Bassiri to be unable to think of what to say; his strength had always been his ability to read people and to find the words that needed to be said. But with Tristam, he was lost. He was always lost.

Tristam finally spoke. "I've been avoiding you."

"I know." Bassiri did his best to keep the hurt from his voice. Hadn't he deserved to be the first person Tristam came to see?

"I'm a coward, Bass." Bassiri looked over at Tristam and he could see the shame he felt on his face. It didn't change anything, though.

"Yes, you are."

Tristam looked at him, hurt in his eyes. He didn't get to look that way. He didn't get to make Bassiri's heart ache for the pain in those eyes. "Bass, I'm sorry." Tristam shook his head slowly. "So sorry. I am the worst kind of man." His voice caught and he looked away. Were those tears Bassiri saw?

"It's in the past now, Tris. It was a long time ago."

"It wasn't that long ago."

But it was for Bassiri. Every day Tristam had been away he'd felt taut with longing for him, even though he had hurt him so deeply. The pain at first had been so encompassing that Bassiri didn't think he could rise from his bed, do his duty to his Queen. But he had. He had carried on because he'd had to. And Tristam — what had Tristam felt as the oceans stretched between them and he'd danced and drank with the nobility from every realm?

"Bass?" Tristam's eyes were pleading. "Can you forgive me?"

He didn't know. Looking into the eyes of the man he'd loved more deeply than he thought was possible, he knew he still loved him, that some part of him always would. But that love was wrapped up in heartache and misery and he didn't know if he had the capacity to forgive him for the agony that still lay within his chest. Tristam was a reckless, selfish man who, if he wanted, could reel Bassiri back in and break his heart beyond repair. Which is why he didn't know if he could forgive him. He really didn't know.

Chapter Twenty-Three

YEELA

Errol had slept on the floor. It was strange how quickly Yeela had become used to him sleeping beside her and she'd struggled to fall asleep without his warmth. To her shame, she had almost given in and begged him to join her. But she was a soldier and she didn't need a man in her bed to be able to sleep. Despite trying to convince herself of this, she had still slept badly. Over breakfast she hardly said a word, her brain fogged with sleep and her neck aching from tossing and turning. Her scowl was as deep as Errol's, who clearly hadn't fared much better on the floor.

They walked into the early morning market with Tret describing the history of every building they passed, even if it was only to say, "And that's where your dad pissed against the wall and got chased by the city guard". Everything they passed had some anecdote assigned to it, which was a relief to Yeela as it meant she didn't have to speak herself. She finally began to wake up when the smell of the spice stalls reached her. Baskets of bright, fragranced powders filled the wooden tabletops, along with whole seeds that when crushed between your fingers released their aroma and oils. She popped a cardamom pod at Tret's instruction and rolled the little black seeds between her fingers. The smell was heavenly to her. Seeing her pleasure at the scent, Tret bought some and promised to make her spiced rice that evening. Once Tret had purchased everything he needed from the food market and introduced them to everyone around, gathering gossip to take home, he left to prepare the inn for the day ahead.

Errol led Yeela to a coffee house. They only had teahouses in Maldessa and very few people drank coffee and so she'd never tried it. Inside the small space there were round tables with mosaic patterns on the top. A large silver pot with a long, curved spout was placed on the table in front of them with two small cups. Errol poured her a cup.

Yeela took a sip of the hot, dark liquid. "It's so bitter!"

He smiled, his ears rising in that slightly goofy way that she liked. "You get used to it. Besides, it'll wake us both up." But he pushed some sugar towards her anyway.

She heaped in a teaspoon and tried again. "Oh, that's much better. My father drinks coffee with his friends. He says it reminds him of home. He makes Niseem and me sweet mint tea, though. I think he knows we won't like the bitter taste."

"That's what the sugar is for."

"I think he might be a purist and would want us to drink it without sugar." She took another sip and decided she liked coffee.

"I'll never tell him." He winked at her conspiratorially and Yeela felt strange. It didn't seem right that Errol was being friendly with her.

She cleared her throat. "So, where should we go today?"

"Let's go to the port, hear what's going on around the fish market." Yeela wrinkled her nose; she was tired of the smell of fish markets after having to be on guard at Maldessa's. "But it's the textile market where we'll get the most information." She brightened at that idea. She'd caught a glimpse of it earlier and the colours of fabrics on display had fascinated her. They were far more exciting than her drab brown dress, which was slightly itchy and far too heavy. Not for the first time she missed her black (with red piping, her favourite part) uniform of the Guard, with its fitted jacket, trousers and knee-high boots that she had to keep to a high shine at all times. She enjoyed her nightly ritual of shining her boots; it was how she wound down after a hard day. Her uniform was light, practical — the dress was cumbersome and got caught on everything. She didn't know how the women in Maldessa endured it, although most of them chose to wear less cumbersome clothing, but they'd decided to make Yeela look as traditional as possible to hide the fact her body was muscular, not curvy.

Despite not wanting to go near the fish market, she enjoyed being at the docks. The salty air blowing through her hair reminded her of home and there was something comforting in that. She turned her back to the sea and looked across at the rows of houses and then across to the right, where the land began to rise and she could see the palace. She hoped Ithrael was okay. It was then that she spotted the man watching them. She recognised him; she'd seen him already that day, maybe twice. He was the one she'd sensed following them. She approached Errol and linked her arm in his and told him of what she'd seen. They made their way back towards the city streets and the bustling market. He played the doting husband, holding up fabrics for her, letting her admire the jewellery. She admired a silver bracelet. She didn't wear jewellery as it didn't exactly go with being a soldier, but she liked the delicate chain and the small, bright turquoise stones that were studded along it. She ran her fingers along it and then walked away; she didn't have any need for trinkets. They continued through the market until they reached the food stalls and Errol bought her spiced lamb wrapped in a flat bread. It was delicious. With all the sights, smells and sounds to take in she was beginning to forget why she was there and what her mission was.

They began to make their way further up the market towards the palace. The crowds around one set of stalls were particularly thick and there was a lot of shouting.

"What's going on?"

"Trade auctions." Yeela tried to get closer to see the action and felt herself jostled to the side and then slowly moved further away by the excitable crowd. She turned, trying to spot Errol. He waved to her to signal for her to come to him but she felt a hand on her arm and she knew it was the man who'd been following them.

He yanked her towards him and she was about to fight him off when he whispered to her, "Degat Kureen wishes to see you."

She turned back to where Errol was and mouthed *Kureen* hoping he understood. His expression darkened but he nodded once, telling her to go, get what information she could.

"My husband," she protested to the man, trying to play the dutiful wife.

"We'll bring him along as well." She knew he was lying but the Yeela she was pretending to be was naive and trusting and so she went with him. He led her through the crowds who seemed to part for him. People clearly recognised him, and from their expressions not for any good reason. They finally broke free of the rabble and headed uphill. Yeela hoped he was taking her to the palace but he stopped outside a large house that was a few doors down from the castle gates.

From the outside the house was fairly plain with a beautifully carved wooden door with brass accents. Inside it was something else. Yeela had never seen anything like it. There was an inner courtyard with red pillars topped with white arches, beautifully carved with geometric patterns. In the centre was a pool with a softly bubbling fountain. Chairs were arranged into seating areas and lush plants in pots reached up towards the open sky. It was a haven.

Kureen approached from the other side of the courtyard, wearing loose trousers in a rich blue with a long vest top. He opened his arms out to her. "Yeela, I'm so glad you could come."

She smiled warmly at him, despite them both knowing that her presence was under slight duress. "Degat Kureen, you have a beautiful home. I've never seen anything like it."

She could tell he enjoyed the compliment; he was clearly a man who liked compliments. "I wanted to invite you and your husband to stay with me, as my guests."

She looked behind her at the door. "Where is Errol?" she said, acting perplexed even though she knew he wouldn't be coming.

"He must have been detained — there are so many sights to see and *experience* in the city." Yeela looked forlorn. "Don't be sad. I have just the thing to cheer you up."

A serving woman appeared and led Yeela up some stairs and into a bedroom. There was no glass in the large arches in front of her, and she stepped through the sheer white curtains dancing in the gentle breeze and looked down into the courtyard. The room, she realised, was designed to remain cool by blocking out the sun and keeping the air moving. There were two small windows on the opposite wall with intricate geometric latticework on the shutters. The bed was large with a deep-red blanket and matching cushions. She'd never been in a bedroom like it. In the royal guard she had shared a dormitory with other soldiers when she was training and was now in a two-bed bunk room down at the docks. She had an urge to lie on the bed and roll around but the maid was watching.

The maid stepped in front of her and opened a wooden cupboard and brought out a dress in deep red with gold embroidery all over it. It had a deep V-neck and the waist had a band around it. The sleeves were long and the skirt fluted out slightly. She rubbed the material between her thumb and forefinger; it was light, not heavy and scratchy like the dress she was wearing. However, she didn't want to appear too eager. The maid beckoned for her to follow and led her into a bathing room. Yeela's eyes widened. It was fit for her Queen.

She didn't object to the implication she needed to bathe; she'd always wanted to be able to wash in this way instead of with a pitcher of cold water or in the horrible public baths where you left feeling a little grimier from the knowledge that so many other people were sharing the water with you. She was grateful the serving woman left her to it, because despite being comfortable being nude in front of others (she'd had to get used to it quickly during training) she didn't want the woman to notice her muscle tone. She was proud of her body — she'd worked hard to be strong — but it wasn't what was expected of a trader's wife.

The dress was a lot more comfortable than the one she'd had on before, but she was uncomfortable with the cleavage she was showing. She'd never actually worn anything low cut. She tried tucking her breasts away but they kept popping back out. She tried lifting the dress up but it slid back down. She searched around for her old, uncomfortable, heavy dress but it had clearly been taken away by the maid. She was trapped with her breasts exposed. She hid her face in her hands. It was a nightmare but she had to continue to play the part. She had to find out everything she could. She took a deep breath for courage and made her way down to the courtyard.

Kureen was sitting inhaling fragrant smoke from a bubbling water pipe that he held in his hand. She'd never seen anything so strange.

"What is that?" she asked.

He looked up and the smile that spread across his face said that he enjoyed the new view. She held herself still, not allowing herself to flinch from his lascivious gaze.

"It's a hya pipe." He motioned for her to sit opposite him on the wooden-framed sofa, so she did and he handed her the pipe. It was wooden, ornately carved with a glass bulb near the far end. She placed the mouthpiece between her lips and sucked in and instantly started coughing.

Kureen bellowed with laughter. "Suck on it slowly, like a small sip of wine." He got up and sat next to her, taking the pipe from her hands, his eyes locked on hers. He took a slow, even drag and then passed it back. She did the same and found the sensation almost pleasant. The water vapour rolled into her mouth and down her throat and had a fresh flavour to it. It made her feel slightly light-headed and oddly calm.

"What is it?"

"It's a plant called karool."

"I've never heard of it."

"It isn't grown in Maldessa, the soil is too rich. The karool plant likes our dry sandy soil." He took another drag from the pipe and slowly blew out a puff of smoke. "It takes strength to thrive in this land of ours."

He passed the pipe back to her and she took it, nervous that the effects were going to diminish her ability to do her job. She sucked in some of the vapour and didn't inhale it down, slowly breathing it out. She didn't feel the effects as much that way, which was good.

Kureen gave her a slow smile as she sank into the cushions slightly. "My body feels very relaxed."

He placed a hand on her knee. "I'm glad because there's something I want to ask you."

"Mmmm?"

"It was a strange coincidence that a beautiful Maldessan woman happened to join our party when we had precious cargo."

He moved his hand up her knee and to her thigh. Yeela froze. In all her training, she'd never prepared for this. She felt uncomfortable but she didn't want to tell him to stop in case she made him angry, in case he realised she wasn't who she said she was.

"I don't know what you're talking about. What cargo?" she asked, feigning confusion.

He reached forward, turning her face towards him. "They wanted to kill you on the road but I thought I could find use for you in my household."

He went to kiss her but she turned her face away. "Degat Kureen, I'm married and I really don't know what you're talking about." She stood up. "I should go, get back to Errol."

"That might be difficult, seeing as he's been arrested."

"Arrested?" Her heart pounded wildly. "Whatever for?"

"For spying, of course."

"Spying? Degat Kureen, why would my husband spy? He's a trader."

Kureen clapped slowly. "A wonderful performance, my dear."

"Are you trying to say my husband is a Maldessan spy? He's Hyrathean!" She shook her head and then winced, feigning that the movement made her feel woozy. Kureen stood and helped her back to the sofa. "I don't understand. He can't be. It doesn't make sense."

"Look at me," Kureen said gently. She looked into his eyes. "Tell me the truth."

"The truth? That I'm the wife of a trader. That's the truth."

He examined her face, his expression serious. He brushed his fingers under his chin. "I believe you. But I'm afraid you are mistaken about your husband."

"He can't be ... he just can't." She made sure she sounded confused and distraught.

"Stay here, with me. We'll get to the bottom of this." She looked him in the eyes and allowed her true fear to rise. She felt her eyes water with the surge of emotion. He brushed them away with his thumb and leaned towards her, again trying to kiss her.

She laid her hand gently on his chest. "Degat, he's still my husband."

He placed the kiss on her cheek instead. "Together, we will discover the truth and I promise — I will protect you."

She couldn't hold in her shiver when she saw the possessiveness in his eyes. She felt afraid and she wasn't ashamed by the feeling. It was a warning. She needed to be careful around this man.

Chapter Twenty-Four

AMAREA

Throughout her life Amarea had been subjected to many assassination attempts, and so when she awoke with a knife at her throat, she didn't freeze in fear. Instead, she wrapped her hand around the wrist that held the knife and snapped it. She leapt out of bed as quick and agile as a snow lion. She slammed the assailant against the wall and pulled their face covering away.

It was one of the men from The Fold, his pupils dilated as he beheld her face in the moonlight. Her body was against his whilst she held him and she felt his arousal. She moved back, disgusted.

"Who sent you?"

"My love," he whimpered, trying desperately to touch her.

"Tell me who sent you," she ordered.

"The Vulma Supreme Leader," he replied in desperation to please her. It was what they called the ruler of Vulma — he wasn't a king but a leader who had killed those in his way to gain his power. She used to respect that about him. Used to.

"Why?"

"To give you a message."

She loosened her grip on his windpipe. "Speak."

"Abdicate to him and he will stop poisoning the land, he'll release your lover." Amarea hissed in his face. He began panting with desire for her, trying to touch himself, her. She was repulsed and dragged him to her balcony.

"You're pathetic," she said, and then threw him over the side. She walked back into her room whilst he screamed. She heard the *thunk* of his body as it hit the stone paving three floors below.

Gallia burst into the room.

"What happened?" Amarea turned before Gallia could see her face and pulled on a veil.

"A message from the Vulma Supreme Leader. It's okay, I handled it." Gallia went to the balcony and looked over.

"I don't know why you even have guards," she said as she stepped back into the room.

"I don't either." But her voice wasn't accusatory. "Because I can't always protect myself. You are valuable to me, Gallia."

"Yes, my Queen," Gallia muttered, looking displeased.

"I have a feeling things are about to get worse for my people, and maybe for us."

"I get that sense as well."

Gallia was still in her nightwear having come directly from her room opposite. The duty guard was standing in the doorway looking guilty, and Niseem now appeared with a robe on.

Amarea went to her guard. "Don't worry, Hector, it's not your fault. It happens all the time."

"Honestly, we need to reassess the way you're guarded. No one should be able to get through." Gallia was clearly upset by her own failings as captain.

"I'm not having someone guarding me on my balcony, too." She turned to her guard. "Can you find out if Tristam and Bassiri have returned?"

The guard left quickly, obviously wanting to avoid Gallia's wrathful glare.

"We need to tighten security. If only those soldiers would arrive." Gallia began to pace the room, checking every shadow as though something might jump out.

"They'll be here soon. I doubt we'll have any assassination attempts after that." Amarea rolled her neck. "I'm concerned they're going to target our food stores.

"I'll have the guards doubled." Niseem left to pass the message on.

"Go back to bed, Gallia, there's nothing else you can do tonight."

"I'm not leaving your side." Gallia crossed her arms.

"Gallia, if you don't leave I will make you leave." It was impossible to have a staring contest whilst wearing a veil but Amarea hoped that Gallia felt her gaze. She was sure it was, as her guard stared right back. "Please, I need to think. I need to try and work out what he plans for us, for me."

"Okay, but if you need anything, just scream."

Amarea huffed a laugh. "I will."

THE DARK QUEEN

Amarea stood on her balcony and watched as the guard took away the body of the intruder. It had been a suicide mission; the Vulma Supreme Leader would have known that. He'd already poisoned her land but he wasn't prepared to sit and wait for the effects to cripple her. Why? What was the urgency? He was desperate for something. But what?

She thought about all she knew of Vulma. They imported most of their food as their climate was too cold for crops to grow well. As far as she knew, trade was good; they were known for keeping trade going by their aggressive negotiating tactics — not afraid to blackmail and beat a signature out of merchants and traders. She needed the twins back; they would have answers. She just hoped they were okay.

She stepped back into her room, the cool breeze sending a shiver through her. She suddenly doubled over in pain as though someone had punched her.

"What the—" She felt a stab at her side and the twisting of a knife inside the wound. She looked down but there was no blood. She staggered to her bed. What was happening? Blow after blow came from the invisible force and she felt something inside her tighten. Something was pulling at her, calling her. *Ithrael?* As if in answer, the force tugged harder. "Ithrael," she sobbed. Something was wrong, very wrong.

Gallia burst back into the room.

"What is it?" She knelt down next to her.

"Something's wrong with Ithrael. I can feel it." She put her hand over her heart to where she felt as though the thread that bound them was a physical connection and felt a blow land across her jaw. Her head snapped to the side with the force of it, and the link between her and Ithrael collapsed. She placed her hands on the bed.

"I have to go to him. They're torturing him. Beating him." Her voice shook with rage and worry.

Gallia did something she'd never done before; she hugged Amarea and held her. "You can't go." There was sorrow in her voice.

"I can't leave him."

"You can't go. You know you can't. Your duty is to remain here."

A sob broke from Amarea's lips and then another. Soon she was crying in deep, raking gasps. Gallia held her tightly, not letting go until Amarea's body no longer shook with the agony of having to stay in Maldessa instead of going to save the man she loved.

Chapter Twenty-Five

BASSIRI

They broke through the trees to the site of the old abbey Amarea had burned down as a child. It was true; the earth still looked scorched, as if the fire had only been a few days and not seven years ago. Bassiri and Tristam had hardly spoken for the rest of the ride, and Bassiri noticed Tristam's puzzled expression as he slid down from his horse and walked over the blackened earth.

"How do you feel?" he asked Bassiri.

"As I have done since we rode under the smoke cloud."

Bassiri stepped onto the dead earth and he felt it then, a hollowness in the air, an absence of life altogether. Even though he believed the priests deserved to be punished, what Amarea had done was terrible and her methods were darker than he was prepared to accept. He'd reasoned she'd been young and desperate ... until she had done the same thing again as recompense for the Church killing an entire town in her name. He'd told her he understood her wish for revenge, just not her methods. He always told her when she'd gone too far. Looking around now, at the darkness she'd created, it was no wonder they called her the Dark Queen. This was an unsettled place.

Tristam pulled on his gloves and bent down. "Look at this." Bassiri crouched down next to him and watched as Tristam picked up a piece of the blackened earth. It was solid, almost shiny.

"Resin."

"She was right." Tristam put it into the satchel they'd brought. "And look there."

He pointed to where the abbey had been. The burnt-out husk was mostly collapsed although a few pieces of wall remained standing, but between them were beams of blacked wood. "The same as they used in the tower?" Bassiri asked Tristam as they approached the structure.

"It looks like it." He rapped on it with a knuckle. "Solid, as the wood there."

Bassiri loosed a breath. "So this is how they created the towers and smoke. Mass execution."

"But the sheer amount of resin ..." Bassiri thought he saw Tristam shudder.

Bassiri realised why. "They must have murdered thousands." Tristam had turned grey. "Let's gather what we can and get out of here." Bassiri squeezed Tristam's shoulder on instinct, wanting to offer him comfort. They began searching for small pieces of wood they could take back to the palace.

When they were far enough away from the site of the abbey and near the edge of the smoke, they stopped. Tristam dismounted and tethered his horse.

"How do we tell her that what she did created such a poison?" Tristam asked, hands on his head, his breathing heavy.

Bassiri joined him. "Tris, I think she knows."

Tristam shook his head, tears in his eyes. "If I'd known what they'd been doing to her back then, I would have taken her away. We just left her there. Me, her last remaining family."

"Well, technically she has Aiden."

Tristam let out a surprised laugh. "A useless cousin, an aunt and uncle who abandoned us both, and a feckless half-brother. No wonder she likes to burn things down."

"I worry about her choices."

"So do I, but what do you expect when she was raised by perverse priests and kept in a gilded cage by the Church? She knows only to react with the full force of her wrath." Bassiri understood that, but she had to start being smarter. "It's why she has us, has her council. To keep her in check. She knows that there's a darkness inside her, that it rules her emotions. She's trying."

"I know, but this current threat, it worries me. Especially with Ithrael being gone. He may not reign in her darkest desires but she is calmer, more stable with him around." Tristam stepped towards Bassiri as Bassiri spoke and placed his hand over his heart. Bassiri's pulse quickened. "Tristam..."

"I know. What I did, leaving like that ... I was young. I was scared by what I felt."

"It doesn't change anything." Bassiri's voice was low and rough with emotion.

"Bass, I'm only myself when I'm with you. I left a part of me behind and I know I should have asked you to come with me. I know Amarea would have agreed. I was selfish and stupid. Can you forgive me?"

Could he? He looked into Tristam's dark eyes, the sly slash of his mouth. For all his bravado he was now vulnerable before him. His expression was open. For once, there was no courtly mask of emotion hiding his true feelings.

Bassiri tipped his head forward until their foreheads touched. "I want to be able to, but …"

Tristam tilted his head upwards until their lips were near touching and whispered, "Let me show you every day from now until our last breaths how sorry I am." His breath hitched. "I love you, Bass. I always have."

Their lips touched and Bassiri thought his heart was breaking all over again. He had wanted this for so long, the touch of his love, the taste of an apology on his mouth. He felt like a fool for falling deeper into the kiss. Tristam's kisses were gentle, apologetic at first, and then he slid his mischievous tongue into Bassiri's mouth and he was lost in his lust.

They made love at the edge of the forest with the stars of the night sky blotted out by the poisonous smoke of their enemy, their bodies naked and consumed by their pleasure, lost in one another as their doom hung overhead.

Chapter Twenty-Six

ITHRAEL

Ithrael awoke to find himself back in his cell. There was a metallic taste in his mouth and so he spat out the blood that was coating it. His body hurt, not from the smoke that emanated from the lamp just outside his door but from the beating he'd received from the guards. He touched his jaw tentatively and could feel the swelling from the blow that had knocked him out. He groaned as he sat upright; they'd definitely broken some of his ribs.

He had to admit he wasn't particularly pleased he'd put himself in this situation. He'd been clear and free, but his duty to his Queen and country always came first. He took his time standing and made his way to the bars of his cell. Yuto was leaning against his own cage, whistling to himself. When he spotted Ithrael, he gave him a half smile.

"Welcome back. We have a new guest." He tilted his head towards the cell next to his own.

Ithrael bent forward to get a better look. A forlorn-looking Errol was sitting with his knees hugged to his chest. Ithrael rested his head against the cold iron and closed his eyes. This wasn't good. There was a different guard on duty who was awake and seemed more alert than the other one. Ithrael didn't want to risk speaking to Errol and all he'd got from the other man was a sad shake of the head. Ithrael took it to mean he didn't know whether Yeela was okay and that he was pretty pissed off to be in prison. But he didn't seem panicked; if Yeela was in danger, he was sure he'd be acting differently. He had to assume she was relatively safe somewhere.

He was too weak and sore to attempt a breakout right then and there. Even though he hadn't yet achieved his goal, he was concerned events had taken a turn and they were going to go downhill rapidly. One of the things he taught recruits was once things began to unravel it was time to get out, regroup and try a different tactic. Unfortunately, right then, he wasn't going anywhere. He sat back down carefully and looked up at the lamp.

At least he'd gained one thing from his beating. He pulled out from his sleeve the useless guard's key. He'd been in the room to witness his beating; he'd requested to be there, promising to learn from them how prisoners were supposed to be treated. And then, before the final blow that knocked Ithrael unconscious, he'd moved in to taunt him and Ithrael had taken the opportunity to swipe his key. He just needed to keep it well hidden. The walls to his cell were smooth but in one corner some of the stonework had crumbled away. Whilst the guard was at the other end of the room, Ithrael managed to wedge the key into the loose mortar and cover it with enough dust that anyone entering the cell wouldn't notice it there.

Ithrael stayed awake. Without a window he had no concept of what hour of the day it was. Because of this, he didn't let himself sleep and instead waited. Eventually the guard nodded off in his chair. He removed the key and unlocked his door. Both Errol and Yuto stood and watched with wide eyes as Ithrael reached for the lamp and removed the resin from inside. He returned to his cell and locked the door and dropped the foul-smelling poison down the hole for waste. Both Errol and Yuto were gesticulating wildly at him but he ignored them both and waited. His body needed to heal, his strength needed to return. Only then would he move.

Chapter Twenty-Seven

YEELA

Yeela barely slept despite her luxurious bed. She hated to imagine what they might have done to Errol. She dressed in a deep-purple dress in the same style as her one from the day before but the embroidery was in a black thread. She preferred this one.

Downstairs a servant led her to an elegant study where Degat Kureen was already starting on his day's work. The sun was barely up; he clearly took his position seriously.

"I want to see my husband." She allowed herself to appear as though she had been gathering all her courage for the demand.

He put his pen down. "I'll take you to him, but first, we eat."

The food was plentiful and Yeela ate her fill, not knowing when or where her next meal would come from. She needed to ensure she had enough energy for whatever happened next, and she sensed that it wouldn't be good.

Degat Kureen led her to the palace, two guards at their backs. They were allowed in as soon as the degat was recognised. Inside the ornate, sizeable front doors of the palace was a large white courtyard with more intricately carved columns and arches and a bubbling fountain with water that ran in gullies going north, south, east and west. There were no chairs in the courtyard as there were in Kureen's; this was more for show. Kureen led her to the right and up a set of stairs, down a corridor and knocked on a door. Degat Soligan opened it: the room must be his office.

"Ah, you brought the girl. Good. Let's get started." He closed and locked the door behind him, slipping the key into the right-hand pocket of his loose trousers. It wasn't long before Yeela found herself in the belly of the castle and heading towards what could only be the prison. The smell of the poisonous smoke still hung in the air but it didn't make her feel too unwell, which was a good sign.

Ithrael watched her as she entered with the degats and the two guards. She merely glanced at him, not wanting to give away that she recognised him. He looked like shit. He'd been beaten badly. On her left was a scruffy man who glared at them all with unveiled hatred, and in the next cell Errol stood, his expression defiant.

"Yeela!" He reached out and their fingers brushed, pain and yearning in his voice. Yeela wasn't sure why but she wanted to believe it was real and not put on for show. He looked at the degats. "Why have I been put in here? And what are you doing to my wife?" His voice was low, menacing. It sent a thrill through Yeela; she'd never felt defended before. There was something nice about it, even though it wasn't necessary. She could take care of herself.

"Your wife is in good hands," Kureen said, with his true meaning making Errol grip the bars with such force his knuckles turned white. His eyes were locked with Kureen's.

"Gentlemen," Yeela said, trying to break the tension. "I thought we were here to establish that my husband is not a spy, not to taunt him." She raised an eyebrow at Kureen. Kureen signalled for the prison guard to open the cell. He unlocked the door and dragged Errol out by the iron cuffs on his wrists, then Degat Soligan pulled him to Ithrael's cell.

"Do you recognise this man?" the older degat demanded.

"Of course I do. It's the Captain of the Palace Guard. Or was." Errol sounded exasperated.

"Did you not use your journey to our country to insinuate yourself into our party?" Yeela was impressed — Errol didn't give away a flicker of anything.

"Insinuate myself into your party? What? Why? Our cart got buggered by a rock." He was looking perfectly confused. Yeela could have kissed him but she decided not to think about that considering the precariousness of their situation. Yeela looked over at Ithrael who was acting as though he was struggling to stay conscious, but she had already noticed there was no smoke coming from the lantern. She just hoped the others were too distracted to realise it for themselves.

"And what of your wife? A Maldessan. Pretty convenient, don't you think?" Degat Soligan said to Errol, his fury getting the better of him.

"Kureen, what is this all about? Why is the Captain of the Palace Guard even here? Did he do something wrong? Something treasonous?" She wasn't sure if she'd overdone the helpless tone but seeing Degat Kureen's expression soften towards her confirmed she had played it just right.

"My dear, I'm afraid that your husband isn't the trader you think he is. You see, he's a palace guard. Degat Soligan spent a good few days trying to remember where he'd seen him before. Then it struck him. The last time he was in Maldessa he'd been surprised to see that one of the guards was a Hyrathean, the same Hyrathean you see before him."

"But I know he's been a guard," Yeela said, thinking quickly. She furrowed her brow. "What does that have to do with anything? He stopped working for the Queen after the Blood Moon." She looked at Errol. "I know you don't like to talk of it, my love, but let me … let me explain …" She turned to Kureen. "You see, he's ashamed of turning his back on his duty but what she did that night, the Queen, it sickened him." She looked down at her feet. "It sickened me, too."

There was a low growl of disapproval from Ithrael's cell. "Traitors."

"That's why he went into trade, and why we came here. He wanted to see if his father or uncle could use him for work. We aren't just visiting, we're moving." Yeela looked at Errol, her expression apologetic for supposedly confessing their secret.

"It's okay, my love. It's okay," he said, his expression soft. She couldn't help but feel the way he looked at her to be genuine appreciation for how she was handling the situation. It made her feel proud.

"Really?" Soligan said, a sneer on his face.

"Then it's funny how you were seen with the Captain of the Palace Guard on the night of his capture." Yeela's breath caught; she wasn't sure how she could get out of that one.

"Excuse me?" she asked in a small voice.

"Terron here ..." A third guard stepped out of the shadows and she recognised him instantly. She had been so distracted by everything she hadn't noticed him enter. "... recognised you when you arrived in the city. He's been following you ever since." So that had been her bad feeling: one of the men from the night of Ithrael's kidnapping had spotted her. Well, this made things more difficult.

"What are you saying, Soligan?" Kureen protested.

"That the woman you are so taken with is a soldier."

Kureen looked completely taken aback; he couldn't seem to fathom that a woman could be such a thing. "A soldier?"

"Just look at her. She's not afraid — her stance and physique are all wrong. All this time we had two spies in our camp." Soligan sounded irritated with Kureen.

Kureen looked at Yeela, hurt on his face. "But you ..." He shook his head and then his expression hardened.

"Have her locked up as well. I want you to get to the bottom of this by first light," he ordered Terron.

Yeela was cuffed whilst Errol was returned to his cell.

"Do whatever needs to be done to break her, or him," Kureen ordered as he turned to leave. The duty guard went with them as the cruel-faced Terron turned to her and dragged her to the centre of the room. She knew why.

She screamed for Kureen, begging him to reconsider, to realise what he was doing. He turned back once, pain on his face, but he didn't order Terron to stop as he pulled her dress down over her shoulders, exposing her breasts and holding her arms down. The heavy door at the top of the stairs was shut behind the two lords and the guard. Terron's expression was hungry.

"If you lay a single finger on her, I will gut you," Errol snarled. His face, thankfully, was on the guard, not her breasts. She looked into the other cell where the prisoner was also looking angrily at the guard. She didn't have a chance to see what Ithrael was doing because Terron grabbed the skirt of her dress and began to lift it.

"Don't you fucking dare," she said. She lifted her cuffed hands over Terron's head and moved, lithe and quick, until she was behind him, and with impressive force she snapped his neck. She whipped her hands back over his head and held her arms over her exposed breasts.

"I was coming to save you," Ithrael said from behind. He gently lifted her dress over her shoulders, then helped her out of her cuffs.

"Well, that was definitely why I had a bad feeling. I do not like having my bare skin exposed against my wishes," she said as they freed Errol, along with the shaggy-haired prisoner.

"Are you okay?" Errol asked, genuinely concerned. It was the first time he'd treated her as a woman, not a soldier. Somehow she didn't mind just then. Usually it would infuriate her, but right then, she felt vulnerable and she needed to be seen for what she was, not who she made herself to be.

"I'll get over it," she said, giving him a grateful elbow. He didn't look relieved by her words but he nodded. They had an escape to carry out and now wasn't the time for sentimentality.

"Yuto, fancy showing us to that study?" Ithrael asked.

"It would be my pleasure," the Jair said with a surprisingly white-toothed smile.

Chapter Twenty-Eight

AMAREA

Amarea stared down at the items before her on the table. She felt sick, not from the dark magic that was locked within the blackened remains of the abbey, but for the first time she was truly disturbed by her own actions. She had done this, created this evil within her own lands. She'd never once felt remorse for the deaths of those men, but now ... now it was different.

"Do you think they discovered this magic here? In Maldessa? From this?" she asked Tristam and Bassiri.

"It's hard to say. There was no sign that a large amount had been removed, but a small amount could have been enough for them to uncover what had been created." Tristam had never been one to protect her feelings but he didn't confirm her fear, even though she knew he was thinking the same thing. Her actions had inspired the creation of the dark towers. Inadvertently she had brought about the evil in her lands. For the first time she loathed being known as the Dark Queen. It sickened her. She'd been proud they saw her that way, knowing that she was doing whatever was necessary to ensure the safety and survival of her people. But now she understood. She was the Dark Queen, the cursed Queen. She had brought upon them a darkness greater than any they'd ever known under the Daylarian Church.

Her nails dug deep into the wood of the table and she closed her eyes, leashing her rage. "How many did they slaughter to build their towers?"

"It must have been thousands," Tristam said, pain in his voice. She could tell he knew that she was struggling, that the realisation was too much for her to bear. But bear it she would. She was still Queen. She had a duty, always a duty, and it would always come first.

"When will the army be here?"

"High General Ethea said they'd be here late morning." The sun hadn't even begun to rise yet; it was too far away.

"I won't wait any more. I ride to Vula, with those men."

Bassiri and Tristam shared a look. There was a change between them; she could feel it. "Majesty, I would advise against it," Bassiri said carefully.

"I know you would, but what are we to do? Sit here and wait for the Vulch to slowly tear this country apart with an invisible hand? Enough is enough. If they want to attack us, they do it out in the open instead of hiding away like cowards." Hatred lashed in her voice. She needed to avenge her land, her people. She needed to right the wrongs she had done.

"We don't know the size of their army. No one has ever been able to establish its full extent. What if it's triple the size of ours? They will slaughter our men. And if they use smoke on the battlefield, what then? Are we to lose our Queen?" Tristam's voice was gentle, almost pleading.

"I have to do something!" she screamed as she flung a chair against the wall where upon impact it exploded into splinters.

Bassiri approached her carefully as though she were some wild, untamed beast. "Amarea ..." He hadn't used her name since she'd been crowned, and the sound of it on his tongue, so deep and soft, focused her. "If you act rashly you could doom us all. You chose your council well. Let us help you plan how to deal with this threat. Using our army may be the answer but we must come to the decision together." Tristam stood next to Bassiri, worry in his eyes.

Amarea bowed her head, ashamed of her outburst. "Any word from the House?"

"None." Gallia stepped forward. "But a messenger came. Saia's device is ready."

Chapter Twent-Nine

SAIA

Saia's eyes stung from tiredness and she was barely able to keep them in focus. She had told Gallia the machines were ready, and they were, but she wanted to run one last test, just to be sure.

"They work perfectly," Dideum tried to reassure her. She'd enjoyed working with him; she hadn't realised how lonely it was working by herself. She'd just thought that that's the way it was supposed to be. But having someone with her had been a comfort, especially when the stakes were so high. She enjoyed being able to discuss her ideas and have someone to not only understand them but also to improve upon them. Maybe her mother had been right: she should spend more time with other people.

"Just one more check before you take it to the House." She placed one of the devices at the furthest point in the room to the other. They were a little crude but time hadn't allowed her to create elegant keys and beautifully carved bodywork. They were simple wooden boxes with flat-headed letter keys that were balanced like the keys of a piano. Beneath each letter was a sharp point that when pressed hit one of the blue orob stones fixed beneath the needle. The orob stones had been mined from the Maldessan Mountains and were now an even more precious resource since the outlaws moved into The Fold. They were the same stones Saia remembered seeing in the diagram from a previous design. The impact on the stone activated the dormant magic inside it and sent a signal to its counterpart on the other machine.

That had been the vital element, to make sure the corresponding stone was split from the same piece. The machines had been expensive to make. It was fortunate she was working on behalf of the Queen who appeared to have access to a large amount of orob stones.

Dideum typed out a message and the keys in front of Saia clacked out the words, *"y o u n e e d t o s l e e p"*.

She smiled and replied, *"s o d o y o u"*.

"Can we show her now?" he asked eagerly.

"Yes, we can show her now."

The Queen was talking with Tristam and Bassiri. Saia's heart pounded at the sight of Bassiri. She was so tired and knew she looked a complete disaster and hoped he didn't notice. And then she saw the way Bassiri and Tristam were with each other, always close, always sharing secret looks, as though they were in each other's orbit. She'd dared to hope when Tristam had left and broken Bassiri's heart that one day he'd finally see her, but she knew now her hope was wasted. She felt her throat tighten. Dideum was right — she needed to sleep more; it was playing havoc with her emotions.

She felt a gentle hand on her back and Dideum was there, seeing it all on her face. No one in the room had noticed them enter the large room. She smiled at his gentle kindness. She took a breath and stepped forward, towards her Queen. Two guards followed her, each carrying a heavy machine.

"My Queen, if you have a moment we'd like to demonstrate the communication machines." Saia was pleased her voice didn't quaver when her eyes met Bassiri's.

Amarea's head rose, her posture telling Saia that the Queen was troubled. Her shoulders were rounded, her hands in the shape of claws. "Show me what you have, Saia." Her voice was hollow. Saia was concerned but nonetheless she had the guards set the machines at opposite ends of the table. Dideum stood at the other end of the room and Amarea tilted her head to watch as the message was written. *"i a m r e a d y t o g o t o c a l m a y a".*

"Remarkable," Amarea said. "Saia ... I don't even know where to begin. It's truly wondrous." Amarea placed her hands either side of Saia's face. "But if you're to continue to help me, you must *sleep.*"

Saia laughed softly. "Yes, my Queen."

"Finally, some good news." Amarea stroked her hand over the keys. Saia watched her. She used to find it strange talking to someone whose face you couldn't see, but over the years, she'd got used to the smallest gestures and postures to signal what the Queen was feeling. She watched her reverently stroke the keys and Saia felt proud of her work. She felt proud that this wonderful, powerful woman always believed in her and trusted her to go ahead with her ideas.

Her attention caught on the black stones on the table. "What are those?"

She realised it was the wrong thing to say when Amarea's body tensed once again. "Resin from the fire at the abbey."

Saia frowned. "Resin? But resin is formed from plant secretions." She picked up a piece and everyone sucked in a breath but she barely registered their reaction. She turned it over in her hand. "This is something different."

She felt Dideum come and stand behind her and peer over her shoulder as she frowned at the shiny black substance. She took from her pocket her special glass that enhanced the size of whatever she was looking at. Amarea had had it rimmed in gold and attached to a chain that hung from Saia's belt because she kept losing it.

She examined its black form through the glass. "It's as though it's solidified smoke. It certainly feels and looks like a resin but it's not a natural formation. This is the creation of something else entirely."

She looked up to see Amarea watching her. "A dark act. The murder of hundreds in a fire created this." Saia understood Amarea's mood; she'd created this through her violent actions. But Saia had never questioned or judged her Queen. She believed in her enough to make her own mistakes, forge her own path.

"So they created more through the same methods ..."

"What ... what is it?" Amarea's voice had a slight tremble in it.

"I'm not entirely sure but it makes me wonder ... If a slaughter of fire creates this substance, then what would other slaughters create?" She saw the Queen flinch when she said "slaughter" but didn't hesitate to tell her what she suspected. It would do them no good to hide from ugly truths at such a time.

Amarea sat down in a chair. "What could they be creating?" Her voice was thin, scared. It chilled Saia. She believed her Queen to be afraid of nothing, to be able to fight any enemy.

"I'll figure it out so that you know what you might face."

Amarea nodded absently. "Dideum, I'll need you to speak to the High Mage, tell him we need something to counter the effects of this kind of magic. Anything to give us a fighting chance."

Dideum bowed low, a strange expression on his face. "We will do our utmost, your Majesty."

"Saia, I want you to sleep before you tackle this new problem. I can't have you burnt out and unable to work," Amarea said, her voice firm once again.

"Yes, my Queen." She wasn't sure she could come up with anything in her current state anyway. She felt dizzy from lack of sleep.

Saia watched as Dideum rode away with six guards to protect him and the device. She'd miss his company. Saia sighed and made her way through the marble halls to her room. She'd barely spent any time in there; instead she'd been sleeping on a small cot in the room that had been set up as her workshop. Her room was larger than she'd realised: a room for a high-powered guest. The realisation made her smile. It was Amarea's way of showing she valued her.

The bathing pool in the adjoining room was already full and scented. It was nice to be taken care of. She managed not to fall asleep in the warm water and as soon as she was in her nightwear and in bed, she fell into a deep slumber.

Gruesome deaths troubled her dreams. Thousands corralled together into fire pits. Even children. A lake where thousands more were drowned and the water turned black. A field where others were buried alive and the soil turned black.

She awoke, sweating. She knew how they'd be attacked. She got up and ran from her room to find her Queen. She had to warn her.

Chapter Thirty

ITHRAEL

Ithrael would have preferred more time to regain his strength but he wasn't going to let any harm come to Yeela. He gritted his teeth every time he thought of the way Terron had exposed her and tried to rape her in front of them. The Hyratheans were pigs. He wished he could kill that scum again.

He leashed his anger and opened the door that led up towards the main palace. Yeela had told him it was still morning, but they couldn't risk staying down in the prison and waiting for a new guard or more soldiers to be brought in for his next beating. Yuto led the way, having already scoped out the palace for when he'd come to thieve.

There was a guard standing behind the door, and Ithrael snapped his neck, killing him instantly. His limp body slid to the floor and Ithrael relieved him of his two daggers and sword. He handed the sword to Errol and a dagger each to Yuto and Yeela.

Yeela raised an eyebrow at him.

"You know that you're better with a knife and he's better with a sword," Ithrael whispered to her, irritated. He had trained them, after all. It had taken him a while to remember the days when he'd trained cadets, but seeing how they both moved had brought it back to him.

"I know, just making sure you did, too," she said.

He stalked forward. *Maldessan women were impossible*, he thought affectionately, with a smile.

They made it up another level to another door. Errol helped him dispatch the two armed guards — Yeela helped herself to another dagger and didn't grumble when Ithrael took one sword and Yuto the other. Instead, she slipped a third dagger into the sash she had tied around the waist of her dress. Errol and Yuto changed into the guards' uniforms. The next staircase curved around to a final door, one that led out into the courtyard of the palace.

"No one is going to believe Yuto is a guard — he's too unkempt," Yeela whispered.

The other two scrutinised Yuto. "You're right," Ithrael said and held up a dagger to Yuto. "I'm going to have to tidy you up."

"Fine by me. Sorry about the stench in advance. They didn't let me bathe." Ithrael didn't think he seemed that sorry.

Ithrael made quick work of Yuto's hair and beard, cutting out the most snarled and tangled parts. It wasn't perfect but he looked almost presentable.

"Here." Yeela held up a bucket of water that had a cup in it for the guards. Yuto washed his face as best he could. "Not bad," Yeela said with a smile and Ithrael noticed Errol's expression darken ever so slightly.

"Ready?" Ithrael whispered. He received confident nods in return. Errol chained Ithrael and Yeela's hands behind their backs with manacles taken from the prison. He didn't comment when Errol chose Yeela to be his prisoner; the man's hackles had clearly been raised when the guard had touched her. It was prideful but Ithrael understood it; he would have been the same with Amarea.

The door opened wide to an early afternoon sun. As Ithrael squinted against the light he could make out a guard on either side of the door that Yuto had said led to a forecourt. Yuto shoved him in the back and he stumbled forward.

They didn't say a word as he led them further around the back and in through the tradesman entrance.

"What you doing bringing them lot through here?" a woman yelled. Her clothes were covered in grease and food stains; it was easy to guess she was a cook.

"Degats told us not to bring the prisoners through the front to them," Errol said.

She harrumphed at them, and they continued through the back corridor and up a staircase. The door opened onto a far more opulent corridor than the ones they'd seen so far.

"Straight to Soligan first," Ithrael ordered, and Yuto continued on his march. None of the guards so much as flinched as they made their way up to the rooms the degats held in the palace, until they reached the degat's door.

"What you doing bringing the prisoners out?" one of the guards asked, his voice deep and commanding.

"Degat Soligan told us to bring them up once Terron was done with this one." Errol indicated a shaking Yeela who had tears running down her cheeks. Her entire posture gave off the air of a woman terrified and miserable. Amarea couldn't have sent anyone better to come and rescue him. Yeela had already proven herself to be one of the best soldiers he'd ever had the privilege to work with.

The guard didn't budge. Errol gave off the air of a guard who just wanted to go home. "Go ask him yourself. He won't want to be kept waiting."

The Hyrathean guard turned and opened the door. Soligan was talking to another man when they entered behind the guard, and before anyone in the room could react, Yeela had her manacles around the guard's throat, cutting off his windpipe. Ithrael did the same to Soligan, and Errol had the third Hyrathean by the throat up against a wall. Yuto then went around and gagged each of them. They dragged their prisoners into the adjoining meeting chamber and used the manacles they'd kept from their own captivity and a couple of curtain cords to tie them up. They made quick work of it and then locked the door behind them.

Ithrael and Errol began riffling through the degat's papers to see what they could find. Anything that looked interesting Errol handed to Ithrael who did a quick inspection, and if he thought it was of use he put it aside.

"We need to get to the Dolsan's office — there's not enough to help us here." Ithrael rolled the papers and tucked them into his shirt. "There should be a passage in here." Ithrael had remembered Yuto saying something to that effect before. They all began to examine the wall behind Soligan's desk, tapping on the walls, pulling at ornaments on the shelves, pushing against the wall.

"Here," Errol said as he pulled harder on a gold horse ornament. It was a lever; there was a distant click and part of the wall popped forward. Yuto pulled it fully open and they all followed him into the dark passage softly lit by orob lamps.

At the other end, they reached a single door that had a metal lever to one side. Ithrael listened carefully but heard no sound from within. He pulled the handle and stepped into the Hyrathean king's large study. The desk was wooden and carved. A beautiful tapestry of wild horses — and just as wild-looking men — hung behind his desk. There were chairs upholstered in wine-red fabric around a round table. Although there wasn't much within the space, what was there spoke of the Dolsan's wealth. He wasn't like Soligan who clearly liked to display his position with trinkets.

Ithrael made his way to the desk whilst the others searched the room for a safe. He noticed Yuto head straight for a specific corner of the room where a display case held a variety of weapons, which he doubted were ornamental. He caught Yeela's eye and drew her attention to Yuto. She went to join him instantly; it was worth keeping an eye on the stranger.

Ithrael felt around and underneath the desk. Working for a Queen had taught him that those high up in power always had some sort of secret compartment in their desk. Errol joined him in the search, having already done a quick sweep of the entire room and found nothing.

At the back of the desk he found a small piece of wood protruding; he pushed it in and a hatch opened up underneath the top. He pulled out the documents inside, quickly flicked through them to see the plans for the towers and slipped them inside his top also.

"Time to go," he ordered quietly.

"One moment," Yuto replied, trying to prise open another hidden compartment.

"We need to go," Ithrael said.

"Find the exit tunnel — it'll be behind the tapestry," Yuto replied, still focused on the compartment. Yeela huffed and started helping him.

"Tapestry is a bit obvious isn't it ... oh," Errol said as he uncovered a door. It was locked but he made quick work of it.

Errol held the door open and Ithrael stepped forward to make sure it was safe for them all. Yeela approached them, a grin on her face and an arsenal of weapons in her arms. She handed Ithrael a double-headed axe with a harness for him to wear it on his back. She passed Errol a curved short sword and a belt for it. She appeared to have strapped as many daggers as possible to her body, which was impressive considering her dress didn't seem to have anywhere for her to put them, but she'd managed it. Yuto was wearing a cross-body strap with throwing stars and he had a satchel slung over his shoulder. He'd clearly found whatever it was he'd come to steal.

They made their way through another orob-lit passage. "Where does this come out?" Ithrael whispered to Yuto.

"Outside the palace walls." There was a fire in his eyes, triumphant for stealing what he'd come for all those months ago.

"Don't let your guard down just yet," Ithrael warned as they crept along the passages that slowly wound further and further downwards.

"What's that smell?" Yeela spoke through the sleeve of her dress. The smell was both sweet and rotting at the same time; it made Ithrael's head spin and he saw Yeela slow down a little. They kept going until they walked into a wide cave that contained barrels and barrels of something that smelt so foul, Ithrael struggled not to gag.

Errol popped the lid of one and the smell made them all choke. He quickly replaced the lid.

"Thanks for that," Yeela said between slow, deep breaths.

There was a table of vials of a black liquid, and Ithrael's heart rate increased. It was too much of a coincidence for the smoke to be poisoning them and then for a black liquid substance to turn up.

"Each of you, take one. We need to take these to the House of Mages." They moved through the chamber, not keen to linger, and exited through another tunnel.

They finally broke into the open air, sucking in the freshness hungrily.

"What was that?" Yuto asked.

"Another poisonous weapon, no doubt," Ithrael replied, his head tipped back, drinking in the clean air. His head started to clear. "You feeling okay, Yeela?"

"I am now." She placed her hands on her hips. "I almost puked all over Errol back there."

Errol looked a little sheepish. "Sorry about that."

"They have another poison?" Yeela turned to Ithrael, worry on her face.

"It would appear so. We'd better start moving. Yuto, where've we come out?"

"Can't you smell it? The coast!" He spread his arms wide and walked forward. They followed him up the incline and sure enough, they were near the top of a cliff and below waves broke on a sandy shore. "I have a small boat hidden down there." He pointed to the bay.

"Can you get us to Calla Bay?" Ithrael enquired.

"Of course, and for the man who gave me my freedom, I'll actually keep to my word." His smile was wide and bright.

Chapter Thirty-One

AMAREA

Saia came to her, feverish from what Amarea assumed was a fretful sleep.

"My Queen," Saia said as she entered Amarea's private office where she was trying to make plans with the High General. "I know what the other poisons are."

Amarea rose and led Saia to a chair — she was shaking; she'd never seen her so rattled. Amarea knelt before her as Gallia handed Saia a strong drink to calm her nerves. "They've drowned and buried thousands. I *saw* it." Her hands shook as she brought the drink to her lips, sipping slowly.

Amarea brushed Saia's sweat-soaked hair back from her face. "Saw it? How?"

"In a dream. I saw how they do it. By slaughtering people, they create a dark magic that settles into a new element of its own made of the darkness it was created in. A resin that burns as smoke from fire, a liquid poison from the waters, and raw materials for forging weapons made from the black ore created when they bury people alive." She drank the rest of the spirit in one go. Gallia refilled her glass.

Amarea sat back on her heels. "So many deaths." She shook her head in shock, not disagreement. "How could they do this?"

"Because you have the power, my Queen. Because you have the magic of the goddess in your veins and the magic of a god by your side. If they can't have that power for themselves then they will snuff it out, and they have found a way to do it." Saia's voice had become clearer. She looked around the room and saw the High General and looked a little embarrassed.

"We need to find a way to combat this poison," Amarea said, mostly to herself.

"I'll start investigating it now." Saia stood.

"No." Amarea stood up also and took Saia's hand. "Rest, you've hardly slept."

"I can't go back to sleep now." She squeezed Amarea's hand and turned to leave.

"Wait, we can find someone to help you. You shouldn't do this alone. Maybe they can make notes for you or something?" Amarea asked hopefully, not wanting Saia to be by herself after her haunting vision.

"Okay. Thank you."

"I'll send for someone," Gallia said, and left the room with Saia.

"Gods!" Amarea said as she sat back down in her chair. "If only Ithrael were here."

"Though my son is strong, it is the minds of those like Saia you need right now. Our might will not be enough against this foe." For the first time since she'd known the High General he looked old, tired.

"What are we to do against these new weapons she speaks of? With the air choking us, with weapons that will poison us, how do we defeat them if we cannot find a way to counter their magic?"

"And what will they use the liquid for?"

"Can we even prepare for a war we cannot win?" she asked, her hope tied up in whatever his response would be.

"We have to plan, even if we know the outcome will not be what we desire." He paused. "I know for a man of war this may come as a surprise, but we need to send an envoy to see what it is they want and whether we can negotiate."

"Negotiate?" She loosed a long breath. "High General, has the poison got to you as well?"

"Fortunately I am not blessed with the magic of my son." He smiled. "But right now we need to hear what they have to say. Send an envoy."

The High General left her alone to her thoughts. There were only two people she trusted with such a delicate diplomatic mission, but neither of them she was willing to risk. But it always came down to this: her position meant she had to risk those she loved. She removed her veil, went to the window and looked out over the Waeseah Waters. She shuddered to think of people drowning in waters such as those before her. What madness had brought the Vulma Supreme Leader to this?

Gallia returned with Niseem. Amarea reluctantly picked up her veil and put it on before she turned to them.

"The twins have returned," Niseem said.

Amarea felt elation at the news but then she took in Niseem's expression. "Where are they? What happened?"

"Leonius has been gravely injured."

"Take me to them."

Amarea ran from her rooms as soon as Niseem delivered the news. She was outside the palace within moments and was running towards the lake, towards the two figures, one carrying the other on her back.

"Lisette," Amarea said. She heard Gallia catch up to her and stop. Amarea and Gallia carefully helped the unconscious Leonius down from his sister's back. Blood had dried around his ears.

"How much did he bleed?" Amarea asked as she checked for a pulse.

"Not much. It was his back …" Lisette gulped, suddenly overcome. "They broke his back."

"I'm so sorry, Lisette. I'm so, so sorry." Tears slipped down Amarea's cheeks. If she hadn't sent them to Ruist this horror would never have occurred.

"They had braziers with the poisonous smoke on their battlements which weakened us so we couldn't move as quickly and we exposed our position. They threw him and he landed on his back on a balcony." Her lip quivered. "I thought he was dead."

"You carried him the entire way?" Amarea asked in wonder. Lisette nodded.

"Oh, Lisette." Amarea held the tiny wisp of a girl, for she was still only in her eighteenth year. She should never have sent two so young to their enemy. She was a fool — a cruel, selfish fool.

Gallia had a stretcher brought and they moved Leonius to a room within the palace where a healer bathed and tended to him. Amarea wouldn't leave his side and neither would Gallia, Saia or Niseem.

Leonius stirred. "Lisette?" She reached forward, touching his brow. "You did it, you got us home."

"Rest, brother."

He looked past Lisette and saw Amarea. "My Queen." His voice had been as soft and as lovely as Lisette's but it sounded dry and cracked now.

He tried to move and Amarea could see it in his eyes, the strain. The agony of him not being able to move in front of his Queen was too much to watch. Amarea reached forward and placed a hand on his shoulder. "My brave Leonius, you will have the best care. I will send for a healing mage."

Leonius frowned. "No, my Queen, we must not interrupt their work. Did Lisette not tell you?" He seemed confused.

"Tell me what?" she asked gently.

"The weapons they have, they're like nothing we've ever seen. They are blacker than the darkest night and they gave us a strange feeling, like the smoke does. There is evil in them." He moved his gaze to rest on Lisette. "You didn't tell them?"

She shook her head. "I'm sorry I—"

"It's not her fault," Amarea said. "And we had an idea they were creating such weapons but thank you for confirming it." She paused, wondering whether she should go on. "If it's too much to talk about please let me know, but were you able to find anything else out. Any idea of the size of their army?"

A look passed between Lisette and Leonius. Lisette said, "From what we saw, their army is growing — over ten thousand just in Ruist, all camped together as though they were readying for a battle." Lisette paused. "We discovered from letters we saw in one of the general's chambers." Lisette looked down, seemingly ashamed. "Which I'm afraid I lost on my journey back."

"That doesn't matter," Amarea said.

"The Vulch are biding their time. They need to wait for clans from their outer regions to arrive. And allies. There will be *thousands* of them."

"Gods," Niseem muttered behind them.

"There were priests, too, from the Daylarian Church. They wore their robes."

"Shit." Amarea looked up and at Niseem. "The Daylarian priests must have discovered the dark magic on the abbey grounds … they would have shared their discovery with the Vulch." Amarea felt sick.

"And we saw the Vulma Supreme Leader." Lisette's voice had become so quiet Amarea could barely hear it. She looked to her brother, anguish in her eyes.

"It was as though he was created of the same magic as the smoke and weapons. His armour was made from it but his eyes were fully red." Leonius squeezed his eyes shut at the memory. "We've never seen anything like it."

"Red eyes?" Gallia asked in her surprise.

"Fully red, the entirety of each eye," Lisette said in a whisper.

Amarea turned to Gallia. "We need to go to Saia with this."

"I'll go," Niseem said, gripping Gallia's hand once before she left.

Lisette moved away and allowed Amarea to approach her brother. "Close your eyes, Leonius," she said softly. He did as she bid and she lifted her veil to place a kiss upon his brow. "May Neesoh heal and protect you," she murmured against his brow before dropping her veil back down. "Rest, brave Leonius and Lisette, you have done your country and Queen a great service. It will be remembered and honoured."

She left the room before either one could reply, but she'd noticed some peace on both their faces from her blessing. They had always been devout members of the Neesohan Church; it would help them through this time. She'd send for a priestess to sit with them.

Tears fell as she made her way through the palace to the library where Saia would be working. What had happened to her? Ever since Ithrael had left she'd been unable to control her emotions. She never cried. This wasn't who she was. She suddenly became furious with herself. She didn't need a man to be in control of a situation. He was the one who had walked away: him, not her. She hardened her heart. She didn't need to have a man in her life to be able to handle the nightmare that had befallen them. No. She could do it without him.

CHAPTER THIRTY-TWO

ITHRAEL

They were halfway down the cliffs when they heard the first shout from pursuing guards. They hadn't managed to buy themselves much time. They picked up their pace, scrabbling down the steep scree path towards the cove. Ithrael just hoped that Yuto's boat was still where he'd left it.

Arrows began to fly as more guards gave chase down the path. One hit Errol in the shoulder. He cursed and paused as Yeela carefully held the shaft and snapped it shorter so he didn't catch it on anything. They continued on, running low. Ithrael was grateful for the winding of the path that made them harder targets for the archers. They deserved some luck.

They reached the beach where the tide was low. The sand beneath their feet was soft and Ithrael could see Yuto was struggling to run having been in captivity for so long. Ithrael dropped back and shielded the thief from arrows.

"What are you doing, you fool?" Yuto managed to say through laboured breaths.

"Making sure the one person who knows where there's a boat stays alive!" Ithrael said, his breath also laboured, the effects of the smoke still not having left his system.

They reached the caves at the far end of the cove and Yuto led the way through the dark caverns, stopping at a smooth stretch of sand at the back of the cave.

"Dig." He pulled two shovels from a crevice and threw one to Ithrael. Yeela knelt down and starting digging with her hands, and Errol did the same using his one good arm.

"They'll be on us soon." Ithrael stood and tossed the shovel to Yeela. "I'll hold them off." Errol went to follow him but Ithrael rebuffed him. "You're injured, stay and help."

"I'm no help to them and I can fight left-handed," Errol said as he caught up. It was true: all trainees were taught to fight with both hands in case of an injury during battle. Ithrael just didn't want to risk the young man's life — he was getting far too soft.

Ithrael easily cut down the first two guards with the axe Yeela had given him. Errol took on one of the three who approached, and Ithrael dispatched the next two. Ithrael was enjoying using an axe; he'd have to start carrying one on his back along with his sword. He liked the way it swooped and swung up, slicing off heads from below the chin.

Errol fought off two guards single-handedly, leaving the last for Ithrael. He made quick work of it, not liking the way some people toyed with their opponents. The next lot of guards were further back and so they ran back to the other two to help them dig up the boat.

"You had to bury it, didn't you?" Yeela said to Yuto as she flung sand behind her. She was covered in a thick layer of it. The hull of the small craft was visible. "If we can just lift it by digging down these sides, it'll be quicker."

"Yuto, hand me your shovel." The Jair was fading fast. He handed it over to Ithrael and then collapsed on the sand, panting. Errol joined Yeela as she tried to get her shovel under the lip of the boat. Together, they levered it. Ithrael ran around and joined them, getting his fingers underneath and lifting it high enough for the others to assist him. They managed to lift and flip the rowing boat over, then Yeela jumped down into the hole and retrieved the four oars, passing them up to Ithrael.

Yuto was up again and helped them push the heavy craft towards the mouth of the cave just as a group of ten soldiers burst through the entrance. Ithrael drew his axe and Errol held up his sword but before they could advance, daggers whipped through the air along with throwing stars. In a matter of mere moments, six men were down. Yeela's knife lodged in the throat of another, and Yuto's final star struck a guard in the eye.

"Be my guest," Errol said, holding out his arm for Ithrael to go first. Ithrael rewarded him with a grim smile. He lifted up his axe and spun, his white hair whipping around him, and sliced the heads clean off the remaining two guards.

"I thought you were under the weather?" Yuto asked as they pushed the boat towards the water.

"I am."

"Maldessans, so arrogant," Yuto said with a tut.

"No, he really is. I'd say that today has been his worst performance yet," Yeela said.

"Thanks." Ithrael gave her a levelling look. "I'm still your captain."

They pushed the boat out into the lapping water and climbed in. Ithrael and Yeela took the oars and began to row.

"It's going to take a long time to get to Calla Bay just rowing," Yeela said. She was beginning to get out of breath.

"Let's just get past the headland and then worry about that," Ithrael said.

Yuto was examining Errol's wound. "I have some supplies here. If you let me, I can get the arrow out."

"If you scream I promise not to judge you," Yeela said with a pretty smile that made Errol scowl. *He definitely wasn't going to make a sound now.*

Yuto unlatched the small cubby at the prow of the ship and removed a wooden box and a cloth bag that contained some dried fruit and nuts (which he passed around) and a rice spirit they all had a sip of before he poured a little onto Errol's shoulder. Errol hissed in pain.

"It's only going to get worse," Yuto said, unhelpfully. "Here." He passed him a strip of leather. "Bite down on this."

Errol put the leather in his mouth and Yuto washed one of Yeela's retrieved blades in the sea, then for good measure rinsed it quickly with the rice spirit.

Without warning Errol, he slipped the thin blade into his shoulder, underneath where the arrowhead was, quickly sliced the cut wider on each side and pulled the arrow out cleanly without tearing the skin. Errol had turned grey and was sweating profusely but he didn't make a sound. With a hooked needle, Yuto sewed up the wound, causing Errol to turn a little green.

"I think he's stopped breathing," Yeela said.

"Breathe, you idiot, or you'll pass out!" Yuto said, and Errol took in a slow shuddering breath. "Nearly done."

Yuto took out a small pot of paste and smeared it over the wound and then bound the shoulder.

"Impressive," Ithrael said.

"If you're going into a line of work where you're going to get injured, you need to know how to patch yourself up." Yuto handed Errol the rice spirit and he drank deeply and then let out a long, slow breath. "Better?"

"Much."

Yuto rinsed his bloodied hands in the sea and then the implements, then packed them away tidily and put them back in their cubby. Ithrael watched him with interest. He hadn't expected him to be so methodical, but seeing someone in the state Yuto was in, it was hard to know what he would be like ordinarily.

They reached the headland and Ithrael turned to see two small boats with sails pursuing them. He had no idea where the boats had come from.

"Did you know—?" Ithrael started.

"No, I didn't know they kept sail boats nearby, otherwise I'd have led us to them," Yuto said. "But don't worry, I always have a plan."

He held in his hand a tube he'd pulled from the cubby, which he inserted into a small metal hoop hanging from the prow. "Stop rowing for a moment." He struck a flint and put the spark to the string coming from the end of the tube. Ithrael and Yeela paused, both leaning back to catch their breath and watching as the flame rose and lit the bottom of the tube. It shot up into the sky and exploded with an almighty bang and lit up into a bright red spark. It reminded Ithrael of Mierdas' white fire: useless in battle, but pretty. He wasn't sure exactly what the Jair's plan had been but it didn't seem to have worked.

"Okay, we can keep going."

"Oh, thanks." Yeela rolled her eyes as she made a backstroke. "So good of you."

"I can swap in if you like," Errol said.

Yeela snorted at him. "Maldessan male soldiers are all the same."

"What?"

"Stubborn fools."

Errol scowled. "No we're not."

Yeela's eyebrows practically hit her hairline. "No? So it's sensible for you, having just been stitched up, to row and split your stitches and risk slowing us down?" Errol's scowl deepened. *The poor man's in deep trouble*, Ithrael thought with a smile.

They continued to row towards Calla Bay, Calmaya's main port, with the Hyratheans gaining on them. They kept as far out to sea as they dared to stay out of range of anyone trying to fire at them from the shore. Ithrael was matching his strokes to

Yeela's and she had started to slow down considerably. And, although he hated to admit it, he was tiring as well and wasn't sure how much longer he could continue.

Yuto looked to the horizon, waiting for something. Errol kept his eyes to the stern of the boat and the approaching Hyratheans.

"Yeela, we need you and Yuto to throw. A sword and an axe are no good to us here," Ithrael said.

"If only the Dolsan had had a bow and quiver, or a cross bow. Some kind of a bow," Yeela said.

"Patience," Yuto said with a confident smile.

Ithrael saw a shape break the horizon moments later — a ship. Yuto's face was victorious.

"See?"

"Yes, that's wonderful Yuto, but it's a little far off and the Hyratheans are gaining on us," Yeela said.

Yuto paused to think and then opened up his cubby and pulled out another exploding stick. "Errol, help me aim." They clambered over Yeela and Ithrael to the stern of the boat and Errol lined himself up behind the exploding stick.

"What about your hands?" Yeela asked, genuinely concerned.

"They'll survive … hopefully." Yuto looked like a man saying farewell as he glanced down at his palms. He held the exploding stick out over the water.

"Left a bit … Right a bit … Up a bit," Errol said. "There, hold it steady." Errol struck his flint, double-checked the direction of the exploding stick, then ignited it. "Hold it … Hold it …" Errol stayed in place as the wick fizzed with flame. "Loosen your grip a bit …"

The stick shot from Yuto's hands. He plunged them in the water as he cursed in Jair. They watched as the stick flew straight into the sail of the ship, but it didn't explode, instead hitting the sail and falling into the boat. Yuto cursed again. "Well, it was worth a shot." He turned to them, an apologetic expression on his face. Moments later, there was a loud bang and the boat erupted into flame. Yuto's face transformed from disappointment to elation at comical speed. The crazy Jair had done it.

However, the second boat was approaching and the ship was still too far off to be of any assistance.

"What now?" Yeela asked Ithrael.

"We'll have to hold them off as best we can." Ithrael looked towards the other craft. It shouldn't be too difficult; he just wasn't sure exactly how to go about it.

As he was contemplating the best way to fight in a small craft, he felt the boat tilt slightly and watched as Yuto slipped into the water.

"What on—"

Ithrael silenced Yeela with a look. She caught on quickly and drew her attention away from the man with a dagger clamped in his fist, swimming underwater towards the other boat.

"We're in range of their arrows now," Errol said. They watched as two men knelt and drew back their bowstrings. The arrows flew in perfectly aimed arcs, but the three in the boat were well-trained and neither one hit a mark.

"So we just sit here and dodge arrows until Yuto does what, exactly? Slit each of their throats?" Errol said. His faced was pinched with pain and Ithrael put his irritation down to that.

Yuto was already halfway to the other craft. Ithrael had never seen anyone swim so fast (although the current was in his favour). He was rising in the water and so to distract the boat Ithrael took one of Yeela's throwing knives, much to her consternation, and flung it at the other boat's sail. It pierced the sail blade first and then fell into the boat.

Yeela's eyes were wide. "I've seen you throw before but that ... that must have been ... well, really fucking far."

"I could do better."

She rolled her eyes and continued her arrow vigil, even managing to pluck one from the air. Her returning glare to the Hyrathean soldiers would have impressed the Queen.

Yuto reached the other boat and slipped out of view. They all watched and waited as arrow after arrow missed their mark. The tiller swung suddenly in the hand of the Hyrathean who was steering. Yuto had cut the rope. They watched in amazement as he hauled himself onto the boat, and standing on the side he leapt into the air and latched himself onto the mast. He slashed wildly at the sail as daggers and arrows flew at him. He moved higher up, still slashing, and then flung himself free and dived into the water.

The Hyrathean boat bobbed idly in the water, its sail in tatters, tiller useless. Yuto had bought them some time.

Chapter Thirty-Three

AMAREA

Amarea entered the winter palace library with her heart hardened. Niseem was sitting beside an increasingly exhausted-looking Saia. Gallia followed with near-silent steps behind Amarea. These three women were her most trusted advisers: she believed in them above any man now. Together they would defeat the enemy.

"We all help Saia with this," Amarea said as she sat down opposite Niseem. "Do you believe it's the liquid that causes this strange alteration?"

"I do. It explains why they sacrificed so many for it. He must have to take it as a tonic daily. But even so, the quantity from my dream — he could be making an army of soldiers like himself, and who knows what powers the tonic grants him?" Saia looked at Amarea as though she was staring directly into her eyes.

"Where do we start?"

Saia pushed a book towards her. "We need to understand everything that's known about magic. And not much is known." Saia re-tied her limp hair with a leather cord. "Although the House researches magic they've never found a way for people to control their own, rather it is just part of them. If we can understand our magic it will give us a basis to understand the darker sides to it as well."

When she said "our magic" she touched her heart. Amarea realised she needed to start to learn about her own power and whether or not she could wield it as a weapon. There was little use to being bewitchingly beautiful when on a battlefield, but maybe there was more to what was inside her. Maybe she could be the key to defeating this enemy, and she would do it no matter the personal cost.

It was dark when a further report from the tower came in. Nothing had changed. Amarea rubbed her eyes beneath her veil. As she tired, she felt the nausea from the smoke start to return. Although her symptoms weren't like those she'd experienced in the capital, she was weaker and she hated that the Vulma Supreme Leader had made her that way. In front of her, Gallia and Niseem were opening books, and at the other end of the table Saia was examining the samples of the black resin taken from the abbey fire.

"Do you think the Daylarian Church traded what they knew of dark magic for his support in overthrowing me?" Amarea said to no one in particular, finally voicing her fears.

"If they knew of dark magic it's never mentioned in any of the texts we've been through tonight." Niseem seemed to be trying to make Amarea feel better, but her guilt wouldn't go.

Amarea rubbed her face under her veil again, as though trying to wipe her past ill-conceived choices from her mind. "Okay, let's go over what we've all found out and see if we can connect any of it together." Amarea straightened as she spoke, not wanting to let the others see her flagging.

Saia placed the resin back in a glass bowl and removed the glove she wore to handle it, then joined them at the other end of the table.

"Magic came from Daylar and Neesoh appearing on our land. That is the common understanding," Niseem said. "And it seeped into the earth beneath their feet and made our soil fertile, our land rich beyond any other."

"Has anyone found any accounts of other gods or goddesses in other lands?" Amarea asked.

"There is tell of the Jaien god, Jair, who rose from the sea and gifted their island with the skill of sailing and plentiful waters," Saia reminded them.

"And the Issabad goddess who came from the wind and blew rich spices into the air, laced with gold," Niseem said with a smile, as though remembering the story from childhood.

"And so our land is not the only one blessed with magic, which means Issabad and Jaien could be at risk. It may be worth sending an emissary to each nation — maybe we can forge an alliance against the Vulch?" Amarea said, thinking aloud. The others agreed it was a good idea.

"Okay, so we have the origins, but how do we access this magic and find out what it can do?" Spiced tea and a platter of food were placed on the table, and Amarea tore at the freshly made herb bread as she considered their problem.

"The mages of the House keep the balance through linking the orob stones throughout the kingdom. They drive spikes through large boulders containing the ore, hammering the spikes into the earth and connecting them to the source of power. The rest even they don't understand fully. Mierdas consults the Book of Balance if any issues arise, but mostly he's an alchemist." Saia didn't sound too impressed by the High Mage, and Amarea imagined it was because he hadn't explored the magic in the realm; instead, he just accepted its existence.

"Do you think the stones are the key? You used them in the message machine," Gallia said to Saia, her expression showing fascination in the work Saia was able to create.

"There is definitely something about the stones that is significant, but no, somehow I don't think it's the key. The stones contain magic, just as our Queen does. It's how it's accessed that's important."

Saia stared off into the distance. She was thinking, something starting to connect: Amarea could almost see it all slotting into place before Saia's eyes. Saia stood suddenly and pulled a book from the pile in the middle of the table. She flipped through the pages quickly and began explaining, "When I made the communication device, the old instructions stated that a sharp point must hit the stone to access the powers." She held the book open and pointed at a diagram of the Queen's sceptre. "The magic that held the Queen on the night of the Blood Moon was activated when Aiden twisted the staff, forcing a point into the stone." Saia's finger pointed to the image of the magical staff.

"And the weather is controlled by staffs that have a core of orob stones, and they're hammered into the earth," Niseem said eyes wide.

"So you think that to access the power of the stones something must hit them or the stones can't be used as a method to draw out magic?" Gallia asked.

Realisation dawned on Amarea. "When I was a child, Mierdas used to tell me about ancient medicinal techniques. It used to bore me to death but there were ones that used needles." Amarea stood and followed Saia as she made her way to the back of the library to where the books on medicine were kept. They searched the old spines for what they needed. Saia found the leather-bound book and pulled it out. She brought it to the table and they all leaned over her as she scanned the chapters.

"There." Niseem pointed to the title *Needle Healing*.

Saia turned the pages, her hands trembling slightly. Amarea understood why; it was the anticipation of knowing that they may just have found the answer to harnessing magic.

The first page of the chapter displayed diagrams of the needles' uses.

"See here," Saia said. "*To enhance the efficacy of the instrument some practitioners use a core of blue moon*'. Blue moon is the name of the orob stone in Jaien. It was first discovered by the light of a full moon." Saia was practically breathless in her excitement.

She turned the page and they all read the information below an illustration. "It's not exact — it seems like this was in experimental stages," Amarea said as she finished reading.

Saia frowned and turned the page. It was the last one of the chapter. Disappointment flooded Amarea. *That's it?* The page showed a diagram of the human body with red dots in places.

"These must be the points used to trigger magic healing. It says that every person holds some magic so everyone can be healed with this method." Saia's finger was tracing the points on the page.

"This one, here." Amarea pointed to one in the stomach, just below the centre of the rib cage. "For nausea. Let's try it."

Saia looked surprised. "Now?"

"Yes, I'm nauseated from the bloody smoke. Let's try it." Amarea turned to Gallia. "Have someone collect a needle from a seamstress."

"And tongs from the kitchen — I'll need to sterilise them in a flame," Saia called after Gallia.

It wasn't long before they had what they needed. Amarea lay back on the table, her stomach exposed.

"Are you sure, my Queen? Shouldn't we test this on me first?" Saia's eyes filled with concern.

"You need to be the one to do it, Saia, and I have the most magic. It's best to test it on me." Amarea was direct, ensuring Saia felt no doubt before she stuck a needle into her Queen's flesh.

Saia knelt on the table next to Amarea with the book open at her side. Niseem stood with Gallia, both of them looking on with concern. Saia placed her fingers on Amarea's sternum and used two fingers to find the point she was looking for.

"Ready?"

"It's just a small needle, Saia, stop worrying," Amarea said with a smile, hoping that the smile was evident in her voice and that it reassured Saia.

Saia took a deep breath and stuck the needle into Amarea's abdomen. It didn't hurt Amarea much, but it also didn't do anything.

"Anything?" Saia asked, hopefully.

"Nothing," Amarea said and sighed.

"Wait!" Gallia turned the page and scanned the written text. "It says here you have to twist the needle clockwise."

"Go ahead," Amarea said to a sceptical-looking Saia, but she did as she was bid.

Her delicate fingers gently touched the top of the needle and carefully turned it. Instantly, a tingling sensation flooded Amarea's body. Saia sat back in shock, staring at Amarea's stomach.

"It turned blue!" Niseem and Gallia looked equally shocked.

"I felt it," Amarea said, sitting up. "What happened?"

"When I turned the needle, the point turned a sort of luminous blue, like the light of an orob lamp, and the colour spread across your body in a wave. I've never seen anything like it." Saia was staring at the needle sticking out of Amarea's stomach. Amarea pulled it out and dropped it into the small metal dish beside her.

"How do you feel?" Niseem asked. Amarea wasn't entirely sure why she was whispering but there was a look of awe on her friend's face.

Amarea stilled, considering. "Normal. Fine. Not sick at all." She swung her legs over the side of the table and stood, straightening her clothes. "This could help Leonius, couldn't it?"

Saia's eyes widened. "Yes, yes it could. Depending on the magic in his body we could at the very least make it so he can sit up." Saia scanned the points on the picture. "I'll need to investigate further."

There was fire in Saia's eyes as she glowed from the excitement of discovery.

"Can it just heal, though? Or could it harness my magic to help us defeat the Vulma Supreme Leader?" Amarea could feel energy coursing through her entire body. She was thrumming with it. She would now be able to endure the effects of the smoke, although the remedy wouldn't be enough to face their enemy.

"I need to investigate further, to communicate with the House." Saia's brow furrowed. It wouldn't be long before the machine received its first message. All their eyes fell on it sitting dormant in the corner of the room.

"I'm going to meet with the Primlect and the High General," Amarea said, and swept from the room, energy pouring through her, her mind clear. She needed to apprise them of the new developments and in that moment, she felt she could take on any challenge facing them. The goddess was with her; she could feel it.

Chapter Thirty-Four

YEELA

Yeela helped haul Yuto back into their rowboat. The guards in the other craft were still firing arrows in their direction, but they were beginning to fall short as the current slowly dragged them further away. Despite the ache in her shoulders and the fierce blisters forming on her hands, Yeela re-joined Ithrael and began to row towards the approaching ship. She glanced over to Errol who seemed to be holding up well: Yuto had done a good job on his shoulder. She felt more relieved by that than by their escape, but she supposed that was because she had been trained for combat, not for losing a friend.

The ship didn't take long to reach them and it was the finest vessel Yeela had ever seen. She'd always admired the Queen's fleet in the Port of Saffiere but she could tell that the ship now in front of her was far superior to any the Maldessan navy had. The hull was black, the shape narrower than the large ships she was used to seeing. A gold and red dragon was painted across one side and from its open mouth, curling gold fire spewed. It was magnificent.

"Is this *your* ship?" Yeela asked in awe.

"She is indeed. I'd told her to leave if I wasn't back within five days. She's waited all this time." Yuto shook his head, smiling. "They're in a lot of trouble."

They pulled up alongside the beast of a ship and one by one scaled the rope ladder whilst sailors climbed down to secure the rowboat. Yeela almost offered to give Errol a hand but when she turned to him his expression clearly stated for her to *not even think about it*.

Yeela clambered over and onto the deck, just behind Yuto. A woman approached him dressed in a long robe in black, with red and gold embroidery along the edges of its fabric. It was tied with a sash in blood red, and beneath it she wore trousers (which Yeela instantly approved of). Strapped across her back was a long, thin sword. She bowed to Yuto.

"Captain, what took you so long?"

Yuto laughed and slapped the woman on the shoulder. "You were supposed to leave moons ago, Koharu," he said but with no trace of temper.

"What can I say? We wanted a holiday." Her mouth quirked up into a half smile. "You work us too hard."

Yeela took in the crew standing in regimented attention. The boat was spotless and the men and women sailors looked in perfect health, not like they'd been partying in Calmaya. She noticed Yuto doing the same.

"You should have returned, Koharu." His expression was serious.

"With respect, we heard you were captured, not killed. At least I regarded your request not to send anyone in after you." She tilted her chin up in defiance. She was a bold second-in-command, that's for sure. Yeela liked her instantly. "Who have you brought with you?" Her dark eyes examined Yeela, Ithrael and Errol.

"Just a few convicts I picked up along the way. I promised to drop them off in Calla Bay." Yeela wasn't sure why Yuto hadn't said who they were but she was sure he had his reasons.

"Yes, Captain, I'll set a course immediately." Before Koharu turned to give the orders, she spotted the bag Yuto carried. She looked into his eyes and he inclined his head slightly. Yeela thought she saw visible relief in the woman's posture and expression. Whatever it was that Yuto had taken, it was important.

Yuto led them all to his large cabin. He handed Yeela some clothes and pointed her in the direction of a changing screen and a basin of water.

He frowned at Ithrael and Errol with their bulky frames. "I don't think I have anything that'll fit either of you."

"We'll be fine, thank you," Ithrael replied.

Yeela was pleased to pull on loose-fitting trousers, a short tunic and a robe like the ones the others on the boat wore. She felt more like herself, like she could actually fight. She stepped out from behind the screen and her eyes caught on two long, thin swords hanging on the wall.

"What are they called?" Yeela asked Yuto, as she stepped towards them.

He reached up and took one down, smoothly slipping the thin blade from its sheath. "This is a katana. They are the sharpest blades in existence."

"Beautiful," she said as she admired the gleaming sword. Yuto slid it back into its casing and hung it up once more.

"I'll teach you how to use it sometime," he said with a smile.

"I'd like that," she said, beaming back at him.

Errol cleared his throat. "Any idea how long until we're in Calla Bay?" He had his same old grumpy expression, but this time Yeela felt as though it was directed at her, although she wasn't sure what she'd done to deserve it.

"It won't be long — my ship is the fastest on the known seas."

Out on the main deck, Yeela stood with Ithrael and Errol as Calla Bay came into view. The dangerous part of their journey was coming to an end and she felt oddly saddened that she would no longer be travelling, even though she was headed to safety.

"Where will the House of Mages be staying?" Yeela asked Ithrael.

"The Lead Council will know, and I know her well." Ithrael seemed troubled. There she was feeling as though their adventure was coming to an end and Ithrael looked as though his was just beginning. Maybe he was right; maybe they were headed towards a war.

When the boat docked, Yuto followed them to shore. "You're coming with us?" Errol asked, a little rudely Yeela thought. He'd slung the bag he'd taken from the Hyratheans over his shoulder.

"I have some things I want to speak to Mierdas about."

Errol, Ithrael and Yeela looked at one another, surprise on their faces.

"You know the High Mage?" Yeela asked.

Yuto just shrugged and led the way along the docks, dropping some coins into the hands of the waiting port guard.

"Who is he?" Yeela said in a low voice to Ithrael.

"I don't know, but I think we need to find out," Ithrael said. Yeela looked to Errol whose brow was so furrowed he looked like an angry old man. The thought made Yeela smile as she followed Yuto towards the port guard's office.

Yuto shook hands with the man on duty and slapped another on the back.

"Come to cause trouble again?" the first man asked.

"Not this time. I brought some friends from Maldessa — they need to speak with your Lead Council." Yuto stepped aside and Ithrael greeted the two men.

The first guard squinted at him and cocked his head to one side. "Are you—?"

"Captain Ithrael Ethea." Ithrael bowed his head slightly. Both guards' eyebrows shot up.

"We heard you'd been taken."

"And now I'm back, thanks to my friends." Ithrael smiled genially. "Would you be so good as to take us to the Lead Council?"

"Of course. I'll have a couple of my soldiers escort you to the Seat of Calmaya." The first guard disappeared and quickly returned with a four-soldier escort.

"What's the seat of Calmaya?" Yeela said to Errol in a whisper.

"Their government building. The country is run by elected leaders, and the Lead Council is in charge." Yeela made an "oh" face and allowed herself to be flanked by the guard. It was strange to walk in their protection when she was usually the one doing the protecting.

The Seat of Calmaya was a large, very palatial building in the centre of the main city. It didn't take long to walk there from the port. The stone of the city was similar to that of Hyrathea, but the streets were wider and everything looked better put together. There was a better atmosphere, too.

They were told to wait in an antechamber for the Lead Council to be fetched. Refreshments were brought to them and Yeela drank the fresh guava juice with relish. In the smart clean surroundings, she realised how dishevelled Ithrael was looking. His clothes were filthy, his hair no longer a gleaming white but a dirty-looking dull grey. He didn't seem to notice, though. He merely seemed impatient.

The Lead Council walked in and Yeela was pleased to see it was a woman. She must have been in her fiftieth year, her hair greying and tied back tightly. Her back was straight and her cool grey eyes fierce.

She strode directly to Ithrael and shook his hand. "It's good to see you safe."

"Thank you, and thank you for taking in our mages."

"It was the least we could do. Besides, they're incredibly well house-trained." She gave him a wry smile.

"I need to speak with them." Ithrael's expression was grave and the Lead Council looked as though she understood the importance of what he needed to do.

"I will take you to Mierdas myself."

They followed her out of the room and through a central courtyard, then out the back of the Seat of Calmaya. There was a small stretch of manicured garden before a single-story building with large, arched windows that came into view behind a high hedge. The Lead Council opened the door and to the right Yeela could see a room made up with rows of beds.

"This is our state ballroom and dining rooms — the building has come in incredibly handy." And Yeela knew she was also referring to the time when Hyrathea invaded and extra sanatoria and sanctuaries were needed.

The larger dining hall had been turned into a makeshift laboratory/library. Mages were brewing noxious potions; others were scribbling notes from large tomes.

"They haven't stopped working since they arrived." Her face showed no indication of how she felt about the threat they were now facing, but Yeela imagined that was the politician in her.

At the far end of the room an old man bent over a sluggish brown substance, frowning. They went to him and it took him a good long while to notice their approach.

Mierdas looked thoughtful when Ithrael greeted him. "That took longer than I expected."

"We decided to explore the city before our escape," Ithrael said, and the old man nodded in understanding.

"And was there anything interesting in the city?"

Ithrael placed one of the vials of black viscous liquid into the old man's palm. "We have something here that is dangerous and needs examining. Also ..." Ithrael pulled the papers from inside his tunic and passed them to the old man so he could feel what Ithrael had presented him with. Mierdas laid them out on the table and Ithrael summarised what was before him.

Mierdas muttered something unintelligible to himself as he listened. Ithrael continued in a low voice. "This is from an Atarix brother — they're instructions for the creation of dark magic. The same dark magic that is currently plaguing Maldessa. The Church has been ... busy."

Yeela could hear the fury in Ithrael's voice, despite his tone being even.

"Atarix brother?" Yuto said to Yeela.

"The higher order in the Daylarian Church," she replied quietly.

"We need to get the information to the Queen as quickly as possible," Ithrael told Mierdas.

"You must ride to the winter palace at once." Mierdas looked up. "But first maybe bathe and eat something?" He sniffed the air with humour.

Ithrael huffed a laugh. "It couldn't hurt."

"Leave these with me and I'll have copies made before you leave." Ithrael nodded in agreement and the Lead Council led them out.

"How severe is this threat?" the Lead Council asked Ithrael.

"Very. It would be wise to be on your guard, even though Maldessa appears to be the target."

The Lead Council looked tired all of a sudden. "Will there ever be a time of peace?"

Ithrael touched her shoulder in consolation as they stepped back into the Seat of Calmaya. It was only once they were inside that Yeela realised Yuto had stayed behind.

The Lead Council led them to the suites reserved for state visitors where they were invited to bathe and change into clothes that would be brought and left in the rooms for them. The bathing room was tiled in small, glossy mosaic pieces in a simple repeating pattern. *The effect is elegant*, Yeela thought as she sank into the fragranced water. At least some of Calmaya's beauty had survived the Hyratheans. She'd heard the great gardens had now been destroyed; they were once meant to have been one of the most beautiful places you could ever visit. The thought made her sad. What else would be lost under the current threat?

A dress had been laid out for her on the bed and so she changed back into the clothes Yuto had lent her, tucking her daggers away happily and feeling more like herself than she had since she'd started her journey.

She met the others in the hallway and they made their way back to the temporary House of Mages where food had been laid out for them. They ate hungrily, and even Ithrael, who Yeela had assumed had courtly eating manners, ate like a cadet after a gruelling training session. As they were finishing, a young mage approached Ithrael and handed him the original papers. Yeela was surprised to see Ithrael check to make sure they were all there. Did he not trust the mages? Or maybe being the Queen's Guard has made him overly cautious.

They rose, ready to request horses and be on their way, when Yeela saw a travel-worn mage enter carrying a large box. The other mages began to notice him too, and she saw their surprise.

Mierdas was led towards the young man. "What are you doing here, Dideum?"

"I've brought a communication device from the Queen and copies of writings from inside one of the dark towers." Dideum kept his eyes to the floor when he spoke to the High Mage.

Ithrael stood instantly and walked towards the young mage. Dideum looked up in awe at the towering soldier. "You're free ... She was ... We must send her a message right away."

With shaking hands the young man placed the bulky wooden device onto the nearby table and Yeela noticed he avoided being close to the High Mage. Dideum loosed a shaking breath and pulled down the side lever. Yeela saw that it lit up a small crystal on the side. He waited, and then slowly pressed down the strange flat keys embossed with letters. Yeela watched intently as he typed *'ithraelsafe'*. He paused a moment and then added, *'incalmaya'*.
He paused again. *'leavingforwinterpalace'*.

He stopped and pulled out some paper and a pen from inside the box. They all stood, watching and waiting. The *'q'* key rose upwards of its own accord; the collective intake of breath came out as a gasp that sang through the room. Everyone stood a little closer to the machine as Dideum carefully wrote down the letters as they moved as if an invisible hand were pushing them upwards. Yeela peered closer and noticed that before a key moved there was a faint blue glow from the stone beneath.

Magic. It was true magic.

Chapter Thirty-Five

AMAREA

Amarea ran from her meeting to the library where Saia and Niseem were in front of the communication machine. She stood there breathless as she watched the keys jump, and then her heart felt like it was about to explode as she saw the letters carefully written down by Saia. Ithrael was safe. He was free. Despite convincing herself she didn't need him, that she didn't care, her knees went out from under her and she had to grab hold of Gallia for support.

"My Queen?" she asked with concern.

"He's alive."

Gallia's eyes were bright as she nodded her head, her smile full and joyous.

Saia read the messages to her once it seemed there was nothing else being written.

"What shall I respond?" Saia asked.

"Queen asks for quick return." Amarea thought as Saia typed. "Mages to investigate needles and magic."

Saia slowly and carefully typed out the message. "And the black resin?"

"Three types of black poison. Resin for smoke. Metal for weapons. Liquid to … to …" Amarea wasn't sure of the best or quickest way to describe what it did.

"Drink?" Saia suggested. Amarea supposed it was the simplest explanation.

"Also, mention this is dark magic that comes about through mass killings. They need to know exactly what they're dealing with." Saia nodded and sent the message. They waited and soon got the response that Ithrael had left for the winter palace and the mages would look into what they had mentioned.

"Ithrael brought them some of the liquid. That'll be useful. And he has evidence of the Daylarian Church's involvement," Saia said as she watched the letters in front of her jump.

Amarea's heart thundered; knowing the Daylarian Church was involved confirmed her worst fear. Her actions had triggered all of this. It was all because of her. She pushed her emotions down, focusing on the task at hand. "Ask if they've discovered anything else of use," Amarea asked.

They waited but the response wasn't promising. For all their studies, the mages were further behind in their understanding than they were. Amarea swore. "Useless bunch of old men."

"They didn't have a very useful dream," Niseem gently said to Amarea.

"We're not getting anywhere." Amarea threw up her hands. She couldn't leash her agitation any more.

"I think we've done pretty well in such a short span of time. We didn't know anything about the black resin a few days ago." Niseem's disapproving tone didn't soften.

"We should do more needle tests." Amarea turned to Saia.

Saia gave Amarea a penetrating look, as if she could glean her true meaning. "I'd like to find out as much as I can about the flow of magic and its release before we go down that route."

"So you just want to weaponise yourself without any real planning?" Niseem crossed her arms.

"What is this? Why are you all suddenly so cautious?" Amarea said.

"Because you're not yourself. You're all jittery and that's when mistakes are made." Niseem raised her eyebrow accusingly at her.

"They're right, sweet cousin. Go to the tower and drink in some of that putrid smoke, should calm you right down." Tristam was leaning against the doorway listening in on their conversation. "So your thingy." He waved towards the communication device. "It works, then?"

"It does," Saia said primly.

"Well that's good. I suppose the mages haven't got anywhere."

Although he couldn't see it, Amarea narrowed her eyes at him. "What makes you say that?"

"Because they're stuck in the past. They never want to explore new possibilities. It'll be hard for them to think of magic in a new way." He stepped into the room and read the transcript and a slightly smug expression formed on his face.

"Okay, your assessment was correct." Amarea considered her cousin for a moment. "Tristam ... How do you feel about a little experiment?"

"No!" Saia, Niseem and Gallia shouted in unison.

Tristam raised a single eyebrow. "Well, now I'm interested."

Behind her veil, Amarea's smile was wide and vicious. There was something in their blood that sang to danger and adventure.

The wind by the Waeseah Waters sliced through Amarea's thin clothes, but she'd chosen them so that the needles and pins they'd brought (from a very displeased tailor) could pierce her skin without her having to strip naked.

Saia was sitting on a boulder wrapped up in a thick cloak, a large book open on her lap. "In theory, your heart point is the source of all your magic, but ..." Saia held up her hand, her expression panicked. "If it is, it'll be too powerful to experiment with today."

Amarea lowered her hand and Saia relaxed, but Amarea could tell she was still on edge. "Where do I start?"

"The body is split into meridians. Each is related to a different organ, but there are two that are different." Saia frowned in concentration. "But there's a primary, which runs through your centre, and if I track it ..." She ran her finger over the diagram in front of her. "Okay ..." Saia stood up and placed the book on the boulder. There was an audience — Bassiri, Tristam, Niseem and Gallia all watched as the small woman approached their Queen and held out her hand for the Queen's arm. Amarea placed the back of her hand in Saia's and she pulled back her sleeve.

"I can do it." Amarea went to take the needle from Saia.

"It's better if I do it. I know where the point is." Saia was firm, in charge.

Her finger was cold as she ran it along the exposed skin of Amarea's wrist, and it sent a shiver through her. Saia's finger paused, and she stared down at where her finger lay.

"Gallia, pass me a pen." Amarea held out her hand and kept her eyes on Saia. She felt the pen being put into her open palm and placed a single dot where Saia's finger was. Amarea stepped back and she saw apology in Saia's expression, but there was no need for it. She understood how dangerous what they were attempting was. Saia joined the others further back and Amarea removed a pin from the small wooden box Gallia had handed her before they'd left for the lake.

She stood facing the lake, the water rippling before her. She loosed a breath, and before she could think too much about what she was about to do, she pushed the needle into her exposed wrist, right over the small black dot. Energy coursed through her body in a sudden burst, sparking and coiling up from her core. Blue light shot from where she'd pushed the needle in, twisted it and then removed it. The light arced out as though it was a bolt of lightning, crackling with energy. The force of it made her stumble back. Her heart hammered in her chest.

"Holy fucking Gods," Tristam said from behind her. She turned to her friends and saw the awe and fear in their faces.

"Would Bassiri and Saia be able to do that?" Niseem asked, her face alight with the possibilities that now lay before them.

With hands shaking slightly, Amarea held out the open box of pins to them both. They each tentatively took one. Amarea noticed the shy way Saia looked at Bassiri. Amarea was pleased Tristam and Bassiri had rekindled whatever it was they had before, but she felt for Saia. There was no joy in unrequited love.

They stepped to the shore of the lake and Saia found the point on Bassiri's wrist and marked it for him. Amarea didn't step back; instead, she stood beside them as they held the needles above their wrists.

"Don't forget to twist and then pull it out," Saia said to Bassiri. He simply nodded in response, his expression unreadable. Amarea watched as they each pricked themselves with their needles, twisted, then pulled them out.

Bassiri shuddered, his body glowed slightly and then it faded.

Blue sparks broke out across Saia's exposed skin, her pupils dilated. "Oh!" She put her hand to her cheek. "Remarkable."

Tristam approached Bassiri and placed his hand on Bassiri's elbow. "Well?"

"I feel more alert, stronger. I don't really know how to describe it." He looked intently at Tristam's face and placed his hand on his lover's cheek. "I see so much." His eyes were searching Tristam's face. "So much."

Amarea turned to Saia and didn't have to ask for her assessment. Saia began to speak. "So much energy. That's what magic is, it's an energy, coursing through all of us. I can see it all now, the threads, the veins in the earth." She turned to face Amarea. There was something different about her, as though she was finally awake. Everything about her seemed more alive than before. "How did I not see it before?" She approached Amarea and began to lift her veil.

"Saia!"

"It's okay, my Queen, I can see with eyes unguarded." She lifted the veil and looked upon her Queen's face as the others averted their gazes. "Such beauty. Such power. You are the key to this war, my Queen, you will bring about the end. Blood of your love will fell the tainted." Saia paled and began to sway. Amarea caught her before she fainted. She pulled her veil over her face and Gallia picked up Saia's slight frame.

"What was that?" Tristam asked.

"A prophecy," Niseem said as she brushed Saia's hair back off her face. "It was a prophecy about the coming war."

Saia slept for the rest of the day and when she awoke, she was feverish.

"The point triggers everyone's individual magic and your ability is too much for you to attempt it again, Saia," Amarea said as she held a cool compress to Saia's head.

"But the things I could see — it could win us the war." Her voice was weak and it worried Amarea but the healers didn't have any answers. It was a fever caused by excessive use of magic. It was something they knew nothing of. The only person who would be of use to Saia was Saia herself, but she was in no state to be able to work out how to go about healing herself.

"I will not fight this war at the expense of my friends." Amarea pointed to the guard in the corner. "He's been instructed to physically hold you down if he sees you even look at a needle or expose your wrist. I've even considered metal cuffs welded onto you, so don't test my patience."

"You want to manacle me?" Saia's expression was incredulous.

"If that's what it takes to keep you from doing something incredibly stupid, then yes. I will manacle you."

Saia sank further into her pillows. "Fine."

"Good. You're more use to me as you, anyway. When you were prophesying it was a little ... creepy."

Saia frowned. "Oh, thanks."

"You saw my face and you were okay." Which didn't make any sense to Amarea; only Ithrael could look upon her unaffected because he was part god himself.

"You're very beautiful," Saia said absently.

"So I've been told," Amarea said dryly. Saia began to sweat. "Stop thinking too hard about it. Your body can't handle it right now. You need rest."

"I'm useless like this."

"I know, and that's why I need you to rest and not try anything reckless." Amarea paused and when she spoke again her voice was soft. "I can't lose you, Saia." She took the small frail hand of the brilliant woman lying before her, so fragile now, and squeezed it gently.

"I will do as my Queen commands, and rest, and heal." Saia's smile was small, and there was something there that frightened Amarea. Saia didn't think she'd recover. Dread rose up in Amarea like a wave and she placed a trembling hand over Saia's heart and gave her Neesoh's blessing.

Amarea made her way through the halls of the winter palace in a daze. She felt like her world was crumbling and she had no idea how to rebuild it and no real idea how to fight the enemy before them. She brushed her hand along the cool, smooth marble walls, the sensation soothing her. It was only then that she realised she was alone. She was only ever alone when she was in her private chambers. She'd asked Gallia to leave her alone with Saia but she'd expected her to be outside the room waiting for her. Amarea looked around, not a single person in sight. It was strange to be alone. She wasn't used to it; it felt freeing. She rested her back against the wall and took in a long, slow breath and rested her palms against the cool stone, grounding herself.

It wasn't long before Gallia found her, a slight scowl on her face. Amarea wasn't sure whether it was aimed at her or if Gallia was annoyed with herself for allowing Amarea to be alone.

"I think we should relax your duties. I quite liked those few moments to myself."

Gallia's expression nearly made Amarea laugh. "I'm excellent company, and no fucking way."

"That's no way to speak to your Queen."

"It is when there's a very real, very dangerous, very unpredictable threat."

Amarea sighed dramatically. "I suppose there are things to be done?"

"The Primlect and High General want to see you — they've heard about the developments." Gallia began walking and didn't wait to see if Amarea would follow, although she knew she would. Amarea quickly fell into step next to her guard. Gallia was a little taller than Amarea, her shoulders broad, her red hair tightly plaited. There was a seriousness about her when she was on duty, but Amarea also knew her as Niseem's wife, that her laugh was loud and infectious, that she could drink as much as her goddess-blessed Queen without hesitation, and that she was loyal to the Crown. Amarea felt her pride swell as she considered Gallia. She was fortunate to have such a woman as her protector, even if she really didn't need one.

The High General was bent over the long banqueting table examining maps when he spoke. "We've located two more towers." The Primlect was sitting down looking weary. Amarea was almost tempted to send him to bed.

Amarea looked over the High General's shoulder to where he'd marked their locations. "Four towers. Do you think there are any more?"

He joined up the crosses he'd marked. "If you look at where they're positioned, I expect there to be one on the eastern mountain range." He circled a small section and showed Amarea how the locations connected to encircle Maldessa. "I've sent soldiers to that location and they will send word if they find it."

"Any joy destroying the tower nearby?" Amarea asked as she looked at the ring of terror surrounding her lands.

"No. Nothing has made even a dent in the wood and the resin keeps on burning." She looked at the High General's face and saw Ithrael there. It was a painful reminder, but he was on his way back to her and she had to keep her focus. The High General looked tired, worried even.

"If we can't bring these towers down, what does it mean?"

"It means our enemy is a step ahead. We have to overcome this first obstacle, to give our soldiers hope, to help us understand what's behind this dark magic." He stood and stretched his back.

"We've made some discoveries about our own magic, the magic that lies in Maldessa and in some of her people," she said, trying to soothe his worry, although she was sure that was his job.

"I heard something about needles and it nearly killing Saia." His voice was gruff and the coarseness grated on her.

The Primlect stood. "I understand that times are ... difficult, but, your Majesty, you need to exercise some caution."

Amarea looked at her two most senior advisers with exasperation. "It didn't nearly kill her, it was just too powerful. She'll recover." *She has to.* "We can access our own magic now. We just need to keep experimenting, and we know that the mages access the magic in the earth through the orob stones. Maybe we can create weapons with that same practice in mind — to pierce the enemy's armour."

The High General considered her idea. "That could work. I'll get my best weaponsmith on it. How much of the orob stone can we have access to?"

"All of it, every last chip the Crown owns. I can even have more mined."

He nodded thoughtfully. "The more we can gather the better."

Amarea turned to one of her aides and gave the instructions for the mines to have as many workers as possible sent to them. "There will be farmers without work because of their failed crops. Have them paid properly, well-fed, well-housed, well-rested. This isn't forced labour — this is a job for the Crown and they will be treated accordingly. Understood?"

"Yes, my Queen," he said as he wrote down her decree. He handed her the pen; she read what he'd written and signed it.

"Send out as many riders as we can spare. I want work to start immediately."

"And what of the issue of The Fold blocking the mines?" Primlect Tiemenin unhelpfully pointed out.

"I'll deal with them personally." She would enjoy it, too.

The aide left and Amarea felt comfort in taking some positive action despite still feeling helpless in the face of their enemy.

Amarea had spent longer with the High General and Primlect than she had wanted, as they quizzed her relentlessly about her magic, what she knew of the black resin and the other forms it took. By the time she had left the hall, she'd wanted to hurt someone, which was unfortunate as that was the moment she saw Ithrael again for the first time. He was walking towards her with Yeela and Errol.

She stopped at the sight of him. Gallia, always alert, managed not to bump into her. She didn't know how to greet him; she wanted to run into his arms but it didn't seem right after their last encounter. But she had missed him, had promised herself during the empty nights she would give him what he wanted; she would give anything to have him back. But she was also still irritable from her long conversation. Instead of making a decision, Amarea stood unmoving in the hallway and waited to see what Ithrael would do.

He approached her without a faltering step and knelt, *knelt*, before her. Something she'd told him never to do.

"My Queen, I have information for you." He handed her papers that had been tucked inside his coat, a coat of Calmayan design by the looks of it.

Instead of responding, Amarea bought herself time. She indicated for him to stand and scanned through the documents, one of which showing how the towers were constructed, others showed how deeply involved the Daylarian Church was and how far the Vulch influence had spread.

"I'll pass these on to the High General." She held up the tower schematics.

"He's here?" Ithrael looked behind her as if his father would materialise.

"He has been since you were taken."

Ithrael nodded as if confirming something to himself. "That's good."

"I can take you to him." She half turned.

"If I may, my Queen, we have much to discuss of our time away." There was almost hesitation in his voice. What did he have to say? She looked at Yeela suspiciously but the young guard gave nothing away.

"Very well, we will all convene in the library where it's ... quieter." And she could keep out irritating aides and people fussing over her.

Niseem, Bassiri and Tristam were fetched and Amarea waited in an uncomfortable silence for them to arrive.

"Where's Saia?" Ithrael asked, genuinely perplexed.

Amarea felt her shoulders tense, and fortunately, Niseem explained what had happened by Waeseah Waters. Amarea was so grateful she could have hugged her.

"And this technique, it's the only way to access our magic?" Amarea didn't like his tone — incredulous, maybe even slightly judgemental, but she was a Queen and she was used to speaking to people who were pissing her off without letting them have any idea of what she was really thinking.

"As far as we've discovered. Saia seems to believe it's the only way, especially seeing as it's the technique used in the Balance." He knew her too well and his expression told her he could tell she was annoyed, so she ignored him and continued. "But we still can't disable the towers."

Yeela turned to Ithrael. "Didn't you manage to put out the smoke?"

Everyone's attention in the room focused intently on Ithrael, and Amarea felt like the air had become tight with their anticipation.

Ithrael was silent as he considered — Amarea could see some of the others becoming impatient. "I held the resin in my hand and it didn't go out until it burned through my skin. I assumed I was smothering it—"

"But we've tried every method to smother the flame," Amarea finished.

"Did you bleed?" Amarea turned in surprise to see a sheepish-looking guard helping Saia into the room. She looked terrible, and Amarea couldn't fathom how she was even standing. Her face was grey and sweat covered her brow. Gallia helped the guard and they led her to a chair. She rested her head back, her eyes closed as though she was struggling to even sit upright. "Did you bleed?" she asked again, her voice weak and only just above a whisper.

"Yes, it burned through my flesh and drew blood."

"The blood of the gods will counter the magic in the towers. I know we thought that by using the needle technique we could somehow destroy them, but I'm afraid it's only the blood of those possessed with the strongest magic who can counter the power of the towers." The effort to explain her thinking caused Saia to lean forward with her head in her hands, her breathing ragged. Everyone around the table seemed to be as concerned as Amarea.

She lifted her head. "Use your blood, my Queen." Saia's eyes rolled and she tipped towards the floor. Bassiri caught her and held her up.

Amarea stood and without a word gently took Saia from Bassiri's arms. Saia wouldn't like to know that the man she loved had carried her feverish form to her sick bed. It surprised Amarea how slight and light her body had become. Could she really have started to fade so quickly?

She carried the unconscious Saia all the way to her room. She laid her in her bed and pulled the covers over her shivering and shaking body.

"Contact the House. Have them look into a way to counter the magic that did this to her." Amarea didn't look up as she commanded Gallia, aware that her tone was cold. But she was Queen and those around her were there to do her bidding, and they would do this.

She knelt before Saia's bed, brushed her hair from her forehead, pulled back her veil and placed a single kiss upon her brow and whispered another prayer to Neesoh.

Ithrael was standing in the doorway alone, his expression grave. Amarea left the room and gave instructions to the guard to have her fetched should anything change. As she left, a young healer curtsied as she entered the room to tend to Saia, but Amarea knew there wasn't much the woman could do.

She walked with Ithrael at her side towards her chambers. Having him beside her was a comfort, somehow. She didn't want to think about it too much; what she really wanted was to be held, to be told it was going to be okay. But she was a Queen and she was not weak. She did not crumble in the face of adversity.

Gallia came towards them from the direction of the library.

"The message has been sent. Niseem and a guard will monitor the machine in shifts."

"I'll be in my chamber — you won't be needed Gallia."

"Yes, my Queen." Amarea was relieved to see that Gallia didn't seem to make an assumption about Ithrael going to her chamber.

Ithrael closed the door behind him when they entered her room, and out of habit Amarea removed her veil, relieved to feel cool air on her face.

"I'm happy to have you back." Her voice was tight; it was all she could manage. She looked up into his face and confessed, "When you were beaten, I felt it. I don't even know how." She didn't know why she chose to mention it.

"You felt it?" He paused, maybe to let it sink in. "Mierdas said there may be some magical connection between us."

She didn't want to add that she'd hardly been able to breathe without him. She couldn't even turn to face him.

He walked around her so that they were face-to-face. "I don't want it to be like this between us. I will take whatever you offer — I don't care if it makes me seem less of a man to stand here and beg, but I will do it, Amay. Being without you …" He took her hand in his. "It's not worth being prideful."

Amarea stood frozen and she saw the man she loved, strong in stature and powerful in resolve, buckle to her whim. She didn't want a man to stand beside her because her position was too important. She had been the prideful one.

"You left me."

"I know. I'm sorry."

"And then you got yourself kidnapped."

"Again, sorry."

"Do you have any idea what that was like for me?" Her voice sounded shrill but she didn't care. She would be as shrill as she wanted to be.

He smiled. "Really? I was the one who was kidnapped."

"Only because you're a stubborn ass and walked out when you didn't get what you wanted! I would have given you anything!" She didn't know why she was fighting with him but she couldn't seem to stop herself. She was hysterical.

She saw his muscles tense, and her entire being honed in on the movement. He was spoiling for a fight, too.

"Well, you refused to give me the one thing I actually wanted!"

"Prideful Maldessan male!"

"Stubborn Maldessan Queen!"

They stared at one another for a moment before Amarea, her blood high, threw the first punch. Ithrael blocked it with his fist but she kicked him in the shin. He winced and retaliated by sweeping her legs out. She anticipated the move and landed on her hands and kicked out, landing a blow on his jaw. He hissed out a breath in shock and glowered at her, then pounced like the snow lion he was and pinned her on her back.

"Did you even miss me?" he said.

"Every fucking day."

"Good."

"I hate you."

"I loathe you."

"You'd better marry me then," she said. He pressed a kiss to her lips.

"You are the darkness to my light," he whispered into her ear, before he bit it.

"You are the darkness to mine," Amarea said with a savage smile; she desired none of his godliness, only his darkness. She began to tear off his clothes.

As they lay naked in each other's arms Amarea confessed, "I cannot face this threat without you by my side." She rested her head on his shoulder.

"Yes you can. There is no force stronger than you, Amay. But I will stand by your side and slay and burn those who would harm our people. I will tie a noose around their necks made from their own entrails and watch them swing." Her heart hammered at his savagery, at the horrors he would commit for her, for their people. His soul was the twin to hers, her magic sang to his, her blood beat in time with his.

She kissed him deeply. "Always and forever."

"Always and forever, my Dark Queen."

He was hers and she was his.

In the darkness of the night, the time of her goddess, Amarea and Ithrael stood before a priestess of the Neesohan Church and made their vows — to stand beside one another, as equals.

The priestess left them alone in the small, draughty chapel. Amarea turned to face her husband. "My king."

"Shouldn't it be consort?"

"Only those who do not understand will think a king is higher than a Queen. You are my king."

He lifted her black veil and kissed her. "I will run my sword through anyone who defers to me instead of you. You are the true Queen, the true ruler. I will be the consort."

"But to me you will always be my king."

He kissed her again. "Would it be wrong for me to have my wife in a place of worship?"

"I think Neesoh would be offended if you didn't."

His answering smile made her heart thunder with anticipation.

In the small chapel with walls decorated the darkest blue, the stars of the night sky carefully painted across the ceilings and walls so that you felt you were standing in the heavens themselves, Ithrael laid Amarea upon the alter and showed her how a king would love his Queen.

Chapter Thirty-Six

AMAREA

Amarea had only just drifted off to sleep, tucked in the arms of her husband, when the knock sounded on the door. Her initial reaction was annoyance but it left her abruptly. It was a time of crisis; sleep and contentment could come later.

Ithrael answered the door for her so she could cover her face, and she shamefully realised she hadn't thought about Saia in hours. What kind of Queen ... what kind of *friend* was she?

"A gentleman has arrived, a Captain Yuto. He says it's urgent," announced the guard at the door.

Ithrael had told Amarea about Yuto and she was just as puzzled and concerned as he was when they learned he was at the palace.

Yuto — black, glossy hair, wide, winning smile — was waiting for them in the hall that had since become the war room. Niseem and Gallia were with him and they both looked as exhausted as she felt.

"I heard from the House you may need some help with a problem." He opened his satchel and removed a leather-bound book. "This may be of use."

"This is what you risked your life for?" Ithrael seemed surprised.

"You'll see why." Yuto opened the book and placed it on the table. Inside were intricate maps of the body with points marked out. "This book is an ancient relic of my people. It is the only understanding we have of magic. The Hyratheans took it on the instruction of the Vulma Supreme Leader."

"The drawings look the same as the ones we found." Niseem took the Jair in, assessing him as Amarea was doing.

Yuto turned a few pages and pointed to the open section of the book. "Three needles — one in her leg, one in the abdomen and one just above the heart. That will restore the balance within her system so she can recover."

"Balance." Amarea muttered the word, feeling as though things were starting to fall into place.

"When you accessed her magic it took too much and drained her. The balance needs restoring," he said.

Just like the elements. Amarea examined the diagram. "I'll do it."

"You don't have to," Niseem said gently.

"It should be me." Although Amarea didn't want to be the one to do any harm to Saia, it had to be her. She was the one who wanted to experiment; she was her Queen. There was no one who had any expertise in the matter. It had to be her.

It wasn't becoming for a Queen to be seen running; the previous regent, Zanzee, had lectured her often enough on the subject. It was the only lesson he had given her that she'd felt was useful — a running Queen caused panic. So she made her way with Ithrael to Saia's room without too much haste, despite her heart and feet demanding that she quicken her pace. Every moment was critical for Saia.

Saia's breathing was shallow and there was a new hollowness to her cheeks. Panic seized Amarea. Why had she not been told earlier that Saia's condition had worsened so dramatically? She knelt before her friend and took her hand in her own. Her pulse was weak. The healer looked at the Queen with pained sympathy on her face. Saia was dying.

Amarea ordered everyone to leave except the healer, although Yuto really seemed to want to help. He may have known what to do better than she did, but she couldn't let him look upon Saia's naked form without Saia's permission.

The healer pulled back the covers and lifted Saia's tunic, and Amarea felt uncomfortable exposing her friend completely but there was no choice. She laid the book on the bed in front of Saia's prostrate body and carefully marked points on her leg, stomach and chest in the places Yuto had told her to put them. He'd instructed her to insert and leave the first needle in the stomach. She was then to insert two more needles, one in the chest and one in the leg, twist both these needles and then remove them. Only then should she remove the central needle.

Amarea clenched her shaking hands into fists. She couldn't allow herself to make a mistake. She tried not to think about Saia as her friend, her *dying* friend. Amarea did what she did best; she separated her emotions from the task she had to perform.

Amarea steadied her breathing and the healer handed her a needle, sterilised by passing it through a flame. It was also still warm, which Yuto had said may assist with the healing. Amarea inserted the first needle in the stomach, twisted it and left it in. Saia's breathing became more rapid but Amarea wouldn't allow herself to panic. A blue hue began to spread from this central point. She inserted the last two needles into Saia's leg and then chest, making sure she twisted them before removing them. Amarea then removed the central needle, and Saia's back arched as the blue hue steadily spread and engulfed her entire body. Amarea began to tremble violently; had she killed her friend?

Saia collapsed back onto the mattress and Amarea quickly pulled down her tunic, giving her some dignity in her final moments. The healer rose and placed her hand upon Saia's brow, placed her ear against her chest. "Her fever has broken. Her breathing is no longer laboured."

"It has?" Amarea took Saia's hand in both her own.

"I've never seen anything like it." The healer looked at her Queen with wonder.

Saia's eyes fluttered and then opened, her gaze somehow finding Amarea's eyes despite her veil. Amarea never understood how she did that. "Did you just see me naked?" Saia's voice was hoarse so the healer carefully held a cup to Saia's lips so that she could take a sip.

"Sorry about that." Amarea laughed through tears of relief. Tears again. She didn't recognise this new emotional version of herself.

"I forgive you."

Amarea rested her forehead on their clasped hands. "You're too generous." She sobbed out another laugh. She felt a hand on her shoulder then and looked up to see Ithrael. He must have heard Saia wake.

"It's good to see you, Saia," he said.

"You, too," she whispered. "I'm sure you have lots to tell."

"Do you remember last night?" he asked, perplexed.

"Last night?" Saia looked to the window where the early light of morning was beginning to leak through the sides of the drapes.

"About our blood?" Amarea reminded her gently.

Niseem and Gallia had also entered the room. "No," Saia said, confused.

"It doesn't matter now. You need to rest," Amarea said in an uncharacteristically soothing voice.

"No, I feel my strength returning." Saia sat up and Amarea noticed that colour was coming back to her cheeks. "Tell me what happened."

"You were feverish," Amarea said. "It's no wonder you don't remember. You told us our blood, Ithrael's and mine, will counter the resin."

"I did?" Saia frowned. "That makes sense but I still don't remember."

"That's okay. We tested it on some smaller pieces we lit." Amarea grimaced at the memory of the sickly-sweet smoke. "One drop from either of us extinguished the flame. We're going to the tower at first light ... Well, now I suppose."

"I'd like to come." The room had now filled with everyone who had been waiting outside and they all protested in unison. "Gods! Calm down, I'll bathe first. Honestly, do you really think I'd go out like this?"

"You need to rest."

"I've rested enough, I feel fine." Saia's voice was firm.

"Well, I don't. I need some sleep. We'll go mid-morning instead," Amarea said.

Saia didn't seem pleased but agreed. They left her to sleep and instructed the healer to make sure Saia rested and under no circumstances allowed to even look in the direction of a book.

Having managed some sleep, Amarea met the others down at the stables. It was there that Ithrael took his father aside and told him their news. She saw the High General firmly grip his son's shoulder in pride. The only time she'd seen true emotion from the High General was the previous night when he'd held his son after his return.

The party mounted their horses and Amarea was surprised to see Saia do it with ease. Ithrael had insisted Yeela, Errol and Yuto join them.

"You came alone, Captain?" Amarea asked Yuto.

"I need my second to keep my sailors in order. They're a rowdy bunch."

"Thank you for bringing something that is sacred to your people to save my friend. She wouldn't have survived without your help."

"If I'm completely honest, I wasn't sure if it would actually work."

Amarea turned in her saddle to look at him. "You know my reputation?"

"Oh, I know it well — you'd have ripped out my throat with those talons of yours if your friend hadn't made it. It was worth the risk though, don't you think?" He didn't seem nervous by her, as some would. Amarea realised that she liked this arrogant Jaien captain.

"It was." Saia rode up beside them. "And thank you."

Amarea couldn't believe the change in Saia. Her hair was shining, her cheeks no longer hollow and there was brightness back in her eyes, eyes that always sparked with intelligence. Amarea realised then how much she'd missed the light in them.

"I'm glad I could be of assistance."

"Would you be willing to allow me to look at your book? It may help us in this fight."

"Actually, I have another motive for coming. I'd heard the best person to interpret the work was a brilliant woman named Saia. It seemed prudent to try and save her."

Saia laughed, delighted by Yuto's charm. "I'd be happy for us to work together."

Amarea rode ahead and let them talk.

She led the party, Ithrael at her side, up the mountainside towards the tower. Silence fell over the group as the sickly smoke began to affect those with magic. Bassiri looked particularly unwell so Amarea insisted he stay further back with Saia, who she didn't want to risk inhaling too much after her ordeal.

Amarea stood before the black tower and pulled out her jewelled dagger. She entered the structure with Ithrael and sliced open her palm. She passed the blade to him and he did the same. They held their bloody hands over the brazier and they both clenched their injured fists and watched as their blood dripped onto the burning resin. Amarea began to feel dizzy, the smoke becoming too much. Nausea rose up in her. But their drops of blood hissed and spat as they fell upon the black, unnatural substance. Amarea couldn't say how long they stood there, their essence slowly putting out the flames, the drops making the blackness turn grey. It's what had happened with the smaller pieces, and once they were fully grey they couldn't be re-lit — the dark magic having left them.

The nausea and dizziness slowly left her and she looked down to see the entire slab of resin had turned grey. She opened her palm and saw that the cut had stopped bleeding and her magic had started to return.

"Well, that was rough." Ithrael pulled her into a side hug as he looked down at the inert mass before them.

"We can't travel the country to do this. We'll have to extract our blood and send it to the sites."

"I agree." He looked up at the tower. "Question is, do we use more blood to dismantle this structure or leave it?"

"I have an idea."

They went outside where Amarea picked up a discarded axe and sliced it across her forearm, coating it in her blood.

"A little extreme?" Ithrael said under his breath.

"Symbolism — you can never be too extreme when it comes to symbolism." She swung the axe back and round and it sliced cleanly through the blackened wood of the tower. Amarea bent down and picked up another axe and threw it to Ithrael. "As my *consort*, you should be seen doing some of the heavy lifting."

Ithrael laughed and sliced his own forearm. Together they hacked at the tower whilst the others looked on until it collapsed before them.

"That was ... interesting to watch," Niseem said as she handed Amarea a cloth to wipe some of the dried blood from her arm.

"Apparently, it was to do with symbolism," Ithrael said as Amarea passed him the cloth.

"Well, no one will question your physical strength, that's for sure." Gallia had crossed her arms, as though she was feeling a little jealous of their show of force.

"If you're lucky, a rumour will start that you simply removed your veil and it collapsed." Yuto had his customary grin as he addressed Amarea.

"I think that was her plan all along." Ithrael turned to Amarea, laughter dancing in his eyes.

"I don't know what you're talking about." However, it had been her plan; she knew how news travelled and she hoped that it would reach the Vulch and they would begin to fear the Dark Queen of Maldessa.

Amarea rode with Ithrael to The Fold. Boothrod stood where he'd greeted her the last time she'd visited.

She spoke without preamble. "We need access to the orob mines."

"It'll cost you." He crossed his arms, his stance wide.

"Boothrod, don't make me slap you in front of your people again. We have a shared enemy. Join us in this fight — not for me, but for your niece, for the people of Maldessa who have done no wrong." The line of his mouth was hard. He was a stubborn ass.

Catarina stepped forward. "I don't know how someone as boneheaded as you became leader," she said to her son as she passed him. She addressed Amarea, "We will join your fight, Queen. We'll even grant safe passage to the mines. I can't promise how things will be after all this is done, but for now, we'll join your fight."

"Mum!" Boothrod's expression was incredulous and Amarea fought hard to hold in her laughter.

"Don't make me cuff you, boy." Amarea and Ithrael left before Boothrod's humiliation became so great he throttled his own mother, and made their way back to the palace.

Amarea and Ithrael sat patiently side by side as a healer used a hollow glass needle, attached to a glass bottle, to extract their blood. The needle had been invented by

Mierdas when he'd realised that cutting Amarea's vein for medicinal bloodletting didn't work because she healed too quickly (she had later come to realise that it wasn't medicinal bloodletting but the Daylarian Church running tests on her magical blood; Mierdas had been furious when he'd found out). The needle was as thin as the glass artisan could make it, but it was still large and Amarea tried not to flinch when it pierced her skin.

After the healer had filled two bottles of blood from each of them they were allowed a break, mainly because they were both beginning to feel a little dizzy.

"I'll have some honey pastries brought to you and some sweet tea," the healer said as she left the room.

Amarea lay down to try to stop the room from swaying. "So, my king, what's next? We've found a way to defeat the towers, we're mining for more orob stones and developing weapons we hope will counter their own, but what do we do now? I hate waiting."

"Now, my Queen, we continue to explore this needle technique to access our magic and we train, as we have always done, but in a different discipline." He lay down next to her. "But maybe when there's actually some blood in my veins."

Amarea shuffled closer to him. "I would drain every last drop of my blood if it were to save my people," she said quietly into his neck.

"I know you would, but I won't let you sacrifice yourself. I'm your husband now, and I have a say in these things."

"Oh, really? Is that how it's going to be?"

"Me not letting you die? Yes, that's how it's going to be."

Amarea stilled. "I'd forgotten that our life forces are tied now, since our union."

"We don't know that for sure. It's an ancient tale." He kissed her veiled nose. "But my life is nothing without you, and so I'm okay with it."

"I'm not sure I'm okay with dying if you get killed on the battlefield." She wasn't sure if he could hear the smile in her voice.

"Oh, my Dark Queen, you're so romantic." He laughed as he kissed her shrouded mouth. "I'm a lucky man to have such a compassionate wife."

"Wife?"

Amarea broke away from Ithrael and looked to the doorway where Niseem was carrying a tray of honey pastries and sweet tea. She put the tray down and placed her hands on her hips. "*Wife?*"

"So ... there's something I need to tell you ..." Amarea felt incredibly sheepish under Niseem's glare.

"You two got married and didn't tell me? Or *invite* me?" Amarea understood Niseem's anger; she was Amarea's closest friend.

"It was a spur of the moment decision." But Amarea knew that wasn't a good enough excuse.

Niseem glared at them and Ithrael cleared his throat. "No one else was invited, except the priestess who performed the ceremony."

Niseem's glower didn't waver. "Well, there'll have to be a proper announcement. And a party."

"We're about to enter into a war!" Amarea protested.

"The people need this." Niseem's eyes lit up. "Once the towers are down we can return triumphantly to Saffiere and have a royal wedding. The people will go crazy for it."

Amarea buried her head in Ithrael's chest. "Make her stop."

"If you'd invited me in the first place then it wouldn't have come to this," Niseem said haughtily. She left the room and Amarea sat up and grabbed two small pastries, passing one to Ithrael.

"I think I fear Niseem more than the Vulma Supreme Leader," Amarea said with a hint of complaint.

"The others won't be happy either," Ithrael said as he popped the pastry into his mouth.

"It's just a wedding, what's the big deal?"

Ithrael choked on his food. "Thanks for making me feel so incredibly special. And for nearly killing me repeatedly with your refusal for 'just a wedding'."

Amarea pulled back her veil and kissed him. "I didn't want anyone else there. It was about us, no one else. I'm just uncomfortable with this spectacle."

He cupped her face in his hand. "She's right, though. A royal wedding after it appears we've had a victory will really boost morale." He brushed his thumb across her lips and made a low sound of pleasure.

"You don't have enough blood in your body for that."

"Don't be so sure."

Amarea rolled her eyes. "Eat and drink first."

"My wife, such a nag."

Amarea snorted and shoved another pastry into his mouth.

Chapter Thirty-Seven

YUTO

Yuto examined the book Saia had brought to him.

"There's not much here. I'm surprised you were able to discover what you did."

"We took a risk," Saia said nonchalantly, her hair falling over one eye. She seemed annoyed by this and re-tied her hair with a thin leather strip. He thought he'd like to see her with her hair down, but there was something about the way she was practical and annoyed by the existence of her hair that he liked.

"Pretty big risk." He rested his head on his hand and took her in. "Didn't you think it could go wrong?"

"For my Queen? No, she's too powerful. I don't think she even realises how much." As she spoke, she seemed far away, as if she were seeing something. He'd heard she'd spoken a prophecy that day; was she seeing it again? "As for myself, it was worth the risk. I had to know how it felt. It seemed only right that I experience it too." She looked at him then, truly looked at him, and he felt unsettled, as though she could see something deep within him. "You have magic as well. Not any I recognise though."

"Jaien magic comes from the Jai, who emerged from the sea and gifted our small island with his powers."

"It sits differently to the magic here. I suppose the best way to describe it is that it's more fluid."

He narrowed his eyes at her. "So you can see other people's magic?"

"Apparently so. It's new and a little ... distracting." She looked at him then shook her head as if to clear away what she was seeing.

"Fascinating. You must have awoken some part of your ability when you nearly killed yourself." He watched her expression change to one of surprise and wondered who this incredible, unassuming woman was. He'd never met anyone more fascinating, aside from her Queen, but he had no interest in a woman who could bewitch him.

"Well, hopefully it'll be of use." She pulled her chair close to his and lifted the precious ancient Jaien tome towards them. "Now, tell me what you know about the contents of this book."

"They are the teachings of Jai, carefully recorded and added to over time. The beginning is the knowledge of magic he shared with us, and from there it's our own exploration into it. Although ... some of it has never been deciphered."

He could tell her interest was piqued. "Which parts?"

"The darker parts, where you can shatter another's magic ... or steal it."

She looked at him intently then, and for the first time he knew she saw him as the thief Ithrael had found in the Hyrathean cells. Nevertheless, she didn't say anything more; instead, she placed her hands on the ancient tome then carefully, reverently, opened the book, her hand trembling slightly as she touched the first page. "I can feel some of his magic in this book."

"His teachings were that there is magic in all of us but only a small amount. When the gods arrived, they brought pure magic within their beings and they shared it with us. He made our seas abundant, our shipbuilders skilled beyond any others, and gave our sailors the ability to tackle the harshest waters, to swim underwater for a great length, at speed, even against a current. He gifted everyone equally." He opened to a page that had a depiction of Jai and a blue mist engulfing the people around him. "But what the book doesn't say, but it's in our history, is that he didn't account for the greed of man. And there was a war amongst my people as only the elite wanted the gift of a god. They felt only they deserved it." Yuto couldn't look at her as he told their shameful history. "The rich slaughtered the poor, and only those within the royal family could reproduce magic with magic. Everyone else had to 'dilute' the seed with people of non-magic blood." He looked up and her keen expression told him he had revealed too much to someone with such a sharp intellect.

"And that practice continued, didn't it?"

"Yes."

"Does Ithrael know? Does anyone?"

"That I'm dishonoured? They don't need to know." He felt oddly embarrassed: not that he was dishonoured but that she knew him to be a prince. Somehow, he didn't want her to see him that way.

She didn't seem affected by his admission but instead focused on the book again. "And what did your people discover about accessing magic, about needling?"

He was surprised she didn't ask why he was dishonoured. He'd been ready to tell her, but he appreciated that she didn't ask. "The royal family had the original texts scoured for clues and discovered the meridians in the body were important to accessing the magic and that these could be 'triggered' with a needle. The needle is like turning a key to the magic — it taps into it and releases the power. Each person's magic is personal to them, which is why you had a different reaction than your Queen and Bassiri. You have a lot, you must do, but the power of what you saw drained you. Draining, they discovered, is a huge risk when needling."

"And that's why you have to keep a balance?"

"Exactly." He turned the pages to show her the diagrams of the human body. "Every point has a counterpoint. When you access your energy directly, you need to anchor it with another point." He indicated a point on the opposite shoulder on the picture.

She examined the page closely. "This point here?"

"The heart point."

"What does it mean when it says governing point?"

Yuto ran his hand through his hair. "There's a lot of disagreement about the governing point. There is no anchor to it — it is said to be where the purest magic is held and if accessed it will spill the life force from someone and they will die."

"And their magic? Where does it go?"

"No one knows. It's always been deemed too dangerous to be attempted." He noticed she had paled slightly.

"What is it?"

"I need you to promise me something." She looked at him with such open pain that he would have promised her anything.

"Of course."

"Do not speak of the governing point to anyone, especially not to my Queen or Ithrael."

He paused as he took in her words. "What did you see in your prophecy?"

"A woman who would give anything, everything, to save her people."

Realisation dawning on him, he looked at the governing point, the mark over the heart, and understood. Saia had foreseen her Queen dying to save her people.

Chapter Thirty-Eight

ITHRAEL

Ithrael and Amarea were alone by the edge of the lake. She'd asked to be free of her veil, and no one else seemed to want to be near them when they trained with their magic and so she stood with her face exposed and looked as though the touch of the cold air upon her cheeks was the greatest pleasure in the world. He loved seeing her like this, his wife.

He examined the paper Saia had given him with written instructions and a drawing of where the points they should try were on the body. He opened the box of needles and held them out to Amarea.

"Too afraid to go first?"

"I was being a gentleman."

"Really? I'm pretty sure what you just did with me wasn't very gentlemanly." He loved her feral smile. He loved to look upon her without the veil; she really was breathtaking, although he knew she resented her beauty, the power it had, and he understood that. She deserved to be seen for who she was, not for the mask she had to wear, the brand of the Dark Queen that she now bore. But she bore it well, like a true ruler: a great ruler.

"What does the magic feel like?"

"Like waking up to yourself for the first time." He saw excitement in her eyes then, almost a need to access the power within. It gave him pause. Could they be treading down a dangerous path towards something that would become a drug to them, an addiction? He knew that even if they were, they couldn't stop. They didn't have a choice.

"We should do the points to ourselves, right? Otherwise we can't use them when needed," she said as she pulled back her tunic, which he couldn't help be distracted by.

"Yes, and I think we need to make the markings permanent. We can't waste time measuring out the points each time." He placed a dot on her shoulder and then her wrist.

"Good idea. Let's make sure we know which points are worth using first, though." She held up her needles to him. "Ready?"

"Ready."

They both faced the water and inserted the first needle into their shoulder points. He felt both grounded and alive with energy at the same time, like something was building inside him. Amarea looked over at him and nodded once. He inserted the second needle into his wrist and twisted. A golden ball of fiery energy burst from the point, rose into the sky and then plummeted into the water with a hiss of steam. He was too distracted by his own experience to fully take in the arcing bolt of blue crackling energy that Amarea emitted.

"Holy fucking Gods." He stared out at the water. He'd never felt so alive. He removed the needle from his shoulder and placed it in the box for used needles. The healer had been very strict with them about reusing needles. Apparently, it wasn't sanitary and she needed to place them in a special fluid before they could re-use them. He'd decided not to point out that as descendants of a god and goddess, they probably didn't need to worry about such things, but they'd agreed to her instructions.

Amarea's eyes were burning bright with the use of her power. There was a luminous blue hue to them he'd never seen before. It was intoxicating and he wanted to have her right there. He could tell she felt the same but they held themselves back; there would be people watching from the castle and it would be inappropriate for their Queen and her consort to start tearing each other's clothes off in front of them.

His attention snagged on two figures approaching so he pulled himself together and waited. Yuto and Saia arrived deep in conversation, barely aware they had reached them.

Saia looked at them first. "We've been reading the book and watching you and, well, we think we've figured out a way for you to direct the magic."

"Instead of it just erupting out? That would be useful, to have some control." Ithrael noticed then that Amarea had replaced her veil as she kept her back to Yuto and Saia.

"So, if you clench your left fist before you put the needle in, it will hold the energy that's generated. Opening up your palm should release it. That way you can aim at a target." As Saia spoke, Yuto in his excitement was exuding as much energy as Ithrael had just released onto the lake.

"You'll need a target," Yuto said, looking around. He pointed to a cluster of rocks. "How about those?"

"Sure." Amarea took two clean needles from the wooden box and handed them to Ithrael.

"After you," he offered and moved aside so she was opposite the largest boulder. "And you two should probably stand further back," Ithrael said over his shoulder.

Yuto and Saia stepped back a couple of paces but didn't move any farther. *Well, it's their limbs they're risking.*

Amarea pierced her shoulder and then her forearm, her fist clenched, and she twisted and removed the needle. He saw the blue light shooting down her arm and fill her curled hand until the light turned from blue to white. He could tell she was straining against the power. When no more light filled her closed palm, she raised her arm and aimed at the boulder. She opened her hand in a quick action and the magic she'd held there fired out as a white-and-blue crackling ball of power that moved faster than any crossbow bolt. It hit the boulder dead in its centre and the stone exploded instantly. Small pieces of rock rained down on them, but it had mostly become a fine dust. She'd completely obliterated it.

Ithrael turned to Amarea, wonder on his face. "Handy trick."

She was breathing fast, from exhilaration he imagined. "One to show off at our wedding ceremony?"

"It'll certainly impress the crowds," he said with a smile as he inserted the anchor needle into his shoulder and then turned to face the next biggest boulder. He closed his fist and inserted, twisted, and removed the second needle. He could feel the magic rushing through his body and down his arm, into his closed hand. He watched as the blue light turned golden as it seemed to fill his hand with raw magic. Golden illumination for the man who embodied Daylar, God of the Light. He strained against the building power, holding it back, feeling its need to escape. When he no longer felt the power rushing to his palm, he raised his arm and released the golden ball of energy. It hit the boulder but instead of an explosion, this time the rock glowed red and began to collapse, molten.

"Incredible — it's just like the liquid fire from the volcano on the island of Teeoh." Yuto stepped closer to the oozing mass of super-heated rock.

"It doesn't have quite the same impact as an explosion, though." Ithrael removed the needle from his shoulder and watched the rock melt.

"But it's super-heated. This could be incredibly useful against an army." Saia was standing near the orange-and-red moving mass crusted with black. "Honestly, it's fascinating how your magic manifests differently. It's a good thing, too — it makes it harder for the enemy to defend against."

"You could liquefy half the Vulma Supreme Leader's army whilst your Queen explodes the other half," Yuto exclaimed whilst shaking his head in disbelief, although he looked like he was in the presence of the greatest moment of his life.

"I don't know how I feel about liquefying people …"

"Also, I don't think you have the range, sorry my love." Amarea laughed when she saw Ithrael's reaction to her thinking he didn't have the power to liquefy half an army. She knew he didn't accept any kind of inadequacy.

"Do you think our power could be effective against their dark armour?" Amarea asked Saia.

Saia thought for a moment. "We should try it on the resin first. We'd need some dark armour to be able to test it properly. This is the best we can do for now."

Gallia and Niseem brought from the palace what little resin they had left from Bassiri and Tristam's visit to the site of the old abbey.

"Is there anything in the book which says how we can reduce the amount of power we use? I can't exactly throw a ball of energy at this tiny sliver of resin," Amarea said.

"Oh, yes, I think I saw something …" Yuto sat down on the ground and opened the book in his lap. He looked like an excited schoolboy. "Here it is." He turned the book to show Saia, who carefully read the instructions.

"Okay, so you put the anchor needle in the point just below your thumb on the side of your wrist …" She placed a dot on Amarea's wrist with a pen. "And then at the tip of your index finger, and your magic should release from there. Once you remove the needle you can press it against your thumb to hold it back and then extend it when you want to release." Saia's explanation was clear and precise. She drew the same points on Ithrael.

Said placed two pieces of resin side by side on a flat rock, and together Ithrael and Amarea performed the process as Saia had described. Their magic didn't come out as a ball of energy this time; instead, it was a short stream of power. A small area on the rock around the resin turned red and molten when Ithrael used his power on it, but the resin was left unaffected. Amarea's piece of resin was left unchanged as well.

"Well, at least we can keep draining our blood to take down the towers. That's something I suppose." Amarea sounded disappointed and so Ithrael reached out and took her hand in his.

"We already know what works on the resin. The weapons and armour may be different," he said.

"And I'm confident that the weapons we're creating will pierce their dark armour," Saia added.

"Then what use is this magic of ours if we can't use it in the fight against our enemy?" Amarea rolled her shoulders. Ithrael could tell she was feeling weighed down by everything and gently squeezed her hand.

"I do have one idea," Yuto said.

Saia spun to face him. "No."

Everyone seemed equally surprised by the vehemence in Saia's voice. He held up his hands and seemed to say something to her with his eyes but Saia was still tense.

"You know how the elemental balance is kept by using the staffs?"

Saia suddenly seemed curious and no longer wary. "Yes?"

"So there's magic in the ground, magic that can be tapped into. What if Queen Amarea and Ithrael draw from that and have it work for them?" There was fire in Yuto's eyes as he explained his idea to Saia.

Saia bit her lip in concentration. "But what of the balance?"

"Can't your House take care of that? It's not like they've been of much use otherwise."

Amarea cleared her throat in warning and Yuto had the good sense to look apologetic for speaking ill of the mages.

"It could be possible." Saia turned to Amarea, a hopeful expression on her face. "If you want to try it?"

"We need to speak to Mierdas first. I don't want to disrupt the balance any more. Our people's livelihoods have been affected enough. But if he thinks there's a way to anchor the power, then yes, we should try it."

Amarea looked to Ithrael, and he knew she was checking with him, making sure he agreed. He nodded once and her chin lifted. "We'll contact Mierdas immediately."

That evening, Ithrael and Amarea sat together as a healer used a needle dipped in special ink to tattoo small starbursts on the points on their skin where they were to insert the needles. The technique was the same as the one used by those in The Fold to tattoo their heads. The effect was that of a small constellation across their skin. As they went to bed that night, Ithrael made sure to kiss every star that covered his wife's skin.

Chapter Thirty-Nine

AMAREA

The next morning, Amarea stood at Leonius' bedside. Lisette looked like she hadn't slept since they'd returned. Worry creased her young face, and Amarea wanted to reach out and smooth the worry away.

Mierdas had agreed to look into how they could anchor the magic they wanted to try, and so whilst they waited, Saia and Yuto had begun to look into how to help Leonius. They were now talking in hushed voices as a healer turned Leonius onto his side. He was unable to even sit up. All he could do was lie motionless in his bed. It was heartbreaking to see; he'd always been so light on his feet, so graceful, like his sister.

Yuto and Saia seemed to have come to some kind of agreement about how to proceed. Carefully, Saia marked out points across Leonius' back and then stepped back, and Amarea was surprised to see that Yuto was to be the one to use the needles. Not only that but he removed two from the inside pocket of his jacket. They weren't like the ordinary sewing pins and needles Amarea had been using. These were slightly larger, more ornate.

"What are those?" she asked.

"These are needles with an orob core. They'll be more effective," Yuto said.

"They're Jair?"

"We still practice the ancient technique — it wasn't lost to our island." Amarea found this fascinating, that her own country could have lost this skill and his hadn't. "They'll work better, particularly if someone doesn't have a lot of magic already."

Amarea watched intently as Yuto ran the needles through a naked flame and then quickly and deftly needled Leonius' back. Small areas of blue light spread and then faded as he worked. Higher up Leonius' back, the light spread but at the bottom of his spine, the light faded quickly. Yuto dropped the needles in a clear liquid the healer had brought him. Amarea watched captivated as the blue light slowly receded from the top of Leonius' back.

The healer gently turned Leonius onto his back once again.

Lisette looked at him expectantly. "Anything?"

He lay there frowning. "I felt a tingling." His eyes went to his hands and then he raised his head slightly. Lisette's hands went to her mouth and her eyes filled with tears as she watched him slowly begin to move his fingers.

"Take it slowly." Yuto spoke gently. "The damage to your lower spine was extensive. I don't think the magic was able to heal it, I'm afraid."

Leonius looked up at Yuto and smiled. "I can feel my hands."

Yuto smiled back at him. "That's good. I'm hoping you'll at least be able to sit up on your own. Just be patient as your body heals."

"I will." His head rested back on the pillow but the smile didn't leave his face.

"There is a man in Jaien who was unable to walk and so a chair with wheels was built for him so he could move around. I can draw the design up." He turned to Amarea for confirmation.

"I will make sure it gets built as quickly as possible," she assured the twins. Lisette rushed to her then and hugged her. Amarea was so surprised that it took her a moment to reciprocate. "You will both be taken care of, I promise you that. You will always have a home here." In that moment, Lisette was once again the young orphaned Vulch girl Amarea had taken in, not the young woman who was skilled at slipping into the shadows. Amarea didn't like to think too hard over decisions that were ugly, but this one haunted her. Particularly now. She'd ensure that if anything happened to her in the coming war, they would want for nothing. It was the very least she could do.

"My Queen." Leonius turned his head slowly to look at her. "We did it for you, for the queendom. We made the choice and we'd do it again. Well, I would if I could."

Lisette stepped back and wiped her eyes with the backs of her hands. "We saw what was there. We will always fight for you, our Queen."

Amarea didn't know what to say. She wanted them to blame her for Leonius' injuries, for them to hate her, anything but forgive her. She didn't know what to do with forgiveness.

"I am your Queen, I used you both ill. I will never be able to repay you but I won't have you involved in any of this any more."

Lisette frowned. "But my Queen, I want to try the needles, and so does Leonius. We may be able to help."

"You will not be involved and that is the end of it."

Lisette looked like she'd been slapped but bowed her head. "Yes, my Queen."

Mierdas' instructions came through as Amarea and Ithrael were giving up further bottles of their blood. Niseem brought them the news.

"He said that each palace has spare rods in the mages' workroom and to try and spear three into the ground in the shape of a triangle. That should work as an anchor."

"Seems simple enough," Amarea remarked as she watched her blood slowly pouring out of her vein. It was oddly mesmerising, that or they'd already taken too much and she was getting ready to pass out.

"Yuto thinks he knows which points to needle to access the magic." Niseem stepped forward and placed her hand under Amarea's elbow. She hadn't realised she was swaying. "I think you've given enough for today," Niseem said gently to a panicked-looking healer who quickly removed the glass needle from both Amarea and Ithrael, who was faring a little better. "But maybe we shouldn't attempt anything new until tomorrow." She handed Amarea a cup of sweet tea as Ithrael helped steady her.

"Probably for the best."

By morning, Amarea felt fully restored and the first bottles of their blood had been delivered to the nearest tower. They had successfully neutralised the black magic that was billowing noxious smoke. Only two more sessions and they should have collected enough to neutralise the rest of the towers.

"Do you think we should collect some more bottles of blood, as spares?" Amarea asked Ithrael as she lay naked in his arms.

He ran his hand along her bare back lazily. "Yes, although I'm doing it reluctantly. It took me far too long to restore enough blood to my system to be able to bed my wife."

"Sometimes when you speak you sound like a complete arse." She kissed his chest and slipped out from under his arm. She walked to their bathing room, knowing he was watching her, wanting her again. And knowing he was thinking of her in that way excited her. It wasn't long before he joined her and they slipped into the bathing pool together to enjoy each other's bodies for the second time that morning.

Back out at the lake, Yuto was hammering the large metal stakes used by the mages into the ground. He'd used string to measure out the triangle so it was perfectly symmetrical.

"One point has to be facing north," he said to the group, which consisted of nearly everyone close to the Queen and unfortunately her half-brother Aiden, too. She contemplated making him test out his magic but she knew it was too cruel; he was a weak little thing.

"Saia, is it safe for all these people to be here?" Amarea wasn't sure if she was concerned for their safety or for looking a fool if it went wrong, or didn't work. Her reputation was important as Queen, even in front of those within her inner circle and council.

"I'll make sure they stand back, and whichever direction you face will be the direction of the ... well, the magic." Saia's hesitant smile wasn't encouraging. "Now with this, you have to open up your channels to receive the magic so you can become one with it, but two people will need to needle you at the same time for it to work."

"Okay." Amarea could feel Ithrael's solid presence behind her; she wanted to lean into him, to feel reassured. But she had to be strong. She couldn't show weakness at a time like this.

She stood in the centre of the triangle created by Yuto and held her arms out, palms facing up. Saia marked each of her wrists with a single point.

"We'll use standard needles today, just to be safe," Yuto said as he handed Saia hers. "Once we remove the needles you need to place your palms on the ground and focus on the magic there, and draw it up. I'm hoping it'll be instinctual because nothing in the writing of the ancients spoke of how to wield the magic." He rubbed the back of his neck, clearly feeling a little uncomfortable that they didn't have a full set of guidelines on what she was about to do.

Amarea looked back at Ithrael. He stood stoic, not once suggesting he should be the one to take the risk. It was one of the things she loved most about him. Saia placed her hand under the back of Amarea's hand and she turned back to see the worry in her eyes.

"Okay, I'm ready." She focused on not allowing her hands to tremble, on not letting her apprehension show. She was about to draw upon something she knew nothing about. She didn't even understand her own magic let alone the power that ran through her land. In perfectly timed movements, Yuto and Saia inserted, twisted and removed the needles. Amarea didn't feel the rush of energy that she'd felt before, and instead her body felt alive with it. It was eager, waiting. The others stepped back as she knelt to the ground and placed her bare palms to the earth.

At first there was nothing, and so in her mind she asked for Neesoh's guidance. That's when she felt it, a stirring. She focused on the feeling and dug her nails into the earth and she spoke to it. She told the earth of their need, of the darkness that had descended on their land. And the currents that lay beneath her answered. They were tentative, unsure. She coaxed them forward, asking for her to try, to see if they could defeat this dark enemy together. Slowly the power rose up and into her fingertips. She drank it in, but not too much: she didn't want to frighten it away. This was a gift, a chance. She had to be careful, be respectful.

When she felt like she had taken enough, she stood and she knew what to do: maybe because the power she had borrowed spoke to her, maybe because some part of her already understood the magic she bore. She raised her arms up, her hands splayed, and released the well of energy within her. A web of power burst from her palms, creating a net of energy in the sky, alive and deadly. It hung suspended, dancing in the air that it was part of, this magic of the elements. She snapped her right hand into a fist and it contracted in on itself and exploded in mid-air. It seemed like a cheap parlour trick, but Amarea understood. This borrowed power could lay waste to an army.

Chapter Forty

YEELA

Yeela watched in awe at the wall of pure magical energy that Queen Amarea created before her, and she did it as if it was hardly any effort at all. She was pleased to have been put on temporary guard duty supporting Gallia as it meant she was able to witness magic.

"There's no way we'll lose this war now." She spoke quietly, not wanting to break the spell of the moment she was witnessing.

"Don't be so sure. She may be powerful but she's just one person."

Yeela thought this was a typically pessimistic comment from Errol. "What about the captain? He has almost as much magic as the Queen."

"Maybe, but two powerful people against an army built on dark magic?"

She didn't appreciate the look he gave her; it was almost patronising, which was unlike him. "What's got you rattled?"

"The more we find out ... the more I realise what this coming war will take."

"It may not even come to war." But even as she said it, Yeela knew it to be untrue. War was what the Vulma Supreme Leader was seeking. There was no turning away from it.

"Are you going to try it?" he asked.

"Saia wouldn't have asked if she didn't think it was safe."

He looked down at his feet, that scowl back on his face. "You don't know what will happen."

"She says it enhances the magic you already have."

"And you have good instincts."

She supposed he was implying that her instincts were a magical gift that could become more finely tuned. "Besides, it healed your shoulder, didn't it? That's a good thing."

"That's medicinal though. That's a practice still used in Jaien. I'm not sure all this experimenting is safe."

She didn't understand his reticence over using this new technique to fight their enemy. "It could help. Anything I can do to help, I'll do it." Her voice was firm; she was feeling irritated by him. Why was he questioning her? He'd never done that before. "What is it about this that bothers you so much?"

"It's so unknown. We don't know how to control it or the repercussions of such magic — look what those mass murders created. Such things shouldn't be tampered with." He was serious, and was she reading him right? Was he concerned for her safety?

"But in times of great darkness we have to fight with whatever we have." She didn't know why it was so important for him to see things the same way as she did, but it was. She needed him to see that what their Queen was doing was the only way and the right way.

"And what if that's a darkness in itself?" he countered.

"It's all about intention. With the right intention, the darkness will be kept at bay. You have to believe that."

He looked over at the empty space where the Queen had just made the magic implode. "Can we ever really know another's true intention?"

Fury rose in Yeela's heart. "Never question her," she said harshly. "She is our Queen. My sister wouldn't stand by her side if her desires were anything but for the good of our people."

Yeela stormed away and felt so irritated that her throat felt thick with emotion. How could anyone ever question Queen Amarea's intention? How did he not see she always put Maldessa first and so what if her methods were unorthodox? Sometimes a leader had to make difficult choices for the greater good.

Yeela approached Saia. "I want to learn to use the magic that I have."

"I'm going to be teaching some others in the Guard's training grounds. I'll see you there at high noon."

Yeela turned and walked back to the winter palace and didn't even glance at Errol.

Yeela trained with the others every day until it was time for them to return to Saffiere. Every one of the towers had been dismantled, and rumours of the Queen and Ithrael's powers spread rapidly throughout the queendom.

As they were about to set out for Saffiere, Gallia approached Yeela. "I've promoted you and Errol to the Queen's Guard." Yeela beamed — no more freezing, stinking docks. She was finally the soldier she wanted to be. "You've both shown tremendous skill by assisting the return of the Queen's consort. I hope you'll both continue to put our Queen and her consort first at all times."

"Without even a moment's hesitation."

Gallia smiled at her and then relaxed her shoulders. "Niseem nearly throttled me when I told her about your promotion."

"My father …"

Gallia grimaced. "I'll leave that conversation to you."

"Does he even have to know?"

Gallia elbowed her. "You're supposed to be a brave protector of our glorious Queen."

"There's bravery and then there's facing my father."

Gallia snorted. "Rather you than me."

She left her to saddle her horse, the smile never leaving Yeela's face, until she saw Errol. She'd been avoiding him since she'd last spoken to him at the lake. And now he was to protect their Queen when he doubted her.

"Yeela," he said, his tone tentative as he helped buckle the straps on her saddle. "You know our Queen and country come first for me, always."

"When it comes to protecting her, would you hesitate because of your distrust of magic?" Her gaze was fierce, challenging.

He looked taken aback. "Never. My issue with magic is nothing to do with my duty."

"I hope so Errol, I really hope so." She mounted her horse smoothly and rode out to the rear of the carriage that the Queen, Ithrael, Saia and Yuto would be travelling in so they could continue to discuss and investigate the needling techniques. She sat tall on her mount and didn't turn when Errol's horse stopped next to hers. She was on duty now. The time for difficult conversations was over.

Once they had passed the mountains and were heading towards Saffiere, Yeela began to see the devastation the poisonous smoke had caused. Fields contained blackened, rotted crops. Farmers, hoping to start anew, had even cleared some of them. The landscape was barren, scarred. It made her feel sick to see the destruction the Vulch had already caused, that they would target innocent people just so they could gain power. She turned to Errol and saw the same horror in his eyes. She hoped that now he would begin to accept the need for magic, but if he didn't it was no concern of hers. She would do whatever she had to when it came to fighting for her home.

People had filled the streets by the time they entered the city. The Queen had ensured everyone was still being fed, despite the crop failings. She'd managed to strike up trade deals for food imports that would keep her people from hunger until they could replant. All of this was at a cost to herself, to her treasury. Yeela knew the Queen had wealth beyond imagining, but with feeding her people and having to finance new weaponry, she would surely deplete her treasury greatly. She felt honoured to ride at the side of her carriage as the people cheered their returning Queen. They still whispered of her darkness, Yeela knew that, but now they whispered of it with awe. Their Queen was powerful, unbreakable. She would provide; she would protect. She would use that dark power to defeat their enemy.

The palace was in chaos when they finally made it inside the walls. People were running around making frantic preparations for the ceremony that would take place the following day. Yeela recognised the Lead Council from Calmaya as one of the dignitaries arriving for the celebration. She didn't stop inside the palace to see the decorations being erected in the great hall; instead, she went straight to the barracks where she was to report to Commander Denmer and receive her new orders. The excitement in the city and the pride in her new position had Yeela's heart racing as she walked alongside Errol. She wanted to turn and hug him, to squeeze out some of the energy that was coursing through her, but she managed to hold herself back.

The commander instructed them that because of the recommendation from the consort himself, they would both be part of the Queen and her consort's personal guard during the celebration. It was a great honour to receive such a position and Yeela couldn't help the flush that rose in her cheeks when the commander delivered the news.

She spent the rest of the day running around, carrying out errands given to her by Gallia — to check all the windows were locked in the bedrooms for dignitaries, to ensure that there was a guard stationed at each door, to clean the buttons on her uniform ("They have to shine, Yeela!"), to deliver messages and to make sure she sharpened her blades. By the time evening fell, she was too exhausted to introduce herself to her new roommates and climbed into her bed and fell straight to sleep.

The morning of the ceremony was much the same and she had to rush to dress in her ceremonial uniform, her fingers trembling as she did up the buttons. She wasn't sure why, but she felt on edge. The feeling didn't leave her as she made her way to the grand hall where Gallia was to brief them.

She stood at the back of the group of guards, the worry not leaving her. Saia entered the room, talking with Niseem. Yeela kept her eyes on her, hoping to draw her attention. Eventually she did. Saia read her mood instantly and leaned forward to whisper in Gallia's ear, interrupting her. Gallia's eyebrows rose a fraction.

"Yeela, you're needed. Please go with Saia and then report back to me here," Gallia ordered.

Yeela silently followed Saia into the Queen's study. "What is it?" Saia asked, concerned.

"I don't know ... *something*."

Saia opened a drawer in the Queen's desk and pulled out the small wooden box that the Queen used to keep her needles in. "Are you sure?"

"Something is going to happen," Yeela said. Saia hesitated and Yeela's instincts screamed at her. "If you try it again you'll die," she said firmly, despite speaking to a member of Queen's inner circle.

"I know." Saia looked down at the box and took a deep breath. "Unfortunately I'm unable to disobey our Queen." Her smile was rueful.

"But we know that the needles don't drain me. I'm not at risk and maybe ... maybe I can help," Yeela said and held out her hand. Saia took a small velvet pouch from her pocket and emptied some needles into it and then tied it shut.

"Each needling should last a couple of hours — I'll do one now. Are you okay to do the others yourself?"

"I'll explain to Gallia. She'll allow me to slip away."

"Good. Ready?"

Yeela nodded and unbuttoned part of her uniform so Saia could mark and then insert the needle into the anchor point. Yeela held out her left arm and Saia triggered Yeela's magic. The rush of tingling warmth that engulfed her body was like nothing else she'd ever felt. She closed her eyes as her senses shifted, sharpening. She was getting used to it now and better at reading the signs that her naturally acute instincts sent her when she was under the influence of her magic.

"Any idea yet?"

"The air, it tastes different ..." Yeela's heart squeezed in her chest. "It tastes sweet."

"I'll tell the Queen." There was an edge of panic in Saia's voice.

Yeela felt fear then, true fear. Whatever was coming was laced with dark magic. She returned to the hall, her senses tingling at every movement and every sound. Something was coming. Something terrible.

Despite her feeling of foreboding, the wedding ceremony went smoothly. The Queen entered in a sleeveless gown of pure black, the shoulders structured to give them a sharp, straight edge. There was a high collar at the back that dipped as it came around the front, a cinched-in waist, a rippling skirt that pooled behind her. The front was cut low, with gold leaves edging the *v* and spreading over the shoulders. She wore her crown and only a gold mask to hide her face. There was something terrifying, magnificent, otherworldly about her Queen. She walked as though she were gliding, her head held high. Pieces of gold leaf adorned her arms, heavy bangles covered her wrists, a ring on every finger and, as always, each nail was tipped with a golden claw.

Queen Amarea stood by her throne and then Ithrael entered. He wore a uniform similar to the formal guard one, but it was pure white with gold plating in places. His hair was plaited down the centre and in smaller braids across the sides. The central plait was long and hung down the middle of his back. Despite it being a wedding ceremony, he wore his great sword across his back. He reached the platform where Queen Amarea stood and knelt, bowing his head. The High Priestess of the

Neesohan Church stood next to the Queen and placed Ithrael's hand in Amarea's. She performed a blessing and the youngest priestess from the Church brought forth the crown that belonged to the late king. There was a low murmur throughout the entire throne room as people came to understand the significance of the Queen giving her consort a king's crown.

Once the crown was upon his head, he stood by his Queen's side and the High Priestess proclaimed their union blessed before the goddess. A cheer erupted in the room and Yeela's stomach twisted. Something had been set into motion.

Her eyes scanned the room as her skin prickled. There was something amiss within the room; she just had to find it.

"What is it?" Errol said to her, so quietly no one else could hear.

"Something ... something dark." She wished she knew another way to explain it, but her instincts couldn't tell her what it was she was sensing. Errol began to scan the room as well but Yeela could already feel her magic waning. "I'll be right back."

"Where are you—"

She'd gone before he could finish. She ducked out of the room into an antechamber and carefully inserted her anchor point. She focused on her arm and inserted the second needle, feeling the rush of power as she twisted it.

"What are you doing?" Errol said from behind her. She'd been so focused on her technique that even with her strong instincts she hadn't noticed him enter.

"I'm hopefully going to find out what's going on." He stared at the needle in her hand. "Not now, okay?" She didn't keep the challenge from her voice.

He focused on it for a moment longer and then looked up and into her eyes, a new expression there. "Okay, I trust that you're doing the right thing. Your instincts have never been wrong and so if you think this is the best way to go forward, then it's the best way."

She couldn't believe he'd changed his mind so quickly. "Really? Just like that?"

He shrugged. "It's logical, really. I trust you."

It was all she had wanted to hear from him but she didn't have time to thank him, or saying anything kind; she sensed a change in the air. "We have to go, something's about to happen."

Errol snapped instantly into action — a soldier through and through.

Back in the throne room, guests were filing out into the ballroom where a banquet lay and where there would be an evening of entertainment and dancing. The sounds of people celebrating in the streets could be heard when Yeela and Errol passed by the large windows, both of them scanning the room for whatever it was that Yeela was feeling.

Gallia stopped them when they approached. "It's here," Yeela warned.

Gallia didn't speak. Instead, she motioned for more guards to approach. She ordered them to fan out, to look for anything that resembled the dark magic she'd told them of.

As they entered the ballroom, one part of the room drew her attention.

"There, in the far corner." There didn't appear to be anything out of the ordinary going on, just a handful of guests taking their seats. Yeela and Errol made their way around the back of the table and Yeela stopped, her heart hammering. The smell, the sickly smell. She took a step back and approached the chair she'd just passed.

A woman with a tall updo and an excessive amount of diamonds around her neck sat before Yeela. The stench was coming from her. Yeela leaned over the lady and spoke quietly. "My lady, I've been told to inform you that you are to be moved higher up the table."

The woman preened and every movement sent more of the stench into Yeela's over-sensitive nostrils. She held her breath as the woman rose from her chair, her chin high. Yeela and Errol escorted her towards the head table and then deftly out a side door.

"What is the meaning of this?"

"It has come to our attention that you have brought a substance into the palace that is forbidden," Errol said smoothly.

"What nonsense," she said with a sniff.

"Please excuse the intrusion," Yeela said as she began to pat down the protesting woman.

There was a pocket hidden in the folds of her voluminous skirts, so Yeela slipped her hand inside and removed a small, silver, cylindrical container. She held it up to the woman. "What's this?"

"My husband's medicine." The woman's face had turned purple with rage after Yeela's inspection.

Yeela unclasped the top and sniffed the contents. The smell hit her so hard she nearly retched. She passed it to Errol who smelt it and grimaced.

"Where is your husband?"

"On the high table of course," she said.

"*Who* is your husband?" Yeela pressed.

"The representative for Saffiere, a member of the Queen's own selected council."

Yeela swore. Errol turned to two guards on duty outside the door to the ballroom. "Detain this woman."

They burst into the banquet, which was now underway. Tables were laden with the finest foods from the Daeneah Realms. They wove their way through servants carrying trays of steaming food and jugs of wine, trying to get to their Queen. As they approached the head table, the smell hit Yeela. It was masked by something else, something stronger, but by being close she could smell it clearly.

Yeela saw him then, leaning towards the Queen, and she saw the weapon, too — a black spike sticking out from the cuff of his sleeve. She didn't even take a moment to consider what she was doing; she acted on instinct alone. Her dagger was in her hand and released within a breath. It whipped through the air before anyone could notice what was happening and slammed into the man's back. Screams rose then, as Yeela and Errol forced their way through now-panicked dignitaries. Ithrael had leapt up to protect the Queen. The Queen grabbed the man, now gurgling his last breaths, and lifted him by his collar as she stood. Wearing the gold mask, Yeela could see the cold fury in her eyes. Queen Amarea looked down at his hand and ripped the black blade from his sleeve. As she got closer, she heard the hiss of fury emitting from her Queen's lips.

"Get the Queen out of here!" Ithrael bellowed, and the guards who were trying to calm the crowds sprang into action. But instead of running, Queen Amarea stood on her chair and then onto the table. She kicked away the goblets and piles of food that were in her way.

"Show yourselves," she said. Her voice was deep and carried through the room, although she didn't shout. All eyes turned to her. And then Yeela saw it. Somehow the redness of their eyes had been masked, but she saw it then; whatever magic had hidden them was fading. They were everywhere, men and women under the spell of the Vulma Supreme Leader. Ithrael rested his hand on the pommel of his sword and Yeela and Errol took up position by their Queen's side on the ground, Gallia the only person between them and the Queen. More guards gathered, some protecting the consort. Those who were unaffected by the dark elixir of the Vulma Supreme Leader were fighting their way out of the room. Screams ricocheted off the walls as people were pushed out of the way or trampled by those trying to escape. But those who were affected by the taint of dark magic stood their ground and faced the Queen.

"At least we know they die like mortals," the Queen said under her breath.

Yeela reached into her pocket and passed the pouch containing the needles to Gallia, who handed them to the Queen. Standing atop the table, Queen Amarea plucked out a needle and inserted it into the point that was now tattooed onto her shoulder — a tiny black starburst. She took out a second needle and passed the pouch to her consort. He also placed an anchor point in his right shoulder. They stood there, poised with their second needles ready, waiting.

Errol removed Yeela's dagger from the now dead body at their feet and wiped the blood away on the man's tunic and handed it back to her, his eyes never leaving the room and the imminent threat. Yeela's blood sang with the tension in the air; she could feel it about to snap. She closed her eyes and focused. She felt Amarea turn and focus on her, waiting for her to tell her when the moment came.

"Now," Yeela said and opened her eyes to see Amarea and Ithrael use their second needles. Their power burst forth into their closed fists, filling them with light, just as weapons made of black magic began to fly through the air, directed at the proud Queen standing atop the banquet table, the ends of her dress covered in food and wine, her eyes pale blue fury, shining through her mask of gold.

Amarea and Ithrael lay waste to the weapons and those who wielded them. Having spent a few days practising they were able to use their power in bursts. First Ithrael's magic melted the weapons that were flying through the air, whilst

Amarea made them turn to dust. Yeela watched in veneration as Amarea split the ball of power and held it in each palm and Ithrael did the same. Yeela had no idea they were able to do this. They threw their magic at those tainted with dark magic. Men and women were vaporised before Yeela, into either a mist of blood by the Queen or a burning mass by her consort. It was horrifying. It was magnificent.

But some of the men were unaffected, and of those that Ithrael hit, their clothes melted away to reveal the black armour of the Vulma Supreme Leader.

It was as they had feared; their magic was useless against the armour.

Yeela wanted to turn to Errol, to find reassurance in him, but she had been trained to never turn away from an enemy, to protect her Queen at all cost. She kept her eyes facing the now approaching enemy and tried to think what to do. From the corner of her eye, she saw the Queen look to her consort and she bent down and drew a dagger from a garter strap on her thigh. Something blue flashed in Yeela's periphery and she looked at the dagger properly: it had a blue core. It must be one of the first orob stone weapons created. The Queen spun it in her hand and Ithrael drew his sword from his back, a blue core now running through it as well.

Two weapons. Yeela's panic dampened slightly. In the hands of the two greatest warriors in the Daeneah Realms, they might actually stand a chance against the advancing red-eyed soldiers. Yeela loosened her grip on her daggers slightly, awaiting the order.

Ithrael took command. "Hold fast until I give the order. Look for breaks in their armour." His voice was deep, commanding.

A calm settled over Yeela as she picked out her first target, locating areas of exposed flesh. The Queen and Ithrael would have to fight in direct combat as they couldn't afford to lose their weapons. It was up to the Guard to be the first line of defence for them. It was up to them to stop anyone getting close to them. She would die for her Queen, her country. She'd always known it, but in that moment it was clear; it was her purpose.

"Release," Ithrael ordered, his voice booming through the great hall.

Yeela's first blade hit her mark in the neck. They went down instantly. The second sliced through her other target's ear. She quickly pulled out another set of knives and corrected her mistake, the sharpened blade puncturing through the woman's eye socket. Yeela's attention was drawn completely to her own task and so she didn't see the blackened blade that whipped through the air, directly for her Queen. She would think about the moment often afterwards, about how Gallia had seemed to be aware of the entire room at once and had seen the threat before anyone else, even before the Queen and Ithrael. About how she'd moved, leaping onto the table and throwing her body in front of the Queen.

The dagger struck true, straight into Gallia's back and into her heart.

The blade hitting Gallia registered with Yeela, despite her instincts still being sharp; somehow they'd missed that blade. She would forever question why they had. Yeela mounted the table and moved to Gallia. Errol shouted after her and began to follow her, defending her from the coming attacks. She watched as Gallia's body sagged in the Queen's arms, and Yeela heard the Queen say Gallia's name as she lowered her body to the ground. Ithrael stood beside her, parrying away any attacks.

Yeela knelt beside her sister-in-law. She felt as if the air had been taken from her lungs, that there was no oxygen left in the entire room. Gallia was too still. Yeela watched as the Queen's hands trembled as she pulled open the small pouch Yeela had handed her earlier. Yeela stared at it. What was the Queen doing? How dare she just leave Gallia and return to the fight. Anger rose up in Yeela's chest, hot and sour, but somehow her sharp instincts managed to break through and tell her to wait, to watch.

The Queen pulled out five needles and held them in her mouth as she tried to undo Gallia's jacket, but her hands were shaking too much. Understanding dawned on Yeela and she took over, unbuttoning the stiff formal guard uniform and ripping open her cotton undershirt. The Queen didn't hesitate with the first point, right above the heart. She twisted the needle.

"Pull the dagger out, Yeela." Yeela looked up at her Queen and for the first time ever she locked eyes with her. Amarea's eyes were still glowing with the blue of her magic; she'd never seen anything so mesmerising, but there was no way she could refuse her Queen, Neesoh's descendant.

Yeela put her hand around the handle of the dagger, and saying a quick prayer to the goddess herself, she pulled out the dagger. Queen Amarea quickly put a needle above and below the wound, twisting. The bleeding stopped instantly but the wound was wide and so Yeela tore strips from Gallia's already ruined shirt and packed the wound. The healers would clean it and stitch it later — she just needed to stop any bleeding that might happen if the Queen's plan didn't work. Assuming that she had a plan.

The Queen held the last two needles in her hand, her eyes seeming to lose focus as she looked down at Gallia's prone body. Yeela reached out and did something she never thought she'd do: she rested her own bare hand on top of her Queen's arm. She locked eyes once more with her Queen and she felt she saw gratitude there. The Queen put both needles in simultaneously, one to the left and one below Gallia's heart.

Gallia's entire body jolted and white lightning bolts ran through her body. She gasped, her mouth open in a wide, silent scream and then collapsed back. Yeela felt for a pulse. It was there; faint, but there.

"Get her to Saia — there's more healing to be done." The order was to Yeela and someone behind her. She looked back to see Errol still standing guard over them, deflecting any attack. She felt an overwhelming sense of gratitude towards him.

He helped lift Gallia and they carried her from the melee. Yeela noticed as she carried Gallia away that she'd left a bloody handprint on her Queen's arm.

Chapter Forty-One

AMAREA

Amarea stood, Gallia's blood on her hands, and violent anger roiled through her body. No one should have to sacrifice themselves for her. She jumped down from the table and began plunging and slicing her magic-infused knife through any exposed flesh she could find. Blood sprayed over her gold mask, dripping down her neck as she cut a path through the intruders in her home. How dare they enter her queendom. How dare they threaten her people. How dare they hurt those she loved. She would show no mercy. The Vulch would pay for this. And even though she knew that's exactly what the Vulma Supreme Leader wanted, for her to start a war, she would give it to him gladly just to see the stain of his cursed magic driven from their lands.

To her right Ithrael joined her, his sword slipping through the dark armour as if it were merely scraps of cloth. Together, in the centre of the room, they fought every last Vulch until none were left alive. Amarea's breaths were ragged; around her were dismembered limbs, blood, and bodies piled on top of each other. The scene before her was horrific but that's not what raged in her mind. The violation of her home, the audacity of the act: that's what roared through her. Her eyes caught Ithrael's and she could see the same fury on his face.

She looked around the room. Some of her guards were injured or dead. Her hatred for the Vulma Supreme Leader rose. If Gallia didn't survive, she would take her time killing him — a very long time.

The guards had removed those in her inner circle; it had been her orders to Gallia when she'd warned her of Yeela's fears. If she were to die, she needed people she trusted to see her country through. She kept hold of her blood-slicked blade as she picked her way through the bodies towards the chamber where she'd instructed the others to be held.

Niseem and Saia weren't in the room, which meant they were with Gallia. *Good.* They didn't need to see the horror of their Queen bathed in the blood of their enemy. They weren't warriors.

Guards had filled the room, as per her instructions. All eyes in the room widened when they saw their blood-soaked Queen and consort. The High General looked particularly furious at having been removed from a fight by order of his Queen.

Amarea held up her hand before anyone could speak. Ithrael stood to her left, allowing her to be Queen, not interfering. "You were protected for good reason. If either of us should have fallen, we would have needed a strong council to rule this nation. And that includes a High General capable of fighting the enemy before us."

At the back of the room she saw Lisette with Leonius in his specially made chair. Saia had told her that Lisette had been participating in magic training, despite her expressed wish against it. She'd allowed her training to continue and hadn't considered using Lisette's newfound talents in the coming fight. But as she looked upon the young face, her heart sank because she knew she'd use her for their gain. That despite her not yet being a woman, despite her promise to protect her, to keep her and Leonius from harm, she was going to send her straight to the Vulma Supreme Leader himself.

She bowed her head, her dagger still in her hand. "The Vulma Supreme Leader will expect an instant, aggressive response. Instead …" She took a breath. Was she really going to ask this of those she cared for? She had to; she was Queen. Her chin lifted slightly. She was the one who would always have to make the difficult decisions. It was her burden to bear. She would do as the High General had suggested. "Instead, we are going to send a delegate to Ruist." Her eyes fell on Bassiri and he inclined his head. He would accept this dangerous task without question. "And Bassiri will have someone posing as a servant travelling with him." She spotted Lisette who stood up straighter when she noticed her Queen's attention was on her. "Someone who has a unique and special gift, someone who I know can get them both out alive." Somehow her voice stayed even, despite her heart breaking.

"Bassiri, you are the only person who could even begin to unveil their plans and tactics, but if you feel to be in danger at all, get out. You are there as an emissary of peace."

"I will do as my Queen desires." His bow was low, respectful.

"High General, once Ithrael and I are cleaned up, we shall begin to plan this war. Gather everyone together."

Ithrael and Amarea took a longer route around to her chambers, not wishing to cross through the scene they had just left. She wanted to check on Gallia but she needed to remove the tainted blood from her skin. Yeela's small handprint of Gallia's blood felt like it was burning her skin. What had she done wrong as a ruler to bring this upon her people?

Behind the closed door of her bathing room, Amarea knelt on the floor and her body silently convulsed with agonising sobs. She still controlled her pain so that no one could hear their Queen was broken. Ithrael knelt before her and removed her mask, and using a wet cloth began to carefully wipe the blood from her face and neck. He removed her clothes, gently removing the traces of the dark magic that had stained their halls. Her entire body shook and so he stripped her down and carried her to the now filled and heated bathing pool. He washed her hair as though she were a child, and the tenderness was too much for her. She clung to him and sobbed into his chest.

Ithrael sat back in the pool with Amarea tucked against his side. "They'll be fine. Lisette is a ghost, remember? And Bassiri can read people, a room, like no one else. And Gallia will live. And we will defeat this enemy. You don't have to do this alone. I will share this burden. I would have done the same, made the same choice. It's the right choice, the smart choice." He placed a kiss upon her brow.

She took his face in her hands and looked into his eyes. "I don't know if I can do this. Lead us into war. Risk you, risk everyone."

"We are going into war, together. You're not risking me, or anyone. You are defending our realm."

"I'm afraid," she confessed, and the confession made her feel sick. How could she call herself Queen when she had such fears?

He kissed the top of her head. "It would be strange if you weren't. That fear is your love for your people. That fear will make you plan wisely. You have already protected those that needed protecting to ensure the safe running of our country. Your fear grounds you when your rage tries to rule. And you have surrounded yourself with people who will share this burden and plan this war. You are a great Queen because you don't rule alone."

"I'm also a very smart Queen for having you as my king." She kissed him tenderly but nothing more. There was too much to do and she needed to see how Gallia was.

Gallia was with the healers, who had stitched her wound. Niseem, Saia, Yeela and Errol were in the room with her as the healer placed a poultice over where the dagger had entered her back.

"How is she?" Amarea asked the room.

Saia answered, "I managed to use some needles to encourage rapid healing. If you hadn't done what you did ... It's too soon to say but she's doing well." Saia's voice was thick and she looked away, blinking back tears.

Niseem couldn't meet Amarea's eyes and it felt like a dagger in her own chest. She'd given Gallia the position of her personal guard, a position that meant sacrificing her life for that of her Queen. Niseem blamed her, just as she blamed herself.

Yeela turned to her. "What's happening now?"

"All the intruders have been dispatched. Bassiri and Lisette are to travel to Ruist, Bassiri as emissary." Niseem's attention snapped to Amarea, cold anger behind her eyes. Amarea held her stare, even though Niseem couldn't know she was doing it. She was upset, yes, and part of Amarea felt she deserved that anger. But Ithrael's words from moments before came back to her. She was Queen: she had the support of her council and she wouldn't be cowed, even by her friend's pain.

Amarea approached Gallia's sleeping form and gave her Neesoh's blessing before leaving, her heart aching at the thought of losing Niseem's support. She buried her hurt and made her way with Ithrael to the war council meeting to brief Bassiri and Lisette. That day was one of her hardest as Queen. She knew that harder ones were to come.

Chapter Forty-Two

BASSIRI

Bassiri and Lisette set out as soon as they had their instructions. He barely had time to say farewell to Tristam. They were given a large escort to the pass that led into Vulma and it was two days before they reached the pass. There the escorts left them, and Bassiri looked over at the small girl by his side and wondered whether the Queen had made the right decision. She was a mere wisp of a thing, but Amarea had insisted and he understood enough to trust her decision.

Once they were through the narrow pass, a group of guards clad in black armour halted them.

"I come as emissary to Queen Amarea Saffiere of Maldessa. We wish to speak with the Vulma Supreme Leader." Bassiri removed the sealed letter from the Queen and held it out to the approaching guard.

Bassiri gave Lisette a reassuring smile as the guards made them dismount their horses and escorted in a tight guard towards a nearby camp. The site of the camp was disturbing. The Vulch were definitely preparing for a war if they had an entire army unit near the pass.

The guards led them inside the largest tent, which was also black. Bassiri felt they were really taking the whole dark magic theme a little far — it was a bit too obvious.

A tall Vulch stood in the centre of the room examining the letter from Queen Amarea. "You wish an audience with the Vulma Supreme Leader?" His Maldessan was thickly accented.

Bassiri bowed and in perfect Vulch replied, "I have a message from our Queen which she wished to be delivered in person." Bassiri's voice was smooth, the unassuming tone of a courtier.

The Vulch examined Bassiri carefully but he barely glanced at Lisette, the slight serving girl sent to accompany her master.

"You will be escorted to his camp, a day's ride away. But we have to insist your hands be bound and you be under guard at all times." There was a slight smile on the man's face.

"Bound hands? I am an *emissary* to the *Queen*." Bassiri did his best haughty offended noble impression.

"It's that or you can head straight back home to your Queen."

Bassiri sniffed. "As it's for our Queen, we shall accept your terms, but she shall hear of this treatment."

"I'm sure she will," the Vulch said, already disinterested. He passed the letter back to Bassiri and he was led back out of the tent with Lisette following behind.

Their hands were immediately bound outside, the ropes unnecessarily tight, but he noticed Lisette had clenched her fists just as he had done so that once the knots were tied they didn't chafe too badly. He caught her eye and they had a hard edge to them. She was annoyed but not rattled; she was stronger than he'd given her credit for. Although they had worked on assignments for the Queen before, as Lisette wasn't one for talking and was always sent to skulk in the shadows, he didn't feel he knew her, and he could get an idea about almost everyone very quickly. That's why his Queen had sent him on this mission — a mission he'd taken gladly knowing he could be of use to Crown and country. Finally she was making the right choices as a leader.

The journey to the camp took a further day and was incredibly uncomfortable, but Lisette impressed Bassiri by her ability to sit straight in her saddle and look completely at ease. He wasn't sure how she did it. Every part of him ached from being in one position for an entire day and he hadn't been able to sleep in the few hours they'd stopped for a rest.

Bassiri struggled to keep his composure when he first saw the camp ahead. It was much larger than he'd anticipated. Every soldier he saw wore black armour made from dark magic. Every piece of it he saw, he thought of the lives that had been taken just so they could wear protective plating in battle. It sickened him. He noticed something else, too. All the actual soldiers, unlike the guards, had blood-red eyes. They were drinking the dark elixir as well.

From the corner of his eye, he saw Lisette shudder when she noticed the red eyes. Her brother had nearly died the first time they'd come across this horror; it was no wonder she was now clenching her fists until her knuckles were white.

The guards pulled them down from their horses once they were inside the camp, so Bassiri continued his act and protested greatly over his treatment, and he kept it up until they led him into an unnecessarily large tent. They handled Lisette so roughly she fell to her knees once inside. Bassiri thought this odd; he'd never met anyone more sure-footed. He swore at the guards and went to help her up. She kept her head down, a meek serving girl, and he saw her pull four needles from her boot. She slipped two into his hand. Of course she hadn't fallen. He didn't know why he'd doubted her, as he never had before. The situation they were in had unsettled his senses.

"I would like my hands to be unbound and to freshen up before I am to meet the Vulma Supreme Leader," Bassiri demanded to no one in particular. He pulled at his collar to show his distaste at the state of his clothing and slipped his anchor needle in and twisted. He managed to move his bound hands to insert the second needle into his wrist, which he rotated and removed just as a man entered the room.

He was tall, with jet-black hair, pale skin and eyes the colour of freshly drawn blood. But it wasn't the Vulma Supreme Leader who stood before Bassiri. "I'm afraid this is as high up as you get within our chain of command. I'm

General Kuzman — the Vulma Supreme Leader has asked me to meet you on his behalf. He's rather busy these days."

Bassiri held up his hands, indicating he wanted removal of his bindings. The general flicked two fingers to his side and a guard came to unbind him.

With his hands free, Bassiri removed the letter from Queen Amarea from the inside pocket of his jacket, pulling out the anchor needle at the same time. He stepped forward and handed the general the paper. His observational skills had always been good; it's why he'd always been such a strong asset to the Queen. But when he triggered his magic he saw every detail and could interpret the meaning instantly. The general's eyes were red, but fading, which meant he was due more of his elixir. There was a slight tremble in his hands, withdrawal from the potion, which meant it was addictive. And then there was something else, as he read the letter ... Bassiri watched him as he mumbled the words to himself and then closed his eyes, as if listening. But listening to what? And then it was there, the slightest of nods, a nod in answer to something. Bassiri could see it in the slight crease of his forehead as he listened, the firming of the line of his mouth as he received the order. He knew then what the elixir did; he had what his Queen needed. But first, they had to get out of there alive.

"Your Queen wants to negotiate peace?" General Kuzman smirked. "For what reason? We are not at war."

"The attack on the royal wedding would indicate otherwise."

"A rogue group who oppose your Queen, ever since the night of the Blood Moon. Must be something personal. We'd be happy to uncover any other such groups, seeing as your Queen has her hands full with a terrible frost, or so I hear." The tremble in his hands increased.

"But she's managed to resolve the issue and we're set to recover quickly. She's resourceful." Bassiri straightened his jacket, running his fingers down the braiding.

The smirk didn't leave the general's face. "So we've heard. Very resourceful, your Queen. I hear she's gathered her army, fifty thousand soldiers. So many — it's as if she were feeling threatened."

Bassiri's focus honed in on the general's non-verbal clues — panic seized him; he had to be reading the general wrong. Could they have so many?

"And it would appear that she has every right to be. This army camp is very near the border with Maldessa." Bassiri's tone was firm, less the courtly fop and more the man accustomed to political manoeuvres.

"A training camp." The general licked his lips. He was really beginning to feel the effects of the lack of the elixir, and Bassiri wanted to keep him talking, see what happened when he was deprived for too long, but the general didn't seem bothered that they were in the room. He went to his desk, which was laden with rolled maps and papers, and uncorked a vial and drank from it. Bassiri watched as the red in his eyes intensified. His skin seemed to tighten slightly, his stance strengthen. The potion appeared to have an added benefit to the user: it made them stronger.

"As for you, as emissary, I believe the message we want to send will be best served through you." General Kuzman faced him and the effect of his eyes so close up was horrifying. "You're a favourite of the Queen's, aren't you? The man who fucks his way through society as her spy. How base of her to make you whore yourself for her queendom."

He stepped forward and gripped Bassiri by the chin, taking in his full lips. He licked his own and pushed his groin against Bassiri's. Bassiri felt the general's erection then. He recoiled from the man before him.

"What? Suddenly shy?"

He grabbed Bassiri's groin and acting on reflex Bassiri punched the general in the jaw. He was there as emissary but he knew that his Queen would have torn the heart out of the man who dared to touch Bassiri against his wishes. She would be furious he'd merely punched him. Bassiri felt Lisette behind him then, could feel her energy, vibrating with anger.

The general licked away the blood from his split lip. "An emissary striking a general? Well, that's a punishable offence."

Bassiri's heart sank. He'd played right into his hands. The guards surrounded them in seconds. The general stepped forward and grabbed the back of Bassiri's head and forced his lips upon his. Bassiri could taste the general's coppery blood, and when he pulled away, Bassiri spat the taste from his mouth onto the general's jacket.

"It'll be a shame to dismember you and send you home in pieces. You fit together rather nicely. I'd have enjoyed taking you for myself, but I wouldn't want to disrupt the Vulma Supreme Leader's plan." General Kuzman adjusted himself, his eyes never leaving Bassiri's. Bassiri felt violated by the entire encounter and he'd never wanted to leave somewhere more.

"Guards, have him and his servant taken to those who have gone feral." Bassiri understood his meaning; some who took the elixir were badly affected. "Just make sure they leave some pieces recognisable. We wouldn't want his Queen to question whether it really is her beloved Bassiri being returned in a box." He flicked two fingers at the guards and in that same moment, Bassiri felt a small hand on his shoulder: Lisette.

A tingle ran through his entire body. He looked down and couldn't see his torso, his legs. She'd made them disappear. She must have triggered her powers when the general was distracted taunting him. They'd discussed what they would do if it came to them having to escape. Bassiri was to hold Lisette's hand at all times, and he felt her small hand slip into his and pull him downwards. They watched as the guards looked around in confusion. There was a momentary break in the circle and they darted towards it, ducking low. They waited for a guard to open the tent entrance before slipping through, leaving the illusion that they'd vanished into thin air rather than become invisible.

Bassiri let Lisette lead the way as she wove through the tents and avoided any soldiers. As they passed, he noticed a large tent with priests from the Daylarian Church entering. They were still involved with the Vulch's plans, then. They continued forward but they were in need of horses — Bassiri worried it would give them away. It would take them days just to make it back to the pass. He needed to get back to Saffiere and pass on the information he'd discovered.

Lisette tugged his hand and she took them in a different direction across the camp. He didn't want to speak and question her, but she seemed to have a purpose and he had no choice but to have her lead the way. He chose to start trusting her; he'd already come to realise he'd been unintentionally unfair towards her, mistaking her youth for inexperience. Lisette was in control of the situation — remarkably so.

She led them towards the horses and his heart sank. There was no way they could take a horse without being noticed. She wove her way through the nickering animals — they seemed aware of their presence — to a huge black stallion. It was easy to guess that the beast was the general's. Lisette pulled Bassiri down and released his hand.

"You're going to have to get on first," she said quietly.

He didn't question her and instead helped her saddle the horse, which stomped and huffed. They waited until the coast seemed clear and Bassiri mounted, held his hand out to Lisette and pulled her up. As soon as her legs were around the horse, it disappeared too. *Clever girl*, Bassiri thought. He hadn't realised the range of her magic.

They made their way slowly to the edge of the camp, which had multiple search parties looking for them. He didn't encourage the horse into a gallop until they were far enough away that they couldn't be heard. With the horse travelling at speed, Bassiri knew they would be at the pass by first light.

Lisette's magic slowly faded as they rode, and so before they reached the outer guard of the camp at the pass, they dismounted.

"They'll hear the horse if we go through on it. We'll have to let it go. Besides, there are people waiting the other side with horses for us," Bassiri said.

"Hopefully it will lead anyone tracking us away." She turned and slapped the horse on its behind and it galloped off. Lisette deftly triggered her magic and reached up and placed her small pale hand in his large dark one. He looked down at the contrast between them as his fingers began to disappear, along with his hand and arm. They were so different and yet the girl beside him had the strength of a man better than he, for he would have faltered if she hadn't been there.

It took them a while to make it to the centre of the camp, and there was a lot of activity. They appeared to be planning something. Lisette pulled him towards the main tent; she was clearly as curious as he was. They hunkered down outside and listened.

Most of what they heard wasn't of much use until Bassiri recognised the voice of the guard in command.

"The Vulma Supreme Leader's camp is approaching the mountains. They'll be at the Great Salt Plains two days hence. He needs a stronger defence there — there'll be spies trying to get through the clearest path. We have to be vigilant."

He tugged on Lisette's hand and they stood together, picked their way carefully through the camp and entered the pass.

Halfway across, Lisette's magic began to fade. Bassiri released her hand and they quickened their pace. They had to get to the horses waiting for them and back to Saffiere, and fast.

Chapter Forty-Three

AMAREA

Bassiri hadn't yet returned when the messenger arrived.

"My Queen." The messenger knelt before her, breathless. "Daylarian priests from across the realm have been found murdered."

Amarea stilled. "And what is being said?"

He kept his head down, not brave enough to face his Queen with the news he carried. "The Vulch have announced that as friends to the Daylarian Church they are to rid the Daeneah Realms of a Queen who ..." He took a breath for courage. "Who 'would continually slaughter such a peaceful institution'."

"Is that so?" She wasn't surprised. She knew they'd find a way to insinuate the coming conflict was her fault.

"They have declared your actions an act of war."

"And so it begins," Ithrael said at her side. He was sitting on his throne, which she had insisted be placed next to her own.

Bassiri and Lisette arrived soon after the messenger. He was practically feverish as he relayed his news to Amarea. She didn't hesitate.

"High General, have the army sent to the Great Salt Plains."

"I will need the consort with me to help oversee everything."

"I will of course join you," Ithrael replied instantly.

Amarea didn't say anything because she knew Ithrael was needed, but secretly she wished he could stay with her. Shamefully she acknowledged that having him around gave her courage.

"I recommend we keep a small contingent of soldiers in Saffiere, as a precaution," the High General said.

"I agree. We need to be prepared for whatever the Vulch may attack us with. By now I have come to understand not to underestimate them or to expect conventional methods." Which worried her. She had no idea what was coming.

A day later, after all preparations had been made, Amarea arrived at the newly erected camp in a small valley hidden in the hills that stood between them and the Great Salt Plains.

She entered the command tent where Ithrael and the High General were speaking with the other generals and commanders.

"Have the weapons arrived?" she asked without preamble.

"Some have, more are coming. We're bringing in carts of orob stone and having weapons made here as well," the High General informed her.

"Good." She looked down at the map spread across the table. "Bassiri estimates the Vulch Supreme Leader has two hundred thousand soldiers." She looked at the carved block on the map that indicated where the Vulch army were positioned.

"At least a hundred thousand are already there." Ithrael's voice was hard as he picked up the piece that indicated the Vulch, turned it over in his hand and placed it back upon the map.

Amarea spent the rest of the day visiting troops with the generals and commanders. It was important for them to know that the Queen and her consort were there with them, that they were entering this battle alongside them. By the evening she was exhausted, not from the day's work but from worry. What if all those faces she had seen that day had the life drawn from them. Could she really ask them to go to their deaths?

Ithrael took her to bed, even though she wanted to go over every plan they had at least a hundred more times. He made love to her slowly that night, his touch feather light and tender. It made her heart ache, the care he took with her, as though she were something precious and fragile. Even though they both knew she wasn't.

They rose at first light and Amarea dressed in her black-and-gold outfit from the night of the Blood Moon. She pulled on her gold filigree gloves with her sharpest gold talon extensions, and her crown of black-and-gold thorns, raven feathers and roses. Lastly, she secured her smooth gold mask over her face. She would be the nightmare the Vulch cannot escape after this day. She will haunt all of their dreams.

Final preparations were being made when the entrance to the command tent was pulled back and Mierdas entered. She always forgot how short the High Mage was; for some reason he was never short in her mind. Maybe because of what he represented.

"Mierdas?" she said in surprise.

"My Queen," he said without bowing. "I have brought the House with me. We have something to show you." She was taken aback. He'd brought the *entire* House to a battleground — it was unprecedented.

He led her, Ithrael and the High General to a covered cart. Amarea was always amazed how he was able to navigate around so easily when he could not see. He pulled back the oiled cloth to reveal a huge pile of rods with blue orob cores.

"How? When?" Amarea asked, confused.

"This is Calmaya's contribution. They no longer have much of an army, not one they can spare anyway." Amarea understood; they were still recovering from the Hyrathean invasion.

"What do they do?" the High General asked as he examined one of the rods.

"They are based upon ones we already use, but these ones ..." He held up a thinner stake. "Will trigger and direct lightening. This one ..." He pointed to another, thicker rod. "...will make the ground tremble."

"I thought the house was a peaceful establishment." Amarea couldn't keep the surprise from her voice.

"We're about keeping the balance. The balance is unstable if there is dark magic in the world. We are readdressing the balance by creating these weapons." His unseeing eyes seemed to bore into Amarea's. "The balance is at great risk if these are ever used for any other means. If they are then we have gone against our beliefs."

"Then I promise you, once this battle is won we will destroy all of the weapons you have created and every single scrap of information on them so they can never be used again." She turned back to the cart and looked in wonder at what Mierdas had brought her, and there she was thinking that a House of Mages was of no use to them in the coming war. How wrong she had been.

Chapter Forty-Four

YEELA

Yeela stood on the ridge looking out over the army of their enemy, clad in black armour with eyes the colour of blood; demon eyes she would have to face. She gripped her daggers, one in each hand, cores made of blue orob stone. She would strike true. She wouldn't falter. She just hoped that once she'd triggered her magic, her heightened instincts would keep her and Errol alive.

"Before it all starts, there's just one last thing I want say before—" Errol said in a low voice beside her.

"Don't even think this is it." She looked him dead in the eyes.

He ignored her comment and continued. "It's an honour to fight beside you, Yeela."

She smiled at him, glad that now, when they faced death, they could be true friends, putting all their past disagreements behind them. "It's an honour for me, too."

His ears stuck out when he grinned back at her and she decided she really did like his face. She was about to walk into the hardest fight of her life and yet, at that moment, she'd never felt lighter because she was surrounded by friends. She was part of something great and she knew she was fighting on the right side.

Queen Amarea had sent them to join the soldiers who were to approach from the west of the battlefield. They were to wait until they were signalled to join the fight, once the Vulch had moved their army forward. From their vantage point, Yeela could see the size of the army they were to face and the sheer magnitude of it was enough to make even the bravest soldier turn and flee. But they all stood their ground because below were their Queen and her consort, she in an outfit of black and gold, he in white and gold. Neesoh and Daylar reborn and there to fight for their people. It was that sight that gave Yeela hope. It was that sight that made every soldier hold their position, pride beating in their chests. The gods were on their side.

Chapter Forty-Five

BASSIRI

Bassiri stood next to his Queen, Tristam at his side.

"You're sure that killing the Vulma Supreme Leader will break his control over his soldiers?" Amarea said again.

"I'm sure." And he was. There was no doubt in his mind that that's what he'd seen in the general.

"But how do we even get to him?" Amarea said as she looked out over the Great Salt Plains.

"I think that's the point," Ithrael said. "Two hundred thousand bodies between you and him so you can't break his controlling bond."

"We'll get to him."

But Bassiri could hear the doubt in the Queen's voice. He'd seen their weapons; he knew they only had enough orob blades for the first few lines of soldiers. He just hoped the mages and the Queen's magic were effective enough weapons, because the hoards before them would be hard to defeat.

THE DARK QUEEN

He made his way back to the command tent with Tristam where Saia and Yuto were still working feverishly to find as many things as they could to help with the on-coming battle. Bassiri sat down beside Yuto.

"Wouldn't you rather be back at your ship than be in this fight?"

Yuto seemed surprised. "If I go back to my ship I have to return home with the book of the ancients. It is my duty to my country. You need this book. Besides, I wouldn't get to test out any of this in Jaien." His eyes lit up as he smiled. Saia snorted.

"It's all for his own gain. He wants to experiment and pretend to be a hero." Despite her words, Bassiri noticed that Saia couldn't hide her small smile, but he wondered if she realised how much truth there was in her words.

"Have you found anything about linking magic?" Bassiri asked.

"Sorry, nothing yet." Saia looked at him directly when she spoke. She hadn't been able to do that for a long time. He was aware she'd had an attraction towards him for a while and had always been careful not to mislead her about their friendship. Something had changed and he suspected he knew what it was. He was relieved. He'd always been close with Saia, both of them feeling like they didn't truly fit in when they first started working for the Queen: he a rich lord's son sent to live in the palace because his father didn't want him around and thought it would be good for relations with Assisa if he made the young princess Amarea fall in love with him; and Saia, taken from her position as a servant by a young princess who saw something in her and moved her to a room within the palace. Together they had found a way to make the grand halls their home. Her friendship had given him confidence in his abilities to manipulate people into telling him their secrets, and she hadn't judged him when he'd first confessed to her he'd slept with someone to gather information. She'd told him that so long as he was comfortable and the Queen didn't ask it of him, then it was okay, he was free to act as he wished. He'd always felt accepted by her and it meant a lot to him that she was now able to speak to him again.

Dideum joined them, who Saia seemed particularly thrilled to see.

"Did he forgive you?" she said.

"Did who forgive him?" Bassiri asked.

"Mierdas. He expelled Dideum from the House."

"What?" Bassiri and Tristam said in unison. They'd allowed him near their Queen. How had Bassiri missed such a thing?

"Oh, calm down. All he did was sneak into Mierdas' lab to run an experiment. It was unfortunate that he nearly burned the whole place down." Saia actually *giggled* then.

"He's forgiven me," Dideum said sheepishly. "But I've got to learn to do as I'm told and I've been told to stay in here and out of the way so I don't cause any trouble."

"That reminds me — why are *you* dishonoured?" Saia asked Yuto. Bassiri really needed to pay better attention to those around him; he'd been missing too much.

"I was drunk and the book was stolen from right under my nose." Yuto rubbed the back of his neck in embarrassment. "That's all you need to know."

"I definitely want to know more," Tristam said with a wicked grin, but they were all aware of what was happening outside the tent, and so they returned to researching and trying to think of ways to use what information they found.

They sat in the command tent, he, Tristam, Yuto and Saia, whilst generals came and went, trying to see whether there was anything else they could contribute to the fight. None of them were soldiers, so they would have to provide what they could. Bassiri had never felt so useless.

Chapter Forty-Six

AMAREA

Amarea sat atop her horse, a beautiful black mare. Beside her on his white stallion was Ithrael wearing a small gold crown. The outfits, the colours, all spectacle, but he looked like a true king, a true leader. He turned to her, realising she was looking, and smiled.

"Don't get too lost in the fever of battle, my love."

"I have far more self-control than you do, my king." Humour danced in her eyes and he gave her a returning smile.

Along the cuffs of their sleeves, they'd had special holders made so they could keep needles there and have easy access to them. Amarea ran her finger along the ends of the pins, reassuring herself that they were there, that she had access to her magic.

Behind them were the mages. Amarea wasn't comfortable bringing them into battle but had agreed they would deliver the first strike and then retreat, keeping them out of any direct combat. In the distance, Amarea could see they were burning braziers of black resin, which was slowly starting to drift across the battlefield. A horn blew from across the white expanse before them and the Vulch riders began to thunder towards them, white salt dust billowing.

Facing the battlefield Amarea remembered the only time she'd met the Vulch Supreme Leader. It had been back when Zanzee was her regent; he'd invited the newly appointed Vulch leader to Maldessa. He had twenty years on Amarea. He was tall, reedy. His hair was black with a crisp widow's peak. His eyes were sunken in their sockets and yet they were alert, piercing. He'd barely spoken the entire time but had watched her. It had unnerved her. Reflecting on it she realised he'd been assessing her. How long had he been planning to take her queendom for himself? Anger ignited inside her. He wouldn't have her land, her people — not whilst magic pulsed through her veins and her heart beat in her chest.

Ithrael, to Amarea's right, raised the thin staff Mierdas had handed to him. He drew back his arm and thrust it with great force high into the air with the skill that matched a great spear thrower. When the staff reached its zenith, there was a crack of thunder and the sky split with pure white lightning. This dancing light followed the path of the javelin as it descended, where it landed in front of the lead rider from Vulma. The lightning, a second behind, hit the ground and huge vicious sparks of energy spiralled out from the epicentre. Those closest to the impact were killed instantly by the overpowering energy. A short distance away those with black armour were saved, as when the lightning hit the metal it appeared to dance across the surface and vanish, leaving the soldiers unharmed. Those without armour still further away from the strike point were only temporarily incapacitated.

Now other soldiers who had been selected as javelin throwers released their staffs skywards. There was an ear-shattering boom, which made the earth tremble all around them, as the staffs collectively reached their pinnacle. The resulting lightning seemed to light up the whole heavens and Earth with a fierce, piercing white light.

"Mages ready," Ithrael said, waiting to see the effects of the first assault. Riders still approached but they had made a significant dent in their number. "Now!" And behind him the mages hammered their spikes into the ground. Tremors ran beneath them, shooting towards the still-approaching Vulch. The closer the tremors got to the riders, the more the ground shook and started to crack. The terrain beneath the riders opened up and Amarea watched in fascination as they plummeted into the bowels of the earth. Nearly half their number fell, but those that made it through continued to charge towards them.

"Mages fall back," Amarea said.

"Riders at the ready," the High General bellowed at Amarea's left.

Amarea and Ithrael inserted their anchor pins into their small starburst tattoos, their armour having been adjusted so they could easily access them. They triggered their magic, the thrill of it running through her body, begging her to use it, *use it*. To destroy with it. To release herself onto the world in cold, unmerciful fury.

The order to charge was given by the High General, and using only her right hand on the reigns, she and Ithrael rode to the front of their riders. When they were close enough, she released the reigns, trusting her horse and splitting her power between her hands. Then she released it in unison with Ithrael. Blue and gold fury rained down on those approaching her soldiers. Her people. She would do all she could to prevent harm coming to those who rode behind her in defence of her realm.

She aimed at flesh, knowing that she would have no effect on their dark armour. Ithrael did the same and around them bodies burned and exploded. The deaths they caused were horrific, but they continued unrelenting, merciless. When she had used her magic, Amarea unsheathed the two short swords on her back that had orob stone cores. Ithrael drew his own sword and together they cut a path of bloody vengeance through the mass of Vulch riders.

The battle sang through her blood and she didn't relent from slicing, cutting and stabbing at her enemy.

"Fall back," the High General shouted across the battle ground. Amarea turned her horse and returned with her soldiers to their lines. When she spun her horse back around she was able to take in the devastation before her. Her heart hammered — so many of their own lost. She looked to each side. *So many.*

Her eyes met Ithrael's who she could see was feeling the same thing. The enemy were too strong, even with their new weapons. They had the added strength of the elixir, and the smoke was starting to weaken some of her soldiers.

They'd been so caught up with fighting the approaching horses that they hadn't seen they'd moved their entire army further forward. They were advancing as one, hoping to overwhelm them with sheer numbers.

Amarea swung her leg over her horse and untied the three rods attached to the side of her saddle.

Ithrael dismounted. "Now? You're sure?"

"They'll overpower us. We need to delay."

He looked across at the field as the High General spoke. "The Queen is right. And any fear we can strike into their hearts is a bonus."

They sent a runner to fetch Yuto and Saia to assist them. Ithrael removed his own rods and stepped out with Amarea towards the advancing army. Yuto and Saia had created a template they could place on the ground and they speared the stakes into the ground at the points that were marked out.

By the time they were done setting up, Yuto and Saia had joined them, both of them out of breath. Amarea held out her arms palms facing up, and Saia and Yuto triggered her magic. Saia and Yuto then triggered Ithrael's points. They then quickly left the field of battle.

Ithrael and Amarea stepped into the centre of their anchors and placed their hands on the ground. Amarea had explained to Ithrael how she had spoken to the earth's magic and asked for its help. She did the same again and it answered quickly, speaking of its fear, of the horrors of the bodies that had died as one. Her voice joined with Ithrael's, the thread that bound them uniting their plea, and she could feel the earth giving itself to them, begging them to stop the darkness that was starting to corrupt her own magic. They took what the earth gave and brought it forth before their enemy. A giant net made of fire and energy knitted itself together in the sky — they stood together, darkness and light, and released hell upon the cursed soldiers. It fell upon their heads, and even their dark armour could not protect them from the combined might of the magic of the earth and those with the power of the gods.

The screams were haunting; even Amarea with her hardened heart couldn't shake the feel of their terror. She knelt to the earth again, wanting to draw more power — they hadn't taken out even half of the Vulch army — but the earth could not give any more; if she gave more, the balance would tip, and that was far more dangerous.

"Thank you," Amarea whispered and tried not to show the raw magic her disappointment.

She retreated with Ithrael and remounted her horse.

"What now, General?" Amarea asked.

"Now we advance, as an army. We flank them." His confident tone was what she needed. They had planned for this; she had to trust in that.

The battle raged for hours, Amarea and Ithrael staying at the centre of it all, never relenting. Amarea's armour was slick with fresh blood that ran over the dried coats of those slain hours before. She'd come off her horse hours earlier and was on the ground, shoulder to shoulder with her own soldiers, fighting amongst them.

At one point she was fighting beside Yeela and Errol and felt pride as she watched the young woman fight. She had known of her through Niseem, a proud big sister, and here she was, a fearsome warrior, defending her land from invasion. She even saw some of the mercenaries at intervals, their skill outmatching many of her soldiers. It felt good to be there with them, with her people, to show them that if their lives were at risk, so would hers be.

Chapter Forty-Seven

YEELA

Yeela was locked in battle. Her senses were overwhelmed by the threats that were closing in on her. Dread filled her — death was coming. When she thought all was lost, Errol came to defend her. Yeela looked over at him, relieved for his aid until she realised too late that death wasn't calling her: it was coming for *him*. The black blade pierced Errol's chest as he stepped in front of the man who was about to thrust his sword through her side. She watched in horror as the light instantly went from his eyes. Yeela screamed. Images of his scowl, of his ears sticking out when he smiled, flashed furiously through her mind. Yeela unleased her fury as she hacked down her friend's killer. As grief gripped her, she felt a familiar presence by her side. Her Queen fought by her side, letting her know that she wasn't alone, despite her loss. It was the only thing that kept her present in the moment, that made Yeela continue to fight. Her Queen had come to her. Pride and loss swirled through her as she fought on, relentless.

Chapter Forty-Eight

AMAREA

They didn't stop fighting until they heard the horn that sounded for retreat. The High General had stayed back to manage and coordinate the battle from behind their lines. Amarea couldn't understand it; what was he thinking? They couldn't retreat, but she saw Ithrael turn and so she did the same. They had to fight their way back to the safety of their camp.

Her head was still fogged from the battle as she walked towards the command tent. She passed her horse, happy to see it had returned to camp safely. She rubbed its nose affectionately and it nickered, pleased to see her. That small moment began to bring her back to the present, to ground her a little.

Ithrael reached out and squeezed her hand before they entered the tent. Inside the tent, the High General's face was grave.

"We've sustained heavy losses, my Queen."

"How many?" Her voice came out thick. She swallowed, trying to force down the fear that was rising. She was tired in a way she'd never experienced before. Weary from battle, from loss.

"Two thirds of our entire army." She placed a hand on the table to steady herself. The dried blood of her enemy coated her entire hand.

"There's no way to get through to the Vulma Supreme Leader and stop this madness — there are just too many of them. If we'd had time to form alliances, maybe we'd have had a shot, but it all happened too fast," Tristam said, knowing that would be Amarea's next question. She was surprised to see Aiden in there, blood covering his armour, his arm in a sling. He'd joined the fight? She'd never even considered that he would do such a thing. For the first time she didn't hate her illegitimate half-brother and realised that the Primlect was a good influence on the young man.

She bowed her head at the High General's news. She didn't know what else to do. They had done everything they could think of to defeat their enemy, but they were too great. They hadn't had enough time to prepare. She didn't want to say it, couldn't say it, but she had to say it.

Amarea lifted her head. "I will not see any more of our people lost in a fight we cannot win. I will go and speak to the Vulma Supreme Leader."

"We go together," Ithrael said, his hand resting on her shoulder, and she nodded in agreement. She couldn't do this alone. She couldn't beg for mercy from her enemy by herself; it was the only thing she couldn't do alone.

Silence fell over the tent and Amarea couldn't bear to face them all. She had let them down. She had failed her people. She turned and left the tent with Ithrael and they made their way through the camp, through the injured and the dead, to see whether their enemy would show mercy, to see if her life was enough for him to spare her people.

When they reached the edge of the battlefield, they heard feet running towards them. It was Yuto.
"What is it?" she said, too tired to be patient.
"There's something you need to know ... about the prophecy."

Chapter Forty-Nine

SAIA

Saia sprinted after Yuto when she realised he'd gone. Panic clamped over her heart as she ran.

When she reached him, she saw that she was too late. Saia hammered her fists against his chest.

"What have you done? *What have you done?*" Saia screamed at Yuto as he held her back. Saia watched as her Queen and her king knelt before each other on the blood-soaked battlefield, the twin needles inlaid with orob stone in her Queen's hand, the needles that belonged to the Jaien Crown: Yuto's needles. Helpless, Saia witnessed the Queen unbutton her top and expose the top of her breast as Ithrael also exposed the top of his chest.

Saia struggled against Yuto. "It's their choice, Saia. It has to be their choice." And she saw loss in his eyes and through the haze of her grief she realised, whatever Yuto's true motivation had been for helping them, it was lost along with her Queen and king.

"You *promised* me."

"And I will never break another promise to you, ever." He held her face in his hands, his eyes fierce. "But this wasn't my promise to keep. They're their people." There was true feeling when he said "people", for he must understand their need, as though he had his own to worry about. "There is no other way."

And she knew then that he must be right, because whatever he'd sacrificed, it must have been great. Saia collapsed to the ground and Yuto continued to hold her.

"She's my Queen. My friend. She saw me when I was nothing. *Nothing.*" Her sobs felt like they were cracking open her ribs and she continued to watch, unable to look away, as her Queen and king raised the needles that would end them.

Chapter Fifty

ITHRAEL

"If we die, we die together." Her voice didn't shake as she handed him the needle.

"Together," he promised his love, his life.

She removed her mask and looked upon his face. He saw, then, mirrored in her eyes, the fear he too felt. There would be no recovering from what they were about to do. He pressed a quick, final kiss to her lips and did as she would: he focused on saving their people and pushed his fear aside.

With their eyes locked as one, they rammed and twisted the needles directly into the centre of their hearts. Ithrael pulled Amarea towards him as their magic erupted into blue and yellow light. He felt his entire being pulled from him as though his self was being torn from his body, and he could feel her pain, too. The bond that tied each to the other's death ignited between them, amplifying their suffering. They roared in agony as they clung to each other, giving all they had, all they were, to save their people.

They collapsed to the ground as the tsunami of their magic rolled over the Vulch camp. Black armour disintegrated under the force of the magic. Those with red eyes vomited blackness until the poison was expelled. As the magic reached the Vulma Supreme Leader's tent, it seemed to draw itself together. It poured through the entrance and he stumbled backwards when he saw what was coming for him, but he couldn't escape it. He screamed as it entered through his nose, his mouth, his ears. It tore through his cursed body and destroyed him from the inside out, until nothing was left.

Chapter Fifty-One

AMAREA

As Aiden strode out onto the battlefield, resplendent in his gleaming armour, heroic with his arm in a sling and the blood of battle adorning him, proving his worth, Amarea, scarcely conscious, was suddenly all too aware how the story would go.

The young son of the late king came to Maldessa and found his way into the court of the Dark Queen. He became trusted, learning all he could so that he could take back what was rightfully his. And when darkness fell over the land, brought on by the Queen's evil, he stepped up and fought their enemy, winning the war, becoming king.

With her eyes heavy, barely a single breath left in her chest, she watched as Aiden strode back across the battlefield, the Vulma Supreme Leader's iron helmet in his bloodied hand. Had she the breath to spare, she would have laughed at the brilliance of it. He truly was her brother, after all.

Amarea gazed across at Ithrael, her husband, her king. His breathing was shallow but his eyes were open, locked on her. They had been in it together from the start, and she supposed it was a poetic ending. But in that moment, at the end, she wished it could have been different. She wished they'd had more time. She wished she could have saved him. For the world needed him, his strength, his goodness; it could probably do without her brutality. Grief overtook her but she didn't take her eyes from him. A tear slid down his cheek as the colour drained from his lips. It was over for both of them. She only hoped Neesoh would reunite them in the heavens.

Amarea closed her weighted eyelids, relieved to give in, finally. To accept defeat. The silence in the aftermath of such magic was complete. On the edge of the Great Salt Plains, now stained red, two bodies lay unmoving, one in black and gold, one in white and gold. They had once been the two most powerful people in the known world. Now, they were nothing but a man and a woman lying side by side.

A lone figure walked past the two individuals who had sacrificed everything to save their people. He didn't even spare them a passing glance.

ACKNOWLEDGEMENTS

This book is really for all the women in my life. Amarea has some badass lady buddies and I'm fortunate enough to be blessed with equally badass ladies.

Michaela Pannese, you've got me through the worst times, you've made me laugh more than is medically advisable, and you still want to talk to me after spending time with me when I'm in full book-stress mode. I wouldn't be in one piece today if it wasn't for you. This book definitely wouldn't be written, edited and published if it wasn't for you. Thank you.

Natalie Flynn, I am thankful every day to have you in my life. You help me through all my crazy and *you totally get me, dude*. Your work inspires me and your friendship is incredibly precious to me. Thank you.

Imogen Gray, you've been supportive from day one and I value everything you do to help me not lose my shit. You would totally be a badass Maldessan warrior woman; in fact, you already are. Thank you.

Samantha Baldwin, your bravery and strength over the past year has been inspirational and beautiful to see. There is no one more badass than you.

My sisters, Sara and Rachel, I don't think I can fully express how much I love you both. How inspirational you both are to me. You guys are my jam.

My mother, for fixing the intricate details in magic-laden scenes so that it makes sense to you, the reader. For teaching me that it's not about how you fall, it's about how you get back up. The strength I've found recently was planted by you. Thank you.

Cressida Downing, as soon as I get an edit back from you I feel like my book is going to make it. Thank you.

Pam Firth, I mean, you even have to copy-edit your own acknowledgement, that's how much I need you! My books would be incomprehensible without you. Thank you.

To Claire and Chris at Eight Little Pages for making this book's insides look as good as its outsides.

And now for the men.

For my Dad for hashing out the plot for this book (and all my books) with me, for being strict on timelines, and for being an excellent roommate (it's temporary! I swear!). I really hope you and Mum never read this book.

My brother James, I'm sorry you always get left out of the 'sisters' stuff. We love you; you're just rubbish with WhatsApp.

Simon Hawes, for the typography and formatting of the cover. You're good. Real good.

And to Chima Mgbemere, for coming into my life at a time when everything was a complete disaster and not turning around and instantly running away. I know now it's because you hate running, but still.